"PLEASE DON[...] MARY MURM[...]

Her dark eyes were pleading, and D.A. sank into their depths. "Are you sure?" he asked.

"Yes," she sighed. "Yes, I'm sure." Her hands unfastened the remaining buttons of his wrinkled shirt. "Yes," she whispered, and her fingers slipped beneath the fabric and caressed his chest with the lightness of a mountain breeze. *"Yes."*

She trembled beneath his kiss, and felt his hand move to undo her sweater.

"We can't turn back," he said softly.

"I know," she replied, her fingertips reaching up to brush his lips. He tasted them with his tongue, and she sensed his desire.

"You're so beautiful, Mary. I want to make love to you. I have for a long while, but the time wasn't right."

"And now?"

His hand wandered to her breasts and drew circles around each rosy crest. "And now the time is right."

ABOUT THE AUTHOR

Montana author Sally Garrett liked the characters from her first Superromance so much that she decided to do a spin-off for her second. Readers agreed. *Until Forever* received the most complimentary fan mail of any Harlequin novel in 1983.

Books by Sally Garrett

HARLEQUIN SUPERROMANCE
90—UNTIL FOREVER
139—MOUNTAIN SKIES

These books may be available at your local bookseller.

Don't miss any of our special offers.
Write to us at the following address for
information on our newest releases.

Harlequin Reader Service
P.O. Box 52040, Phoenix, AZ 85072-2040
Canadian address: P.O. Box 2800, Postal Station A,
5170 Yonge St., Willowdale, Ont. M2N 5T5

Sally Garrett

MOUNTAIN SKIES

Harlequin Books

TORONTO • NEW YORK • LONDON
AMSTERDAM • PARIS • SYDNEY • HAMBURG
STOCKHOLM • ATHENS • TOKYO • MILAN

Published November 1984

First printing September 1984

ISBN 0-373-70139-X

To my sons, the Bible Boys
James Andrew, Christopher Adrian,
Garrett Alan and David Anthony—
The D.A.s in my life.

PROLOGUE

THE SURLY DARK-HAIRED MAN scowled as he applied the brakes to the family's Wagoneer and rolled to an impatient stop before turning onto the gravel road that led into the town of Dillon. His wife braced her hand on the dashboard and shot him a cautioning glance.

"Ed Russell, be careful. The girls are with us," Julie reminded him.

"Yeah, daddy," his youngest daughter Lisa cried. "Mary wants to stay alive until after lunch, and I want to get my new shoes you promised me."

"Sorry, ladies," Ed replied, a smile softening his ruddy features as he touched the brim of his black western hat.

"We forgive you, daddy," Lisa said, reaching her hand to the rounded crown of his hat and making an indentation in it.

"Cut that out," Ed growled, and quickly reshaped the felt into its desired style as Lisa giggled.

"Look!" Lisa cried, pointing to a vehicle in the distance. It appeared and disappeared as the road wound its way along the curves of the foothills of a rugged mountain to the southwest of the Rocking R Ranch where the Russells lived.

A horn honked, and a maroon European compact car rolled to a stop near the driver's side of the Russell station wagon.

Lisa nudged her sister Mary. "It's D.A. McCormack!" she whispered as they craned their heads to get a look at the new arrival.

"Hello, everyone," called the blond man behind the wheel.

Mary Russell's breath caught in her lungs as she tried to catch every movement the man made. He opened the car door and slowly unfolded his athletic form until he stood before them. He was tall at six foot two and threw a shadow over Mary as she moved beside Lisa and hung her head out the window of the rear door.

The young man leaned against his car's front fender and folded his arms across his chest. Sunlight reflected off the shiny stainless steel of the prosthetic device he wore on his left arm. The brightness momentarily blinded Mary, but she resisted the urge to shield her eyes for fear of embarrassing him.

His cable-knit ecru sweater matched the color of his hair, and his curls, unruly in the spring breeze, fell across his forehead. Unconsciously he brushed them away from the wire-rimmed glasses he wore, all the while continuing to chat with Ed and Julie Russell. He shifted his position and crossed his long denim-clad legs, then changed his mind and sat on the hood and fender instead.

His movements brought his face into closer range with Mary's line of vision, and she let out a sigh as she admired his angular features and searched for the flecks of rust in his sage-green eyes.

Lisa elbowed her and giggled, and Mary's face reddened with embarrassment. She didn't want D.A. McCormack to see her as a silly seventh grader even if it was the truth.

Mary's face was starting to lose its childish flatness. The contours of cheeckbones with slight hollows beneath were beginning to emerge, highlighting her oval face and her dark shiny hair, which she wore in two long braids.

She was unaware of D.A.'s thoughts as he spoke to her family, but her heart tripped when he smiled down at her.

Her gracefully arched brows frowned slightly as she stared back at him, then finally she smiled. D.A. nodded in reply, and her dark lashes swept down to hide her brown eyes.

He asked the girls about school and laughed when they told him about a recent practical joke that had backfired on their brother Steven. Steven had tricked Mary into missing the only school bus that traveled south of town, and had found himself stranded with her when the bus had driven away.

"He had to call home and ask for a ride for them both." Lisa laughed, her blue eyes sparkling with mischief.

D.A. smiled at both sisters, then turned his attention to their parents.

"Did you get our birthday card?" Julie Russell asked.

"Yes." he replied with a nod. "Thanks. It arrived right on time a few months ago."

"Happy twenty-two," Julie remarked. "I'm glad to see you've finally put some weight on that frame of yours. You were always so thin. You look great now. What do you do to stay in shape?"

D.A. laughed good-heartedly. He'd known the Russells for ten years. He'd been twelve years old, five foot ten, and skinny as a rail from a jackleg fence when he'd first met Julie. She'd been trying to fatten him up ever since. Now at his full adult height, maturity had added the muscles and hardness that she had been unable to accomplish.

"Thanks for the compliment," D.A. said, and he slid the prosthesis into his jeans pocket and out of sight.

Mary's eyes flew to his face. Her parents had explained years ago that he had been in an automobile accident when he was six years old. The car his mother had been driving had hit a bridge abutment; she was killed instantly and D.A. was thrown through the windshield. His left hand had been hopelessly mangled and amputated above the wrist.

He'd worn a prosthesis with either a stainless-steel terminal hook or a cosmetic hand ever since. Occasionally he went without the appliance. He had seldom talked about his missing hand, so Mary and her sister and brothers had accepted him the only way they'd ever known him. Their curiosity waned as the bumps of the buckles on the leather harness he wore under his shirt became a normal part of his appearance.

"I play a wicked game of racket ball," D.A. said. "I took first place in a city-wide tournament last month in Missoula. You're looking good yourself, Julie, and these two daughters of yours get prettier every day."

His glance flicked across the two sisters. "It's too bad I'm so far away. This is a nice area to live, but it's hard to make a living unless you want to shovel manure."

Ed Russell laughed and held up a cautioning hand. "That's not just manure we shovel, boy. There's a hell of a lot of money in this manure-shoveling business. Where would you city dudes get those hamburgers at McDonald's and Wendy's if we didn't raise the beef?" He arched his dark brows knowingly at D.A.

"I suppose you're right, Russ," D.A. admitted, "but dad runs the place with a tight rein, and it'll be more so if he retires from work and ranches full-time. I've always wanted to be partners with him, but I'm not so sure about working for him as a cowhand. Do you think he'll actually follow through with his plans to make the ranch a profitable operation?"

Ed Russell shrugged his husky shoulders.

"I think so," Julie said confidently.

D.A. missed a joke Lisa had told while his mind wandered momentarily. He realized he'd been staring at Mary. In order to lighten the mood, he winked at her.

"D.A.," Julie said, "if I were twenty years younger and weren't married to old Ed Russell here—" she leaned across to kiss her husband's smooth-shaven cheek "—I could really go for a handsome young man like you."

"Don't let these flirty women of mine get to you, boy," Ed warned. "They usually want something when they're sweet-talking like this. Keep your guard up."

Lisa giggled, Julie poked at her husband playfully, and Mary continued to stare in admiration at D.A. McCormack.

"Maybe it's a good thing you don't live in Dillon," Julie said. "The girls at the college would go wild for those blond curls. They'd all call you a hunk!"

"Oh, mom, don't say things like that to him," Mary whispered.

"That's all right, brown eyes," D.A. replied. "If you were older, maybe I'd make a play for you." He reached out unexpectedly, took her hand and gave it a squeeze.

Her eyes grew round. She gasped, then her face flushed and she ducked her head.

"Have a good Easter, folks," D.A. called as he returned to his car.

"Same to you and your father, D.A.," Julie said, waving as her husband started the engine.

Goodbyes were exchanged, and soon the Russells were on their way to town, and D.A. McCormack drove off toward his father's ranch farther up the Blacktail Road in the mountains of southwestern Montana.

SEVERAL INCHES OF SNOW had fallen in Missoula, and D.A. McCormack was glad he'd decided to skip his usual visit to his father's ranch two hundred miles to the southeast. He'd spent the Christmas holiday revising the final draft of an interim report on his acid-rain project, the result of a government grant he'd been awarded upon graduating from the University of Montana. His growing concern for the effects of sulfur dioxide on the environment had been spurred by a research project he'd done for an honors chemistry seminar during his senior year.

If the devastating effects of the compound from the industrial plants of the Midwest could destroy the New England forests, why wouldn't the same thing happen to his home state in the Northern Rockies from emissions from plants in Portland and Seattle and even as far away as heavily industrialized Japan. The question had been intriguing enough to earn him a grant for research and part of his living expenses for the next two years.

Christmas dinner had consisted of three pieces of fried chicken and biscuits from a nearby fast-food restaurant. As he cleared away the plastic cutlery and the paper cartons and shoved them into the trash can, he grimaced inwardly at spending such a family oriented holiday alone.

His father had recently remarried. Most of his friends from university had taken jobs out of state. The young woman he'd dated casually the past two years had recently accepted a marriage proposal from their mutual best friend.

Only one woman had caught his eye since, and she had disappeared as quickly as she'd entered his life. Technically she was his stepsister, the daughter of his father's new wife, but the thought of her being his sister made him laugh aloud in the quiet of his studio apartment. He'd met her on his father's ranch a few months ago. She'd come bouncing toward him across a small pasture behind his father's stable. A tight pair of jeans had hugged her long legs, the form-fitting fabric accenting each rounded curve of her hips and thighs.

She was a tall woman, over five nine, and voluptuous. Her full breasts had obviously been unrestrained by a bra, and her ski sweater accented their movements. Her eyes were the darkest shade of blue he'd ever seen, almost a blue violet, surrounded by long dark lashes. Dark wavy curls had cascaded just past her shapely shoulders. Her lips were pink and her complexion had glowed with youthful good health.

He'd quickly learned that her name was Sarah, she was a few years younger than he was, and she was busy living life to the fullest in her own uninhibited style.

A wave of desire had surged through him as they'd chatted in the pasture, with only a few milling horses, a nearby barking dog, white patches of snow and the mountain skies above to know they'd discovered each other. He'd been jolted back to reality twice when her gaze had returned to the terminal hook on his left hand. He was sure he'd convinced her it was nothing to be concerned about, and by the time they'd parted he suspected the attraction was mutual. She'd kissed him once, tantalizing his lips with the tip of her tongue, but he hadn't had time to respond the way he would have liked.

They'd parted company that same evening. He'd been able to give her his phone number in Missoula, but she wasn't sure of her destination. Other than a promise to stay in touch, she had disappeared without a trace. He knew he'd find her again. He'd never met a more attractive woman, sensuality flowing with every move of her body.

The only problem he could foresee was the effect of their relationship on his father's marriage. He knew his father and his new bride, Sammy, had had several heated arguments regarding Sarah, but they seemed reluctant to talk about it.

Sarah had his phone number. It would be her decision now to make the next move. It'd better be soon, he thought, and he clenched his jaw so tightly that is face ached.

He flipped on the television set and dropped into a chair, staring blankly at the football game being broadcast, but thinking about Sarah.

The day after Christmas his phone rang.

"I have a collect call from a Miss Roberts," came the operator's crisp voice. "Will you accept the charges?"

"Roberts?" he asked, momentarily confused by the unfamiliar surname.

"D.A.!" Sarah's sultry voice resounded over the line.

"Please, miss," the operator cautioned. "Sir, will you accept the charges?"

"Of course," D.A. exclaimed, his pulse pounding with anticipation.

"Hi, big brother," Sarah's melodious voice burst through the receiver. "Guess where I am?" Before he could respond, she rushed on. "San Diego! I just went bodysurfing in the Pacific Ocean. Can you imagine?"

D.A.'s mind was instantly filled with an image of Sarah's voluptuous form being caressed by the frothy surf of the ocean. "Yes, Sarah, I can imagine." He laughed.

"What a fantastic way to spend Christmas! What's it like in Montana? Cold?"

"It's always cold in Montana at Christmastime, Sarah," he replied. "I thought you were staying in Phoenix."

"It was so dull we could only take it for a week."

"We?"

"Paul, silly," she said. "Remember Paul...my boyfriend? He has a brother living here, so we have a place to crash for a while. We ran out of money, though, and the creep is starting to complain that we're freeloading and not chipping in our share. He's wrong, of course. We're both looking for jobs, but nobody is hiring over the holidays."

D.A. shook his head, amazed at her carefree approach to life. "So what are you going to do now?"

"I don't know," Sarah replied. "Paul and I aren't getting along. He's so jealous. He smothers me. If I had some money I'd take off, maybe for San Francisco. I could get a job there.''

"How about coming back up here?'' he suggested.

"What would I do there?''

"Stay with me. Be my *companion* for free room and board.''

"You're joking, big brother.'' She laughed. "Missoula doesn't sound like a swinging town. I think San Francisco is the place for me.''

As she chatted he reached into his small desk and withdrew his savings passbook and scanned the balance. After all, she was his stepsister.

"Sarah, if I send you some money, would you get out of there...leave Paul...and let me know where you go?''

"Oh, D.A., would you?'' Her voice changed to a lower husky pitch. "I didn't want to ask. I promise to pay you back...and yes, I promise to keep in touch. I'll check in on a regular basis just as if you're my parole officer. Oh, D.A., I love you! You're my savior. When can you send it? How much?''

"I'll wire it tomorrow morning,'' he promised. "Check with the Western Union office in San Diego. Now listen, Sarah, you'd better keep your promise and get out of there alone. If I find out that you've given any of it to Paul, I'll personally come and get you,'' he threatened.

"Is that a promise?'' she teased. "How much can you send?''

"Sarah, this is serious. I'll send eight hundred. That should take care of a bus ticket to Frisco or wherever and some for food and rent until you can get a paycheck. If you need more, just call me." He listened for a few minutes to her voice as she jumped from one trivial subject to another. The changing tones of her voice brought a growing response in his body until finally he jerked his glasses off and wiped the sweat from his brow. God, he wanted her. The thousand or more miles separating them seemed an insurmountable barrier keeping her away from him. Her cry interrupted his reverie.

"Goodness, D.A., this is costing you! I'd better sign off."

"Sarah," he said, "call me when you get the money. I'll be working tomorrow in the lab at UM, so take down this number.... Now call. Promise?"

"Promise, big brother. Really! And thanks," she whispered, making a kissing sound to him over the phone. "If I were there, I'd show you just how much I appreciate this. Bye."

He sent the money, but it was three weeks before he heard from her. She was in San Francisco and working as a cocktail waitress.

She described her uniform, and he pictured her busty, long-legged figure in the skimpy outfit.

"D.A., thanks again," she said. "I left without telling Paul where I was going. I mailed you a fifty-dollar money order yesterday. Sorry I took so long to call. I wanted to prove I could take care of myself before I got in touch again."

They chatted about the San Francisco nightlife and the Montana weather and then said goodbye.

D.A. buried himself in his acid-rain research project and the months passed by. He'd been a graduate teaching assistant since his own graduation and was now given three classes of his own: introductory agronomy, a biology class normally taken by non-science majors and a chemistry class open only to agriculture majors. His teaching career was firmly launched. Thoughts of working with his father on the five-thousand-acre cattle ranch were pushed from his mind as preparation for class lectures and the ongoing research project captured all his waking moments.

His birthday was acknowledged with the customary package from home, a card from the Russells and a fat envelope from Mary Elizabeth Russell, the oldest daughter of his father's neighbor.

She had carefully folded a key chain with a good-luck charm in several pieces of facial tissue and slipped it inside a funny birthday card. She'd also enclosed a wallet-size photo, her eighth grade picture. He smiled as he noted her emerging beauty. He suspected she'd always he petite, but her expressive brown eyes were gradually coming into proportion with her oval face. She displayed an unusual balance between her mother's warm fair features and her father's dark ones, and the blend was striking.

Mary wrote him a short note, explaining that she'd earned the money for the gift by baby-sitting and doing chores, and that her grades had been all A's on the last report card.

He hadn't seen her since her birthday the previous

summer, and he wondered if she had grown any taller or started to fill out. Her slenderness gave her an air of fragility that reinforced his protective attitude toward her. He reread the note several times, recalling the many occasions during his youth when he'd taken her horseback riding and sheltered her from the sometimes abusive teasing of her older brothers.

He slipped the photo into his wallet and tossed the card onto the pile of correspondence he'd accumulated since the holidays. He would reply to it all soon, he promised himself.

Sarah hadn't called for several weeks. Maybe he'd give her a buzz if he could find her number. He'd written it on a scrap of paper and tossed it onto the pile of letters just after her December call. She had phoned him once since, but that had been more than a month ago.

He searched through the stack of envelopes, but the slip of paper with her phone number was missing. He called directory assistance in San Francisco, but there was no listing for Sarah Roberts.

"Damn," he cursed, and pounded the desk with his fist. He hastily called the home ranch and asked Sammy if she knew her daughter's number. He was surprised and puzzled by her cool response.

"No, I have no idea where Sarah lives," Sammy said. "She leads her own life. It's best for all of us that way."

He ran his fingers through his blond hair in frustration. If he ever saw her again he'd wring her neck for becoming such an obsession in his thoughts. She interfered with his ability to concentrate on his lectures in the classroom, as well as his research project.

In early April he acted as best man for a friend's wedding but left the reception early after dancing with the radiant bride, shaking his friend's hand and wishing them the best of luck. The phone was ringing as he unlocked the door of his apartment.

It was Sarah.

"Just checking in, big brother," she said. "I'm sending you some more money. I'll bet you thought I'd never repay you, but I'm getting good money and the tips are fantastic." She laughed, and he could imagine the expression on her face. "All I have to do is smile and move right and the tips roll in. I'm sharing an apartment with someone...no, it's a woman. Here's my new address and phone number."

She rattled off the numbers quickly as he frantically searched for a pen to write them down.

"Sarah, give them to me again. I couldn't...."

"Got to go, D.A.," she whispered breathlessly. "My date is here. Bye, you darling brother."

"Sarah!" he cried, but it was too late.

CHAPTER ONE

"BYE, MOM," Mary Russell called over her shoulder as her fingers flew up the front of her quilted pale-blue parka.

She pulled the long rope of brown hair from the inside of her parka and tugged a matching blue knit cap down over her ears for protection from the windy April breezes. "Hope your idea works." She crossed two fingers on her right hand and beamed a smile at her mother. "Gotta go now." She slipped a pair of blue knit gloves on her slender hands and sailed out the door. Her boots clicked a light rhythm on the worn wooden slabs of the porch that covered the entire front of her family's sprawling house.

She skipped down the four steps to the ground, then raced to the stable. She saddled her Appaloosa mare and was on the road before her father and four brothers had finished their breakfasts and returned to the barns. She didn't want to hear any of their teasing comments this morning. For thirteen years they'd picked on her, calling her the Russell-family runt, making fun of her overly large brown eyes and her toothpick-slim arms and legs.

Why did it matter that she was not yet five feet

tall? Someday she'd grow. Two of her brothers were already six feet tall and the others promised to follow suit.

Her two oldest brothers were home from Montana State University at Bozeman for the weekend. The other two attended the local high school in town. They were all helping their father with late calving and inoculations, and tending to other responsibilities related to running three separate cattle operations in different parts of the valley. They didn't have time for her problems and would only make fun of her anyway.

She had found herself in a predicament this month, and her father's refusal to help had compounded the problem. Perhaps the McCormacks, who lived on the neighboring ranch, would help. Time was running out. The chickens would arrive in seven days.

Less than an hour later she slid from the saddle and flipped the reins around a hitching rail near the McCormacks' log home.

She knocked on the front door and waited only a few seconds before it was opened by an attractive woman in her mid-forties.

"Come in," Sammy McCormack said. "Your mother called to say you were on your way. David's out admiring his new pets. He'll be back in a few minutes." Her blue eyes shone as she mentioned her husband's name.

"Thanks," Mary replied, shedding her parka, cap and gloves and smoothing her hair.

"Let's go to the kitchen," Sammy suggested.

As Mary followed the older woman down the hallway, she wondered if she would ever be as tall and attractive as Sammy McCormack. Sammy was only about five-foot four herself, but she didn't have the matronly appearance Mary had noticed in some of her mother's other friends. Sammy's trim figure allowed her to wear jeans and knit tops, and today a woolen sweater in subtle earth tones highlighted the gray frosting in her short curly brown hair.

"I have tea, milk, lemonade or orange juice," she offered. "What would you like?"

"Tea," Mary replied.

"Hot or cold?"

"Cold, thank you," Mary said, and she became aware of a large black-and-white cat rubbing against her pant leg. "What did you mean about new pets?" she asked, recalling Sammy's comment. "More dogs? Or a kitten to keep Duke company in his old age?" She scooped the huge cat into her arms and carried him a few steps.

The cat rubbed his massive head against Mary's cardigan and purred contentedly as he twitched his ears, encouraging her to scratch them again.

"Oh, Duke," Mary cried, glancing down at the front of her blue sweater. "You're shedding!" She lowered the cat to the floor and brushed frantically at the sweater, then slipped if off and hung it over the back of a nearby chair.

Sammy let the swaggering cat outside. "I should have warned you," she said, laughing. She offered

Mary a tall glass of iced tea and joined her at the table. "Duke has adjusted so well to his new home. I think he loves it as much as I do, Mary."

Mary found herself drawn into Sammy's infectious high spirits. "You make me feel good just coming here," she said. "You. . . you smile a lot. You're very happy, aren't you?"

"Very," Sammy replied.

"Is it getting married. . . and all?"

"Not getting married, although that was certainly part of it," Sammy explained. She looked pensively out the window. "It's easy to fall in love, but staying in love requires something more. David and I have had problems—especially where my daughter is concerned—and I've made them worse with my impulsive actions, but . . . but David's wisdom overcame my doubts. Our love is having a chance to grow now and strengthen."

"You must love him very much," Mary commented, caught up in the romantic atmosphere.

"Very much," Sammy said. Her eyes grew shiny with emotion. "I don't think I could live without him." She blinked several times before smiling at Mary. "Now, your mother warned me you were coming. Tell me more about your problem. It involves chickens?"

Mary's slender shoulders drooped a little as she tried to explain the consequences of her own impulsive actions. "I'm always doing homemaking projects in Four-H, and my friends say all the time that I want to grow up and be a mother! That's not true, but what if I did? Is anything wrong with that?"

"Of course not," Sammy replied. "Full-time motherhood is a wonderful career, though I never had the chance to enjoy it. My first husband always thought I should work and help bring in the money, but he also made it very clear that the housework and caring for our four children were also my full responsibility. When we separated, he had the nerve to clean out our joint savings account. It wasn't very much, but still...." She frowned, her sky-blue eyes turning stormy with the memories. "He used to say that the money was his and the children were mine. I never realized how serious he was until...." She brushed her curly hair nervously. "Well, after my divorce, I had four children to raise and I decided that if I didn't keep the wolf from the door, no one else would."

She jumped from her chair and busied herself at an old-fashioned bread box. Mary frowned as she watched her friend, puzzled over her sudden burst of energy.

When Sammy returned to the table a few moments later she placed a small plate of cookies before Mary. "Sorry, Mary. I suppose we all have memories we can never erase. The years between my divorce and finding David are the black ones for me. Oh, Mary, I'm so fortunate to have found him after all these years." She smiled at Mary. "Well," she said with a sigh, "some of us mothers had to work outside the home, but I've always envied those lucky wives who could stay home. But how does that relate to your problem with the chickens...and your father? You're much too young to want to get married. Have you decided to have chicken babies instead of human babies?'' She laughed.

"Yes! How did you guess?'' Mary cried.

"I...I'm not sure,'' Sammy admitted. "Why don't you explain.''

"Well,'' Mary began, feeling rather sheepish, "I decided to have a project this spring that was different from my usual homemaking. I chose chickens. I know I should have talked it over with daddy, but he's never said no to me before. When I explained it to him, he said, 'Absolutely not!' He says with the coyotes, hawks and the weather, no baby chick can survive in this country for long. But he's wrong, Sammy. The Inneses on the Sweetwater have chickens.''

"Chickens aren't free,'' Sammy said. "How can you afford the project?''

"I saved my allowance for months, plus the prize money I won at the fair last year and...and mom gave me some extra. So...I went ahead and ordered three hundred baby chicks from a hatchery in Idaho Falls, and they'll be here next Saturday! And now I have no place to put them,'' she cried in desperation.

"They're all paid for in advance?'' Sammy asked.

"That's another problem. I paid half when I ordered them and thought I'd borrow the rest from my father and pay him back when I sell the fryers. But he refuses to loan me the money. He said I'll have to refuse delivery and either try to get my money back or forfeit it. Oh, Sammy what can I do?''

Sammy studied the young girl before her. "I have an idea,'' she said after a few moments.

"Mom said you might," Mary admitted.

"Let's talk to David," Sammy suggested. "I'll call him on the intercom. He's at the barn."

"Oh, you said he was with his 'new pets.' What did you mean?"

"His Simmental heifers." Sammy laughed. "One is due to calve any day. He's been baby-sitting her as though she were his own child. Let's explain the problem to him, and if he agrees, you can keep them here in our barn. We'll need his help. I'm not very good at building poultry brooders." She dialed the extension and waited. Her face glowed as she talked to her husband.

"Yes...thank you, darling...me, too...could you?" She turned toward Mary. "Yes, she's here now."

Several moments later David McCormack arrived. Mary watched as he took off his muddy overshoes and left them just outside the kitchen door. His long legs carried him quickly to his wife. When he reached her, his arms encircled her waist and pulled her close against him.

Mary watched, enraptured, as his mouth grazed Sammy's. Somehow the tenderness of his light kiss was much more sensuous than the drawn-out open-mouthed kisses she had studied on television. David kept his arm around Sammy as he turned to Mary, a smile warming his rugged features.

Sammy leaned against him, her head and hand momentarily resting against his chest, her fingers toying with the tiny pearl snaps of his blue denim shirt.

David whispered something under his breath that caused Sammy to laugh and push away from him. He came to the table and took the chair next to Mary.

"Well, young lady, what can I do for you this fine day?" he asked. His green eyes flickered back to Sammy once, then concentrated on Mary as she explained her predicament.

Within the hour arrangements were made. David had agreed to build a brooder in a corner of the stable, Sammy insisted on providing half the money in return for half the profits anticipated when the fryers were sold, and Mary pledged to give the chicken project proper attention.

As she said her goodbyes, Sammy and David stood on the porch, their arms around each other, waving to her. As she rode away, Mary felt a wave of gratitude well up inside her. Their love showed in their lives. Although her own parents sometimes kissed in front of their children, her father more likely would pat her mother on the behind than brush her forehead with a kiss. She was glad she knew the McCormacks.

THE FOLLOWING SATURDAY MORNING, Ed Russell delivered his wife and daughter to the McCormack ranch, along with three hundred cheeping Rhode Island Red chicks, then drove away without a word.

Soon the area under the infrared brooder lamps in the barn was filled with bobbing golden heads pecking at the trays of starter mash. After a few pecks at the food, the chicks scurried to the galvanized steel water founts and dipped their beaks into the fresh water. They would raise their small heads upward to the heat lamps overhead to allow the water to run down their throats, and then race back to the trays for more mash.

A car engine sounded outside the barn, and David McCormack left the building.

"Aren't they cute?" Mary said as she stood between her mother and Sammy.

"Very," Sammy agreed.

The chicks gradually settled into clusters, fluffing their coats of rust-and-yellow down and closing their eyes. Only an occasional cheep sounded as the barn quieted.

Mary was thinking about her future wealth, trying to decide between a new sweater or more chickens, when a tall shadow fell over her. Her mother and Sammy stepped aside.

"Hi, brown eyes," D.A. whispered near her ear.

"Oh!" she gasped. He was the last person she'd expected to be there. She whirled around and stumbled over his father's forgotten toolbox, twisting her ankle so sharply that she heard the snap of fragile bones. She crumbled onto the straw. Excruciating pain brought a wave of nausea. She clutched her leg, tears running unchecked down her cheeks.

D.A. knelt before her, holding her leg steady with his prosthesis as he slipped off her shoe and sock. The swelling had already begun.

"Bring a board," he called. "It may be broken."

He whipped off his leather belt as the board was handed to him.

"It hurts terribly," she whispered, an unnatural pallor around her mouth.

"I know, honey," D.A. replied. "I'm so sorry. I didn't mean to scare you...I...." He stopped trying to explain and busied himself with her leg. He used Sammy's proffered sweater to cushion her leg, then quickly bound it to the board with his and his father's belts. "Let's get her to the house," he said as he carefully lifted her in his arms and strode through the stable doors.

Halfway across the yard he slowed down.

"You're as light as a feather. Hold on now," he told her as he adjusted her weight slightly to relieve his left arm.

Her arm went around his neck for extra security and she trembled slightly when he whispered near her ear, "You're safe."

"You're very strong," Mary replied softly. She knew she was being carried to safety by a giant of a man. She had not been this close to him in years, and now as she laid her bobbing head against his shoulder, she heard the steady deep beat of his heart. Her own heart was bursting with joy, leaving her breathless.

Mary hadn't seen D.A. since her thirteenth birthday, and suddenly she realized that her hair was pulled back with the red-and-white scarf he'd given her that special day.

The thought made her blush, and she felt the heat

on her cheeks. She hoped he didn't notice the heightened color; it would only reinforce his opinion that she was still a child. She was almost fourteen, but he was a man. She would love him always, she knew, even when he married. It was inevitable that he would marry one day, and the idea pained her sensitive feelings.

Only her mother and sister knew how she felt. One quiet afternoon, shortly after his birthday gift arrived, her mother had found her crying on her bed. D.A. had sent her a friendship card with a picture of a tiny pink shrimp looking up at a huge ugly lobster. Although it was meant to be humorous, she had burst into tears, because the card proved that he hadn't noticed she was no longer a shrimp. So what if she was short? Surely he could see other proof of her maturity?

She had decided that day that she would never get married. Since she couldn't marry David Alan McCormack, she would just become an old maid and take care of her aging parents and her yet unborn nieces and nephews. *Old Aunt Mary,* she had concluded, and the tears had flowed.

Now here she was experiencing the surprise of her life—being carried to safety by the very man who was responsible for her spinsterhood.

They entered the kitchen and he set her on the table, steadying her while her mother hurried to the telephone to call Dr. Morrison, their family physician.

Mary tried to catch her breath, but D.A. was

standing directly in front of her. He had the most striking sage-green eyes, flecked with splinters of rust. Someday she wanted to see them without his glasses. She would peer into them and...she had missed what her mother was saying as she stared into his eyes, but she heard him speak.

"Since I caused it, I'll drive you to town. Ready for another trip, honey?"

She found herself in his arms again, but instead of going out the door, he just stood there holding her, right in the middle of the McCormack kitchen. She shyly lifted her eyes to admire his face, and noticed the light stubble of blond beard on his firm chin. Blond curls edged around his ear and the side of his muscular neck. He was so handsome.

Her hand slid upward and caressed his hair. A sigh escaped her when she felt its softness, but as she touched the curls he turned, and she thought he was losing his hold on her.

"Oh!" she gasped, clutching at his shirt.

"Hey, I wouldn't drop you, honey," he said.

His wide lips came closer to her face. What was he going to do? *Kiss her? Where?* She had never been kissed on the mouth before. She waited breathlessly, then in an instant of disappointment felt his lips touch her cheek.

"I love you, Mary. You're a doll." He tightened his arms slightly. "Dad, can we take your truck? My car is a little snug."

"Of course," his father said, nodding. "Here are the keys." He held the door open, and Julie grabbed the keys and hurried toward a blue four-wheel-drive pickup truck parked near the hitching rail.

Mary was in the truck leaning against D.A.'s right arm, her splinted ankle propped across her mother's lap, before she realized that she had forgotten all about her throbbing injury. Each shift of the gears brought his arm and shoulder rubbing against her. She tried to give him room, and as he glanced down at her, her heart stopped.

"You're okay, honey. I'll manage," he said, his voice husky with concern.

He carried her into Dr. Morrison's office, stayed with her during the X ray and cast placement, then carefully eased her into the truck cab for the trip to her own home.

As they went over the drainage ditch into the Rocking R he hit a bump and she cried out in alarm, grabbing for support. Her hand found the denim of his pant leg, and she clutched it until she realized what she was holding. Quickly she released her grip.

"Are you okay, honey?" he asked, looking down at her again. He smiled and a delightful tingling feeling swept through her.

"Yes," she replied. "My ankle hurts, but I'm fine. Thanks for taking care of me." She tried to balance herself on the seat between her mother and D.A., her plaster-coated ankle propped on two pillows the doctor had lent them.

She knew she probably would never have another experience quite like this. It was worth the broken ankle to ride with him and be carried by him. He was very tall and strong, and the handsomest man she knew.

He carried her into her house and followed her mother into Mary's bedroom, where he laid her on the purple quilted bedspread. Her family swarmed around her, trying to get details of her accident.

As her mother began to shoo her brothers and sister out, Mary looked anxiously around the room in search of D.A. McCormack, but he had disappeared without a word.

DARKNESS HAD FALLEN by the time D.A. drove over the culvert into his father's place. He chuckled to himself as he thought back over the day's unexpected turn of events.

When he'd entered the barn that morning, the cheeping sounds of the baby chicks had filled the stable.

"How many are there?" he'd whispered to his father.

"Three hundred, give or take a few that may have escaped."

D.A. had spotted the two women and Mary. She looked pencil slim as she stood between the two older women. Her dark hair had fallen just past her waist, and D.A. had smiled when he recognized his red-and-white silk scarf holding back her long shiny hair.

She had turned slightly, bending to retrieve a chick that had escaped from the brooder. As she reached for the scurrying chick, he had seen the slight swell of newly forming breasts. Her movements had reminded him of a ballet dancer in a leotard, or, as he re-called her image now, perhaps a rose about to un-fold. He wanted to see her someday in full bloom, but he knew that would be years away. Now she re-mained a tender bud of a girl with only a hint of the womanly form to come.

Thoughts of Sarah Roberts swept the image of Mary away, but the rosebud symbol did not fit Sarah at all. Perhaps a giant colorful dahlia, but never a delicate rosebud. Ah, Sarah, he thought, now there was a real woman.

Hunger gnawed at his stomach, and he realized that he'd missed lunch with the excitement and urgency of Mary's broken ankle. He parked near the kitchen door and took the steps two at a time. He rushed through the door but stopped abruptly when he found his father and Sammy embracing. His father's hand had disappeared under her sweater. There wasn't a spot along their bodies that was not in close contact.

D.A. heard her moan. Why hadn't he knocked? He whirled away. "I forgot something in the car," he mumbled, and left the room as quickly as he had rushed in.

He stayed outside and smoked a cigarette. Seeing his father expressing his desire for his new wife made D.A. uncomfortable, and what he had just witnessed had definitely been a bit of sensual foreplay.

"Damn it," D.A. murmured as he faced the hard cold fact that in his own life he had no woman to give him love or affection. Was Sarah Roberts the woman to fill the void, he wondered.

He smoked another cigarette. When he returned, knocking before entering, Sammy and his father were at the table, acting as though everything was normal.

Near the end of the meal he told them about his calls from Sarah. He didn't mention the loan, only the contacts. He could tell he had opened a wound in their relationship and wondered if there were things he didn't know.

He shrugged his shoulders. Their difficulties with Sarah were their concern, just as his keeping in touch with her was his.

D.A. McCormacks's summer was filled with drafting and revising the results of the first phase of his research project. He quickly wrote the summary paragraph that proved his hypothesis and tossed his pencil down onto the desk. He started when the phone rang.

Instinctively he knew who was calling.

"Hi, big brother," Sarah's velvet voice surged through the instrument like a tidal wave.

"Hi yourself, little sister," he said, laughing, trying to sound casual. "Why this call after all these months? You're hard to keep track of, did you know that? I lost your number, but my letters never came back, so I assumed you were still there in Frisco."

"Why didn't you come find out for yourself?" she teased.

"I should have, but—"

"Well," she said, cutting him off, "John and I want to come see you."

"John?" he asked, seething at the thought that she would have the nerve to bring a new boyfriend with her and still visit him. "Who the hell is John, Sarah? Don't you think...?" He glanced at himself in a nearby mirror and saw that his eyes were blazing with anger. Feeling foolish at such a visual proof of her effect on him, he quickly dropped into a chair and blocked out his own image.

"He's your brother, silly," she chided him lightly.

"I'm an only child."

"Not anymore. Not since your father married my mother," she reminded him. "D.A., for a guy as intelligent as you're supposed to be, you're a little dense tonight. Want me to come there and teach you how to think straight?" Her voice slowly changed into a sensual purr.

He tried without success to recall the names of Sammy's children. "Which one is he?" he asked, growing tired and frustrated with her game.

"He's my baby brother. He's here on leave from the navy and wants to meet you."

D.A. heard a man's laughter in the background, and he wondered if she was telling him the truth about her guest.

"Will you meet us at the Missoula airport if we fly up?" she asked.

Arrangements were quickly made, and the following morning D.A. met them at the airport. Sarah flew into his arms as if they were long-lost lovers, and he only wished it was so. He shook her brother John's proffered hand.

John bore a family resemblance to Sammy and had inherited his mother's soft blue eyes. His sandy brown hair lay neatly on his high forehead, its short crisp cut announcing his military enlistment. His lean wiry build made him appear taller than his six-foot height, and the moment he smiled, D.A. knew he was Sarah's brother.

Again Sarah hugged D.A., and he forgot John's presence. Sarah had taken on an air of sophistication. Her clothes were expensively tailored and made of a silky clinging material he couldn't identify. Her casual unpolished image was only in his memories, and she was even more beautiful than he remembered.

Each touch of her hand or brush of her body against his as they drove to his apartment brought a new surge of desire for her. Her smile and subtle whispering near his ear as he maneuvered through the traffic kept his self-control barely in check.

D.A. took them to a nightclub that evening for dinner and dancing. When the music began, he asked Sarah to dance. The band played a medley of country swing with a heavy beat. They were both perspiring lightly when he returned her to the table, where John had been waiting for them.

"It's hot in here," Sarah said, twisting her body and shedding the short jacket of her navy-blue jump suit. The spaghetti straps on the silk jersey bodice held up the few inches of material covering her breasts.

John's eyes grew round and teasing as he evaluated his sister's attire. "Don't sneeze," he warned, grinning at D.A. and winking.

Sarah took a few sips of her frosty coconut drink and caught her breath. John grabbed her hand and returned her to the dance floor, leaving D.A. behind to stew as he caught glimpses of their undulating forms in the crowd.

When the music ended, Sarah returned to the table.

"I love it!" she exclaimed as D.A. handed her a soft napkin to wipe the moisture from her face. She was flushed with the excitement of the dance.

After the band broke for an intermission, the music changed to easy-listening and slow-dance numbers.

"Dance with me again," D.A. said.

"Of course," Sarah replied.

He led her to the dance floor, and she moved into his arms. The only time he really regretted losing his left hand was when he was with Sarah. He wanted to hold her with both hands, feel the warmth and softness of her skin, take her away to some private intimate world and never let her go.

She danced slightly away from him, watching his face. Suddenly she smiled. "How tall are you?"

"Six foot two...and you?"

"Five foot nine...and a half inch."

"That's good," he whispered, drawing her closer. Her breasts pressed against his chest, and he desperately wanted to touch their creamy smoothness.

The dancing continued, and he brushed her cheek with a kiss. She nibbled the sensitive skin on his neck, kissed him, and leaned closer into his hard body. He knew she felt his arousal as they continued dancing slowly and intimately.

"This music does something to a person, doesn't it?" he whispered near her ear. He wanted to slip away with her, but knew they couldn't leave John. Each time the music stopped, he felt a simmering resentment, which quickly changed to pleasure when she remained with him, holding his right hand, waiting for the band to resume. At the first strains of the instruments her body returned to its rightful place against him, and the dancing continued without a spoken word.

In spite of his age and experience, he was reluctant to express his feelings, fearing she might laugh at him, so he merely held her close. She seemed to have taken his self-confidence away, yet her movements suggested so much, teasing him with a promise of fulfillment.

The evening ended in the wee hours as they drove the quiet streets to D.A.'s studio apartment.

"You can sleep in my bed, Sarah," he said as suitcases were opened. "John can have the sofa, and I'll take the floor in my sleeping bag."

When she returned from the bathroom, he was again struck by an avalanche of desire. The champagne-colored satin of her peignoir set seemed to be molded to every curve as she sauntered toward him. John disappeared into the bathroom, leaving them alone for a few moments.

"If John weren't here," she cooed, drawing her index finger down his lean cheek, "we could...." She ran two fingers back and forth over a taut muscle in his jaw, and it quivered before relaxing. "Good night, big brother," she whispered.

As she slithered out of her robe and slid between the sheets of his bed, he glimpsed the soft curves of her sensuous body.

The next day she disappeared from his life again. He called the number she'd given him during her short stay, but received no answer. A week later the number had been disconnected. He wrote her a letter urging her to call him collect, but it was returned marked, "Moved, no forward."

A money order paying off her loan arrived three months after her visit. It was drawn on a bank in Bakersfield, California, but the envelope carried a postmark from Lake Havasu, Arizona. She was on the move again.

CHAPTER TWO

"MARY!" A MAN'S VOICE CALLED through the crowd of Christmas shoppers in the department store.

Mary Russell turned, but all she saw was milling shoppers in overcoats and parkas. Perhaps she'd imagined the call.

She was trying to choose a knitted hat for her sister Lisa from the many different styles. Finally she selected a royal-blue-and-white cap with tiny antelope bounding around the border. Fumbling in her purse, she headed to the checkout counter. She had one more stop to make before phoning her mother for a ride home. She'd stayed in town after school to complete a research assignment in the high-school library for her freshman English class, then impulsively had decided to finish her shopping for the holiday.

As she dropped the cap and her money on the counter, she glanced toward the door and groaned inwardly at the falling snow. The sky had been threateningly overcast all day.

"Thank you," she murmured to the clerk as she dropped her change into her open billfold. Three coins missed their destination and tumbled to the floor. Mary knelt to retrieve them, embarrassed at her clumsiness. She heard the people in line start to chuckle, and she tensed with irritation at herself as well as at the other shoppers.

A large hand picked up a dime before Mary could reach it. "May I help?" a familiar voice asked.

She looked up into D.A. McCormack's smiling face, and her irritation and embarrassment were instantly replaced with light-headed disbelief.

"Thank...thank you," she stammered, stepping away from him.

"Wait," he said, and he paid for a package of calculator batteries. They walked together to the exit, and he held the door for her. The movement of the crowd swept them away from the protective storefront. The northern latitude brought an early dusk to the area in winter, and lights from the traffic shimmered through the snowflakes, lending an unearthly beauty to the street.

A change in wind direction showered Mary's face with powdery snow, and she hunched her shoulders and pressed against the wall of the stone building. D.A. lifted the lapels of his fleece-lined coat and tried to protect her from the elements, then he unbuttoned it completely and built a sheltering wall around her.

"Don't move," he said. "It'll pass in a few moments."

Mary felt his warmth as she stood motionless within this makeshift cocoon. She was torn between utter delight that he was there with her and bewilderment that he was in town at all. She hadn't seen him for several months. He'd sent her a teasing get-well card and asked about her ankle, and mailed her a birthday card in July, enclosing cash instead of the usual gift.

Mary had realized he must have become tied to his career and graduate studies at the university. During a recent visit Sammay had told the Russells that he'd received his master's in agricultural chemistry and was now working on his doctorate. Just the thought was a little intimidating to a high-school freshman.

"What are you doing here?" she asked now, her voice croaking slightly with excitement.

He leaned closer to her face to hear. "I came for the weekend. I have some Christmas gifts to deliver. I'm spending the holidays in Missoula," he explained, smiling at her upturned face. "Did you miss the school bus? Are you stranded in town?"

"Mom's coming for me when I call," she replied. "I didn't think the weather would be this bad, though. I hate to have her drive in for me. I guess I could stay with my grandmother, but I'd planned to work on a special assignment this evening.

"Let me give you a ride," he offered.

"I have to go to the Country Gallery for some poster board and felt markers," she explained, "and I'm so hungry I thought I'd get something to eat." She held her breath and decided to give him an out. "You're probably in a hurry," she murmured, glancing up to catch his reaction.

"Come with me," he said, and grabbed her gloved hand. Soon they were nestled in his maroon automobile and heading to the art shop. He waited patiently as she selected several colors of large poster board and two packages of markers. He stowed the bulky packages behind the driver's seat as she climbed back into his car. He slammed his door and turned to her.

"If you're finished shopping, how about having dinner with me in town?" he asked. He laughed at her surprised expression. "Dad and Sammy aren't expecting me, and I hate to drop in for dinner unannounced. I was planning to eat in town and call from the restaurant," he explained. "You said you were hungry. You can call your mother and tell her I'm bringing you home. It'll save her a trip."

Mary's brown eyes sparkled. She nodded her head, afraid if she spoke another word this scene might evaporate like a dream.

D.A. drove to a nearby restaurant and hurried her to the door, draping his arm around her shoulders to protect her from the storm. He brushed the snow from her coat before removing it from her shoulders and hanging it on the coatrack near the door.

They made the phone calls to their respective ranches while waiting for the hostess to seat them. D.A.'s hand rested on Mary's waist as he escorted her to their table. When he withdrew it to pull her chair away, she missed its warmth. She glanced around the room, seeing if she recognized any of the other diners in the subdued lighting. D.A. waved to a couple across the room.

She suspected she was out of her element when she glanced at the customers, all much older than herself.

Her feeling was confirmed when she picked up the menu.

She grabbed her small clutch purse, hastily scanned the worn billfold inside, and let out a perplexed sigh. "I...I spent all my money, D.A."

"Why do you need any?" he asked, lifting a blond brow in question.

"My meal...I...should pay for...I spent more on the art supplies than I'd intended." She felt a wave of heat burn her cheeks and grew restless under his continued gaze.

"I invited you to dinner, Mary. You're my guest. Did you really think I'd make you go Dutch, honey?" He smiled at her misunderstanding. "I guess you're too young to have boys asking you to dinner," he observed. "But be patient. You're getting to be a very pretty young woman, Mary. I'm sure the high-school boys have noticed that. Right?"

She smiled. "Perhaps a little," she murmured, "but Lisa is much prettier. She's fair...I'm too dark. She's almost as tall as I am and she's four years younger!"

The waitress took their orders and left. Mary tried desperately to think of something witty to say, but her nervousness kept her speechless.

Their salads arrived, and her fork felt like an icicle when she touched it. She fumbled, lost her grip, and watched helplessly as it fell to the floor. The waitress hurriedly brought her another and left.

"Relax, Mary." D.A. smiled. "It's only a meal and we're old friends. You'll make me think you don't want to be here with me. Pretend that you're my date for the evening. You're out to dinner with an *older man*."

His laughter and charm soothed her inner turmoil.

"Now what shall we talk about?" he asked as the waitress removed their salad plates. "You or me?"

"You," she said.

"Ask away."

"Sammy told us about their trip to Missoula and your getting your master's degree," she said. "Tell me about working on your doctorate. I don't understand. You must love school to keep going yourself even while you teach."

For several minutes he explained the program he was following. He told her it would enable him to someday become a full professor at a college or university around the country, and that although he liked teaching, it was the research he loved most.

"I think I like the problem solving best. It's all in my hands to find a solution. If my first attempt doesn't work out, then I try again...and again, until finally I get what I want." He studied Mary intently, his eyes changing to a stormy dark green. "It's like searching through a forest looking for the perfect tree to meet your needs. Haven't you ever wanted something so badly it made you ache with the want?" He reached across and took her hand.

"Yes," she admitted. She could barely breathe as she stared down at their clasped hands, and she gave thanks that he was actually sitting across from her. "And sometimes, just when you know it's so hopeless, suddenly you find it right in front of you, or as though it's fallen from nowhere into your lap.''

His look held admiration. "You do understand, don't you? Mary, you've always been so easy to talk to, and now that you're growing up, even more so. I'm glad we're still good friends.'' He withdrew his hand and took a sip of coffee.

She dropped her hand into her lap, unable to resist the urge to touch the skin he'd held.

"Remember some of those summer trail rides we used to take?" he asked. "The years have flown, haven't they?''

"Yes," she said. "You would let me ride double with you, and my brothers would groan and complain about me tagging along. Gee, D.A., if you hadn't let me ride with you, mom would never have let me go. That's when you started calling me 'shrimp.' You used to be able to step right over me with your long legs. You'd toss me up in the air and spin me around and catch me before I'd touch the ground.'' She frowned thoughtfully at him. "That was a long time ago.''

She turned her attention to the steak before her, and as she ate, she mulled over the years they'd known each other.

"Do you date?" D.A. asked, startling her from her reverie.

"No," she replied. "Daddy won't let me. He says I'm too young.''

"He's right. If you were my daughter, I'd want to hide you away from the boys around here.''

"Do you?" she asked.

"Date? Some," he replied.

"Still Betsy?"

"No," he replied. "Betsy married a mutual friend last spring. I received a Christmas card from her. She's expecting a baby next summer." He grinned. "She turned out to be rather domestic. She changed a lot when she met Jason."

"Who's Jason?"

"Betsy's husband. They live in Berkeley, California."

"Do you date anyone special?" she persisted, needing to know if there was one particular woman in his life. "Have you ever been in love?"

"Not really...until...I don't really know. Perhaps if we could see each other more often," he said contemplatively.

"Oh, dear, there is someone special, isn't there?" Mary said.

"Possibly."

"Oh, please be careful, D.A. Don't rush into anything you might regret. Mom says that...." She dropped her head.

"What does your mother say, honey?" he asked.

Her brown eyes widened with concern. "That sometimes people marry the wrong person...for the wrong reasons."

"Why do you think two people should marry?"

"For...love. The kind that lasts and lasts. The kind that grows and gets so strong that even the most terrible problem can't break it apart. Daddy says that's a silly attitude to have. That I'm being romantic and unrealistic. What do you think, D.A.? Do men marry for love?"

"Perhaps," he replied, "and a few other things probably more basic. After all, a man gets a maid and cook when he gets a loving wife. Didn't you know that behind every knight in shining armor, there's a castle waiting to be cleaned?"

Her eyes widened as she puzzled over his words. "I hope you're joking...a little?" she asked, and was relieved when he grinned at her from across the table. "Don't women get anything out of this marriage thing?"

"Sure," he agreed. "Women get love and security and children...and sometimes heartache."

"Don't men get heartache?" she asked, taking a sip of her soft drink to hide the conflicting emotions she was feeling about this discussion.

"Sometimes," he admitted. "Maybe that's why I'm a little gun shy. I have some friends who married, divorced and then remarried again. They left their first family and started another, kids and all, without a backward glance at what they left behind. I know a few of the wives and children abandoned for another woman. That doesn't seem right. I wouldn't want to be guilty of that."

"That's terrible!" she agreed. "But you'd never do a thing like that. If you loved a woman enough to marry her, wouldn't you try to stay with her?"

He nodded. "Marriage should be forever."

"Oh, I agree," she said. "So who's special in your

life?'' She frowned. ''I think you've been giving this marriage business some extra thought. Just be careful, D.A. Forever is a long, long time.'' She envied the woman he chose. ''Tell me about the woman in your life. Is she someone at the university?''

''Not really,'' he said. He laughed awkwardly. ''It's someone in my family, you might say.''

''Who?'' Mary asked. ''A cousin? That's not... very good.''

''My cousins are all six-foot men, Mary,'' he explained. ''It's Sammy's daughter.''

''Who?''

''Dad's wife's daughter. Her name is Sarah Roberts. I've only seen her a few times, but... God, she's the sexiest woman I've ever met.'' He glanced at Mary's startled expression. ''Oops, that's a little strong for your innocent ears, isn't it? She visited me in Missoula, but she moves around a lot. I've lost track of her lately.'' His face was shadowed by a seriousness and it clouded the pleasure she had been feeling in his company.

''Well,'' he said as he set his coffee cup down. ''Tell me about you, Mary. How's high school? Do you like it? What courses are you taking? College prep or...?''

''Some college prep and some home economics. I can't decide what to do.'' She let out a deep sigh. ''D.A., why do girls have to have fancy careers?''

He frowned at her. ''What do you consider a fancy career, Mary?''

''Oh,'' she hesitated, chewing on her lip. ''You'll

think I'm being silly. I got into an argument at school a few days ago with my teacher and the principal and some other students." She took a sip of her drink. "You see, I'm our freshman-class vice-president. I ran because no one else would...and I won!" She laughed, her eyes dancing as she told him about the class elections.

"Anyway, now I'm on a committee of freshmen to do some displays for a careers day next spring. Each grade is doing part of the presentation. When I read through the list of careers being featured, I got upset. They were all things like medicine, law, accounting, engineering, computer science. You know...so I asked why there wasn't one for a woman who wants to be a wife and mother." Her voice faded.

"And what was the reply?" he asked curiously.

"They said...they said being a wife and mother was no career, that it was just what women did if they couldn't do anything better."

"And?" he coaxed.

"And I told them they were wrong...that some women do that best. My home-ec teacher suggested I do a display to prove my case." Her face lighted up. "So that's what I'm going to do with the supplies I bought. I'm going to prove that homemaking is just as worthwhile a career as those other occupations."

"Perhaps," he agreed, "but homemaking requires something the others don't."

"What?" she asked, relieved that he wasn't making fun of her.

"A husband."

Her shoulders sagged.

"It makes good planning sense, Mary," he explained. "You set goals, but you allow for alternatives. You're a farm girl. You know it's never wise to put all your eggs in one basket. Don't let yourself become dependent on a man. Have something to fall back on just in case things like marriage don't work out. Be realistic."

"You're probably right," she agreed reluctantly.

"You're an old-fashioned girl, Mary," D.A. said as he reached for the check. "I like that, but in this day and age it might be dangerous. There are no guarantees in marriage in today's world. Some fellows just walk out when they get tired of the responsibilities. You need protection from that possibility."

"You make it sound a little scary."

"I didn't want to frighten you, just make you leery. When some young cowboy sweeps you off your feet in a few years, think of me and our discussion tonight. Be prepared." He gave her a sloppy salute.

"I suppose you're right, D.A. But you're wrong about part of it."

"What's that?"

"No cowboy is going to sweep me off my feet. After living with four brothers who track mud and manure into momma's kitchen, I've decided I want someone who's...different."

"How about the clean-cut types who teach at universities?" he teased. "Or bankers or insurance agents, maybe a computer programmer or a lawyer."

"Don't make fun of me, D.A.," she said, frowning. "I'm not the little shrimp you still think I am." Her fists were clenched in her lap, but they slowly relaxed when he smiled across at her.

"Sorry, Miss Russell," he said as he dropped a generous tip near his coffee cup. "Ready to brave the elements, honey?"

"I suppose."

"Don't give up, Mary," he said as he helped her into her coat. "There's a husband out there somewhere. You're too young and much too pretty to worry about being an old maid."

He held the door and together they stepped into the storm. Her pulse quickened when he put his arm around her shoulders and pulled her snugly against his side, shielding her until they reached his car.

He turned to her as they pulled into the traffic. "Sammy has a wall plaque that reads 'Believe, because dreams can come true,' " he said, glancing at her pretty profile. "Are you a believer, Mary? Will you find the perfect husband someday?"

"Oh, yes," she cried.

"You sound very positive," he said as they left the town and headed south.

"I am," she replied. But as they drove silently through the darkness and up the winding gravel road, she knew that as far as she and D.A. were concerned, time was working against her.

"TELL ME ABOUT SARAH," Mary said, glancing at Sammy as she handed her an armload of books.

They'd spent the day rearranging the library in the small Baptist church where Mary's family worshipped each Sunday. The other volunteers had left for the day.

As they slid the remaining children's picture books into their new location, Sammy's hand trembled slightly.

"Why?" she asked.

"Oh, someone asked me about her," Mary hedged. "And since I've never met her, I thought maybe you could tell me about her. Mom said once that she... caused trouble between you and David."

Sammy sighed deeply. "She did, but I was partly to blame, because I let her. She and her boyfriend came to stay with David and me when we were first married and almost took over our home. I became upset when David implied that it was my fault my daughter had turned out the way she had—and I was jealous of all the attention Sarah was lavishing on her new stepfather." Sammy ran her fingers through her curly hair. "Sarah's very beautiful."

"Is she blond or dark, blue or brown eyes, tall or short, thin or fat?"

"My goodness, you are curious," Sammy said, laughing. "She's tall, several inches taller than I am. Her hair is brunet, her eyes are dark blue." She shook her head in disbelief. "Where she gets her figure from, I don't know."

Mary's eyes grew round. "What do you mean?"

"She's very... well endowed. She's twenty-one now. I'm sure men find her quite attractive."

"Did she go to college? Does she have a career?" Mary asked.

Sammy laughed aloud. "She's never been academically inclined. She was kicked out of high school several times, mostly for smoking in the rest rooms. She considered it a big joke. The classes she did earn credits in were all with male teachers. She's intelligent, but unscrupulous.

"Sarah is a manipulator," she explained. "If she's nice it's because she wants something. She left friends scattered around Phoenix like litter. Two of her brothers hate her so much they won't have anything to do with her. Only my youngest son, John, has stayed in touch. Throughout school she used her brothers and took advantage of them, and even stole from them when they wouldn't give her something she wanted."

Sammy shook her head. "I feel sorry for the man who falls in love with her. He'll have to be very blind to stay with her for long."

Suddenly she turned to Mary, her eyes tear-filled. "I tried to raise all my children the best I knew how, but something went wrong with Sarah. Every moral principle I believed in and tried to instill in her was thrown back in my face. She called me a prude. I know for a fact that her first sexual experience was just after her thirteenth birthday." Her distraught expression forced Mary to drop her eyes.

"The boy's parents called me early one morning and accused Sarah of seducing their son. They told me I should control my daughter, that she was the talk of the neighborhood boys. I found out later that day that she'd sneaked out her bedroom window the night before and joined a kegger party at the park near our home."

"I'm so sorry," Mary murmured. "I wish I could help."

"Just having someone to talk to helps," Sammy replied. "For some reason I've hesitated to tell David about this period in my life. Maybe I was ashamed, maybe I'm afraid he'd think I was a real failure in raising my children. It's been eating at me for years." She pressed the heels of her palms against her eyes. "I used to think that if you tried your best to raise your children they'd automatically turn out right. But with Sarah, I've had to change my beliefs. Once when they were about fifteen and seventeen, my oldest son had a terrible fight with her. He didn't know I was home from work. He told her she was known as the East Phoenix whore. Oh, Mary, it was so awful. She actually smiled at him, stuck her chest out and flipped her hair, and told him the north side was next."

"Has it been a long time since you've heard from her?" Mary asked.

"Not since her visit to the ranch, but my sons and I agreed to keep each other informed if we heard from her. John's always been loyal and protective of her, so I'm not sure he'd tell me if he saw her, but the others would.

"My son Lawrence called me a few weeks ago and said he'd run into her in Las Vegas. Out of curiosity he bought her a drink and asked her what she was doing. Oh, Mary, she's a member of the Follies Bergère at the Tropicana on the Strip. They dance nude from the waist up! Can you imagine dancing with your breasts exposed to an audience full of strangers?''

Mary crawled around the stacks of books and scooted over to Sammy's side. "I'm so sorry, Sammy," she said, patting her shoulder and trying to console her. Yet she felt torn with an even stronger concern for D.A.'s driving desire to find Sarah. Apparently Sammy was unaware of D.A.'s obsession with her daughter.

"That's not all," Sammy whispered hoarsely, wiping her eyes and nose with a piece of tissue. "Oh, Mary, I shouldn't burden you with my problems, but I haven't been able to tell even David about my son's call. Lawrence said she was dressed very well and wore expensive jewelry. He said she hinted that she was making most of her money on the side. When he asked her how, she only smiled and said that she'd finally found a profession that paid for what she did best. She even bragged to her own brother that she was good and wanted to be known as the best in town. Mary," Sammy said sadly, "it sounds like she's a call girl or prostitute or...."

Sammy turned pleadingly to Mary. "Where did I go wrong with her? I tried so hard!"

Mary patted her shoulder again reassuringly. "Sometimes the kids just decide to do what they want. I don't think it's fair to blame the parents. Maybe sometimes, but not always. I certainly don't blame my mother for what my older brothers do when they're in town for the weekend. They think I don't know, but I keep my ears open. They think I'm still a little kid, but I'm not! Oh, Sammy, I'm sorry I asked about her."

"It's all right," Sammy replied. "I feel better just sharing my problem. I'm sorry I dumped it on your shoulders. Please don't tell anyone, especially not your parents or D.A. or David. I...I'll just have to learn to live with the fact that my daughter and I have different standards."

Sammy squeezed Mary's hand. "She's still my daughter, and I love her. Maybe that's why I *hate* what she does!"

She slowly got to her feet and brushed the dust from the seat of her jeans. "Well, I think if we sweep the floor we'll be done for today. Next Saturday we'll finish in time for the open house."

As they finished their work, Sammy smiled. "I'm glad your mother talked me into volunteering to head this project. I guess it's my Leo instinct to take charge." She put the brooms away and reached for her coat. "Let's go eat before we drive home."

During dinner they discussed high school, the ranches' calving problems, Julie Russell's latest quilt design and D.A.'s determination to live in Missoula...everything but Sarah and the turbulence she had brought to the McCormacks.

CAREERS DAY WAS HELD the first week in April. Except for a few snide remarks from several boys and a few girls, Mary's homemaker career display was a hit, especially with some senior girls who had their eyes on selected boys.

"It's about time," one girl told Mary.

"I think it's great, but I'd never have the nerve," another whispered.

"That's all well and good, Mary," her friend Jackie said, "but who's going to pay the rent? No wife gets paid for her services. She's a slave...work, work, work, cleaning up after some sloppy man. My dad says a woman doesn't need any modern appliances, that that's what women are for. My mother spent years cooking on a wood stove because my dad was too tight to spend the money on her. Cows yes, new tractor yes, but his own wife, hell no! No one appreciated her until she got sick last year. My father didn't even believe the doctor when he told him she had cancer. He told my mother she was just getting lazy. Well, she fooled him. She escaped—she died... and now he wants me to take her place!" Her jaw tightened and she whirled away.

"I'll get married someday," Mary's friend Joannie said, "but not until I get my law degree. I'm going to be the first woman lawyer in my family...actually the first college graduate. I'm not going to clean up after anyone but myself...unless he's gorgeous like...." She named several television stars who met her requirements.

"I hate men," Mary's cousin Michelle Innes announced. "If they're all like my brothers, then you can have them. I prefer my horses. You can trust them and train them to do what you command. I like to be in command.''

The day ended with Mary's display winning a first-place award in the freshman division.

CHAPTER THREE

"LET'S RIDE TO THE MCCORMACKS," Lisa said as the Russells enjoyed a leisurely Saturday-morning breakfast. "We can tell them about your two triumphs."

Mary smiled. Steven gave her a thumbs-down sign. Her other brothers ignored the conversation.

"Hey," her oldest brother Paul said. "Check this! D.A. made the *Montana Standard*. It says here he was invited to speak at a symposium sponsored by the University of Nevada at Las Vegas. That's great!" He glanced at the calendar on the wall nearby. "He spoke Wednesday and Thursday. He's probably on his way home by now." He tossed the paper on a nearby chair and left the room.

Mary reached for the paper, but her brother Steven grabbed it away and tossed it in the garbage can, which he then took outside.

"Let's go, Mary," Lisa called, gathering up her lightweight jacket. "The McCormacks have a ranch, e-i-e-i-o," she sang as she skipped out the door.

As they mounted their horses, Lisa giggled. "You tried to make the McCormack place into a chicken farm, remember? Do they still have some of your chickens?"

Mary laughed. "Yes, six hens and a rooster."

As they cantered up the dirt right-of-way along the gravel road, Mary tried to put her concern over D.A.'s visit to Las Vegas into its proper perspective. Las Vegas was a large metropolitan city. The likelihood of D.A. meeting Sarah Roberts was extremely remote.

She and Lisa were invited to stay for lunch with Sammy and David, and during the meal Lisa prodded her sister into telling about her recent successes.

"They saw the pictures of the display," Mary said.

"Tell them the other thing, too," Lisa said. "It's the best!"

"It's not much," Mary replied with a blush.

"It is too!" Lisa insisted.

"What is it, Mary?" Sammy asked, her blue eyes giving Mary encouragement.

"Last week I tried out for the junior varsity cheerleading squad. You have to be a sophomore next fall...and I made it."

"That's great, Mary," Sammy said. "I'm very pleased for you. David," she said, turning to her husband, "can you bring me the green album in our bedroom?" He left the room and she explained, "I was a pom-pom girl my last two years in high school. Pudgy legs and all, but I loved it. It did wonders for my self-esteem. Let me tell you something that happened during one game...." She stopped and turned her head toward the door, listening. Footsteps and a loud knock sounded.

Sammy frowned. "I wonder who that could be. Mary, would you get some more iced tea?"

As Mary got up from the table the knock sounded again.

"Come in," Sammy called.

Mary turned away from the refrigerator as the door opened and D.A. McCormack entered the room, his arm around the shoulders of a tall, voluptuous young woman in her early twenties. Mary's expression froze on her face at the sight of them.

"Sarah!" Sammy gasped.

David McCormack entered from the hallway carrying the album as D.A. closed the door.

"Who's that?" Lisa whispered.

The silence in the room grew awkward.

"Well, hello," David acknowledged their presence at last. "You're probably the last two people we expected to come through that door, especially together. What brings you here? Sit down, sit down. Coffee?"

Mary was the first to notice the light reflecting off the simple gold band the young woman wore on her left hand. A tortured expression tore across her pale features and her gaze slid to D.A. She began to chew her lower lip. Her chin moved, but no words were uttered. She watched helplessly, waiting for D.A. to make the fateful announcement that her broken heart knew would come.

David looked at Mary and Lisa. "I don't think you two girls know Sammy's daughter, do you? Sarah, this is Mary and Lisa Russell, our neighbors and D.A.'s friends since they were small children."

Mary stared at the woman's deep blue eyes and

couldn't help but admire their shining beauty. Shoulder-length dark wavy hair surrounded her face and gave her the appearance of a professional model, yet she wore only a hint of makeup. Her waist was made small by the most ample breasts Mary had ever seen.

Mary glanced down at her own chest and her heart sank in dismal disappointment. She now wore a bra, but its size was embarrassingly small. She had passed the five-foot mark and weighed ninety-five pounds. Her new goal was one hundred pounds, and she was hoping to reach it before her fifteenth birthday in early July.

She had been betrayed, not only by her beloved D.A. but by her own inadequacies. She wanted the earth to split open and swallow her.

D.A. seemed to be speaking through a megaphone, and his words deafened her ears.

"Sarah and I were married yesterday in Las Vegas."

Sammy's eyes flew to the gold band on Sarah's hand, then she turned to David in disbelief.

"Don't everyone speak at once," D.A. said, his voice sounding huskier than usual. "I know it's a surprise, but we just decided not to wait any longer."

"Any longer?" Sammy asked.

"We've seen each other a few times over the past couple of years," D.A. explained. "We met again in Las Vegas. It's what we wanted."

David was the first to react. He slowly walked to his son and shook his hand, then embraced his step-daughter and now daughter-in-law as well and kissed her cheek.

Mary's eyes filled with tears. Her feet were leaden weights that held her in this room of despair. Suddenly she revived and dashed to the door, leaving her younger sister behind.

"Mary? Wait!" D.A. shouted as she slammed the door behind her. She ran to her mare and tried to mount, but her foot slipped from the stirrup, and D.A.'s heavy hand fell on her shoulder.

Mary stumbled against him but pulled away when he tried to steady her.

"Mary, let me explain," he said, grabbing her arm.

"No," she cried, plucking at his fingers in a futile attempt to free herself.

"Don't cry, honey," he said. "Please look at me." She shook her head as he turned her around. "Mary," he said, tilting her chin to see her face. "We married because we love each other."

"You said one time that you loved me," she whispered.

"I do love you, but as a friend. You're still my cute little shrimp, but you're just a kid. You're not even through school."

His cruel words tore at her.

"Mary, try to understand. I told you months ago how I felt about her. I found her again quite by accident. . .where she worked. Just like we said, honey, I searched and searched, and there she was where I least expected her. She. . .oh, hell, Mary. Why am I explaining my own marriage to you? Sarah and I are both adults. We're about the same age. We've known each other long enough.''

"She's so beautiful," Mary sobbed.

"She is, isn't she?" he agreed, the pleased smile on his face only adding to her grief.

"But she's your sister."

"Not really. Just because she's Sammy's daughter doesn't mean. . . .''

"I've heard bad things about her, D.A." Mary's face contorted in anguish as she recalled Sammy's words.

"What bad things?" He shook her thin shoulders. "Who said things?" he demanded.

Tears streamed down her face. "My mother. . . and Sammy. I won't tell you what they said. You'll find out!''

"Mary, I don't want to hurt you," he said. "You're my favorite little friend."

She stomped her boot hard against the ground. "I'm not your little friend anymore. I'm not little! I'm growing up." She choked, gasping for breath. "You're dumb, D.A. I always thought you were so smart, but you're stupid. . . and blind, too!" She wanted to regain her composure, but a wave of shuddering sobs shook her.

D.A. drew her to him and held her, engulfing her in his arms.

"Oh, D.A., why did you do it?" she cried. Her arms encircled his waist, her hands clutching at his back.

He held her tightly, gently patting her shoulders, and the moisture from her tears dampened his shirt-front. "Mary, please don't cry." He kissed her flushed forehead, then rested his chin lightly on the top of her head. Her convulsive sobbing slowly subsided.

"Mary, you must try to understand and accept this. She's my wife," he said quietly.

Mary withdrew from his arms and turned to her horse. D.A. helped her mount. As she settled in the saddle, she turned to him.

"It's wrong, D.A. Even if she's not your sister, it's wrong. She's not the one. You'll see. Someday you'll wake up and realize the horrible thing you've done."

She yanked the reins from his hand and kicked the mare's flanks viciously. The horse leaped ahead, leaving D.A. behind to puzzle over her words.

He shook his head in bewilderment and reentered the silent kitchen, a heavy frown on his face.

"She's changed. I just don't understand her anymore."

Lisa gave him a scathing look and ran out the open doorway. D.A. turned and watched as the eleven-year-old mounted her horse and rode off in pursuit of her sister.

He turned to face the others. "I don't know what's the matter with her. Maybe she's just going through a phase. Teenagers do that, don't they?"

THE BUSTLE OF SUMMER lulled the pain away, soothing Mary's wounded emotions. The ache in her heart flared up only when bits of information about D.A. and Sarah filtered through to her. She'd learned they were living in Missoula in a two-bedroom apartment near the university when she overheard her mother reading her father the thank-you card they'd received from D.A. for the Russells' wedding gift. And once again the pain had returned.

Mary helped her mother and a young woman from town when they worked in the cook house. The quantity of food needed to feed the hungry, hard-working men in the branding crews was staggering, yet she found solace in meeting the demands of her job.

She grew an inch, but lost five pounds. When haying began, she volunteered to work on a haying crew, but her father rejected her offer, saying she was too young and too small. Although just fifteen, she knew how to operate some of the ranch vehicles and took over the noontime job of delivering lunch to the haying crews in the fields.

Once haying began, it continued nonstop seven days a week until the meadows of wild grasses and fields of timothy or alfalfa lay in windrows that snaked over the ground. After being dried by the August sun, the hay was piled into giant stacks, the process aided by tall Beaver Slides that hoisted the loose hay onto wood-slatted platforms. The platforms were slowly elevated by winches, then tipped, and the hay dropped on top of the growing haystack.

The method had been in operation almost as long as haying had been done in the country. The Beaver Slides were unique to the area and represented the most economical way to provide fodder to the live-stock during the often harsh winter months when the range was snow covered and the temperature fell below zero.

During haying season high-school and college students worked on the ranch to fill out the crews. At the end of the summer the Russells had a barbecue for the ranch workers, their families and some of the neighboring ranchers. David and Sammy McCor-mack came to the annual event, but Mary avoided them, not wanting to hear about the newlyweds.

School started and soon Mary was immersed in learning the cheerleading routines for the junior var-sity football season. She received a Christmas card from Mr. and Mrs. D.A. McCormack but dropped it into her dresser drawer unopened.

She thought the wounds were healed until her parents received an announcement telling of the birth of D.A. and Sarah's child. The family gathered around Julie Russell and admired the small color photo of the baby.

Mary left the living room and went directly to her bedroom. She buried her face in the pillow and didn't hear the door open.

"Here," Steven's voice sounded above her. She rolled over, and he dropped the birth announcement onto her chest. "Here's proof that no guy is going to wait around for some runt." He laughed and turned away. "Give up, sis," he said, and swaggered from the room.

Hesitantly she opened the folded announcement

and read the message, noting the time and date, and the baby's weight and length. Then her eyes widened.

The baby girl's name was Annette Elizabeth McCormack.

"We'll call her Annie," D.A. had scrawled as a postscript.

Mary studied the baby's photo, noting the cap of dark curls that surrounded the rosy-cheeked face. Her eyes were closed.

"She's a pretty baby," Mary murmured. "Probably looks like her mother," she added, tight-lipped. In spite of her mood, she searched and found an appropriate card and wrote them a short note of congratulation.

As she licked the flap and sealed the envelope, she mulled over the baby's name. How many other Elizabeths did D.A. know, she wondered? Perhaps Sarah had chosen the names. She smiled in approval at their choice.

"Annie," she whispered, rolling the name of this brand-new baby girl around in her mind. "I want to meet you someday, Annie. We have something in common...your middle name...and your handsome father." She slid the envelope into her English textbook and undressed for bed.

A FEW WEEKS LATER in early March Mary rode her Appaloosa mare to the McCormack ranch to visit Sammy.

"Where have you been?" Sammy asked, giving Mary a warm hug. "Your mother told me you've been very busy with school, but I've missed our visits." She led Mary into the living room. "Now sit down and tell me what's been happening in your life."

"School's fine," Mary said. "I tried out for the varsity cheer squad and made it. A year on the junior varsity helped. I've made the honor roll each semester, and next fall I'll be taking a computer-literacy class. I stay busy. I...I have to...because if I don't...oh, Sammy!" Her brown eyes glistened, and impulsively she spilled her heart out about everything that was troubling her. It all seemed to point toward one person: D.A. McCormack.

"Mary, Mary," Sammy replied. "I had no idea you still felt so strongly about him. I assumed you'd gotten over him long ago. I agree he's a very charming man, quite handsome too, but he's married now...and to my own daughter. Aren't there any boys at school you like?"

"A few," Mary admitted, "but they're just friends. I know how silly it is. It's just that...but it's too late now. How come I feel like life is over for me when I'm just fifteen and a half years old. That's not fair!"

"That's the way I felt when I was nine and David and his family moved away from Phoenix and I was left behind, but look how our lives have changed. What if we'd stayed friends, dated, married each other in our twenties? What if we had been too immature to grow together and instead divorced and parted enemies? The fact that we both had bad marriages may say something about our inability to make wise choices when we were younger.''

Sammy ran her fingers through her curly brown hair, then attempted to smooth it. ''When everything is right, love blossoms. But after it blossoms, it has to grow or die. David and I work at our marriage every day. We don't take it for granted.''

Sammy reached for an envelope and removed some photographs from it. ''Here,'' she said, ''may I show you some pictures of my granddaughter?''

Annie's round eyes stared back at the camera lens as each parent held her. Mary took in Sarah's tall regal beauty and D.A.'s happy expression. ''I hope he's happy. I really do,'' she said.

Sammy patted her hand affectionately. ''He loves her, of that I'm sure, but whether that's enough to keep a marriage strong when problems are already surfacing...I worry about them. I don't know about Sarah's willingness to make a go of it.'' Sammy frowned as she slipped the pictures back in the envelope. ''Sarah didn't want this baby.''

''Oh, no!'' Mary cried.

''She wanted an abortion, but D.A. talked her out of it. Sarah has always been rather self-centered, sometimes cruelly so. I don't know if the responsibility of motherhood is her strong point. She's always wanted to be free or else the center of attention. This baby is very special to D.A. I'm not so sure with Sarah.'' She stood up and brushed at her jeans.

''Now, come into my sewing room and let me show you what I've been working on...and guess what?

David's been thinking about buying a microcomputer. He wants me to write some programs to keep track of the Simmental breeding records. Oh, it's been years since I've done any serious computer programming, and it'll be exciting and challenging.''

Soon they were surrounded with fabrics and patterns, and Sammy explained her ideas for a quilted wall hanging.

"I want it to have our new brand, the Standing SD.'' She drew a quick sketch of a letter *S*. The underloop was closed with a bar converting it into the letter *D*. "It'll have David and his two dogs, and all our children and now Annie. I want to show this beautiful country with its snowcapped mountains and the wild flowers and. . . . Oh, what do you think, Mary? Do you like the idea? I think I'll put you and Lisa in it somewhere, too.''

"It sounds lovely,'' Mary replied, admiring the rainbow of colours in the fabrics surrounding them. "Don't forget to put yourself in.''

Time flew by and finally Mary glanced at the wall clock, then out the window.

"Oops, it's getting dark. I've got to get going, Sammy. Thanks for listening to my troubles. It helps just to talk to someone. Mom's got enough problems of her own, Lisa isn't old enough, and my girlfriends are all madly in love with guys at school.''

"I understand,'' Sammy said. "I'm always available.'' She walked outside with Mary and waited as she gathered her reins and mounted.

"If they come to visit, would you let me know?''

Mary asked, twisting in the saddle to look back at Sammy. "I...I...I'd like to see his baby...I mean their baby. Please?"

"Of course," Sammy promised, and she waved as Mary rode away.

SCHOOL WAS OUT for the summer before the call finally came. Sammy phoned on Friday evening to inform Mary that D.A., Sarah and the baby would be at the McCormack ranch the next morning.

Midway through the morning Mary called to verify that they had arrived. Her face brightened when she told her mother.

"I'm going to see D.A.'s baby. Can I drive the Volkswagen? I'll be careful," she promised.

"Just D.A.'s baby?" her mother asked.

"Well, he'll be there too, and his wife, but it's mostly to see his baby," Mary replied, bobbing her head emphatically.

"It's *their* baby," her mother corrected.

"I know," she said, rushing out the door.

Her heart pounded erratically during the endless drive to the McCormack ranch. As she parked in front of the house, she marveled that she had been able to keep the old car on the road.

She ran up to the door and rang the bell, but when she heard heavy footsteps on the other side, her confidence evaporated. She took a few steps backward.

The door opened slowly, and D.A. stepped through the entrance. She hadn't seen him since that fateful day when he'd announced his marriage and she'd told him what a horrible mistake he'd made. Recalling her brazen words brought the heat of shame to her cheeks. He closed the door behind him and approached her.

"Hello," she said, offering her hand to him in a ridiculously formal gesture. Clumsily she dropped her red windbreaker onto the porch.

He towered over her as he took both of her hands and held them wide. His eyes scanned her face, roamed down to her sandaled feet and slowly returned to her face. Her smile faded.

A grin brought a twinkling light to his green eyes. "You've changed, Mary. You've...matured," he said softly.

Her confidence soared. "Time does that, I suppose." She took a deep breath. "D.A., I'm glad you came outside. I want to apologize. I was grossly unfair and rude to you that day. I really don't know why I would have ever thought that you and I...I was so childish that day...." Her face reddened. "I'm sorry. Please forgive me. Can we be friends again?"

"Of course," he said, smiling. "Oh, Mary, honey, it's good to see you again." His eyes ran down her body once more, and he noticed the definite hint of cleavage above her midriff blouse, her tiny waist showing above her cut-off jeans, and her tanned legs. "You're a very pretty young lady." He stared at the top of her head. "How tall did you finally get, shrimp?"

"A measly five foot two. Even Lisa is already five foot five. I really am the runt of the Russells."

"You drove?" he asked, glancing at the beige Volkswagen parked behind them.

"Daddy lets me sometimes."

"Careful?"

"Very. I want my license next month."

They stared at each other for several seconds. Her brown eyes began to shimmer. Any thought of getting over her love for him evaporated as she gazed at him.

"Oh, D.A.," she whispered.

Suddenly she was in his arms. She hugged his waist. There was a rightness to his holding her, and she was glad the rent in their friendship had been repaired, but it was much more than friendship she savored as she prolonged the embrace. She spread her palms across his back, feeling the rough texture of his shirt.

She drew strength and courage from the muscles that rippled when he tightened, then gradually relaxed his hold on her. She tried to steel herself for the meeting with Sarah. She could endure Sarah in order to see Annie.

He slowly eased her back and tucked his hand under her chin, lifting her face. He studied her features, a smile curling his lips, and then he surprised her by kissing her lightly on the corner of her mouth before turning her toward the door.

"This way, honey," D.A. said, keeping his arm around her shoulders. "You'll want to meet Sarah again."

"Not really," Mary mumbled under her breath.

"What did you say?" he asked, leaning closer.

"Nothing," she replied. "I'm ready for...anything now."

He scooped up her windbreaker, then escorted her into the house. As they entered, Sarah rose from her chair. Mary fought valiantly to overcome a growing feeling of intimidation as D.A. introduced them again.

She was relieved when Sammy called to her from across the room. "Over here, Mary. Come meet Annie. She's four months old already. Would you like to hold her?"

"Hi, Annie," Mary crooned as Sammy gave her the baby. "She's very pretty," she added as the baby smiled up at her. The baby's eyes were a mixture of blue and deep sea green with dark lashes. Mary glanced at D.A. and caught his eye, then pulled her attention away. She walked through the house, whispering soft words to Annie, making the baby coo and smile.

As they returned to the entryway to the living room, Annie laughed aloud. D.A. came and stood beside Mary, admiring his daughter.

"What do you think of her?" he asked.

"She's precious," Mary said. "She's going to have your eyes." She glanced over at Sarah. "If you ever need a sitter when you're here, call me."

Mary and Annie were the center of attention for several minutes as Mary encouraged a few more giggles from Annie.

A shadow suddenly fell across them.

"I'll take her," Sarah said, and whisked the baby from Mary's arms.

"What's wrong? Did I do...?" Mary asked, but D.A. laid a cautioning hand on her shoulder. She kept her rising anger under restraint as he guided her to the sofa. He insisted that she sit beside him and soon had her talking about school and her plans for the summer. She stayed for another hour, but Sarah held the baby all the while.

"I really must go," Mary said, glancing again at Sarah, who still held the baby possessively. She grabbed her purse and windbreaker and rose from the sofa.

"I'll walk you to your car," D.A. said, following her to the door.

They chatted about marriage and babies and school, and as he held the car door, Mary turned to him.

"Are you happy, D.A.?" she asked, shading her eyes from the bright sunshine overhead.

"Of course," he said, laughing. "What made you ask that, Mary?"

She dropped her head. "I just wanted to be sure you have what you wanted."

"Sometimes what we want doesn't make us happy," D.A. replied, staring beyond her to the mountains.

"What does that mean?"

"Oh, nothing," he insisted, looking at her once again. "Every marriage has its ups and downs. Husbands and wives have their differences."

"Like...?"

"Like children." He frowned. "Sarah didn't want any children. You could say little Annie was an accident, but a delightful one at that."

"I agree," Mary said. "When...if I get married, I'd like to have several children. Children change a marriage into a family."

"Is that Mary Russell's philosophy of life?" he teased.

"Part of it," she admitted, then reluctantly she turned to enter her car.

"Wait," he said, stepping closer than before.

She held her breath as he touched her cheek with his fingers and tilted her face upward.

"I'll miss your next birthday," he murmured. Without warning his lips brushed her cheek and settled on her mouth. Just as quickly he pulled away. "God, I'm sorry, Mary. I didn't mean...."

Her senses were still whirling when he pulled away and hurriedly walked toward the house, his long strides covering the ground rapidly. He paused once to turn and glance at her.

She touched her mouth, still able to feel his lips. The banging of the screen door brought her to her senses.

"Damn you, D.A.," she muttered as she dropped into the driver's seat and began the long drive home.

CHAPTER FOUR

MARY'S REACTION TO D.A.'S KISS had erased her promise to baby-sit for him from her mind. Months later when a call came from Sammy McCormack, Mary wasn't sure how to answer.

"D.A. and Sarah are here for the weekend," Sammy said. "They're in town having dinner with the Morrisons. May Morrison has asked us to join them, but Annie is fussy. I was going to feed her dinner and put her to bed. I know it's short notice on a Saturday night, but could you come sit with her?"

"I was just going to shower," Mary said, thinking of her date with Johnny Nielsen, then she said impulsively, "Of course, I'm free. I'll be there in less than an hour." She returned the receiver to its cradle and stood contemplating her predicament. "He'll understand," she whispered under her breath. "I hope." She reached for the phone again and dialed a number.

"Johnny? This is Mary," she said. "I'm sorry, but I can't go with you tonight. I'm really sorry, but something's come up." She listened to his rising voice. "Johnny! You know I wouldn't break our date unless it was really important." She let him ramble for a few more moments. "Next Saturday? Sure. You're sweet to be so understanding. See you Monday at school."

She hummed to herself as she began to shower. Being sixteen was proving to be interesting. Her success in making the varsity cheerleading team last spring had brought her an abundance of offers for dates. She'd quickly learned which boys were too aggressive and tried to avoid them. Johnny Nielsen was one of the few boys she dated with any regularity.

As she shampooed her waist-length dark hair, her thoughts meandered back to the time she had broken her ankle and D.A. had carried her, then flowed to her unexpected encounter with him while Christmas shopping several years ago. His not-so-sweet sixteen kiss came blazingly alive as she rinsed her hair and she touched her lips, recalling the pressure of his mouth. A tightening sensation surprised her, and she glanced down at her breasts. They weren't as big as she would have liked, yet for her stature they were full and high, definitely larger than she'd expected a few years ago.

Thoughts of D.A. continued to whirl around in her fantasy. She felt an ache in her body and a return of the tingling in her breasts. She glanced down and was alarmed to see her nipples erect. She turned on the spray to its fullest force and the painful impact released some of her tension.

She imagined a whole evening with Annie. The only person missing from the imaginary picture would be *him*, and he would be with Sarah. It wasn't fair!

An unpleasant image of her beloved D.A. with his wife floated through her thoughts. Her fantasy changed, and it was her own slender body with him. He was long and lean. He put his arms around her, and his mouth made a slow-motion descent toward hers. She removed his glasses, and he stared at her with his piercing gaze.

She murmured, "I love you," and he responded, "I love you, too. Not Sarah, but only you, Mary." And he pulled her to him. Their legs were entwined, and his sensuously wide mouth crushed hers. "Mary..." he breathed, running his hand through her loose flowing hair.

"Mary! Aren't you ever going to get out of there?" Steven pounded on the bathroom door, and all the images of the erotic fantasy evaporated.

Her face reddened. "Sorry, Steven. I'm almost finished," she called. "Give me five minutes."

She finished quickly and dressed in a pair of snug jeans and a bulky-knit crimson sweater. As she used the blow dryer on her thick hair, she thought of D.A. Her love for him had become a cushion for all that happened in her life. In spite of his marriage, he continued to send her humorous friendship cards, usually with short notes describing something about Annie or his research projects.

He was now Dr. D.A. McCormack. He'd written once that he wasn't sure if he was proud of the title or a little embarrassed at the overuse of it by a few of his students. She sent him the local newspaper's listing of the students at school with *A* averages and had underlined her own name.

She unlocked the bathroom door.

"A mighty long five minutes," Steven complained.

She stuck her tongue out at him and ran to her room, grabbed her coat and purse and was soon on the road. The air was crisp and cold. Traces of an early snowfall lingered across the countryside.

She chatted with David and Sammy for a few moments before they left. The evening was spent playing with Annie, who was now eight months old. They played finger games, and Mary sang a few nursery rhymes. When Annie began to point to Mary's face, Mary carefully enunciated the words for eyes, mouth, nose and ears.

"Let's rock," Mary said, scooping Annie playfully up in her arms and carrying her to the bentwood rocker nearby. Mary crooned a few lullabyes, and Annie's eyelids drooped and closed. Soon her head of dark rust-brown curls was nestled against Mary's breast. Mary continued to sing softly until she was sure Annie was asleep.

Mary remained in the rocker, using her foot to keep a steady rocking motion going. She rested her head against the back of the chair and let her mind wander.

She was still in the rocker with Annie when the McCormacks returned. The door banged against the wall and Mary started.

Annie awoke, frightened by the unexpected disturbance, and began to cry. Mary tried to console her, but her own mind was foggy with sleep. Before Mary could recover herself, Sarah strutted to the rocker and whisked the baby out of her arms.

"She's been crying," Sarah said, frowning threateningly at Mary. "She's wet, too. She's probably been neglected most of the evening." She whirled around to D.A. "I told you we should never have left her in the care of some incompetent teenager." She strode away with the sobbing baby and disappeared.

Mary grabbed her coat, refused the money David offered her and angrily ran out the door. She heard the door bang again and hoped no one was following her.

She was trembling as she reached for the handle of her car door, but D.A.'s large right hand on hers prevented her from opening it.

"Leave me alone," Mary demanded.

The prosthesis on his left arm clasped the side mirror, trapping her against the car. "Sarah didn't mean what she said, Mary. She's been irritable lately. Please forget what she said." His voice was soft against her ear.

She shoved at his chest, but he stood firm.

"I would *never* neglect Annie...or any other baby. I played with her and changed her and gave her a bottle...and sang to her...and...and...." She tightened her mouth to stop the quivering of her lips.

The moonless night surrounded them, isolating them in a cloak of intimate privacy.

His right hand slid up her coat sleeve to her shoulder. "I know you'd never neglect my little girl. I'm sure you treated her as though she were your own." His fingers touched her thick rope of hair, and unconsciously he tugged at the piece of yarn tied around it.

"Sarah's lucky to have Annie...and you, too," Mary said.

"Sarah's not the best mother in the world, but she tries. She's changing. I think any woman can learn to be a good mother, don't you?" He paused, giving her a chance to answer. His finger touched the skin on the side of her neck, and he marveled at its softness.

"I've been trying to help her," he continued, his voice sounding huskier than usual. "At times I think I understand Annie better than Sarah does. Sarah's used to thinking of just herself, and now with Annie taking up her time...God, Mary, sometimes I think she resents us both, but...." He exhaled slowly. "I shouldn't have said anything. Problems should stay within a marriage." His hand fell to his side.

"Sometimes problems need to be shared, D.A.," Mary replied, touching his hand. "They're not so heavy that way."

His hand encircled hers. "Another of Mary Russell's philosophies?" he asked, a small grin twisting his mouth.

"Perhaps."

"Mary Elizabeth Russell, I think in lots of ways you're mature far beyond your years. And you're very pretty, too. I always did have a weakness for big brown eyes." He squeezed her hand before releasing it. "Many boyfriends?" he asked unexpectedly.

"A few," she said.

"Anyone special?" he asked. "Are you in love, Mary Russell?"

"Perhaps," she conceded.

"Who is he? Do I know him?"

"I'd rather not say," she said.

"Wouldn't you like to have a confidant?" he asked.

"At times," she admitted.

"Is it me?"

Her mouth fell open in surprise.

"I mean, am I the wrong person for you to confide in, Mary?" he asked, his hand touching her cheek.

Mary turned her face, allowing her cheek to fully caress his palm.

"Damn it," he mumbled. "I'm tangled in your yarn."

"Oh," she cried, as she realized that his prosthesis had become caught in her hair as well as the yarn. She pulled the yarn loose, and the rubber band holding her hair snapped and fell away.

"There," he murmured, lowering his left arm. "I think I'm free from you."

Her hair tumbled around her shoulders, and his fingers slid through the silken strands.

"The Bible says that a woman's hair is her crowning glory. Now I understand what was meant." He brushed the hair away from her face. "When was the last time you cut it?"

"I...I don't remember...I...trim it...occasionally," she stammered.

"You've changed a lot these last few months, Mary," he said.

"Some things never change," she replied, and her heart ached as she thought of Sarah inside the house. Suddenly she didn't care that Sarah was his wife. She had known him long before Sarah had barged into their lives.

"Would you kiss me?" Mary asked.

She half expected to find a teasing grin on his face when she glanced up at him. Instead she found that he was frowning, and his eyes had darkened to a stormy forest green.

"I'm sorry," she said. "I don't know why I said that."

"That's all right. I'll kiss you. But why?"

"Because I...we don't get to see each other much anymore. Because you've always been special to me," she replied.

"And you to me, Mary." His right hand tunneled through her hair and his left arm surrounded her, easing her closer.

Her mouth was closed when his lips first grazed hers. She was terrified that she would respond incorrectly and tightened her lips involuntarily.

He pulled away slightly and smiled as he studied her rigid face and closed eyelids.

"Relax," he said, and her eyes flew open.

"I'm not very good at this."

His finger traced the outline of her mouth. "Open

your lips a little, even your teeth. Your lips should be full and soft, not pursed like an old prude...soft... full.''

She was hypnotized by his voice as his mouth came closer. This time her lips were responsive as his mouth covered hers. Her hands flew around his waist, hugging him tightly. His kiss deepened, her lips parted, and she was aware of his tongue tracing a pattern over her teeth.

She stretched on her tiptoes to give him access to her mouth, hungry to experience the full essence of her growing desire.

Suddenly he pulled away, breathing heavily. ''Damn it, Mary,'' he said huskily. ''I'm sorry. I don't know what came over me. I didn't intend to...I got carried away. You're a friend, and a very young one at that.'' Yet he pulled her close again and held her securely in his arms. He nuzzled her hair, then brushed a few stray strands from her cheek.

''Please don't apologize for kissing me, D.A.,'' she murmured. ''I know you didn't mean to lead me on. I trust you. Sometimes when we're troubled or unhappy we do things....'' She stretched her hands to his face, touching the smooth-shaven skin of his cheeks and the rugged plane of his jaw.

''I care about you,'' she said. Her lips were soft and full, just as he had taught her, when she kissed him again before withdrawing from his arms. ''Sarah is probably wondering why you haven't returned to the house. Goodbye, D.A. McCormack.''

She quickly slid behind the wheel of her car, started the engine and drove away, aware of the dark shadow he made as he remained standing in the yard.

D.A. McCormack used the toe of his shoe to knock on the apartment door. "Sarah, open the door," he called. "I'm loaded with Christmas presents and can't use my key. Hurry."

A gray-haired woman wearing an apron around her ample waist greeted him.

"Mrs. Creswell, what are you doing here?" he asked.

Mrs. Creswell held the door wide and helped him with the boxes. He turned and saw Annie toddling to him, her arms outstretched.

"Dada, dada, dada," she squealed. Her green eyes sparkled when he scooped her up in his arms and hugged her.

"Hi, sweetheart, how's my girl? Got a kiss for daddy?"

She laid her mouth against his cheek and held it there for several seconds, then threw her body backward. He caught her and she giggled.

"Annie, don't do that," he cautioned. "Sometimes I think you're a little spoiled, but I love you anyway." He hugged her again and carried her over to the sofa. He sat down and positioned Annie on his lap, then looked at Mrs. Creswell.

"Where's Sarah?"

Mrs. Creswell shook her head and wiped her eyes with her apron hem. D.A.'s apprehension grew as she pulled up a chair close to him.

"She's gone."

"Gone?" he asked. "I don't understand. Gone shopping?"

"No, dear. She gone. . . left Missoula. She took the afternoon flight out."

"My God," he cried. "Why? When will she be back? It must have been an emergency. Was it someone in her family? Did Sammy call?"

Mrs. Creswell laid a cautioning hand on his. "I don't think it was an emergency, D.A. She was gone when I got here."

"I don't understand. She left Annie alone? How did you know to come?" He slid Annie to the floor and stood up. "What the hell is going on?"

"Please sit down and I'll explain the best I can," Mrs. Creswell said.

D.A.'s head was throbbing as he dropped back onto the sofa and tried to concentrate as Mrs. Creswell began to recount the afternoon's events. Annie tugged at his pant leg, and he unconsciously helped her climb into his lap, cradling her in his arms.

"I called the university, but you'd already left," Mrs. Creswell explained. "I received a call from Sarah about three hours ago. She said she was at the airport, that she had a ticket on the flight to Las Vegas that was leaving in a few moments. She asked me to look in on Annie, that the door would be unlocked. She'd had enough. That's all she said, D.A. She hung up before I could say a word. It took me about fifteen minutes to get here and I found Annie. . . oh, it was so terrible!"

She glanced at Annie and, in spite of the seriousness of the moment, smiled back at the bouncing little girl. "It was terrible, yet comical too. You naughty girl!" she said, waving a finger at Annie, who giggled.

"I found her in her crib," Mrs. Creswell explained. "She had messed her diaper and had somehow gotten the pin unfastened and removed her diaper. Oh D.A., she'd managed to soil not only herself but the linens and crib, as well. It took me over an hour to clean up the bed and room, to bathe Annie and wash the sheets. My dear, you know more about Sarah's mental state than I do, but I've known for months that things weren't right. Whenever I'd sit in the afternoons, Sarah would walk out without a backward glance at Annie. When she returned, she'd usually ignore Annie and instead go light a cigarette and mix herself a drink."

Mrs. Creswell took a deep breath. "I'd usually stay another half hour or so until I felt Annie would be attended to. Poor little Annie. It would tear at my heart to see her go to her mother and cry for attention and be shunted aside. I didn't want to mention it, but did you ever wonder about the bruises that Annie sometimes had on her forehead and arms and legs?"

"Yes, but Sarah said she'd fallen when she was learning to walk," D.A. replied sharply, his anger rising at the baby-sitter's insinuation.

"I don't usually interfere in these matters, D.A., but frankly I don't think she had much of a mothering instinct," the older woman cried indignantly. "Children are a gift, they're precious." She wiped the corners of her eyes with a tissue.

"I agree," D.A. said quietly as he sat holding Annie, mulling over Mrs. Creswell's remarks.

"I prepared a tuna casserole," she told him. "It's ready if you'll come into the kitchen. I'll stay and clean up."

He ate the dinner without tasting anything. When Mrs. Creswell touched his arm, he started.

"I'd be glad to stay the night, D.A. I can call Henry."

"No, no, that's okay. Thanks for coming when you did." He stared at her and frowned, his eyes filled with shadows. "Why, Mrs. Creswell? Why would she do this. Was it me? How could a mother just walk off and leave her baby?"

"I don't have the answer," she said. "God works in mysterious ways, my son. You have a lovely sweet baby, and she's very fond of her daddy. Now you listen to me. Until you get things straightened out, you bring Annie over to our place. Henry and I will play grandparents. Frankly, we'll love the opportunity. You bring some diapers and a bottle, and we'll do the rest." She patted his hand, gave him a hug and quietly left the apartment.

D.A. played with his daughter on the floor until she grew tired, then he undressed her and put on her night diaper and a pair of blanket sleepers. He had trouble using his prosthesis and chided himself for his clumsiness.

As he rocked Annie in the wicker chair he'd given Sarah at their daughter's birth, he thought of the irony of the gift. Sarah had never used the chair with the baby.

Annie fell asleep in his arms, and he continued to rock her. He studied her round face, her dark lashes lying gently against her cheeks, her pink lips occasionally making a nursing sound. He knew her face was a small replica of Sarah's, and his vision blurred.

He continued to rock her. The steady movement soothed him, but the pain he was feeling made rational thought difficult. She'd really duped him into thinking she loved him. Finally he got up and carried his sleeping daughter to her crib and laid her down. As he covered her with a blanket, he made a vow to take care of her no matter what the future held. He touched the soft curls near her rosebud ear and tried to still the trembling in his fingers.

Snow was falling outside. He felt a black cloud settling over him. Christmas was just four days away. He'd talked Sarah into spending Annie's first Christmas at the ranch south of Dillon.

D.A. found Sarah's note in an envelope by the telephone. He read it over and over again.

D.A.,
I liked it for a while, but things have changed. I've had an offer from an old friend in Vegas that I just couldn't refuse.
    You're great in bed, lover, but I can't forget

the arm. Oh, how I've hated those repulsive scars.

Motherhood is definitely not for me. I told you so, but you wouldn't listen. The dirty diapers, the runny noses, the sour milk and sloppy eating.

I tried to handle it, but I can't. Maybe you two should go to Dillon and let little Mary babysit for her two lambs. I'm sure she'd love to have you two all to herself.

I'll file for divorce. I have plenty of money, and I'll pay for it myself. You're free, I'm free. Don't try to find me. It wouldn't do any good. Say something kind about me to Annie when she's old enough to understand.

                                    Bye lover, Sarah

MARY'S STOMACH DID A SOMERSAULT when her mother made the announcement at dinner a few days before Christmas.

"The McCormacks are coming for the day," Julie Russell said.

"David and Sammy?" Mary asked.

"All of them," Julie replied. "D.A. and Sarah and little Annie, too. I've only seen Annie once, and that was during the summer. We'll all have a wonderful day together, just like one giant family."

Christmas arrived, and snow fell heavily all morning. An hour before dinnertime the phone rang at the Russell home.

"Hello," Mary said.

"Hello, Mary," came David McCormack's deep voice. "Is your mother or father there?"

"Daddy's outside and mom's taking pies from the oven. Can I take a message?"

"Well," David said, "we won't be able to have dinner with you. It's...well...something has happened. See if Julie can come to the phone. I'd better explain to her."

"Mom," Mary called, and her mother picked up the kitchen extension. Mary hung up her line and joined her mother, listening to the one-sided conversation. Her stomach tightened into a hard knot of concern as she watched her mother's face grow pale. Finally Julie said goodbye.

"Mom, what's wrong?" Mary asked.

"It's...D.A. and Sarah."

"Has something happened?" Mary cried.

"Yes."

"There's been an accident? Oh, no, have they been hurt?"

"No."

"Then what? Why can't they come?"

"D.A. did come," Julie said.

"Alone?"

"He brought Annie."

Mary frowned. "Where's Sarah?"

Julie turned away.

"Mother," Mary cried, tugging at her sleeve. "What's happened? Has something happened to Sarah? Is she sick? Why would D.A. bring Annie and not his wife?"

Julie wiped her hands on her flour-dusted apron. "David would only say that Sarah is now living in Las Vegas, that she left Annie alone in their apartment in Missoula one day last week and flew to Las Vegas. She...she apparently wrote D.A. a note and said...she didn't want to be a wife or mother anymore." Julie shook her head in disbelief. "D.A. must be devastated!"

"What else did he say?" Mary asked, shaking her mother's arm.

"Nothing. Just that it would be best if they stayed home today. That they'd see us for coffee on New Year's."

"She never loved him, did she?" Mary said, a grim expression on her face.

"We don't know," Julie replied.

"No woman who really loves a man would leave him. What kind of mother abandons her baby?" she cried. She was unaware of the tears flowing down her cheeks. "I want to go to him. Maybe I can help him, maybe I...."

"No!" Julie said. "Don't get involved in this, Mary."

"But I...."

"You'll only get hurt. You're not old enough to understand their problems."

"But I do understand," she pleaded. "He and I have talked."

"No!" Julie whirled away, but immediately turned back to Mary. "David asked that we stay away...for a while. D.A. needs time to adjust."

"But I could. . . ."

"I said absolutely not!" Julie replied. "Later per-haps—when no one will misconstrue your motives." Suddenly she hugged Mary. "Oh, darling, I know you care for him. We all do, but getting involved in a triangle of broken hearts would be like a nonswim-mer jumping into the middle of a deep lake. You'd be out of your element. Try to understand."·

"But. . . ."

Julie clasped Mary's drawn face in her hands. "I love you, Mary. I don't want to see you hurt." She forced herself to smile. "Now go wash your face. Dinner is ready early so we'll eat. It's still Christmas for the Russells."

Later that night Mary lay in her bed unable to sleep. Her thoughts were with D.A.; she could sense his agony and heartbreak. It didn't seem to matter that his grief was for another woman.

CHAPTER FIVE

HEAVY OVERCAST SKIES shrouded the countryside on New Year's morning when David and Sammy McCormack arrived at the Rocking R for brunch.

The conversation skirted the subject of D.A. and Sarah as everyone gathered around the harvest table in the spacious but cozy kitchen. Julie set a platter of ham and scrambled eggs on the table, followed by cottage-fried potatoes and a plate of fresh-baked cinnamon rolls. Mary served coffee.

When everyone had finished the meal and lingered over coffee and second helpings of cinnamon rolls, Mary glanced at her mother and then turned to Sammy.

"How are D.A. and Annie?" she asked. "Did Annie enjoy her first Christmas?"

"Annie had a delightful time," Sammy replied. "I think she had more fun playing with the empty cartons than with the presents inside. And D.A...." She turned toward David before continuing.

David dropped his arm around Sammy's shoulders. "He's much better now," he said. "He needed a few days to start healing. Coming home from work and finding himself a single parent so unexpectedly knocked him down for a while. I think he's back on his feet now and is wondering what hit him. It's rough to think it was his own wife.''

"Who will take care of Annie?'' Julie asked. "Will he leave her with you at the ranch when he returns to Missoula?''

"We offered,'' Sammy said. "But he's fiercely protective of her. He says she's his responsibility, that he has no intentions of abandoning her like her own. . .mother did.'' Sammy's mouth set tightly.

David pulled her closer and kissed her cheek. "It's going to be all right, love.'' He glanced around the table. "We McCormacks are sturdy stock. We bounce back from adversity. You know that.'' He squeezed Sammy's hand before releasing her and reaching for his coffee mug.

"Do you think it would be okay for me to visit him?'' Mary asked, ignoring her mother's nudging knee under the table.

Sammy's face brightened. "I think he'd like that. Just avoid mentioning Sarah if possible.''

"Of course,'' Mary murmured, rising from the table. "Excuse me,'' she said, and she hurried from the room.

She quickly changed into thermal-lined beige woolen slacks and a cable-knit sweater. As she tugged on black snow boots, her mind raced over what she would say to him, determined to keep the visit as cheerful as possible. There was always his teaching or the research project he'd completed. She tried vainly to recall the facts about sulfur dioxide's devastating effect on the environment but gave up. Perhaps Annie would be the best subject for them both.

She zipped up her parka, adjusted the fur-lined hood around her face and reached for her gloves. The temperature was below zero and the sting of the cold air brought tears to her eyes as she unplugged the electrical cord from her car's engine heater and climbed in.

When she arrived at the McCormack ranch, she parked near the kitchen and plugged in the car heater to one of the electrical outlets in the hitching rail. She didn't want to risk car trouble and be stranded there. She smiled as she speculated on such a pleasant prospect, then chided herself for making light of the reason for her visit.

She surveyed the snow-covered area between the stable and house and, seeing no one, hurried toward the kitchen door. But something stopped her and caused her to turn again toward the stable. She saw him standing in the shadow of the building smoking a cigarette.

She froze as she watched him drop the cigarette into the snow and crush it savagely with his boot heel. He straightened, took a few steps away from the shadowy wall of the stable, then stopped abruptly when he spotted her across the yard.

Her decision to come to him was made out of friendship, she tried to convince herself. Anything more was wishful thinking.

He waved.

Her heart pounded erratically as she approached him. "Hi," she said, trying without success to keep her voice calm.

"Hello yourself," he replied. He towered over her, and reaching down, he took her gloved hands in his. "I suppose my father and Sammy told you I was here."

"Yes," she said, looking up at him. His strained features lent an unexpected hardness to his angular face. The usual sparkle in his eyes was buried beneath stormy pain.

He continued to stare down at her as he held her hands. "Thanks." He broke the visual contact and looked off into the distance. "It's terribly cold. I was thinking about going for a ride when dad and Sammy returned, but I don't have the heart to take old Bay out of his warm stall, so I gave him some fresh hay instead." He gazed down at her again. "Want to walk?"

"Yes," she said, and he guided her around the stable and through the gate to the south pasture.

The ground was frozen and covered with several inches of packed snow. One of her boots collided with a small boulder and she stumbled. He caught her, then put his arm around her shoulders and pulled her against him as they continued slowly to the fence at the end of the pasture.

Just a friend, she reminded herself as she felt his arm press into her small shoulder. She tried desperately to keep her rioting emotions under control.

"How have you been?" he asked.

"Fine...and you?" Immediately she wanted to withdraw the words. "Oh, D.A., I'm sorry," she cried, stepping away from him.

"It's okay, honey." He smiled, but the twist to his mouth belied his words. "I'm better. I'll make it. I've made it through worse," he said, and motioned toward his left arm.

"Of course you will," she agreed.

Sarah's name never came up as they chatted about the bitterly cold snap of weather they were having, the football season at the local high school and college, a recent television special they'd both seen.

She watched as he pulled his leather glove from his hand and reached for his pack of cigarettes. His hand trembled slightly, and his glove fell to the snow. Unconsciously she bent to retrieve it.

"I'm clumsy," he apologized, and suddenly she was showered with cigarettes. "Damn it," he growled. "I can't even handle a box of smokes anymore. I need two hands." He bent down beside her and groped for the scattered cigarettes.

"Here," Mary said, shoving the empty box into his hand. "Let me help."

"But...."

"No buts," she insisted. "Let me help." She quickly gathered up the filter-tipped cigarettes.

He sat back on his boot heels and watched her carefully insert them into the box. When she had finished, she slowly withdrew one and offered it to him, and they both stood up again.

As he lit the cigarette, she said, "You know, smoking isn't good for you." He nodded his head in agreement. "It's not good for Annie, either."

"I'll quit one of these days...but not today. It seems to help."

They talked a while more about school, child care and D.A.'s plans for the future. When he had finished with it, D.A. flicked the spent cigarette into a nearby snowbank.

Mary turned to him. "What are you going to do now?"

"I could stay at UM or make a clean break and leave the state. Maybe it's time to leave teaching and go into research. I've had a few enticing offers." He paused and glanced at her. "What do you suggest?"

"Seriously?"

"Of course. I value your friendship and good judgment."

Her heart sank a little at his reminder of their platonic relationship, but she replied, "You've omitted one. I think you should consider teaching at Western Montana College. You'd be close to your father and Sammy. I'll even baby-sit for you... whenever you want to go out...on dates." She studied his face, waiting for his reaction to her recommendation. She wanted to reach out and touch him, to erase the tension and fatigue she saw. Tiny lines she had never noticed before were etched around the corners of his eyes. The sensual fullness of his mouth seemed permanently narrowed into a grim straight line. Her concern and affection for him welled up anew when he smiled.

"I'll consider that. Good thinking, shrimp." He smoothed the fur of her hood away from her face, leaned over and kissed her cheek.

Her heart was racing again, making her feel slightly giddy. Perhaps she would faint in his arms, and he would once again carry her back to his house. She smiled to herself. In spite of her small stature, she was disgustingly healthy and had never fainted in her life.

"What's so funny?" he asked.

"Oh, nothing," she said breathlessly. "Remember when I broke my ankle and you carried me to the house."

"Yeah," he recalled. "That was a long time ago, wasn't it?" He glanced toward the house. "Want to see Annie? She's been napping and should be waking up soon. Come with me to the house. If you're going to stumble, I'll carry you. I certainly don't want you to break a leg again on my account."

She gasped. He must have been able to read her thoughts. "I'll be careful, silly," she said, hoping her cheeks weren't flushed.

He took her hand and led her across the snow-covered yard and into the warm house.

As they entered, she heard a voice calling, "Dada, dada, dada."

"She's learning to talk," Mary exclaimed. "Oh, how exciting, D.A.!" She followed him into the bedroom.

Annie stood in the crib. When she saw D.A., she clutched the rail, bouncing and giggling.

"Hi, Annie," he greeted her. To Mary he added, "She's a little tigress. I suppose I've spoiled her just a bit. Excuse me, I'll change her."

"Let me," Mary said, spotting a stack of clean folded cloth diapers near the bed. "You don't use disposables?"

"Sometimes, but these are much more economical. Two years of throw-away diapers adds up to a staggering amount of money and a lot of litter to be...." He laughed. "I'm an environmentalist at heart. It must be my agricultural and down-home upbringing. Go ahead. She's all yours." He stepped away.

"Hi, Annie," Mary said as she approached the crib. "D.A., do you think she remembers me? It's been a few months since I saw her." She felt him move to stand behind her.

"Let's see," he said, resting his hand on her shoulder. "Annie, this is Mary...Mary Russell. Can you say *Mary*?"

Annie's green eyes gleamed. "Mama, mama, mama," she said in a toddler's lisp, and held out her hand to Mary.

Mary blushed and tried again. "No, Annie. Say *Ma-ry*."

"Mama, mama, mama."

D.A. laughed. Mary felt his breath stir her hair.

"She's hopeless," he said. "They do sound a little alike. Shall we call you Momma Mary? That *would* confuse her. Lie down now, Annie."

Annie dropped to the bed, stiff legged and expectant, awaiting the removal of her wet diaper.

Mary smiled as she made the change.

"You do that like a pro," D.A. said.

"I like babies," she told him. "I think they're wonderful." *Especially this one,* she thought. Aloud, she said, "You've got her trained to obey. Is she always this good?"

"Usually," he said, laughing, "but she does have a stubborn streak once in a while."

Mary finished the final adjustments of Annie's clothing and lifted her up. She turned to D.A., holding his daughter in her arms. "I think she's sweet. If you ever get tired of her, you just call me, and I'll take her home for keeps."

Mary kissed Annie's smooth cheek.

Annie grinned again and said, "Mama, mama, mama," then pointed at D.A. "Dada, dada, dada."

"She's always grouping words in three's," he said. "Well, come, Mother Mary, let's go to the kitchen and feed this hungry girl."

Mary watched the meal, impressed by the gentleness D.A. showed as he patiently fed his daughter. When the bowl was empty he wiped her mouth and hands and handed her a vanilla wafer. "Now," he said, turning his attention to Mary. "Would you join me in a grilled cheese sandwich?"

"Thank you. Can I help?" she asked.

"Nope. This meal is on me."

He quickly prepared the sandwiches and joined her at the table. As he took the last bite of bread and melted cheese he began to stare at her.

Mary wondered what was going through his mind

but didn't know quite how to ask him. She started when his hand suddenly reached out across the table and touched her cheek.

"I'm glad you came, Mary. You're what I needed right now."

She helped him with the dishes and played with Annie for several minutes, and then she knew she should leave.

"Drive carefully," he cautioned as she zipped up her parka and pulled on her warm gloves. "There's a lot of ice under the snow."

"I know," she replied. "I have new snow tires. My dad would be furious if I had an accident. He's paying my insurance until I get a job next summer." She paused, reluctant to leave him alone. "Take care, D.A. Stay in touch. When you get back to Missoula, don't forget you have friends back home."

He nodded, but the grim tightness had returned to his mouth.

MARY RUSSELL ARRIVED HOME from school late. She was running behind schedule because of her varsity cheerleading practice. Her third year in high school was hectic, and as the spring break fast approached, the pace escalated. Cheerleading tryouts were scheduled, and she had volunteered to help. She parked her VW and rushed through the kitchen door.

"Hi, mom, I'm starved," she said, grabbing a fresh-baked cookie. She turned toward the hallway, but her mother grabbed the apricot sweater tied around her shoulders.

"Wait, my dear. You have a package."

"Me? No one would send me anything. I didn't order anything...I..." she stammered.

"It's from Missoula," Julie Russell said, smiling as she handed Mary a large padded envelope.

"Oh, mom, it's from...."

"Yes, darling."

Mary pressed the envelope to her chest and made her way down the hallway. She'd sent both D.A. and Annie birthday presents earlier in the month but had expected nothing in return.

In the privacy of her bedroom she carefully opened the packet. "Oh," she gasped as she peeked inside. A portrait, matted in linen and framed in distressed walnut, slid into her hand. She gazed at the face of her beloved D.A. His green eyes had caught the photographer's light and a slight smile curved his mouth. The shading accented the angular planes of his cheek and jaw. His blond hair had grown and now brushed the collar of his burgundy velour pullover. She touched the soft curls showing near his ear and imagined their texture.

He was holding Annie on his lap. Her auburn curls covered her ear. He had tied a pale-pink bow to form a curl on top of her head, and her dress was a matching shade of pink. Her sparkling eyes were copies of her father's.

Mary blinked to clear her eyes as she placed the photo on her dresser. She returned to her bed and shook the envelope. A note fell out and another smaller manila envelope. She opened the envelope and found something wrapped in several pieces of cotton and tissue. Her hands shook as she uncovered a thin gold ankle bracelet with the letters M, B and M engraved on it. The lettering puzzled her. All she could think of was Mary Beth McCormack, and that was impossible. She unfolded the note.

Dear Mary,
Thank you for the thoughtful birthday gifts. You deserve a present yourself. The ankle bracelet is for your ankle, which I made you break. The initials stand for "Mothered by Mary," as the two people in the photo certainly are whenever you visit. Annie's baby-sitter talked me into the photo.

Love, D.A. and Annie

Mary reread the note and stared at the initials on the delicate bracelet. The letters became blurry, and then she began to cry.

An hour later her mother knocked on her door, calling her to dinner. Mary opened the door a few inches.

"You stay here," Julie said when she saw her daughter's flushed face. "I'll bring a plate to you."

Several minutes later Julie knocked again. She carried a tray of food, a damp washcloth and a towel. As Mary picked at the food on the tray, Julie sat on the corner of the bed.

"Can I help?" she asked.

"I think it's hopeless," Mary said. She tilted her

dark head to one side and frowned at her mother. "Mom, do you know why I joined the cheerleading squad?"

"To enjoy the games, because you wanted to, for the prestige...." Julie stopped when Mary shook her head in disagreement.

"I joined the squad to keep busy and forget him." She pointed to the portrait on the dresser. "Sometimes I'm so miserable, I just want to die, but then I'm afraid I'll miss seeing him. Oh, momma, why did I have to be born so many years after him? If I were older, I know he'd see me differently. Sometimes...sometimes I just ache for him, and I don't understand it. I don't want anyone else to touch me and he won't."

"He'd better not!" Julie declared emphatically.

"He still calls me a shrimp and...it's so hopeless." Mary buried her face in her arms.

Julie gently patted her daughter's shoulder reassuringly. "My poor darling. It's developed into a chronic condition, hasn't it? Have you talked to him lately?"

Mary looked at her mother. "He called right after he received the birthday gifts, and last Saturday just to say hello." She sighed.

"What did he talk about? Does he date?" Julie asked.

"I don't think so," Mary replied. "He tells me about things he's done with Annie, and this older couple who take care of Annie when he teaches. He never mentions women at all."

"I'm sure he still hurts very much from Sarah's leaving him," her mother said. "He loved her. You must be prepared to accept that." She reached out to touch Mary's hand. "If you were several years older and something did develop between you two, there would always be Sarah. As unlikely as the situation might be, would you want that memory from the past coming between you?"

"I don't know." Mary frowned at her mother. "Momma, why did she do such a cruel thing to him? I'd never do anything to hurt him. You can't do such wicked things to someone you love, can you?"

"Sometimes love can be very one-sided," Julie said. "You should certainly know about that. There's a big difference between loving someone as a friend and loving someone as a man and a woman can love. I'm afraid when love and sex get tangled, it's different, Mary. It can be very wonderful, with deep meaning and caring for each person."

"David and Sammy have that, don't they?"

"Yes, I believe they do," her mother agreed. "Somehow with D.A. and Sarah, I think it must have been different. You're right, Mary. Healthy love shouldn't hurt the people involved."

"How old do you have to be to love that way, mom?"

"I don't think age has much to do with it," Julie said. "It's something that just happens. It develops over a period of time and withstands the trauma of separation and problems and crises and grows deeper. A bond develops that gets stronger over the years and. . . ." Suddenly Julie stopped and studied her daughter's face. "I really goofed, didn't I? I came in here to convince you that your feeling for our young Dr. McCormack was just a passing case of adolescent love." She sighed. "Who knows what the future holds. . . but there's also the possibility that Sarah will come back. What would happen if she did?"

"Do you think she might?" Mary asked. She grimaced. "I hate that woman, even if she is Sammy's daughter. How could a nice woman like Sammy have a child like that? Why she's a. . .*bitch!*" She covered her mouth in a futile attempt to erase the profanity. "I'm sorry, mom. That woman makes me so mad!"

She stared at the photo for a few minutes. "What you said about real love? Real love. . . ." A dreamy mood softened her eyes. "That's how I feel, but I've never told anyone but. . .you. . .and Sammy. Please don't tell daddy or—" her brown eyes grew round with concern "—my brothers?"

"Of course not," Julie replied.

Mary smiled again and hugged her mother. Julie kissed her cheek, gathered the dinner tray and linens and said good-night.

DIVORCE PAPERS ARRIVED in mid-February, giving D.A. custody of Annie. He didn't contest the action and in March received the final decree.

A month later he received an envelope containing a clipping from a Las Vegas newspaper. It was a photo from the social page, showing several people at a cocktail party. He recognized Sarah immediately. He searched for her name and froze.

> Cocktails and dinner were hosted by the newly-weds, Sid and Sarah Lansburgh.... The well-known area contractor and businessman and his bride, the former Miss Sarah Roberts, were married in the home of mutual friends....

The newsprint blurred. He crushed the clipping and threw it into the kitchen trash can. "Damned whore!" he muttered under his breath.

BEING A SINGLE PARENT came easier to D.A. than he'd expected. He'd always helped with Annie's care, and Mrs. Creswell became his regular baby-sitter until he made some decisions about his future.

He made inquiries through the university about Western Montana College. His department chairman listened to his explanation and agreed to contact his counterpart in the science department in Dillon, who in turn suggested that D.A. send his résumé. There were no openings at present, but when springtime musical chairs began for the faculty, he would keep D.A. in mind.

A week later the chairman from Western Montana College called D.A. to ask for additional information. He was impressed that D.A. had grown up in the area and that he had received his doctorate at such an early age. He also asked D.A. if he had ever taught biology.

"For two semesters, sir," D.A. replied. "Most of my classes have been in agriculture and chemistry. I have the requirements though. It would just take an initial effort to prepare. I'm definitely interested."

D.A. didn't hear from the science chairman at the college until late April, when he called and asked if D.A. could come for an interview.

"An opening has developed for the fall semester," he said, "We're looking for someone to teach a freshman class in biology and agriculture. You know this college was originally a teachers college, but recently we've expanded into business, computer sciences and natural resources. Now we've been given approval and funding to implement some agriculture courses. It certainly makes good sense, since we're in the heart of cattle- and sheep-raising country. You'd be coordinating an extension program that involves working with some of the ranches in the Big Hole Basin."

D.A. drove to Dillon on a Friday in early May and left Annie with May Morrison, the wife of the McCormack's longtime family physician. He met with the dean and several other officials and was offered the position.

"Dr. McCormack, welcome home," the science chairman said.

D.A. spent a quiet weekend at the ranch with his father and Sammy.

"Please leave Annie with us," Sammy suggested. "It'll be much easier to pack and settle your affairs without her underfoot. Now that she's walking, I'm sure she's into everything. And we'd love to have her, wouldn't we, David?''

"Of course," David replied. "It would only be for three weeks.''

D.A. agreed and returned to Missoula. The walls of the quiet apartment began to close in on him, and he was glad to be leaving. He moved in early June, and his plans were to stay at the home ranch for the summer and help his father with the purebred Simmental breeding program.

He'd bought himself time to breathe and to think.

CHAPTER SIX

"HAPPY BIRTHDAY, SHRIMP," D.A. McCormack's velvet voice came flowing over the phone line.

Mary's heart tripped at his greeting and continued to beat rapidly, interfering with her hearing. "You remembered?"

"Of course," he said. "How have you been?"

"Fine," she replied. "Are you calling from Missoula?"

"No, honey. We've been at dad's place for a month. We'll be there for the summer. I'll start looking for a place in town in August."

"In town?" she cried. "You've...moved?"

"Sure. Didn't you know? I've accepted a position at WMC. I'll be teaching this fall. I took your advice. Sorry I forgot to write, but I've been very busy."

"I'm glad," she said.

"So what have you been up to?" he asked.

"I've been working in town at the printing shop," she told him, "but they gave me the day off because it's my birthday."

"What do you do there?"

"I set type using one of their new computer terminals. See, D.A., I've learned to type and do something other than just homemaking and *mothering*. I took your advice, too," she laughed.

"Good. Now, do you have plans for today?"

"Just the usual family party tonight. Why?"

"Annie and I thought you might like to go on a lazy July birthday picnic with us orphans. Sammy has already packed the basket with fried chicken and all sorts of goodies. Can you come?"

"Sammy? Are Sammy and your father...?" She held her breath.

"No, honey, just the three of us. It's not every day a girl turns seventeen."

"Of course, I'd love to go," she said, relieved at his answer. "What can I bring?"

"Something to sit on and pillows," he said. "We'll relax when the tigress naps. I'll bring her playpen for a corral. Dress light, because it's going to be warm. We'll be there about ten. Sorry for the short notice."

Mary was ready by nine-thirty. As she waited for him in the living room, she caught a glimpse of herself in a mirror. She sprang up from her chair and ran to her room, yanking the thick green yarn from her hair. She tried a yellow grosgrain ribbon and finally settled on the red-and-white silk scarf D.A. had given her years ago.

"Mary, calm yourself," her mother said when she came back into the living room. "It's only a picnic."

"But it's not. It's with *him*."

D.A. arrived precisely at ten o'clock, and she rushed through the door, calling out a goodbye to her mother as an afterthought.

As his car pulled out of the Rocking R yard, Mary turned to him. "Welcome home, D.A." She glanced back at Annie, who was strapped into her child-restraint seat. She was seventeen months old and at the moment was trying to figure out how to get out of the straps and buckles that held her safely in place.

At least D.A. was here and not two hundred miles away, living with a woman who...Mary thought of her conversation with Sammy that afternoon in the church library and the shock of hearing about Sarah's life-style in Las Vegas. She glanced over at D.A. and vowed never to be the one to tell him.

Annie squirmed again, and Mary laid a calming hand on her toe, shaking it playfully.

"Momma Mar," Annie said, and D.A. laughed.

"Have you been coaching her?" Mary asked.

"Me?" He feigned innocence and concentrated on his driving.

"Where are we going?"

"Over toward the Sweetwater area, or maybe to the Ruby—anywhere away from the crowds," he said. "Do you realize I've been away from here for eight years, Mary?"

"I know. I was nine when you left."

"You remember?"

"Of course." Her heart ached as she added, "Friends don't forget."

They turned onto a narrow dirt road that began to climb, and the valley below them started to take shape. They stopped to allow Annie to exercise her chubby legs and to make a quick diaper change.

"I've got to get this kid toilet trained one of these days," D.A. said. "I just don't know quite how to begin. Perhaps the sitter I hire in town this fall can help." He picked up Annie and held her in his right arm and pointed out some objects in the distance.

"Mary, come here and see the ranches. They're like little dollhouses, aren't they?" When she joined him, he put his left arm around her shoulders and drew her against him.

She glanced at his hand, wishing for his sake it was real. He had changed, and she couldn't put her finger on it. He seemed sensitive about his artificial hand and had apologized when it touched her during the diaper change.

"It doesn't matter," she had replied. "It's just you."

"But it does," he had said, and then changed the subject.

She moved restlessly beside him now.

"Are you okay?" he asked, and tightened his hold on her. To keep her balance, she slipped her arm around his waist. It felt hard and flat. The close contact did little to calm her.

"Yes, it must be the altitude," she said, laughing nervously. "We'd better go, D.A." She quickly withdrew from his embrace.

They found a spot near a creek where the land was level enough to make camp for the afternoon. The playpen was set up and Annie placed in it while they carried the food and blankets from the car. When she was set free, Annie began an immediate exploration of the area. She fell into the shallow creek, crawled out and stood up. The weight of her wet clothing unbalanced her, and she plopped back into the water. D.A. joined her.

"What are you doing?" Mary called, approaching them cautiously. D.A. flicked cold water on her.

"D.A., you're just a big kid yourself," she said, shrieking when he repeated the teasing trick. She whirled away and ducked her head.

Suddenly he was behind her. He grabbed her and clutched her to him, laughing and playfully covering her face with his cold wet hand. She collapsed against him in shock at such intimate contact, and she received a further shock when he kissed her cheek and released her.

He returned to the creek to get Annie, who had discovered some evasive darting water creatures swimming in the pools near the muddy creek bank.

Mary turned and watched the laughing blond giant of a man dunk his daughter in and out of the water, washing the mud and dirt from her as she writhed and squealed at his tickling.

"Can you bring a towel and a change of clothing for this messy kid, Mary?" he called.

Any task was better than the sweet torture of standing silently by and watching him, she decided, and hastened to the car to find dry clothes for Annie.

After lunch, Annie fell asleep in her playpen. D.A. and Mary spread another blanket beside the one still covered with dishes.

"It's getting warm," D.A. said, unbuttoning the cuffs of his long-sleeved shirt.

"Go ahead and take your shirt off if you want," Mary suggested.

"No, I don't think so...my hand...the...." He frowned.

"Take that off, too." She was puzzled by his reluctance to remove the prosthesis.

"I don't want to offend you."

"Good grief, D.A. I've known you for years. I've seen you without it as much as I've seen you with it. Now if you're hot, take it off...take it all off." Suddenly she broke into lighthearted laughter, warmed by his own smile. "Well, I didn't mean exactly *all*, not your clothing, just your...oh," she said, sighing in exasperation. "You decide for yourself, and I'll get the pillows from the car."

When she returned, he had shed his shirt and harness. He stood straight and tall, dressed only in faded cut-off jeans and canvas running shoes. She was enthralled by the picture he made. He seemed very relaxed, yet her own emotions were at such an explosive point that if he touched her for any reason, she would either throw herself into his arms or faint away.

She approached the blanket, hugging the pillows to her bosom. He removed his glasses, and she saw the rust-colored flecks in his eyes. He smiled a lazy smile and she blushed.

"You look like you've got some sun already," he observed. "Perhaps we should move the blanket into the shade."

"No, no," she replied breathlessly. "Here, have a pillow." She playfully tossed one to him.

He dropped to the blanket, tucking his left arm under the corner of the pillow and draping his right hand across his waist. He lay on his back watching the white clouds dance on the high breezes in the bright-blue Montana sky.

She stood at the edge of the blanket, unable to decide where to sit.

"Come down beside me," D.A. invited, a softness rounding the edges of his words. He continued to study the sky.

Hesitantly Mary moved toward him and carefully stretched out beside him, keeping several safe inches between them. She propped herself on her elbows and tried to find something to concentrate on, but she had no interest in the natural things surrounding them. Her eyes were drawn to four long scars on the front left side of his neck. Without thinking, she touched the fine ridges.

"What are they from?" she asked. "The accident?"

His right hand came up to his neck, trapping hers and pressing it against him. She felt the muscular cord and pulsing vein under her fingers. She frowned at him, trying to interpret his actions.

"I almost lost my head one time," he grimaced. "Quite literally, dad says." He closed his eyes. "Apparently my mother was driving back to Butte from Missoula. She was very drunk and took out her anger for my father on me. I've pieced together information over the years, plus what I can vaguely remember of that night. I think she tried to hit me. I crossed my arms for protection and the next thing I knew I was being hurled through the windshield with glass and blood everywhere." He turned to look at Mary.

"Dad tells me she hit a bridge abutment near Butte, but I must have lost consciousness then, because except for a few faint memories, I remember nothing until I awoke in the hospital about three weeks later. I had missed slicing the jugular vein in my neck by a hair's breath, both my arms were in slings... and I had no left hand. Damn it all, why did it have to happen?"

"How awful," Mary cried. "I'm just glad you lived and moved here near us."

"Maybe it would have been better if I had died that night," he murmured.

"Never say that," Mary told him. She wanted to comfort him but didn't know how.

"Some people think my disfigurement makes me a freak," he said, staring at her.

"Oh, no, they're wrong! You're... very special. I think you're very handsome, too."

"It doesn't matter. Handsome freaks are still freaks." Painful emotions tore at his features. "I couldn't satisfy her. I tried. I tried like hell. Never again," he vowed, and he closed his eyes.

An invisible thread held her gaze on his face. She eased her hand from under his and he opened his eyes, but returned his attention to the sky. The silence became unbearable.

"Happy?" he asked, still not looking at her.

"It's beautiful here, so peaceful, so quiet. Listen...only those squirrels in that tree...and the wind."

He turned his head, but before his eyes reached her face, his line of vision was drawn to the scoop neck of her blouse, which had pulled down to reveal the edge of a lace trimmed bra, her full young breasts heaving gently with each breath. When had she become so fully developed, he wondered. A fleeting image of Sarah raced through his mind, and he quickly moved his eyes to her face. The realization that she wasn't a little girl anymore disturbed him.

Mary glanced down at herself and quickly adjusted her blouse front to cover herself. The heat of embarrassment burned her face. His fingers touched her cheek, and his hand forced her face up so she had to look at him.

"Sorry," she murmured.

"I'm the one who should apologize...for looking," he said, still holding her chin as his thumb lightly stroked her cheek.

"It's okay," she replied, and leaned over to kiss him lightly on his mouth. Her lips were slightly parted and her heart raced, causing her breath to come in tiny gasps.

Suddenly a groan sounded deep in his throat, and he took the initiative. He rejected her offer for a conciliatory kiss and replaced it with one of soul-wrenching passion. She fought for air, frightened by his change.

"Please," she cried against his mouth. "Don't hurt me." Her eyes were burning with bewilderment as he gradually released her head. He pulled her down against his bare chest and held her without a word, his left arm lying across her back as his right hand massaged her shoulders. She could hear the rapid vibrations of his heart beneath her ear, and slowly her fear evaporated.

"I'm sorry, Mary," he whispered. "Truly sorry. I didn't mean to scare you. Forgive me, please."

"You didn't frighten me," she lied. "I know it's been difficult for you and Annie. And you *are* special. I meant that," she whispered, and her arm slid around his waist. She wanted to kiss him again and tell him how she felt, but she knew he wasn't ready to accept what she was willing to offer. Her confusion was soothed away as he continued to hold her. She felt his chest expand with a deep breath of air, and he began to speak.

"I told you once long ago that marriage should be forever, and I meant it. I tried very hard to make her happy, but the more I gave her, the more she demanded. I couldn't satisfy her."

"You mean... at night?"

"No," he laughed cynically. "She said I was great in bed. She said once that I was the greatest one-handed lover she'd ever had." His voice faded away, and he grew quiet for a moment.

"That was the crux of our relationship," he went on, his voice muffled against her tousled hair. "She loved my body but hated my ugly wrist scars. I tried to keep them covered. I used to wonder why she preferred to make love in the dark, until one day I stepped out of the shower with only a towel around me. For the first time I saw the revulsion in her eyes. I don't know who felt worse—her for having to see me that way or me when I saw the truth in her eyes. She wanted the one thing in the world I couldn't give her. A whole man."

He continued to caress her shoulders, even when a stream of tears fell from the bridge of her nose and formed tiny puddles on his chest. She turned and reached for his left wrist and pulled it to her breast.

"She was a fool," Mary whispered, and D.A. tightened his arm around her.

The shadows slowly moved across them as the sun began to slip behind the tall pines. His right arm fell away from her and thudded softly onto the blanket. She knew from his deep breathing that he'd fallen asleep. She eased away from his embrace and sat nearby, cross-legged and moody as she studied him in his sleep.

She didn't know just when she'd begun to love him as more than just a neighbor and friend. Throughout her life he'd always been there: the young boy with curly blond hair who could swoop her up and toss her in the air when she was still a preschooler, bringing a squeal of delight from her; the high-school-basketball star forward who still found time to protect her from the teasing of her older brothers; the college student who never forgot her birthday. Somewhere along the years her hero worship had evolved into a steadily growing love for the man he'd become. If only she'd been born several years earlier, if only. . . .

Annie stirred from her nap. Mary slipped away, changed her and set her free to play, then she busied herself with the food on the blanket, trying to decide if she should pack it away.

"Not yet," D.A. said near her ear, startling her. "It's too early to go home. I like it here with just the two of you." They watched Annie play for several minutes until he said, "Mary?"

"What?" She turned expectantly to him.

"Can you hand me my shirt?" His eyes smiled as he spoke.

Her heart sank. "Sure," she replied, and reached across the blanket for it. It was just out of reach. She stretched and was almost prone when suddenly she was showered with dried grass and dirt. She collapsed on the ground, blinded by the dust and debris.

"Annie, no," D.A. shouted, and a whimper came from the little girl as Mary heard a soft spanking sound on Annie's diaper. "No, Annie, that's not nice."

Mary sat up and tried to see what had happened. She spied D.A. lifting his daughter into the playpen.

He returned to Mary and helped her up. "You're a mess," he said, pulling her against him and reaching behind her to brush the dried grass from her hair and shoulders.

"What happened?" she asked, as she leaned against his chest.

"Little Miss Annie was playing like Ruth the

gleaner. She had an armload of debris and dropped it right on top of your pretty head." He released her. "I can't get it out. Here, sit down. I'll get you tissues for your eyes. I'll tend to your hair while you take care of your face. Where's your comb or brush?"

"In my purse."

Her eyes were watering from the dust particles so she obediently sat cross-legged on the blanket. D.A.'s long legs appeared on either side of her as he slid into position behind her.

He untied the red-and-white scarf. "Is this my birthday scarf?" he asked.

"Yes," she replied.

"You were thirteen—a new teenager."

"Yes, a long time ago," she said.

He began combing the debris from her long dark hair and as the dried grass and dust fell out, the sheen returned. The texture became like spun silken strands in his fingers.

"Dada, pease?" Annie called.

He glanced up at his repentant daughter and smiled. "I'm a sucker for a pretty face." He laid his hand on Mary's shoulder. "Don't move, Mary."

Mary listened to D.A. scold Annie before he released her. "Be good, or back you go." Then he returned to the blanket.

His long legs reappeared on either side of her and she felt his hand again in her hair. He used his left arm to hold the hair away from her neck as his right hand brought the comb down in long sweeping motions.

"You have such healthy hair, Mary. It's so shiny." He stopped momentarily as he exchanged the comb for a brush.

Even when all the debris was removed he continued performing the pleasant task, reluctant to move away from her as she sat quietly between his legs. He leaned forward and impulsively kissed the exposed soft skin on her neck.

She took a sharp breath of air. "Oh, D.A.," she sighed.

Her nearness brought an unexpected surge of sensual desire to him, startling him momentarily, and he quickly suppressed it. He concentrated on brushing her hair. Annie toddled over to them and stopped directly in front of Mary, her small hands hidden behind her back.

"No, Annie," D.A. cautioned sternly. "Don't you dare do that again."

Annie gleefully waved her empty hands and fell tumbling against Mary, pushing her back against D.A.'s chest. D.A. reached around Mary's waist to steady a giggling Annie. She wanted to continue the game and again fell limply against her. This time he was ready for her and caught her chubby body before she hit Mary.

"No, Annie." He stood her up, then pulled back, and his hand brushed against Mary's breast. Sarah flashed through his mind—such a stark difference between her and this innocent teenager he held casually in his arms. Again he felt the wave of desire, but immediately suppressed it. He quickly jumped to his feet. Reaching for her hand, he helped Mary to her feet. "We'd better go," he murmured. "It's getting late. Don't you have a dinner party to attend?"

"Yes," she sighed, looking at his muscular bare chest.

"Oh, damn it," he exclaimed. "I forgot to get you a birthday present."

She beamed and, surprising herself at her own assertiveness, stood on tiptoe and kissed his mouth soundly.

"The picnic was more than enough," she assured him, and quickly busied herself packing the food away, trying to restore her composure.

D.A. FOUND A TWO-BEDROOM APARTMENT near the campus and moved from the ranch the first week in August. Two of Mary's brothers helped him move in some newly purchased furniture.

Mary asked for the afternoon off from her summer job at the print shop and kept Annie out of the way. Feeling in the way herself, she volunteered to organize the kitchen.

After her brothers left, Mary stayed and helped arrange Annie's room. She knew she wouldn't see D.A. for a while now that seventeen miles separated them.

Later, as she washed the dinner dishes and he dried, she turned to him. "Remember my offer last New Year's? I meant it, D.A. Call me and let me baby-sit when you want to go out . . . date . . . whatever."

"Sure, but I don't want you to have to drive in all the way from the ranch."

"Call me the night before, and I'll drive in and come here right from school. Didn't you say you've placed Annie in the community play school?"

He nodded.

"I'll pick her up for you. I'll help with dinner if you want. That way, it will be easier for you to get away."

"I don't want you to be my housekeeper. You can't neglect your schoolwork. Senior year is important."

"I've already been given a four-year scholarship to WMC. I'll do my homework here before you get home."

"Any nights excepted?"

She tilted her head thoughtfully. "Fridays and Saturdays. Fridays are football games and I have to cheer. I . . . I usually have a date on Saturdays."

He stopped drying the plate in his hands and frowned down at her. "Do you date a lot?" he asked.

She shrugged her shoulders. "What's a lot?"

"Are the boys knocking at your door in droves?" he teased.

She stared up at him. "I usually have more than one to choose from. Why?" she challenged.

He set the plate on the counter and reached for another. "I just wondered. Anyone serious?"

She couldn't think of an honest answer, so she gave none.

"I assume that means yes," he speculated.

Her eyes flew to his face, but still she remained speechless.

"What do guys and girls do on dates these days?" he asked.

"I assume the same things they did in your day," she replied.

"Good Lord!"

"I don't know what you're implying, D.A.," she retorted angrily, "but if you mean do I fool around, the answer is *no*."

"Saving yourself for Mr. Right?" he teased.

"What's wrong with that?"

"Old-fashioned?" he hinted. "Mary—" he leaned back against the counter "—some day you'll meet some guy just right for you who'll sweep you off your feet, marry you and give you all the best in life. But you might meet someone not so right who'll sweep you off your feet and right into his bed." His hand cupped her chin and tilted her face upward. "Just be careful, honey. I wouldn't want you to get hurt." He dropped his hand. "Now, are you sure you want to commit yourself to Annie and me? We're a package deal, you know."

"I know." She gave a deep sigh. "I'll adjust my own dates around our two schedules."

"Good," he said. "I don't want you to neglect your own social life just because of me. You're sweet, though. I trust you with Annie, and I appreciate your offer."

CHAPTER SEVEN

MARY'S OFFER TO BABY-SIT was made to ensure that she would see D.A. occasionally, but she hadn't expected him to make use of it quite so often.

For two months straight she received a call on Wednesday, asking her to come the next evening. She stayed in town, picked up Annie, went to D.A.'s house and started dinner. Sometimes she'd find money on the counter with a note to go buy hamburgers. D.A. had become rather uncommunicative. He usually ate his meal quietly, allowing Mary to make the small talk, and he would glance up at her occasionally. But once when she described a comedy she'd seen with a college freshman student, he had shot her a piercing look of concern.

"I know the guy. He's not your type, Mary."

Mary laughed nervously. "He's only a friend."

"You don't understand," he said. "He got his last girlfriend pregnant and then left her high and dry. Just be careful."

"D.A., he's only a friend."

After dinner he would kiss Annie goodbye, wave to Mary without really seeing her, and rush out the door, never telling her where he was going or with whom he was spending his time. He returned promptly at ten, thanked her for sitting, insisted on paying and walked her to her car. He never discussed his evening activities with her.

Finally, after the end of the football season, her curiosity got the best of her. One evening she grabbed Annie, ran to her car and followed him. If he was having some hot and torrid affair with a beautiful woman, she just had to know so she could try to forget her own feelings for him. She'd note the address of the house or apartment he entered, swallow her pride and find out who lived there.

She could hardly believe her eyes when she ended up at her own high-school gymnasium. She watched as D.A. removed an athletic bag from the trunk of his car and disappeared into the gym.

The next Thursday evening during dinner she confronted him. Annie had fallen asleep in her high chair so Mary had put her to bed. She and D.A. were alone at the table.

"D.A., where do you go on Thursday nights?" she asked.

"Out."

"Out where? With whom?"

"Just out," he said.

"But where?"

"Why do you ask, honey?"

"I just wondered. What if something happened to Annie? I might need to get in touch with you."

He frowned, and a stray blond curl fell over his forehead. She wanted to brush it away.

"Why didn't you ask when I first started having you sit?"

"I don't know...."

His shoulders sagged slightly as he looked at her. "Since Sarah left...." He stopped. It was the first time he had mentioned his former wife's name to her.

"It's all right," she interrupted. "You don't have to explain your actions to me. I said I'd take care of Annie. I didn't say you had to play true confessions in order to have my services. I'm sorry I brought it up." Her hand shook as she lowered her fork to the table.

"Your social life is your business and mine should be my business, didn't we agree to that?" he said.

His words cut her, and her eyes burned with unshed tears. She shoved her chair back, tipping it over. It crashed to the floor as she rushed from the room and ran to the bathroom.

He followed her and shoved the toe of his nylon-and-suede jogging shoe in the doorway, stopping her from closing and locking the door.

"Go away, please," she cried, turning her back to him and leaning against the wall.

"Turn around, Mary."

"No! Go away. I didn't mean to pry."

He took a firm hold on her shoulders and turned her to him as he surveyed the crowded room. He needed someplace to sit so he wouldn't be a foot above her. He spied the only seat in the room, kicked the lid down with his toe and grabbed her wrist.

"Come here, little one," he insisted, and pulled

her down onto his lap. He yanked a handful of tissue and wiped her face.

He smiled. "Isn't this romantic?"

"Don't tease me, D.A.," she cried. "You've got a mean streak sometimes, and I don't like you when you make fun of me." She started to sob again.

"I'm sorry, love." He pulled her head against his shoulder and held her until her crying ceased. He rocked her gently until he felt the tension leave her slender body, but that release kindled reactions in himself that he didn't like, sensations that had troubled him during their picnic the previous summer. The last thing he intended to do was let himself get involved with the young daughter of his father's best friend. He'd known her too long for that.

"I was about to explain, Mary," he began. "Since Sarah left, I haven't felt like dating other women, not yet. Perhaps in the spring. There are a few single women on the faculty who would probably say yes if I asked them out. I knew I had to get out and do something, so I joined the city basketball league and was assigned to a team that practices on Thursdays. It's really been good exercise, and the other guys are great. Two of them are old high-school buddies of mine from years back. We play every Saturday afternoon. The wives of the other players watch Annie, and she gets to play with other children. I didn't tell you because I thought you might be disappointed by my unexciting social life. Besides, I like your company for dinner." He laughed softly. "It's a little like playing house without all the burdens. It's sort of the high point of the school week. Do I disappoint you?"

She straightened her head and looked up at him, her brown eyes shiny from tears. Her lashes lay in thick spikes against her cheeks. "You could never disappoint me," she said, and her attention moved from his somber green eyes, past his straight nose, to his wide mouth. Her free hand gained a will of its own and brushed across his lips to settle on his cheek.

He applied the slightest pressure with the arm in which he held her, and she kissed his mouth.

There was a sweet innocence to her kiss as she slowly withdrew. "I had to," she whispered, and defied him to challenge her. "I'm not a child, D.A."

He touched the smoothness of her cheek, and again she stared at his sensuous mouth. Her heart beat erratically when she became aware of his own response to their closeness.

"Oh, God, Mary," he breathed as he pulled her to him. His wide sensuous mouth descended on hers, covering her lips in a way she had never experienced before. The subtle pressure grew harder, forcing her mouth to open. When he met the resistance of her teeth, he eased away and finally withdrew.

He pressed her head against his throat and held her. Her petiteness brought out the old protective instincts he'd always felt for her, but they were swept away as his hand explored the rapid rise and fall of her breasts. He cursed under his breath and forced his hand to settle on her waist.

"I love you, D.A.," she whispered, keeping her face hidden against him.

He tightened his hold on her. "This can't be, Mary. You're much too young for me. I'm too experienced for you. I'm divorced with a child to raise. You have your whole life ahead of you. Don't get caught in something that would only hurt you. I don't want to hurt you, Mary. I could easily take advantage of you, but I won't. Damn it," he groaned.

His expression determined, he slid her off his lap and led her into the living room. "You'd better go home. I think I'll skip practice, and I don't trust myself tonight with you here. Do you understand why?"

He shook her shoulders, but she didn't answer. "I'm a normal healthy male, Mary. I've never had to be celibate for long. There are always available women, but I only want one woman at a time. I was faithful to Sarah, but I haven't been with a woman since. For some ungodly reason, Mary, you make me feel alive again, but it's all wrong!"

His brows furrowed as he studied her face. Her mouth was full, her lips parted. Unconsciously she licked her dry upper lip. The subtle movement of her moist pink tongue was his undoing again. He jerked her to him and pressed her body hard against his, knowing she would feel his rekindled arousal.

His kiss was painfully rough. It frightened her until he eased the pressure. When he finally spoke, his mouth was still inches from hers.

"I'm sorry, my love. I'm very sorry. This could have been so good if things had been right." His lips met hers again, and then reluctantly he withdrew. "Go home," he said raggedly. "For both our sakes I wish I could say don't come back, but you're the only one Annie will stay with. She screams her pretty head off when I bring in any other sitter. Come next Thursday. I'll have everything under control. Maybe I'll even have a real date by then."

He guided her to the door and gave her one more kiss, a light touch on her cheek, implying they were just friends again.

THE THURSDAY-EVENING ARRANGEMENT CONTINUED, but now an attractive blond woman arrived shortly after they finished eating. She would honk her horn in the driveway and give him a ride to the gym. One evening she joined them for dinner.

"Mary, this is Danielle Everett," D.A. said. "Would you believe she's the granddaughter of the school nurse who took care of me once when I got into a vicious fight in the eighth grade? Danielle plays on one of the women's teams."

As the introductions were made, D.A. casually draped his arm around the woman's shoulders, and Mary died a slow death as she surveyed the beautiful and statuesque Danielle.

CHRISTMAS PASSED, and Danielle was replaced by Jennifer, who was tall and brunet, but not so curvaceous. As the snows gave way to hardy spring flowers, Jennifer disappeared and Rose Marie took her place. Rose Marie was just slightly taller than

Mary, but she was so much more voluptuous that Mary was glad she wore bulky sweaters to hide her own petite form.

Rose Marie was the scorekeeper for D.A.'s team. Her red hair and blue eyes proved to be accurate reflections of her personality. D.A. commented one evening that she was either cool as blue ice or hot as a flame, and Mary's heart froze, fearing the depth of his involvement with this volatile woman of fire and ice.

Saturday was normally her night for dating, but D.A. called her early one week in May and asked for extra duty. Rose Marie and he had something special planned. Mary didn't ask what.

She rang the doorbell twice before she received any response from within the apartment, and then it was a barely discernible movement of the door handle. She cautiously turned the knob from her side and eased the door open.

Two-year-old Annie was standing on tiptoe jiggling the knob. A smile brightened her chubby face when she saw Mary.

"Hi, momma," she said, and held up her arms.

"Oh, Annie, what am I going to do about you?" Mary murmured softly as she picked up the little girl. Mary kissed her rosy cheek and then whispered in her ear, "I wish you were mine." She gave her a squeeze and Annie giggled.

"Where's daddy?"

"Here. . . ."

Mary heard D.A.'s voice coming from the hall

where the phone was located. She stuck her head through the living-room opening into the hallway and waved, then she joined Annie on the floor, handing her blocks as she needed them. Mary concentrated on the tower Annie was building and tried to ignore the steadily rising tone of D.A.'s voice.

"I'm sorry, Rosie, I can't."

"No, Rosie, don't ask me to."

"Sorry, sweetie, but if you give me an ultimatum like that, the choice is obvious. I choose her over you. Sorry."

"If that's the way you feel, Rose Marie, I think you're right."

There was a long pause, then he shouted, "Same to you, you—"

He slammed the receiver down, and Mary glanced up as he entered the living room. She had expected him to be irate, but a lazy smile spread across his slightly flushed face as he dropped onto the sofa. One of his shoes touched her bare thigh just below her cut-off jeans when he stretched his long legs.

"Oh, excuse me, honey." He grinned good-naturedly. "Rose Marie just called me an SOB. Can you imagine that?"

"Considering what you were about to call her, yes I can." She smiled and handed another block to Annie.

"She called me her name first, but I got the last word in...only I think she had already hung up her phone." He laughed and eased his foot toward the teetering tower his daughter had built.

Mary slapped at his long foot. "Don't you dare," she cautioned. "Just because you have a fight with your lover doesn't give you any right to...."

"She's not my lover. She just wants to be."

Mary turned toward him. "I'm sorry. I shouldn't have said that. What happened? Do you still need me tonight?"

"We were going to go to Butte for dinner and a late show—a special review at one of the nightclubs there." He frowned. "She wanted to spend the night in Butte and come home tomorrow afternoon."

Mary swallowed hard. "I would have stayed over... if that's what you wanted," she volunteered, staring down at her hands in her lap.

"No, that's not what I wanted," he replied, watching her where she sat cross-legged on the floor. "She said I had to choose between my daughter or her company...that I couldn't have both."

"Oh, D.A., that's not right of her."

"You're damned right it's not, but I made the choice and told her so. My daughter always has preference over my dates. Damn her for even thinking that...."

She stood up, glanced at him again and started to gather her jacket and purse. "I'd better go."

As she passed the corner of the sofa, he reached out and caught her knee. She stopped abruptly at the sudden warmth of his hand.

"Wait, don't go. Not yet." He stood up. "I know. Let's you, Annie and me do something. We haven't gone anywhere together since last summer on your birthday. How about a drive-in movie? Annie can sleep in the back of the car. Hey, you haven't ridden in my new car, have you? How about it? Will *you* be my date for the evening, Miss Russell?" he asked, bowing deeply as though he were a courteous southern gentleman.

She grinned. "You're hard to resist when you turn on the charm, Dr. McCormack, in spite of what I heard when I first arrived. And it *is* a shame to drive all the way in for nothing." She looked at him again. "Are you sure you want to spend the evening with a lowly teenager instead of hotsy-totsy Rose Marie?"

He threw his head back in good-natured laughter. "You usually don't say things like that."

"I never liked her very much. She was too... blatant about you. She had no class. She hung all over you, even in front of Annie and me."

"Do I detect a little jealousy?"

"Of course not!"

"Just because you've known me for all these years doesn't give you the right to censure my female companions," he teased.

She twitched her nose at him. "Even when I'm right?"

"You might be this time. You're far too perceptive. Still want to go?"

"Sure," she agreed. "It's about time you paid a little attention to your devoted baby-sitter."

He cocked an eyebrow at her. "Oh, I've paid attention to her. I've just tried like hell to behave myself. This will be a strictly platonic date. For companionship." He gave her a dazzling smile that made his eyes crinkle with humor.

"What do we need?" she asked, caught up in the excitement of the evening.

"Pillows, a couple of blankets if it gets chilly. We'll buy some hamburgers on the way and popcorn during intermission."

Ten minutes into the first feature, Annie was asleep in the back of the new station wagon, sprawled out with her favorite pillow and blanket and Julie Russell's handmade teddy bear in her arms.

D.A. had adjusted the seat to its farthest position. Still he moved restlessly, stretching his long legs. Occasionally he glanced at Mary's profile as she watched the movie. The changing colors from the screen cast shadows across her face.

She laughed, and the cool night air carried the musical tones of her voice to his receptive ears.

"This *Greystoke* movie isn't much like the Tarzan ones I've seen on television with Johnny Weissmuller," she said. She glanced at him. Unconsciously she shivered and rubbed her arms.

"Cold?" he asked.

She turned slightly and her dark eyes caught the movie lights and sparkled like shimmering coffee. "A little."

"Come closer. We'll share the blanket."

"Oh, no. I'm okay."

"You're safe. I'll behave. Rose Marie would never have refused an offer like this," he teased.

"I'm not Rose Marie," she said with a haughty

twist of her head, but she couldn't suppress a grin.

"Afraid of me?"

"Of course not," she insisted.

"Then come over here."

She slid slowly across the seat as he held the blanket open for her. He shifted his right arm and pulled her against his side, adjusted the warm blanket against the chill of the mid-May evening, and tried to concentrate on the movie.

He wanted to touch her but forced his right hand to remain on the back of the seat, inches from her shoulder. The windshield became steamy so he opened the window to clear it, then returned his right arm to the back of the seat behind her dark head.

She turned her face slightly away from him and leaned against his arm, her cheek caressing his forearm. He wondered if she was aware of her actions, and he tried to ignore the sensation of her skin brushing his.

He made a concerted effort to concentrate on the movie, but a breeze floated through the open window and blew strands of her loose hair across his face. He took his prosthesis and brushed them away.

She noticed and gathered her hair in her hands. "I'm sorry. It's bothering you. I should have pulled it back with an elastic." She began to search in her purse for one.

Suddenly he opened his door and left her. He stood outside and smoked a cigarette for a few minutes, then reappeared at the other side of the car. He opened the door and slid in to the passenger side.

He studied her as she wound the elastic around her hair.

"Why did you move?" she asked. She grew uncomfortable under his continued scrutiny.

"I had to."

"Why?"

"I needed my right hand."

"What for?"

"Because...." He hesitated, caught up in his desire. His fingers touched her cheek. "I wanted to see if your skin is as smooth as it was that night in the bathroom when I held you."

"Oh..." she sighed.

"It is." His fingertips slid to her mouth and traced its outline. "I wanted to see if your lips are as soft as I remembered." His hand traveled down her throat, gliding to her breast, where it paused for so brief a time they both wondered if it had even happened. His hand settled on her waist. "And if your waist is as tiny as I recalled." His palm was warm on her flat stomach.

"It is." A hint of disappointment sounded in his voice. "Damn it, Mary, I've begun to compare the women I date with you and they come up deficient."

She was caught off guard by his words and sat hypnotized as he brought his hand to her face again. He lightly explored the contours of her cheekbone, the hollow beneath, and on down to her slightly parted lips. "You change each time I see you, and I find you breathtakingly beautiful. You're not the shrimp I've tried to pretend you were."

He slid his hand to the back of her neck. "I'm going to kiss you, Mary, the way I've wanted to since last summer. You do something to me that I really don't understand—" he pulled her closer "—and I'm damned tired of fighting it."

She came willingly into his embrace, and her arms slid around him.

"I want you, but I know I can't have you, so I'm going to settle for this." He kissed her, a long sensuous kiss that forced her mouth to open.

Her response astonished them both. She strained against him as his hand moved down the back of her rib-knit T-shirt. The stretchiness of the fabric provided little resistance to his exploring hand as it slipped beneath the shirt.

Her skin was hot, and her heart was thudding beneath his inquisitive fingers. He knew her vulnerability and reluctantly removed his hand and raised it to her chin, slowly releasing her from his kiss.

Her eyes reflected her own aroused womanly desires, and he knew she was at his mercy. He'd be a fool to get involved with her. He pulled from deep within himself the self-control to suppress his own hunger.

"I could be arrested for what I just did. Damn it, Mary, you're hardly more than a child." He eased her gently away.

When she heard his dreaded words, the old fear choked her, bringing tears to her shiny eyes. "I'm not a child, D.A.," she challenged him, but her voice came out high and immature.

"You're innocent...inexperienced."

"Is that wrong?" she asked.

"You must stay that way."

She stared at him, too distraught to answer.

"It can't be me," he said firmly. He reached out to wipe the lone tear that caught on her cheek. He pulled her to him again and tried to collect his thoughts. "Your family trusts me. Your father and mother and my dad are the best of friends. It's a family matter whose repercussions could shatter everyone involved. What would they think if we...if I...it can't be me. Don't you understand?"

She pulled back angrily. "Do you mean that if I go to bed with someone else, then you'll find me desirable?" She grew more agitated. "You want someone else to do the...the breaking and entering, then you'll be willing to get in the saddle and do some riding? Is that it?"

"My God, Mary, where did you learn to talk like that?"

"It's an expression the guys at school use when they've been successful with a virgin," she said, on the edge of hysteria. "Michael Innes, my own cousin, has a sweat shirt that says, 'Guilty of breaking and entering,' and then underneath it he puts check marks for his successes. He wears it each Monday."

"That's arrogant and crude," D.A. said.

"Maybe it's the real world."

"No," he insisted. "Don't you ever refer to making love as getting in the saddle and riding." He shook her shoulders. "That's just having sex. I'd never have sex with you, Mary."

"Would you ever want to make love to me, D.A.?" she asked, surprising them both with her candidness.

"I don't know. I do know it wouldn't be right, so I try not to think about it," he said. "Damn it, Mary, if things were different, none of this would matter. If we were different people, in another place, we'd just be two consenting adults who found each other mutually attractive and willing. As it is, we both have to find someone else."

"I don't want someone else," she cried, and melted against him. Her arms went around his neck, and as he looked into her dark eyes, he vowed to keep his distance. But his resolve shattered as once again he captured her tender mouth and explored its depth, drinking of its sweetness. His hand roamed her slender body until he touched her bare thigh below the ragged edge of her cutoffs. His fingers slid beneath the fabric but were hindered by the snug fit of the shorts.

A moan escaped from her as she arched against him, giving him access to her throat. Her hands grew bolder and she explored his body. They clutched at his shirt, then his leather belt, and finally his denim covered hips. He wanted to encourage her, but his own control snapped back.

He returned his attention to her face, working patterns over her features, but always coming back to her willing lips. "Mary, my sweet Mary," he murmured huskily.

Something touched the top of his head, but he ignored it and continued to concentrate on the young woman in his arms. The tapping grew more persistent. He bumped Mary's nose and the romantic climate cooled when they heard a small voice.

"Pee, daddy. Go pee. . . hurry!"

Slowly they separated, turned, and spied two green eyes under a tousled auburn head staring at them.

"Hi, momma," Annie grinned.

D.A. turned from his daughter and stared directly into Mary's heaving chest. Impulsively he placed a light kiss against the narrow valley between her breasts and caught her eye.

She smiled. "I'll take her."

"I'll go, too," he said, sighing. "The walk in the cool air will do us all good. I'll get some popcorn and drinks."

On the way to the snack bar he began to chuckle. Mary stopped and turned to him quizzically.

"Rose Marie could never have handled this," he said, and hugged her.

They left the theater early and drove home. As they pulled into his driveway, he said, "I almost forgot to tell you. I'm moving back to the ranch. Dad's new house is almost finished. Sammy has been after me to live out there ever since we returned, but I've stayed away because I have to be my own separate family. Now the old log house will be available. Annie and I will move as soon as school is out, and Sammy offered to baby-sit next fall."

"I'm so happy for you," Mary replied.

"Do you want to car pool when you attend WMC next fall?" he asked as he unlocked his door.

"Sure, if you trust yourself being alone with me every day," she said glibly as they stood in his entryway.

"Am I in any danger?" he asked lightheartedly. "Are you trying to seduce me, Miss Russell?" He touched her chin caressingly. "Be careful, or you might be successful." He suddenly grew solemn as he took his sleepy daughter from Mary's arms.

"Wait, honey, while I put Annie in bed. I'll walk you to the car."

Minutes later he returned and accompanied her to her Volkswagen. His hand stopped her from opening the car door.

"Not yet," he murmured through the darkness. She found herself being lifted easily onto the sloping hood of the car.

She sensed he wanted to talk, but the subjects he chose were trivial. She didn't care. The sound of his resonant voice warmed her. She became aware of a hunger gnawing at her from deep within. She reached out to him, but she lost her balance and began to slide off the sloping hood. He caught her by the waist, and she grabbed his shoulders. He brought his knee up to stop her fall, and she found herself in the awkward position of temporarily straddling his muscular thigh.

Thoughts of their earlier discussion of saddles and riding swept through her like a dust devil skipping across the valley flats.

"Oh, D.A.," she cried, her voice changing from a sigh to a moan of desire as he drew her close. She found herself wrapped in a steel-like embrace, powerless to break free and not wishing to do so. His warm breath brushed her face as his mouth swooped down to cover her eager lips.

She broke away from his kiss, but he took her face in his hands. As he let her slide off his leg, he stared into her dark eyes.

He seemed to read her very soul. Enlightenment filled them both as he released his hold on her face and pulled her roughly to him, holding her protectively but not saying a word.

Time stopped while they clung to each other. She listened to his heavy breathing gradually subside.

"Oh, Mary, my little Mary," he murmured against her hair. "We can't let this happen." But his arms tightened briefly before easing her away. He opened her car door and stood back while she climbed in.

She gripped the steering wheel, wanting to scream at him and plead with him to take her back into his apartment, but confusion held her in its grasp.

"Drive carefully, honey," he whispered. He reached inside the open window and patted her forearm, then stepped quickly away.

She was baffled and angry by the mixed messages he'd been giving her all evening, yet she also knew her own reaction to him had been one that she had never experienced before. Her love for him had changed tonight, and she wasn't sure how to deal with these deeper, more complex emotions.

CHAPTER EIGHT

SAMMY MCCORMACK SMILED APPROVINGLY as D.A. handed Annie to her.

David raised a curious eyebrow. "You look very sharp. Who's unsuspecting heart do you intend to capture tonight? I pity the poor woman going with you. The odds are against her."

"It's Mary Russell," D.A. replied, trying to keep a casual air to his demeanor.

"Oh?" David straightened, and a look of concern settled on his weathering rugged features. "Be careful, son. She's like one of the family, you know."

"It's her eighteenth birthday," D.A. explained. "I promised her a night on the town if she ever got that old." He busied himself at the small mirror, straightening his tie. "We're going dining and dancing at the Eagle's Nest up on the hilltop. I haven't been there for years, and the view is terrific."

David smiled, the tension slowly leaving his face. "How is Mary? I haven't seen her since her graduation. She's become a very striking young woman, but she's always had a thing about you, D.A. You, of all people, wouldn't want to be her...undoing?"

"I know, dad," D.A. replied. "I'll be the perfect

gentleman. This gray flannel suit represents the conservative behavior I intend to practice tonight.'' He saluted, then waved as he strolled confidently out the door.

Eight miles away, Mary Russell confronted her father.

"How do I look, daddy?'' she asked, twirling in the middle of the spacious kitchen.

Ed Russell studied his oldest daughter. She wore a knee-length dress made of a filmy soft material that changed color each time she moved. Its basic pale-lime shade carried hints of rust and orange along with a deeper green. It reminded him of an opal ring he had given his wife Julie long ago.

His daughter was small, petite would be the proper word, he thought. Sheer stockings covered her shapely legs, and she wore white sling-back pumps that boosted her height a few inches. The skirt of her dress was full and accented her tiny waist.

He was a little surprised to see the cleavage displayed above the low-cut bodice. When had his little girl changed from the thin child he remembered to this amply endowed young woman before him? Paternal apprehension clouded his thoughts as he studied her upswept hairstyle. The thick dark hair was coiled loosely on her head, adding more inches to her height and highlighting the beauty of her dark eyes and delicate cheekbones.

The hint of pink lipstick reminded him that women's mouths were for kissing. How experienced was

she? He had never thought about such things before.

"You look...very nice. Who are you going out
with tonight, Mary Beth?"

"D.A."

"The McCormack kid?"

"Daddy, he's twenty-seven years old."

Ed Russell straightened in his chair. "Then isn't he
a little old for you?"

"No! We've been friends for years, and I...like
him."

Silence filled the room until Julie Russell cleared
her throat. "Russ, relax. Who would she be safer
with than D.A. McCormack. You've known him
since he was twelve years old. I'm sure he's a gentle-
men and has no intentions of harming our daughter." She smiled at Mary, who shrugged her slender
shoulders as though to hint that she thought her
mother was probably right.

The doorbell rang, and they heard Lisa answer it
and escort D.A. into the kitchen.

"Hello, Russ...Julie," he greeted them, but kept
his eyes on Mary.

Ed Russell's attention shifted to D.A. His blond
hair had gradually darkened to the shade of summer
wheat. Russ still thought he wore it longer than was
necessary, but the curls were trimmed into reasonably
manageable waves. He conceded that at least the
waves were his own, rather than some permanent.
He'd always questioned the masculinity of any man
who would subject himself to a beautician's hand and

perfumed chemicals. If the good Lord had meant a man to have curly hair, He would surely have made him that way.

Russ understood why women found D.A. attractive in spite of his hand loss. He fairly exuded a natural sex appeal and charm, and at the same time showed a certain vulnerability. The summer on the neighboring ranch had darkened his skin to a deep-golden tan, and his unusual green eyes held the same expressive quality as his father's. Even his own wife Julie had commented on the McCormack men's intriguing eyes. Was his daughter attracted by them, too? He wondered.

But D.A. was also a virile muscular man, a divorced man and a father. He was much too experienced for his Mary Beth.

"Take good care of my little girl, D.A.," Russ cautioned.

D.A. AND MARY HURRIED to the car. Just before he opened her door, D.A. turned Mary's face up to his.

"You look very lovely," he whispered, and he eased her against him and kissed her lightly.

She trembled against him and started to slide her arms around his waist, but he had already released her. She frowned at his receding broad shoulders as he hurried to the driver's side.

He was quiet during dinner. An uneasiness settled over her, and her appetite faltered.

"Let's dance," he suggested as the table was cleared.

The nightclub was crowded, and the music was soft and romantic as they weaved their way to the dance floor. He smiled down at her and slid his left arm around her. She came just to his chin, thanks to her high-heeled shoes.

He felt her breasts against him, and long-suppressed images of Sarah returned to him. His thoughts stayed on her even as he held Mary in his arms. He knew Sammy received occasional letters from Las Vegas, but Sarah had made no effort to see Annie or contact him about her welfare. Apparently she had forgotten her child, and this disinterest on her part helped keep the memories of his life with her securely locked away.

The young woman in his arms was the antithesis of Sarah; untouched, sincere, loving, maternal, and obviously a virgin. He had made himself a promise to keep her that way. He would continue to be her protector.

She looked up at him and smiled, and he leaned down to kiss her lightly, ignoring the curious looks of a few people they knew.

When the dance ended, Mary said, "I'm too warm. Could we go out on the terrace for some fresh air?"

"Of course," D.A. replied, guiding her toward the sliding glass doors of the exit.

A cool mountain breeze drifted across the terrace as they strolled to the wrought-iron railing. Mary drew her lacy shawl around her shoulders. She wondered why he didn't put his arm around her the way he usually did.

He lit a cigarette and offered it to her, but she shook her head and he smoked in silence. She watched his strong profile as he inhaled, and her pulse raced as she speculated on the end of the evening. She was willing to go along with whatever he wanted. She had dealt with her conflicts and reconciled her doubts.

He snubbed out the cigarette butt in the sand of a smoking stand before turning to her.

"Mary?"

"Yes," she replied, wishing she didn't sound so breathless.

"I have something for you." He withdrew a small jewelry case from his pants pocket.

It was the size of a ring box, and the blood throbbed through her veins as he slowly opened it. Her heart sank when she saw a pair of tiny pearl earrings. She forced a smile as he took them from the box.

"Put them on," he said. "I knew they were meant for you when I saw them at the jeweler's."

Her fingers shook as she attached them to her earlobes. She turned her face up to show off his gift, and when she saw his pleased expression she chastised herself for her initial reaction. His hands moved to her shoulders, and he drew her to him. She responded by sliding her arms toward his neck, but froze when he laid a cool brotherly kiss on her willing lips and withdrew.

"What's the matter?" she asked.

"Nothing. You look lovely. Just as I knew you would." Without another word he quickly led her back into the crowded room and onto the dance floor. The band had changed to country swing, and they had no chance to be close.

She stumbled, and D.A. steadied her. The mood had definitely changed. Her heart sank. He'd made it so obvious that he wasn't enjoying her company. Her disappointment changed to self-protection. If he found her this repulsive to be near, she would spare him the unpleasantness of the remaining hours of the evening.

"Let's go home," she said, touching her temples. "I've got a splitting headache."

He was silent on the return trip to the Russell ranch. As the car rolled to a stop, her anger resurfaced, and she was out the door before he had a chance to open it for her.

He hurried to catch up with her, grabbed her elbow and forced her to walk beside him to the door. On the porch he turned her around to face him.

She studied his face as he stared down at her, but she found no warmth, love or desire in his stony features.

"Have a good time?" His mouth softened slightly.

She stared back at him.

"Was I a perfect gentleman?"

"Yes."

"Good." His eyes scanned her face, but he didn't try to kiss her.

"D.A., is there something wrong with me?" she finally asked, a slight tremor in her voice.

"Of course not. You're lovely. Prettier than I've ever seen you."

"Then why are you acting as though you can't stand being near me. As if you find me almost... repulsive, as if you don't even like me anymore...." Her voice broke, and the tears she had tried so valiantly to suppress surfaced.

"Oh, Mary, you don't understand," he murmured, taking her shoulders.

"Yes, you're right," she said. "I don't understand. You've changed."

He shook his head but refused to elaborate. Instead he laid a light kiss on her forehead.

Her dark eyes grew wide with alarm. "You... don't... even like to be around... me anymore," she stammered. "Well then, I'll spare you... the sight... of me!"

She bolted through the door and disappeared into the house. Once she was inside she looked out from behind the curtains and watched him slowly return to his car, his shoulders hunched in the moonlight.

SEVERAL DAYS LATER the phone rang in the McCormack kitchen. Sammy's face drained of color when she finally concluded the conversation.

"Yes, Sarah, we'll be here. Goodbye." Her hand trembled as she returned the receiver to its cradle. "Oh, David, what are we going to do? She's coming here!"

"When?" he asked. "Tomorrow?"

"No, today," she cried, wringing her hands.

"She's in Idaho Falls right now. That's less than three hours away."

She was frantic when she turned to him, and no sooner had his arms settled around her than she broke away and hurried to the kitchen door of their new home.

"Is D.A. home?" David asked.

She looked across the compound. "His station wagon is there." She whirled back to face him. "What are we going to do? She wants to see Annie. What if he refuses? What if he still loves her and wants her back? What if. . . ?"

"Be still, Sam." David caught her passing hand and forced her to stop pacing. He pulled her down onto his lap. "You're jumping to conclusions. Did she actually say why she was driving all this way?"

"No. She flew from Las Vegas to Idaho Falls and rented a car."

"I wonder what she's up to?" he speculated. "When are you going to tell D.A. she's coming?"

"I don't know. Oh, David, he doesn't know about the money! Do you think I should have told him? I didn't want to stir up old memories. I didn't think she'd ever want to face him again after what she'd done. What if she thinks the payments have entitled her to visitation rights? What if she wants to take Annie away?"

David frowned. "She can't. He has sole legal custody. Remember the hearing in Missoula just before he returned here? She didn't appear or contest. She's relinquished all custodial rights. . . I think." He rubbed his chin thoughtfully. "Sometimes legal decisions get reversed. Suppose she's been up to something in Vegas, and we don't know about it. Sammy, just remain calm. Let's reason this out. Yes, I think you were right to not tell him of the money, and yes, I think you were right to just deposit it into a savings account. It may come in handy someday. Frankly, I think it's her conscience money. Does she still insist it's from legal sources?"

He regretted the words when he saw her blue eyes darken. "I'm sorry, love. That was cruel of me. Oh, damn it, Sam, we're getting caught in the middle, aren't we? My son, your daughter and the sweetest little girl in the whole world."

Sammy rested her head against his shoulder. "Sometimes I find myself pretending she's not Sarah's child at all, but ours. I know it's not right, but sometimes, just for a while...." Her voice trailed off into silence.

"I know, love," David said. He nuzzled her curly head. "I've been guilty of the same." He looked toward the door and the house beyond. "But it's not, is it? She's their child, and I wouldn't want her split between the two of them."

"Do you think we should call him?" she asked.

He hesitated. "No, not yet. Let's wait until she arrives, then tell him on the phone that she's here and ask him to come over. Or better yet, one of us can go get Annie.... Then again, maybe he needs time to adjust. But if she doesn't end up coming, we would have saved him a lot of turmoil by not telling him. Is she still married to that Sid fellow?''

Sammy sighed. "Yes, she said Sid flew in with her. He's driving. That might make it easier. I just don't know. At least D.A. won't think she's decided to return to him. David, how do you think he feels about her? It's been over a year and a half since she disappeared.''

"I think the pain killed the love, but that's a pretty devastating way to have it happen," he replied. "Why don't you come into the bedroom and freshen up while you wait for her. I think I'll take a shower. I got rather dusty and sweaty out in the stock pens. Isn't that new Simmental bull a handsome animal? He's performance tested yet he's as gentle as a lamb. Sure beats the disposition of the angus bulls Russ has. I think we made a good choice in raising pure-bred Simmentals.''

He led her out of the kitchen and down the wide hallway to their large bedroom. "Come join me," he whispered as he tugged the front of his shirt out of his dust-covered jeans. "In the shower," he added, and she smiled.

DAVID PULLED ON CLEAN JEANS and a maroon knit shirt. He turned to watch Sammy casually drop her dressing robe and slip into a pair of silky underpants. His heart caught in his throat as he thought about their life together. They would be celebrating their fifth wedding anniversary in a few months. Their years together had only heightened his desire for her, but their physical satisfaction had been augmented by an emotional bonding that strengthened with each passing year. He couldn't imagine living without her. He had recently had his fifty-first birthday and had promised her thirty more.

He stepped behind her and slid his arms around her before she had a chance to adjust the bra she had just fastened. He kissed the side of her neck, and she relaxed against him.

When she turned in his arms, her hands went up to his face. "I love you, David, more all the time. Sometimes it hurts me right here." She doubled her fist and pressed it against her breast, then raised her lips to meet his.

"We'd better hurry and finish dressing," she said as she reluctantly broke the embrace and withdrew from his arms. She glanced at the clock on her nightstand. "Sarah will be here anytime."

Suddenly her eyes opened wide with disbelief.

"I forgot to tell Sarah about the new house," she gasped. "What if she goes to D.A.'s door first. Oh, David, what have I done?"

She scrambled into her clothes and ran from the bedroom, down the hallway, to the kitchen window. An unfamiliar dark automobile was parked near the other house.

"Oh God," she groaned. Sarah was standing on the porch of the other house. Sammy watched horror-stricken as an unsuspecting D.A. opened his door.

THEY STARED AT ONE ANOTHER, momentarily lost in private thoughts. Time hung heavy as D.A. tried to recover his composure. He surveyed Sarah from head to toe. He'd known the most intimate parts of her body, yet it was a stranger who stood before him.

Her dark hair was piled high on her head in a deliberately disheveled style. She wore a royal-blue dress that clung to her, accenting every curve he'd explored. One knee peeked through the deep slit in the front of her skirt, drawing his attention to her long shapely legs, which were encased in sheer stockings. High-heeled white sandals boosted her almost to his own eye level.

Her eyes matched her dress, radiant in their depth, but makeup covered the creamy youthful complexion he'd caressed.

"What are you doing here?" he said, his jaw aching from unclenching his teeth.

"Hello, D.A.," she said, smiling. "I came to see my mother and my daughter...and you." There was a subtle purr in her voice.

He glanced past her to the black car and the shadowy figure sitting behind the wheel, then returned his attention to her.

"Sammy lives in the new house," he said, starting to close the door.

She ignored him. "Is Annie living here with you?"

He hesitated a moment. "Of course," he said savagely. "I wouldn't abandon my own child."

"Is she here?" she persisted in spite of his jab.

"Of course."

"In this house?"

"Yes."

"May I see her?"

"Why?"

"Because she's my daughter." She fumbled in her purse for her pack of cigarettes and lighter, then casually lit a long filter-tipped cigarette.

As he stood there watching he noticed the strangest things. The pastel blue of the paper on her cigarette. The huge diamond on her left hand where his simple gold band had once been. The tiny dimple in her left cheek, which deepened when she smiled. It was barely discernible, but he knew its hiding place. The slight protrusion of her nipples, which her bra couldn't hide. Even her tendency to mispronounce the letters *L* and *R* when she was excited or nervous. Her hand shook slightly as she inhaled.

A swarthy-looking man emerged from the expensive automobile and turned toward the house. Dark sunglasses hid his eyes, and a gray knit shirt enhanced his muscular physique. His shiny black dress shoes were quickly covered with dust from the driveway.

"Is that your precious Sid, Sarah? Is he the one you exchanged your own child for?"

Before Sarah could reply, a young voice called, "Who, daddy?" A curly auburn head appeared in the opening between D.A.'s long legs. Annie scooted out and stood in front of her father.

"Who, daddy? Momma?" Her smile disappeared and her green eyes grew wide at the sight of the strange woman.

Before D.A. could tell her it wasn't Mary, Sarah smiled. "She remembers me!" she exclaimed. She turned to Sid Lansburgh, who had stopped on the lower step. "She called me mother."

The newcomer cleared his throat. "You must be David A. McCormack, Sarah's former husband," he said. "Yes...well, I'm Sidney Lansburgh. If you don't want us to come in, I understand, but could you at least come out so we can talk? Let me assure you we mean no harm, either to you or your daughter." He offered his hand.

D.A. scooped Annie up in his arms and ignored the outstretched hand. "Come in," he said, holding the door open.

The living room was cluttered with toys.

"Sit down if you want," said D.A. "Excuse the mess. A child lives here."

Sarah flinched slightly at his remark.

"Can I get you something to drink? I have iced tea," he offered.

"That would be fine," Sid Lansburgh replied, wiping his brow. "I didn't know it could get so warm here in August."

D.A. lowered his daughter to the floor and went to the kitchen. He concentrated on filling the tall glasses, but his hand shook, and he was irritated at his own lack of control.

Why hadn't he worn his cosmetic hand? Why the

repulsive terminal hook, which had been a constant problem in their relationship?

Annie ran into the kitchen. "Daddy, stay with you," she cried. She clung to his bare leg beneath his cutoffs. When Sarah appeared in the doorway she tightened her hold.

"What did you say to her?" he demanded.

Sarah shrugged her shoulders nonchalantly. "I just asked her if she'd like to come visit me in Las Vegas for a while."

"No," he thundered.

"D.A., don't get hysterical," she said, tossing her head. "It was only a spur-of-the-moment thought."

Annie's death grip on his leg tightened as he turned to gather the glasses in his hands, and he stumbled. One of the sweaty glasses began to slide from his grasp. He was unable to regain his grip, and the three glasses crashed to the tile floor. Broken glass, ice cubes and amber tea flew everywhere. D.A. grabbed Annie up, away from the shattered glass. He was furious when he saw a trickle of blood appear on her chubby leg where some slivers had become embedded.

His embarrassment over the clumsy accident changed to anger directed against the woman standing before him. She was as beautiful as he remembered. He became aware of desire welling up in him as her presence brought back memories of passion-filled nights when he had so willingly led her to fulfillment because he had loved her and thought she returned the feelings. Knowing of other men's intimacies with her did nothing to lessen his physical reaction.

His anger turned to rage at both her and himself. "Get out, Sarah," he shouted. "Get out of my house. Don't you ever again come here and think you can get Annie away from me. You're not fit to call yourself a mother. Get out, you whore!"

Annie screamed, frightened by her father's angry voice. Sid Lansburgh appeared in the entranceway, grabbed Sarah's arm and surveyed the disastrous kitchen. "What happened?" he asked.

"I just suggested that Annie come spend some time with us," she said, arching her shapely brows at Sid.

"Sarah...." Sid frowned. "I told you not to make trouble. We discussed this several times these past months, and I thought you agreed that it just wouldn't be the thing to do."

She shrugged her shoulders, her breasts bouncing with the movement.

Annie continued to cling to D.A., her arms tightly around his neck.

"Get out! Take *her* out of here before I forget that she was ever Annie's mother," D.A. stormed.

"Let's go, Sarah," Sid urged. When she refused to move, he tightened his hold on her arm. "Now!" he commanded, and forced her from the house.

D.A. watched them hurry across the compound to the new house. He glanced down at his daughter, still clinging to him, and noticed the blood oozing from her leg wounds. He slammed and bolted the door.

As he concentrated on finding first-aid items for

Annie, an image of Sarah returned to haunt him. How could he possibly still desire her, knowing what she was and what she had done to him and their child? He felt vile, as though his sense of morality had become warped, and his temples throbbed as he examined the wounds on Annie's leg. Carefully he removed the small slivers of glass with tweezers and cleaned around the wound with an antiseptic. He cut butterfly strips and applied them over the lacerations, consoling Annie all the while. He was relieved that the cuts were minor.

Annie began to sob again when he took away the package of gauze she was holding. He swung her up into his arms and collapsed into the wicker rocker. The steady rocking motion gradually stilled her sobs, and her curly head nodded and bobbed. Even when he knew she was asleep, he continued to hold her and rock. He heard a car start up, then drive away.

A light knock registered somewhere on his numbed senses, but he ignored it, knowing it was probably Sammy, and she went away. The sun set, and a mellow twilight filled the room as he continued to rock.

A pair of compassionate dark brown eyes floated through his mind's eye, and he willed them to disappear. Darkness fell over the house and still he rocked, until finally his own tormented mind went blank.

He awakened to find himself in pitch-blackness. Annie's hand patted his chest.

"Daddy? Daddy?"

He hugged her, but still he couldn't move. "Daddy's here, sweetheart."

"Where's momma?"

"Oh, God," he moaned, and surprisingly Mary's face came to him instead of Sarah's. "Momma Mary's at her house, in bed like you should be."

He carried her to the bathroom, then to her room, where he helped her climb into her summer pajamas, tucked her into her new youth-size bed and kissed her cheek.

He went to his own room and stretched his still-clothed body across the bed. Every fiber of his being ached. Even the missing hand and fingers that had tormented both him and Sarah throbbed from the torment in his soul. It had been years since he'd been troubled by the phantom limb, and the experience had always been unsettling, yet this time it brought a therapeutic healing to him. He closed his eyes.

"Oh, Mary," he groaned. "How I need you right now."

CHAPTER NINE

MARY RUSSELL SAT ON THE STEPS of her front porch, watching the dust from the wheels of D.A.'s station wagon rise in a trail along the winding road as he drove to the McCormack ranch. She knew it was him. She had waited patiently for his car to flash by on his return trip from town.

In the distance the dust-devil whirlwind evaporated into the air. Maybe it was just her imagination. Eight miles was a long way for her to be able to see him. Her heart ached over the unpleasant turn of events. She had been so confident, and one should *never* be too confident. She had certainly learned her lesson about that, only she hadn't expected it to be quite so painful.

She had not seen D.A. since the disastrous birthday dinner in July. The fall semester would begin the following week. She'd already been to freshman orientation and had visited the college's micro-computer center and played with some of the software available. She enjoyed the excitement of working with the computers and had changed her class schedule to include one at the center. Surprisingly, the only time D.A. wasn't foremost in her thoughts was when she became engrossed in the activity on the screen of the monitor before her.

She had made a firm resolution that D.A. McCormack was not going to ruin her life. True, the computer's software was soft in a symbolic way only, not at all like D.A.'s arms when she sank into his embrace, or warm like his lips when his mouth covered hers....

She shook her head to clear his image from her brain, determined to concentrate on her college program. She had chosen her major in secondary school education with a minor in home economics. When she had chosen her first-semester classes in the spring, she had deliberately included freshman biology and crossed her fingers for luck. Now as she looked at the computer printed schedule of her fall classes, she wasn't sure she'd been so lucky. The entry in the column under instructor read "D. McCormack."

She toyed with the idea of dropping out of school before classes started and finding a job in town. She grimaced. He would know what she had done if she failed to appear for class. Maybe he'd come looking for her. He'd grab her shoulder and shake her. She's probably start to cry, and he'd hug her. He'd remind her that no man was worth making such a sacrifice for, that she needed a career of her own, that fulfillment came from within rather than through someone else. She'd lay her fingers against his lips to quiet his outburst, and seconds later he'd forget his lecturing and concentrate on her upturned face and....

A voice from the kitchen interrupted her reverie. She turned as her sister Lisa appeared at the door.

"What is it, Lisa?" she asked listlessly.

"Phone, my droopy, depressed sister," Lisa replied. "I think you should answer it." She winked mischievously.

"Who is it?" Mary asked, irritated at the thought of moving from the steps.

"I think it's your friend who lives up the lane."

Mary didn't make the connection until her tall slender younger sister came outside.

"You dope, it's D.A."

"What does he want?" Mary asked, her brown eyes reflecting her surprise.

"I don't know. Why don't you ask him? He didn't call to talk to me. He wants to talk to you. Now quit pouting and find out for yourself, silly sister."

Mary sighed again. "He probably just wants to ask me to baby-sit so he can go out with some new chesty broad."

"Mary!" Lisa gasped. "Don't be like that. You might be cutting off your own nose."

"Tell him I'm busy," she said abruptly. "Darn you, D.A.," she muttered under her breath. Just when she'd put her feelings for him carefully in the back of her mind and started to concentrate on other joys in life, he'd come back to trouble her. Her shoulders slumped dejectedly, and she gazed out at the setting sun and the mountains to the southwest.

"Okay, if that's what you want." Lisa disappeared into the house.

Minutes passed. Mary heard the door bang again, and Lisa dropped down to the step beside her.

"He wanted to know if you would like to ride to school with him on Monday," Lisa said, her blue eyes twinkling.

"He did?" Mary asked, astounded. "He didn't want me to just sit?"

"Nope."

"Oh, Lisa, I blew it, didn't I?"

"Yup," Lisa agreed. "But I didn't."

"What do you mean?" Mary turned to her sister.

"I told him that you'd love to ride with him." Lisa gave Mary an impulsive hug and then scooted back inside, leaving an astonished Mary to stare at the sunset.

D.A. called later in the day and asked if Mary could be ready at six Monday morning.

"I thought we could have breakfast before classes," he suggested.

"I haven't seen or heard from you since July. Is this a peace offering?" she asked curiously.

"You might call it a white flag in the form of bacon and eggs," he said, chuckled, and she could imagine the sparkle in his eyes. "Will you accept?"

"Yes."

THE EARLY-NOVEMBER SNOWSTORM had grown progressively heavier throughout the day. After classes had ended, Mary had gone to the center to work with a computer illustrator pad and attempt to perfect her artistic expertise. D.A. was counseling two students who'd fallen behind in one of his agriculture classes. An hour later, when it was time to meet him, she made her way to his small office. He was dialing the phone.

"I'm trying to see if we can drive home," he explained, then listened intently to another weather update. "They've closed Monida Pass, and the radio station says the traffic south of town is being stopped. I'll call the ranch."

His features were heavy with concern when he completed the call. "Dad says it's terrible out that way... you can hardly see your hand in front of your face. He suggested we stay in town. Maybe he's right. We wouldn't want to get stuck in some drift and freeze to death. They wouldn't find us until spring."

"You're exaggerating, I hope," she said.

"About finding us in the spring, yes." He studied her face. "Not about staying in town. Would you spend the night in a motel with me?"

Her eyes widened, and her mouth rounded.

"In separate rooms, of course," he clarified, but his eyes continued to flick over her features. He cleared his throat and pushed himself from the chair.

"My parents!" she cried. "They'll be worried."

"Dad's going to call them and explain," he said. "Let's find ourselves rooms for the night. The Canyon Winds is closest, but the man at the radio station said that it was already full. The Montana Inn is nice, and it's just a few blocks from here. We'll get rooms there, but they have no restaurant. Are you hungry?"

"No, not really," she assured him as she began to put on her heavy coat. He came to her and adjusted her fur cap. Two of his fingers touched her cheek as he fluffed the woolen scarf up around her face. He took her gloved hand in his and smiled.

"Ready to fight the elements, love?"

Her heart lurched at his use of the endearment. She could only nod. When they left the science building and made their way to the faculty parking lot, she was blinded by the blowing snow. He continued to hold her hand tightly until they reached his station wagon.

"Stay here," he said when she started to move to the passenger side of the car. He opened the door and motioned her to slide in.

In spite of the nearness of the motel, it took them more than fifteen minutes to travel the distance. A snowplow was trying with little success to scrape several inches of snow from the street. Few vehicles were still on the road, but their oncoming headlights plus the dim overhead streetlights shimmering through the white hazy twilight aided D.A. in his search for the motel. The intensity of the storm was increasing as he pulled into the curving driveway of the motel and parked.

Mary slid out the driver's side, and D.A. immediately put his arm around her shoulders and pulled her close, protecting her face from the wind with his gloved hand. He guided her to the office, and she stood aside as he registered with the harried desk clerk. Several other people were milling around the lobby.

"Two rooms, please. Make them adjoining. D.A. McCormack and Mary Russell." He waited impatiently as the paperwork was completed, used his charge card to pay for the rooms, then turned to her and dangled two keys from his index finger.

"This way, honey." He motioned to her, and they moved down the hallway to the elevator. "We're on the second floor," he said, punching the appropriate button when they entered the elevator. "If we'd brought our swimsuits, we could go swimming." He grinned. "The pool is inside."

The elevator groaned to a stop and he guided her down the hallway, his hand riding on her waist. He unlocked the door of one room and handed her the key. "See you later, Miss Russell," he said, and turned away.

Mary entered the room and took off her coat. She felt very dejected. The prospect of spending the evening alone in the quiet motel room, waiting for the blizzard to blow itself out, wasn't very appealing.

She shrugged off her depression and surveyed the room, her eyes landing on the king-size bed. She walked over to test it. After pulling the sheet and blankets back out of the way, she eased herself down onto the edge of the mattress, then playfully threw herself backward. She stretched and rolled on to her side, arching herself to reach the pillow in the far corner. As she ran her hand caressingly over the smooth sheet, she thought of her twin bed at the ranch.

"I could easily get used to this," she murmured to herself. "Oh, well." She pushed herself off the bed.

It's only until tomorrow morning, she thought. *I can stand being alone until then.* She went to the phone and placed a wake-up call for seven-thirty, then sauntered to the bathroom. She stripped off her clothing and stepped into the shower, and her depression was soon washed away with the soap.

When she had finished she dried herself and slipped back into her bra and panties, then her woolen skirt and sweater. She tucked her stockings and shoes underneath one of the chairs. The lush carpeting felt deliciously warm and cozy beneath her bare feet. She flipped on the television and curled up in an overstuffed chair in front of it. She tried to concentrate on the early-evening news, but her mind wandered to D.A. They had been riding together since school began. The cause of their misunderstanding had been skirted around, and a relaxed friendship reestablished. She'd decided that his company on these neutral terms was better than not seeing him at all.

She started when she heard a light knock. Her heart skipped a beat as she realized it was coming from the door that separated the two adjoining rooms. She scrambled from the chair and rushed to the door, cautiously turned the lock, and then opened the door.

D.A. stood on the other side, laden with small packages of snack foods, two cans of soft drink and some candy bars.

"I've brought dinner, m'lady," he explained with a boyish grin.

She laughed. "Where did you get all that junk food?"

"From the vending machines in the lobby," he said. "I'm very resourceful when I'm hungry, and the machines were emptying fast. May I come in?"

"Of course. Make yourself at home."

He dumped the food onto the white bed sheet and waved his hand. "You choose first," he said as he slipped out of his jacket and kicked off his shoes.

She smiled and reached for a small bag of potato chips and a can of cola and retreated to the over-stuffed chair.

"Delicious," she assured him as she finished the chips.

"Have some more?"

She took a candy bar. "Thank you, sir."

He laughed at her formality. "We're stuck for the night. We might as well relax and get comfortable. Do you mind?" He began to loosen and remove his tie, unbuttoned the top several buttons of his camel-and-white pin-striped shirt, then fumbled with the cuff links at his wrists.

She was out of the chair without realizing what she was doing. "Let me," she suggested. Before he could say a word, she slipped the gold studs from the openings in his cuffs and dropped them to the nightstand, then returned to her chair. She ignored his lingering scrutiny and concentrated on the movie beginning on the television screen.

He was oblivious of his effect on her as she followed his movements out of the corner of her line of vision. He pushed the packages of food aside and fluffed the pillows, then lay back on the bed. As he crossed his long legs, the material of his slacks seemed to mold the muscles in his thighs.

"What's the movie, honey?" he asked.

"Romancing the Stone," she said. "It's a love story. Should I turn to something else? I've seen it twice before."

"No, no. That's all right. Maybe it'll help me relax a little. I guess with this bad weather, Annie's cold and those two students I had to counsel, I'm a little uptight."

She stood up, retrieved her textbooks and moved to the writing desk near the television. "I'm going to read a chapter in my programming textbook. I have a program due Monday. I'll be quiet."

He glanced at her. "How do you like using the micros?"

"Oh, I love them!" she said. "I had no idea you could do so much with a computer. I always thought they were for dry old mathematics or business, but I've learned to write music, synthesize voice sounds, draw pictures, and now I'm writing a game for children to learn their symbols for both numbers and letters." She laughed self-consciously at her own enthusiasm. "I think I could easily get lost in that room."

"Good," he said. "I'm glad to hear that." He asked a few more questions about her program, but soon left her to her assignment as he became engrossed in the movie.

When Mary had finished her reading she glanced at her watch and was surprised to see the lateness of the hour. D.A. had fallen asleep on her bed.

She turned the television off and walked to his side of the bed. He moved and she jumped, but he remained asleep. His head turned, and his glasses were pushed slightly askew. She carefully removed them and laid them on the nightstand. He groaned slightly and settled deeper into the pillow. She tossed the remaining packages of food to a chair, then eased the blanket up to cover him. His arm moved, startling her, and she dropped the blanket, leaving it to rest just below his chest.

She returned to her chair and tried to ignore him. She considered turning the television back on but didn't want the sound to disturb him. Finally she got up and turned out the lamps in the room. A soft glow of light came from the adjoining room. She could easily go to his room for the night, but she was irresistibly drawn to the bed where he lay.

As she looked down at him she nervously fingered the tiny white pearl buttons running along the front opening of the short-sleeved sweater she was wearing. She refastened the three buttons at her throat and tugged the neckline up a few inches.

As though his presence held her captive, she lay down beside him. He groaned and turned toward her. Her heart raced, but his long brown lashes rested motionless against his cheeks. She tried to ignore his deep breathing as he slept beside her. She knew she couldn't leave him. He rolled closer, his arm rose slightly, then settled on her stomach, and she found herself pinned to the bed.

D.A.'s HAND TOUCHED an unfamiliar object...soft, warm and moving slightly, as though it was breathing. A woman. The room was dim and unfamiliar, but when he propped himself up on an elbow to identify her, his disorientation evaporated immediately.

The warmth of their bodies had somehow drawn them to each other in the semidarkness. She was fully clothed, asleep and unaware of his closeness. Her innocent, youthful beauty was the only thing he saw in the room. He longed to touch her face, yet, at the same time, he knew he should leave the bed and room immediately.

A surge of desire filled him. He fought with himself to leave her, but his attempt at denial only heightened his need. Momentarily he closed his eyes, blocking out her image. When he slowly opened his eyes, ready to escape the temptation before him, he met her dark eyes, wide with wonder.

"Please don't leave me," she murmured, her hand moving to rest on his leg. The heat of her flesh seared through the fabric to his thigh.

She seemed to float toward him. Her dark eyes were pleading, and he sank into their depths.

"Are you sure?" he asked.

"Yes," she sighed, drawing closer to him. "Yes, I'm sure." With both hands she unfastened the two remaining buttons of his wrinkled shirt.

"Yes," she whispered, and her hands slipped beneath the fabric and caressed his chest. She raised one hand to his cheek, and her touch had the lightness of a mountain breeze. *"Yes,"* she cried with an urgency he understood.

Her lips trembled beneath his as he joined her in the kiss she offered so willingly. When at last he withdrew, his hand moved to the buttons of her sweater.

She watched his face as he began to undress her. The cool steel of his prosthesis touched the full swell of her heaving breasts and he stopped.

"Does it bother you?"

"No, it's part of you," she murmured. He lifted her from the pillow, and she clung to his neck as he undid the clasp to her bra. As she sat up, the clothing fell away.

"We can't turn back," he whispered.

"I know," she replied. Her hand touched his face, and her fingertips brushed his lips. He tasted them with his tongue, and she sensed his desire.

"Loosen your hair," he said, and her hands freed the thick rope of dark waves from the beaded barrette. Her hair rippled loose, and he arranged it around her shoulders. "You're beautiful, Mary. I want to make love to you. I have for a long time. Did you know that?"

"What about our platonic relationship?" she asked.

"It's never existed," he admitted. "Not for years, but the time wasn't right."

"And now?"

His hand wandered to her newly revealed breasts and drew circles around each crest. He watched them respond. "And now the time is right." His tongue replaced his thumb, bringing a startled moan from her, and she clutched his curly head. "You're so perfect," he whispered.

He eased her back onto the bed, and as he gazed at her nakedness, the last of his doubts fell away. He groaned and lowered himself over her, his hand touching her throat. Her pulse was racing wildly. As he claimed her mouth again, she arched against him, straining to merge with his own body.

His hand caressed her throat and breast before sliding to her waist, where it lingered. She pressed her hips against him hungrily. The heat of her inner thigh distracted him as he brushed the woolen skirt upward.

"Touch me," she moaned, and his hand found the secret core of her womanhood. She gasped and a trembling sigh shook her body. Her hands clutched at his clothing.

"Are you still sure, my love?" he asked.

"Oh, yes," she sighed. "I ache for you. Only you can be the one." She tunneled her hand beneath his shirt to stroke the muscles that rippled across his back.

He massaged her willing lips, seeking out the sweet crevices of her mouth with his tongue.

"I need two hands," he whispered as his fingers grasped the fastener at the waist band of her skirt and tried to undo it.

"I'll help," she said, and quickly she slipped out of her skirt and bikini underpants. Suddenly she was embarrassed by her bold action and pulled the sheet over her.

He laughed softly and left the bed to shed his clothing and prosthesis. She watched him undress and found herself spellbound as the secret male parts of his body were gradually revealed. She had seen her brothers when they were younger, but this was very different. She realized that she was ignorant as well as innocent.

Now that he stood before her she was alarmed, but before her concern could grow to doubt he approached her. The thought that she could satisfy his needs sent sensual waves of desire through her, and her own awakening passions overcame any fear of the unknown. She raised her hand to him.

He joined her on the bed once again and removed the intrusive sheet.

She froze in uncertainty.

He kissed her, nibbling seductively at her lower lip. "What's wrong, my sweet innocent?" he asked, raising his head and frowning.

"I...I'm afraid," she whispered.

"Don't be, honey. I won't hurt you," he promised, and he lowered his mouth to hers again.

She touched his cheek with such tenderness and adoration that he stopped his kiss and stared at her glowing face.

"D.A.?"

"What, my love?"

"I...I don't know what to do. Teach me, D.A. Show me...."

He began to instruct her in the art of making love, and they became teacher and willing student in one of life's most satisfying pleasures. Yet still she was afraid.

"Maybe we should stop," he said, poised on his elbows above her.

Her breasts heaved, and she stroked his upper arms. "Don't stop!" she cried, her eyes filled with torment. "I love you, D.A. I have for so long."

He dropped down beside her and stroked her cheek. "Just relax," he said, and gradually her breathing steadied.

"Touch me," he suggested, and her brown eyes grew round with surprise.

"Touch you? Where?"

He laughed softly and began to guide her hand. "Touch me...here." He groaned as her cool trembling hand caressed him, and she grew bolder in her exploration until he stilled her hand.

"I'm...ready," she whispered, and slid her arms around his neck, responding to his subtle movements.

His hand moved to lightly stroke her face as he warned her, "This may hurt, little one, but only for a moment." His mouth caressed her responsive lips again, deepening the kiss until she pulled away with a breathless gasp of pleasure.

"Help me," he murmured.

Her hands instinctively knew what to do, and suddenly she was filled with a searing shaft of heat that soothed the instant of pain. She fed her own hunger as she ran her hands up and down his spine.

"It's too late to stop now," he whispered, a smile playing across his handsome face.

"I'm glad. You were always the one, the only one." A warm glow began to spread through her as he kissed her again.

"It...it doesn't hurt anymore. Oh, D.A.," she moaned, and she buried her face in his shoulder.

He misread her readiness and began to move, his own need overcoming his patience. Before her body could respond she felt him hold motionless for a split second, and then an intense shudder shook him. He collapsed against her, his heavy breathing muffled by her thick hair.

She felt bewildered by this abrupt ending to their shared passion. He gathered her to him and pulled the covers over them, but she was restless. His hand caressed her waist, then gradually moved up to rest on her shoulder.

"I don't feel good," she said.

"That's okay," he told her gently. "It was your first time. This lovemaking takes...practice. You were tense."

"I couldn't respond. It all happened so fast."

"No, love," he replied. "I was too impatient. I got caught up in the moment and lost control. Sometimes a man's physical needs get the best of him." He pulled her a little closer against his body.

Her hand slid across the flat surface of his waistline, and she felt his fingers brush some unruly strands of hair away from her temple. Confusion blended with desire and love as she clung to him, filled with uncertainty instead of the satisfaction she'd fantasized. She wondered if she had somehow failed him...if her lack of experience had spoiled the moment of fulfillment. She wanted to cry and tried to stifle the impulse, but hot tears slid down her cheeks.

"Did I hurt you?" he asked.

She shook her head against his shoulder.

"You're crying a little," he said, and wiped away the tear that had become stranded on her cheek.

"I don't know why...I just don't want to disappoint you," she said, sighing.

"Don't worry, honey," he said. "You'll be more relaxed the next time. It's difficult to respond when you're so tense. You'll see." He tightened his hold. "And I was very impatient."

"You ignored me for so long," she whispered. "Why?"

"I saw you changing right before my eyes. You didn't play fair. One day I saw you and you were my little shrimp, then suddenly you became a lovely young woman. I tried to make you off limits." He trailed his fingers up and down her arm. "And..." he sighed, his chest rising and falling beneath her head, "I failed miserably. Your father would kill me if he knew what I'd just done to his daughter. He'd probably send the sheriff after me and want me run out of the county." He smiled at the imaginary scene.

Her fingers caressed his chest, tracing the small muscles that flexed when he moved his arm. "Would it matter?" she asked.

"I don't think so, love. Not anymore. Your charms have seduced me, after all. Can't you see the headlines? 'Beautiful freshman college student seduces science teacher in snowstorm.' No one would believe it, would they?"

She sat up beside him to see him better. His sandy hair was tousled and a few curls fell over his forehead. She reached out and pushed them back in the motion she'd yearned to make for years. His eyes darkened, and his face wore a serious expression as he continued to stare at her.

He reached out to push back the silky strands of hair that fell over her breast, circled the crown lightly, then dropped his hand to rest on her bare thigh. "Mary?"

"Yes?" she asked, and followed his hand with her own. She examined his long sensitive fingers, suddenly afraid to look at him.

"You could have sent me back to my room. You should have, you know." His voice was soft, but the words stung.

"No. I couldn't. I wanted it to happen," she said, but sudden doubts in her judgement washed over her.

"We can never go back to the way it was. You know that?"

"I don't want to. I was miserable the way it was before tonight. I was so young...and you were married. It was terrible!"

Still he continued to study her as she sat before him.

"Are you sorry?" she asked, dreading his answer. "I know I encouraged you. It's my fault." Tears began to well up in her eyes again. "I've spoiled everything. Do you hate me now?"

"Oh, no, Mary, no." He pulled her down to him. "No, honey, I loved it. I could never hate you."

Her hair formed a shimmering tent around their faces as he touched her trembling lips. He rolled her onto her back and kissed her.

"I want to make love to you again. Does that sound like a man filled with regret?"

She clung to his arms as he kissed her. He moved his lips to her throat, lingering to taste her creamy skin, then lowered his mouth to her high breasts. Her breathing quickened as his tongue circled the rosy crests, gently tugging and teasing until she burned with a fever of desire.

She knew she would die of ecstasy if he didn't stop. He was killing her with his erotic caresses. She moaned and twisted beneath him, and one part of her mind was shocked at her abandonment as she opened her thighs to receive him again.

"Yes, yes," she moaned. "Help me to know...."

"I want you, Mary," he whispered near her ear. "I need you, in so many ways...again and again." He began to move inside her.

She released all conscious control of herself and soon her hips were matching his thrusts. She knew the movements without learning them. As she wrapped herself around him, she smiled a secret, primitive, female smile.

Just when she could stand the smoldering emotions no longer, she was consumed by ecstasy and lost all touch with reality for several seconds, unaware of his own release.

They lay exhausted, clinging to each other. Finally he eased himself from her, looked into her soft brown eyes, and smiled.

"Feel better?" he teased.

She became embarrassed by her uninhibited display of passion. "I'm sorry," she whispered. "I guess I just got carried away."

"Don't apologize," he said, pulling her close again. "You were all woman. You were natural and spontaneous. You didn't hide what you felt."

"How could I? It felt like nothing I've ever experienced before." She felt the blush warm her cheeks, and she couldn't keep the smile hidden for long.

"I know, sweetheart," he said, nestling her in the curve of his arm. "Now rest. It's late."

The snow continued to fall outside their room, but the heat of his body provided the warmth she craved. She savored it, not knowing how long she would have it.

He'd made no commitment, expressed no true love, but she found solace in his proven physical desire for her. That was more than she'd had before this special night.

CHAPTER TEN

THE JANGLING of the telephone's first ring jerked D.A. back to reality. He reached to silence the intrusion.

"Yes?" he said, as the events of the previous night cascaded through his mind.

"Oh, isn't this Mary Russell's room?" a curious, older female voice asked. "She had a wake-up call for seven-thirty."

"She's asleep. I'll tell her," he replied, and quickly replaced the receiver.

He turned to Mary and found her still deep in slumber. Stretching across to the bedside table, he retrieved his pack of cigarettes and lit one. As he lay back against the pillow he thought about the events of the night.

She had thoroughly satisfied him, and he knew the satisfaction had been reciprocated, yet he foresaw problems. He'd recently decided to never remarry. His first experience had been too devastating to attempt such an adventure again, but what was he going to do? He couldn't just ignore last night.

She was so young, and he knew their age difference would be a source of concern to her family, some of their friends and possibly the college. He could very well lose his job over such "fraternizing" with a student. In many ways, the administration was as conservative as the townspeople.

Annie's smiling face entered his thoughts. He realized that Mary was more of a mother to Annie than Sarah had ever been. He smiled as he thought of his daughter's determination to call her momma. He recalled all those Thursday evenings when he'd become accustomed to finding Mary in his home, his daughter clean and cared for, a delicious meal ready and waiting.

He shook his head. Domestic services were no basis to commit either of them to a relationship that would last...forever. He mulled the word around. Did any marriage actually last forever, he wondered. He thought of his father and Sammy. Theirs appeared to have the makings of a long-lasting relationship, yet she had experienced one broken marriage, and his own father had suffered through two. How could a person know when the partnership was right, he wondered.

He snubbed out his cigarette butt in the ashtray and turned to her. As he looked at her, his worries evaporated. She lay on her stomach, her tangled hair hiding her face. The stark contrast of its dark sheen against the white bed linens made his pulse quicken. As he eased a handful of the unruly hair from her face, her youthful profile turned toward him.

He lifted the sheet and blanket away and admired her slender body. Her back was satiny smooth with faint markings of last summer's swimsuit straps. He resisted the urge to touch them.

Her torso tapered to a tiny waist, then flared to curving womanly hips. Her round bottom was creamy smooth, and her legs slender yet shapely. As his eyes roamed down her sleeping form, he thought again of the way she had been yesterday, and what he had done to change her forever.

She curled onto her side, stirring in her sleep, and seemed drawn again to his body warmth. Suddenly her eyes flew open, and as she recognized the nude man stretched out beside her, she covered her mouth with her hand. Rolling onto her back, she yanked the blankets up to her chin and looked fearfully at him.

"Oh, D.A.! What have we done?"

He leaned over her and cupped her face in his hand, kissing her lightly. "My little Mary, you became a woman last night."

His kisses were feather-light, and her mouth opened as she warmed to his growing promise of passion.

She released her death grip on the blanket, and her hands went to his chest, touching him as though to confirm that he was real. As she slipped her arms around his neck, the blanket fell away. "Yes," she breathed.

She was his and his alone, and he was lost to reason in his desire to know her again. Her willingness spurred him to declare the feelings he had held in check the previous night.

"Oh, God, Mary. . . how I love you."

THE SOUND OF A KEY in the lock brought them both from a sound sleep. Still only half-awake, they sat up in the bed.

"Who is it?" D.A. called, trying to shield Mary.

The door was ajar a few inches. One eye and the side of a woman's face became visible. "Housekeeping?" an amused voice asked.

"Come back later," D.A. said, a curt sound of irritation adding a husky pitch to his voice.

"Yes, sir," the woman replied, chuckling under her breath, but loud enough to let them know she had seen them. The door closed again with a loud slam.

The room had lost its aura of intimacy with this intrusion.

He turned to Mary. "I'm sorry, love." He glared at the closed door. "I should have taken precautions, damn it." His head jerked toward the adjoining room as the banging and clattering of cleaning materials grew louder. "My God!" he hissed, and bounded from the bed like a raging bull. He strode across to the partially opened door and closed it, sliding the dead bolt to make sure their privacy was secure.

He turned toward her, and she lowered her eyes to the bed. Her mortification only increased when he sat down beside her and reached for her hand.

He tried to coax her to look at him, but she refused. "I'm so ashamed," she whispered. "If only...."

He slid under the covers beside her and gathered her in his arms. "Don't be," he murmured soothingly. "What we did last night and this morning is our private affair."

She shook her head in disagreement. "You may be right about it being an affair, but it's no longer private." Her heart was pounding so hard she was sure it would jump from her chest. She began to tremble, unable to control herself until he tightened his embrace.

"Just lie still," he whispered against her hair. "You'll be all right in a few minutes."

They lay in the bed, listening to the voyeur in the adjoining room do her housekeeping. They flinched when her vacuum banged against the connecting door, but finally silence reigned.

"What time is it?" she asked, still pressed against him.

He glanced at his watch lying abandoned on the nightstand. "Noon."

"Oh, no," she cried, jumping upright, the blankets falling away. "What time do we have to be out of the room?"

His hand trailed down her spine. "Eleven."

She turned toward him. "What about my wake-up call? I never heard it."

"I took it, honey," he admitted. "Oh, damn it, Mary. This is all my fault. I took the call, but when I turned to wake you, all I saw was a young woman beside me, one whom I've wanted to love for so long, and I forgot everything except you." His hand settled on the flaring curve of her hip.

"What do we do now?" she asked, touching his chest for reassurance. "She saw us."

He reached for a cigarette, then his lighter, and lay

quietly, mulling over the situation. He stared at her through the rising spiral of smoke. "I'm sure she's seen lots of couples in these rooms. She's been trained to be discreet, to look the other way. She'll probably forget all about us by the time she finishes her work."

"I don't think so," Mary said.

"Why not?"

"She *knows* me."

He grabbed her shoulder and pulled her closer. "Who the hell is she? I've lived here most of my life, and I've never seen her."

Mary sagged against him in despair. "She's Mrs. Lola Sizemore. Her husband is a janitor at the college. D.A., they go to the Baptist church my family attends. They're both terrible gossips. They moved here several years ago from Miles City."

"Maybe she didn't recognize you," he said in a futile attempt to console her. "Sometimes it's difficult to recognize a person when they're in a different place than you normally see them...or dressed differently." He began to chuckle. "We certainly weren't in our street clothes."

She pulled free, her dark eyes reminding him of a wounded doe.

"Be serious, D.A. This could cause both of us terrible problems."

"What's the worst that could happen?" he asked, grinning at her.

She shrugged her shoulders, unable to sort out the worst from the myriad possibilities that bombarded her.

"You could get pregnant, and your father could come after me with a shotgun." He laughed good-naturedly. "The people here can be pretty old-fashioned at times. It wouldn't be the first time some guy was forced to marry a girl he'd slept with."

Her eyes darkened as she studied him. "Are you saying that marrying me would be the worst possible situation?"

"Of course not, honey," he replied, rubbing his hand up and down her arm. "It's just that we don't want to rush into some foolish act that would bind us together forever."

"That is a little scary," she agreed. "I wouldn't want a man to marry me because he felt responsible. Only because he loved me."

He touched her cheek. "I do love you, Mary. It's just that you have school to finish. I've been at WMC for only two years. I think I'm also still getting over my own marital problems. I wouldn't want to burden you with my problems and Annie when you have your whole life ahead of you. We shouldn't make plans unless you...I assume you didn't use precautions."

She shook her head slowly.

"Well, keep me posted. If we're in luck, we'll have lots of time to work things out at our own pace. Now," he said with a sigh, "let's go have lunch and then see if we can make it home. Much more weather like yesterday and I might trade my station wagon in for a four-wheel-drive vehicle. You take the bathroom first, my love. Things could have been worse, you know. What if today had been a school day instead of Saturday.'' He ambled to the television set and switched channels, finally settling on a nature program on the education station before casually walking naked back to the bed.

Embarrassment swept through Mary as he flopped onto the bed. She hurriedly covered his body with the blanket before scurrying away. She dragged the heavy spread from the bed and wrapped it around her, stooping awkwardly to gather up her scattered clothing before disappearing into the bathroom.

A quick shower refreshed her physically but did little to soothe her inner unrest. Her fingers flew up the front of her sweater, restoring her sense of modesty.

''Next,'' she called as she left the bathroom. She kept her eyes averted as D.A. grabbed his own clothing and disappeared into the steamy bathroom.

Mary breathed a sigh of relief when they finally left the motel. The housekeeper was nowhere in sight. Mary's anger rushed from herself to D.A. to Lola Sizemore. By the time they arrived at a restaurant in the north end of town, she was unable to pinpoint who should take the blame for ruining the experience. She wished she could somehow turn back the clock, change the weather, transfer to another college. Yet not having shared such an intimate experience with him was unthinkable.

He apparently sensed her confusion. When the waitress greeted them each by name, he ordered for both of them. He glanced at her several times during the meal until finally he put his fork down and reached across the table to still her restless hand.

"Mary?"

Reluctantly she looked at him. His eyes had become stormy with concern.

"Mary, I have no regrets."

She tried to pull free, but he tightened his hold. "Mary, you shouldn't...."

The waitress reappeared and refilled their coffee cups. He grimaced at the interruption and released her hand.

When they finished eating, he called her parents to ask about the road conditions.

"Where the hell have you been?" Ed Russell demanded. "We expected you hours ago. What the hell have you two been doing? Is Mary okay? We thought maybe you'd slid into a snowdrift. They're pretty deep out this way." He continued to hurl questions until D.A. finally held the receiver away from his ear.

Mary was able to hear her father's angry voice from where she stood. She motioned for D.A. to give her the phone.

"Daddy?" she said, and immediately he quieted.

"Yes, Mary Beth. Are you okay?"

"I'm fine, daddy. D.A. didn't want to start out if we couldn't make it all the way." She listened as he described the aftereffects of the storm. "Okay. We'll be there in about an hour. Yes, daddy, it was very bad here, too."

She returned the receiver to D.A. and gathered up

her coat and scarf. D.A. studied her as he pulled on his own heavy coat, and they left the restaurant.

"You sure calmed the raging father," he commented as they headed south.

"My father is seldom angry at me. Short-tempered at times, but never really angry for long. I don't usually admit it, but I suspect I'm his favorite of his six children. He thinks I can do no wrong." She frowned. "I don't know what he'd do if he found out about us."

"You're an adult, Mary. You shouldn't have to answer to your father anymore."

"As long as I live at home...try to understand, D.A. How would you feel if it was Annie?"

He remained silent for several moments before replying. "I'd better get you home. We'll talk later."

They chatted casually as they drove out of town, but gradually the periods of silence grew longer. Out of the corner of her eye she became aware of the rigid set of his jaw. She tried to find something on which to concentrate. When she realized that her hands were clenched as tightly as his jaw, she gave up and stared at the snow-covered foothills passing by. Her future was as hopeless as the faded wild flowers buried under the winter-white landscape.

He grabbed her coat sleeve as he rolled to a slippery stop near her front porch. "Mary, I meant what I said. If your period is late...or you suspect...just keep me informed. Okay?" He turned her face toward him. "I love you, sweetheart." And he surprised her with a firm kiss on her mouth. "I'll see you on Monday at the usual time."

Two weeks later, nothing had been resolved. They had discussed their predicament several times during the long rides home from school. They continued to drive back and forth together, but other than biology class, Mary avoided D.A. the rest of each day. She was concerned about the consequences to his career if their relationship was discovered.

"I think you're overreacting, Mary. No one knows," D.A. had said.

"Just to be sure, I'm going to spend my extra time in the computer center. I'm working on a game for new readers with learning disabilities. When I'm at the screen, I forget about...us."

"Really?" he had commented in a wounded tone. "I think you've hurt my male ego."

"Don't be sensitive. The minute the screen goes blank, you're back with me."

D.A.'s biggest distraction was having Mary in his biology class. He wondered if it would be best for both of them if she transferred to another section. He'd found it surprising that he could think about her while lecturing on photosynthesis or animal-tissue regeneration or...invariably he'd glance at her and lose his train of thought.

One afternoon, the door of his classroom opened and a young clerk from the administration office entered with a folded piece of paper.

"Excuse me," D.A. said to the class absently, and

he reached for the note and read it. He glanced at the wall clock. Only five minutes remained in the class hour. "Class dismissed," he said abruptly. "See you all on Monday." He stalked out of the room.

Mary watched his sudden exit. Was Annie sick? Surely he would have told her. Had something happened at the ranch? She hurried to the hallway and saw his broad shoulders disappear through the outer doors of the science building. She knew the temperature was just a few degrees above zero, and in his rush he had left his suit jacket behind.

When D.A. reached the dean's office in the building across the courtyard, Dr. Loving was waiting for him. His desk was clear except for a file folder marked "Confidential."

"Sit down, young man," the dean said.

D.A. felt his blood pressure escalate. The note had said to be in the dean's office as soon as he finished his class. The word *urgent* had been underlined. He adjusted his glasses, loosened his herringbone tie, which had begun to choke him, and waited for the older man to speak.

"I hate this kind of thing, D.A. It should never happen."

"What thing?" D.A. asked.

The dean took a deep breath. "There's been a complaint made against you. It's still informal, hopefully just gossip, but I'm afraid it's serious enough to necessitate an inquiry . . . discreetly, of course."

"What kind of complaint?" D.A. wanted to know. "Who the hell made it? I conduct myself professionally on campus. What I do off campus is no one's business."

The dean's face flushed. "It's been brought to my attention—by one of the maintenance men, of all people—that you recently spent a night in a local motel with one of our students. Frankly, I don't care what my teachers do in their personal lives unless it reflects on our college or the students."

"Dr. Loving, who would possibly know or care where I spend my nights or with whom?" D.A. demanded.

"Does that mean there might be some basis to this man's allegation?" The dean frowned, and his heavy gray brows gave him an intimidating look of authority.

D.A.'s anger at the vague accusation grew stronger. Without identifying Mary, and not yet knowing the full details of the complaint, he chose his words carefully. "During that heavy storm two weeks ago, we couldn't get home and spent the night at the Montana Inn in separate rooms. Would they rather we had become marooned on the road and frozen to death?"

"I knew there must be a reasonable explanation, but the accusation is more specific. The man's wife, who is one of the room cleaners, says point-blank that she saw the two of you. The man says they have collaborating evidence from the switchboard operator at the motel, a Mrs. Johnson. She apparently put a wake-up call through to the young woman's room and insists that you answered her phone."

D.A.'s heart sank. "Maybe we exchanged rooms. Did they ever consider that? Those gossips jump to conclusions, don't they?"

"Yes, they probably do. The man and his wife have made trouble before for a few teachers here, especially single men. But I'm afraid because they have made the charge and used the safety and welfare of the young woman as a justification, I'm obliged to follow through with an inquiry."

Dr. Loving stroked his thick gray mustache. "I'm really sorry. I'm afraid that if I drop the complaint, they might make trouble for the two of you and the administration. We've been trying to get additional funding from the legislature, and we just can't let anything color the opinions of those who hold the purse strings.

"I'm so sorry. I'm most pleased with your performance in the classroom as well as the good reports I've received on the program with the Big Hole ranchers. I suspect your being reared on an area ranch adds a certain authenticity to your recommendations with those often stubborn old-time ranchers."

He arched a brow at D.A. "And I've heard you can make college freshmen take an interest in living organisms."

The dean shuffled the papers. "You know how this bureaucratic red tape works. With the coming Thanksgiving holiday, I know it will be sometime in mid-December before I can get to it. I'll handle it myself and hope I can convince these three troublemakers to forget the whole matter. Don't worry, son.

I'm sure it will smooth over, but for goodness' sake, keep your nose clean until then. Stay out of motels with nosy telephone operators, and if you *must* go to one, bolt the door."

A hearty laugh burst from him, but he quickly regained his composure. "I'll keep you informed," he said, somberly. "Until then, just keep on doing a fine job like you've been doing. I'm sure it will turn out all right." He rose and shook D.A.'s hand.

The dean paused at the door. "Of course, we'll have to question the young lady. You understand."

"No!" D.A. thundered.

The dean turned abruptly, surprised at D.A.'s lack of respect.

"Dr. McCormack," the dean cautioned, raising a hand in warning.

"Sorry, sir, but no one is going to make an example out of. . . the woman. I won't stand for her being embarrassed or her family. We were two consenting adults, but if you insist on making a case just to appease these busybodies, then make it with me!" D.A. glanced around for his jacket and realized he'd left it in the classroom. "The next move is up to you, sir. Goodbye." He brushed past the dean and out of the office before the dean realized that he'd been the one dismissed from the meeting.

CHAPTER ELEVEN

MARY GLANCED AROUND Sammy McCormack's kitchen as she entered. "Are you alone? I mean...is D.A. or Annie or David...." She had barely shed her coat when she felt her self-control beginning to crumble.

"What's wrong, darling?" Sammy asked, putting her arm affectionately around Mary's shoulders. "Can I get you something? Coffee, iced tea, cola—" She broke off suddenly as Mary collapsed against her, sobbing uncontrollably.

Sammy waited until the sobs had subsided, then said, "Let's go to the sewing room. There's a sofa in there, and we won't be disturbed."

She led Mary by the hand to the room that had become her retreat, away from the hustle and bustle of the ranch: no men discussing bull performance, no lowing of cows when their weaning calves were taken away, no roar of diesel tractor engines being tested after repair...only the quiet hum of the electronic sewing machine David had given her for her birthday.

"Now," she said, as she and Mary settled themselves at opposite ends of the small sofa, "tell me what's troubling you. I'll listen...and maybe I can help, if you like." She smiled, her soft blue eyes showing concern for this young woman who had become like her own daughter. "I dumped my own problems on you a few years ago. Now perhaps I can return the favor."

Mary wiped her eyes with the damp tissue she held clutched in her fist and then curled up at her end of the sofa. Her shoulders rose and fell as she took a deep breath.

"Your stepson and I...D.A. and I...we...." She took another breath and tried again. "We've... done...something...." She wiped her eyes again. "Sammy, do you remember that night a few weeks ago when the blizzard hit and we couldn't get home?"

Sammy nodded, aware of a growing sense of apprehension.

"We had adjoining rooms, only...we didn't stay in our own room. We...he...we slept together." The words rushed out so rapidly they ran together.

Sammy leaned closer, caught completely off guard by Mary's confession. "You...he...made love? To you?"

"Yes." Mary's hands began to wring the tissue. "Not once, but three times! And now he's... changed."

"Oh, Mary, how did it happen? No, no," she qualified her question, "don't tell me the details, just...I guess you've already told me enough." A new concern came to her. "Are you pregnant?"

"No."

"Sure?"

"Absolutely," Mary said. "I had my period last week. But, Sammy, now D.A. won't talk to me. We ride to school and home again, and all he does is grunt. He says good-morning and good-night, and other than that he just frowns and mumbles. He used to tell me he loved me, but now I'm sure he's changed his mind. It's been that way since last Friday when he was called into the dean's office, but he won't tell me what it was about."

"Maybe he's just worried about his teaching," Sammy said.

"I don't think so," Mary replied. "Something happened at the motel. We...we were still asleep, and suddenly this horrible woman tried to...oh, Sammy it was so terrible. This cleaning woman almost walked in on us. We were...naked and... still in...bed...together." Her voice faded. "D.A. made her stop and ordered her away, but I know she recognized us. Sammy, it was Lola Sizemore, and I think she's making trouble for D.A. I'd never do anything to stand in the way of D.A.'s career or his happiness. I think he's changed his mind and is sorry he got involved with me."

"What can I do?" Sammy asked.

"Help me find out what's bothering him," Mary said. "If it's me, I'll try to understand. But if it's that nasty old gossip from church, then I want to know. I don't want him protecting me and ruining his own reputation. We should face her and make her stop... together!"

Sammy promised to have a discreet talk with D.A. as soon as possible. "The holiday is coming," she said. "I'll find a way to see if I can help you both." She shook her curly head, the frosting of silver sparkling under the overhead light. "Oh, Mary, to think that after all this time the two of you are on the verge of having a future together, and now it's being torn apart so cruelly. I just don't know what to say. I love you both very much. I want happiness for both of you. I hope it can be together, but there could be other problems besides this." She dropped her head, almost afraid to continue. "Sarah came back. It was in August, and D.A. didn't take it very well."

Mary's mouth fell open. "For a reconciliation?"

"No, more to antagonize him, I'm afraid. She brought her new husband and actually tried to suggest that D.A. let her take Annie to Las Vegas."

Mary's eyes grew wide with alarm. "What did he say?"

"He refused. But you see, he's had a lot on his mind for these past few months. He's loved you for years. He just didn't know it," Sammy said, a smile brightening her features. "But right now you might have to give him some time."

"I feel as though I'm on a roller coaster," Mary said dismally. "As though I've fallen from the very top and crashed, and I don't know if I can put the pieces back together again."

MARY TOOK A SMALL BITE of Thanksgiving turkey and thought again of the past few weeks. Her talk with

Sammy McCormack had helped her to understand D.A.'s withdrawal, but it hadn't eased the strain between them. The Monday after she had visited with Sammy, D.A. had stopped his station wagon along the gravel road on their way home and had taken her in his arms, scalding her with heated words of passion and desire. He'd explained that although there was no possible way they could be together at this point, she had to realize that he still wanted her, that he hadn't forgotten the night they had shared.

"I love you very much," he'd whispered, but he'd released her abruptly when a truck from a neighboring ranch had zoomed past them, honking its horn loudly.

The next morning his aloofness had frozen her to the core. She'd swallowed her pride and told him that since she hadn't conceived he was free of any obligations to her and that they could stop riding together if that was what he wanted. He'd only frowned a little more, mumbled words that she couldn't understand and pressed the accelerator. The car had slid on the icy snow-packed road for a few feet, and Mary had to hang on to the handrail on the dashboard. She'd been so frightened by his response she'd been afraid to ask him to repeat his words.

Mary glanced up from her plate when she realized someone had called her name. Her brother Steven had been talking to her father, but Mary had been engrossed in her own problems and had ignored the rising tone of their conversation.

"He's believing in gossip, isn't he, Mary?" said Russ.

"What? I'm sorry, I wasn't listening."

"See, she's not answering because it's probably true," Steven declared confidently, and the tone of his voice brought her head up.

Most of the family members and relatives had finished the meal and retired to the family room down the hall. Mary found herself being scrutinized by her father, Lisa and the one brother with whom she had always had trouble getting along. Steven was twenty, and as far as she was concerned, he was a cowboy bar hopper. Until her oldest brother, Paul, had moved away, they'd been inseparable, returning home late at night on the weekends, noisy and intoxicated after visiting the bars on Montana Street in town. How they'd made the drive home without killing themselves was a miracle. She was jolted back to the present conversation when her father mentioned the name she feared.

"Just because that old Sizemore biddy called me and tried to tell me some lies doesn't mean..." Russ began.

"I'm telling you, dad," Steven interrupted. "She's not the Mary Moral you've always thought she was." He arched a knowing brow toward her. "Isn't gossip usually based on half-truths?" he added philosophically.

"When did Mrs. Sizemore call you?" Mary asked her father.

"A few weeks ago," he replied. "A little after the

blizzard. But I told her to mind her own business and stay out of our affairs.'' He laughed. ''She said I'd be sorry someday if I didn't keep a closer eye on my own daughters!''

''What about Mrs. Johnson?'' Steven asked. ''If two of them say the same thing, isn't that more than just a coincidence?''

''Steven,'' Lisa said, her voice waivering with uncertainty. ''I told you what I had heard because I was worried. I didn't expect you to use it against Mary.''

''Small-town gossip, I'm sure,'' Russ said. ''I know my Mary Beth. Right, baby?''

''What does Mrs. Johnson have to do with this?'' Mary asked.

Her father shrugged his shoulders. ''She's been feeding fuel to the fire Mrs. Sizemore has been building.''

''You've always assumed that I was guilty whenever you heard anything about me, dad,'' Steven persisted. ''Now when it's your favorite daughter who's been accused of sleeping around, you....''

Russ shot up from his chair, his fists clenched.

Steven backed down. ''I'm sorry, dad. It's just that once in awhile you should listen to us guys and open your eyes when it comes to the girls in this family. Maybe they're not as innocent as you and mom would like to think.''

''Shut up, Steven,'' Lisa hissed.

''All right,'' Russ said, sitting down again. ''I'll listen to you, Steven. Just what did your sister tell you?''

"No, Steven, please," Lisa pleaded. "I told you to not tell." Her blue eyes filled with tears, and she turned to her sister. "Mary, I'm so sorry. I was so worried for you, and I was afraid to come to you directly. I know now that I should have. If I'd known he'd blab, I would never have said a thing."

"What the hell did she tell you, Steven?" Russ shouted.

"Lisa said that Joannie Johnson told her that Joannie's mother knew for a fact that Mary spent a night in a motel room with a man in...."

Her father sighed, "Oh, that. That was during the snowstorm, and the two of them had separate rooms. Mrs. Sizemore tried to insinuate...."

"No, dad," Steven said. "This is proof. Mrs. Johnson works the switchboard and called a room and asked for Mary by name, and a man answered and said he'd wake her. Now if that doesn't sound like sleeping around, I don't know what does."

Mary's heart exploded with fear as she numbly realized how public her night with D.A. had become.

"Well, you see," Russ said. "There you are. It couldn't have been Mary. The only night she hasn't been here was the blizzard night."

"She said it was the morning after, dad," Steven said. "Listen up, dad, most of the girls I know aren't virgins anymore. You still think Mary and Lisa are a couple of white lilies in the fish pond of sex around here. Maybe they are...maybe not." Steven tilted his chair back on its back two legs and smiled at her.

"Time of reckoning is here. Want to tell us who he was, Miss Purity?"

Her eyes grew large at his piercing accusation.

"You've probably sworn Lisa to secrecy, right again, Miss Divinity?" Steven asked.

Her father's chair tipped over as he rose to his feet again. "I know you and D.A. wouldn't fool around, so who the hell was the bastard, Mary Elizabeth? I didn't want to believe Lola Sizemore when she said she'd seen you with her own eyes. She didn't know the man, but she said he was big and blond. Damn it all, D.A.'s the only big blond guy I know, so who was it? She said the man tried to hide you. Did he force you to be there with him? So help me, I'll have the man castrated, and I'll do it myself. No one touches my daughters and gets away with it!"

Lisa jumped up and ran from the room sobbing.

Mary looked wild-eyed from her father to Steven, then to her mother, who had just walked in to the room.

"Russ," Julie said, "What's going on?"

Mary slowly rose from her chair. Tears streamed down her face. "You don't understand, any of you," she cried. "I wanted it to happen. I love him! It wasn't D.A.'s fault." She burst into sobs as she rushed from the room.

She ran to her bedroom, grabbed her warm coat and car keys and was out the door, but not quickly enough to avoid hearing her father's angry words.

"That damn McCormack kid has raped my daughter. I'll get him for this!"

D.A. AND ANNIE had returned to their own house after sharing Thanksgiving dinner with David and Sammy when the phone rang in the McCormack kitchen. David answered it and listened silently for several minutes. When he hung up, he turned to Sammy.

"Is D.A. still home?" Before she could answer, he crossed to the kitchen door and looked out. His son's station wagon was parked near the old house across the compound. He glanced again, but there was only one car.

"What was that all about?" Sammy asked. "You're very upset."

He tried to unscramble all the accusations his best friend had made about his son. "Russ has just called my son every vile name I've ever heard used to describe the lowest example of the human race. He's accused him of cradle robbing, child molesting, seducing an innocent virgin. My God, Sammy, he says D.A. raped Mary! I know my son. He loves that young woman. He would never harm her." He frowned at his wife. "Why aren't you excited? This is terrible."

"Is it about the night of the storm?" Sammy asked.

"Yes," he nodded. "Do you know more details? All Russ would do is accuse and shout and threaten. He says she's just eighteen, and she wouldn't do anything like that unless someone had taken advantage of her."

Sammy touched his arm. "I think perhaps, David, they seduced each other that night. They each had a need that could only be filled by the other. Perhaps it was destiny.''

''I don't understand. They insisted they had separate rooms.'' He stared at her. ''I see. They told the truth, just not all the truth.''

She nodded her head slowly.

''They had adjoining rooms,'' he murmured, ''with a door...to allow...? Oh, good grief. You mean Russ is right?''

''I know them both,'' Sammy said. ''It wasn't rape at all. David, do you remember our first weekend in Phoenix, when events seemed to race to a destination neither of us would have dreamed of...as though we had to be united even though we had no intention for such a thing to happen when you first stepped off that plane?''

''Of course I remember, but that was different,'' he said, a smile softening the worried concern on his face. ''We had known each other since we were kids. We....'' She caught his attention again, and suddenly he saw the situation clearer. ''They've been thrown together all their lives, haven't they?''

''Sometimes I feel as though I'm in the counseling business, darling,'' she said. ''You see, several days after that night Mary came to see me. She was very upset, possibly a little guilty about what they'd done, but mostly about changes she'd noticed in D.A. since. Of course, she didn't tell me the details of the night.'' She kissed her husband lightly. ''But if he's anything like his father, I know she had a wonderful and satisfying experience.'' She patted his arm reassuringly. ''Shall I try calling him?''

David nodded and looked out the window again. He listened as Sammy picked up the phone and dialed D.A.'s house.

"Hello, D.A. Sorry to bother you so late. Is Mary there?"

Sammy listened, then asked, "Have you seen her? It's very important, dear."

There was another pause. "Has she phoned you?"

A long period of silence followed, and David watched as Sammy frowned before speaking again. "Her father and mother are worried. They had an argument during their Thanksgiving dinner. I'm afraid it was about that night in the motel. Yes, they all know...at least that you and Mary...oh, D.A., Mary was very upset and she ran away. They can't find her. Russ assumes she's with you. I'm afraid he'll come and try to get her. It could become ugly. His fatherly pride is injured, but it's Mary I'm concerned about. If she comes to you or calls, would you ask her to call me? Perhaps your father and I can run interference for her...and you, if you want."

There was another short pause. "Yes, I know you do, and I feel better just knowing that." She smiled. "Give Annie a kiss from her grandparents. Bye, D.A."

Sammy turned to David. "He hasn't seen or heard from her. He called the Russells about an hour ago, but Julie told him that Russ was on a rampage and that D.A.'s life was in danger if he showed up around there for a while. D.A. says Julie was so upset she started to cry and hung up on him. He didn't know Mary had run away."

Sammy stepped closer to her husband and hugged him tightly around his waist. She rested her head against his chest for a few minutes. Finally she looked up into his face and found him smiling down at her.

"I love you," she whispered. "David, D.A. also came to me after that stormy night and needed to talk. He was in a quandary about so many things... Mary, Sarah, Annie, his teaching career, and this scandal the Johnson and Sizemore women are trying to cause.

"After Sarah's visit last summer he had decided never to remarry. He says he doesn't love Sarah anymore, but I think he's still bitter. He feels he betrayed Mary and her family and even us by their intimacy that night, even though he insists that neither of them wanted to stop. He says he loves Mary, but he can't stop thinking of her as a child, and it makes him feel he's done something wrong. He says he knows she'd accept if he offered marriage, but that people would think he'd married her to give Annie a mother. Oh, David! What can we do?"

"It's their problem, and they'll work it out," David said. "I hate to see tomorrow come, Sam. I'm afraid the solution may be forced on them when our good friend Russ comes looking for his wayward daughter and expects to find her in my son's bed."

ALTHOUGH D.A. HAD TRIED to find her, Mary was still missing when morning came. The sun was well above the horizon when a loud pounding sounded at his door. He knew without answering who his visitor was and what he wanted.

"I want my daughter!" Ed Russell shouted. "You've got her hidden. Get her out here before I call the sheriff."

"She's not here, but come in and see for yourself," D.A. said. He held the front door open and his stocky neighbor charged through the house, flinging wide each door he came to as he searched for his truant daughter.

Julie Russell patted D.A.'s arm as she passed him, on her way to keep a close eye on her irate husband. Russ stood in the middle of D.A.'s bedroom and stared disbelievingly at his neatly made bed, trying to find some evidence of Mary's presence.

"I told you she wasn't here," D.A. said. "I don't know where she is. I tried to find her last night. The people I contacted hadn't seen or heard from her. She didn't call me." He was puzzled by Mary's failure to seek him out.

Annie was sitting on the floor as Russ stormed by her, and D.A. quickly swung her into the safety of his arms. Something about the sight of D.A. standing tall and confident, holding Annie protectively, destroyed Russ's anger.

"Why?" Russ demanded. "Why did you do it? You've always been welcome in my home. Why did you and Mary have to ruin everything? She couldn't have known what she was doing. She's not that kind of girl. I know my little Mary Beth and she isn't...

loose like some of the girls in town. She's special...
isn't she?''

"Yes, she's special," D.A. agreed. "But she knew
what she was doing, and she's not your little girl anymore. My God, Russ, I was going to leave the room,
and she asked me to stay." The words sounded as
though what happened had been her fault, and he
stopped. "Russ, she's a grown woman, with a woman's needs and desires."

D.A.'s insinuations infuriated Russ. "She is not!"
he shouted. "She's my little...you should have
stopped it. You were the older one. Damn it, now the
whole town knows. That gossipy old bitch Sizemore
has the biggest mouth in the county." Russ's face
flushed as he slid the closet door open and then
slammed it closed again. He turned to D.A. "Why
didn't you stop her? Damn it all, you've ruined her
chances of ever marrying in this town."

"Shut up, Russ," D.A. threatened. "That's old-
fashioned. No girl loses her reputation in today's
world because she's lost her virginity."

"It's your fault." Russ glared at him. "You marry
her!"

"You can't force either of us to do something we
don't want. Now get the hell out of my house. Mary
will come home when she wants to. If she comes here
she's welcome, whether it's in my house, my bed or
my life. Just don't try to cram matrimony down my
throat!"

There was a knock on the front door and D.A.
shouted, "Come in."

David and Sammy entered. Russ's mouth clamped shut on the retort he'd been about to make.

"Thought you might need a referee," David offered, an attempt at a smile on his face. "Russ, why don't you and Julie come over to our place. We can discuss this problem over coffee. D.A., if you'd like, we'll take Annie with us, and you can come when you can talk about this...rationally?"

D.A. slid Annie down to the floor and she ran to Sammy, who immediately scooped her up into her arms and started out the door. David put his arm around Russ's shoulder and spoke quietly to him. Russ threw an angry glance toward D.A. but finally agreed to accompany David back to his house across the compound.

D.A. grabbed his pack of cigarettes and headed toward his bedroom. Each step he took made him feel as though he was sinking deeper into an emotional quagmire. How could one night of lovemaking end with all this hatred and name-calling? He didn't want the responsibility of a new wife. His first marriage had been bad enough. Yet what right did Mary's father have to condemn her, a sensitive young woman who meant so much to him and to Annie. Mary was sweet and innocent...until he had changed everything.

He paced the bedroom, pondering his situation. As he stepped into the bathroom off his bedroom to toss his cigarette into the toilet bowl, he noticed the three previously smoked butts floating in the water and realized how long he'd been alone.

Suddenly he knew what he wanted. He walked back into the living room. The silence surrounding him reinforced his decision—he didn't want to live alone anymore. He needed and wanted Mary in his life, not just as a traveling companion twice a day and occasionally for a meal or movie, and especially not as a baby-sitter. He wanted her as his wife.

He collapsed into a nearby chair and tried to sort out the events of the morning and his own reactions to them. He closed his eyes and rubbed the back of his neck, trying to massage some of the tension away. An image of Mary came to him.

"Teach me," she had said that night in her eagerness to learn. He smiled as he recalled how willing she had been to take instruction.

"Oh, Mary," he sighed. He recalled the great satisfaction—pleasure—he had felt knowing that he had been her first. He wanted no man to take his place in her life. Together they could meet whatever lay ahead.

He glanced toward the window as he heard the familiar VW approaching. He knew he had to protect her from her father's wrath. He waited for Mary's knock on his door, relieved that she was now safe. Where had she spent the night, he wondered.

He waited. When the knock didn't come, he looked out the window again. "Good Lord," he muttered, surprised to see her entering the house across the compound. "Mary, no!"

He rushed from the house and ran across the grassy yard. Voices were already raised in anger as he approached the house. He entered without knocking and stopped abruptly at the harsh words.

"Where have you been, girl?" Russ demanded.

"None of your business."

"Don't you sass me. I said, where have you been? I came looking for you. I expected to find you in bed with your lover boy." There was a sneer in his voice.

"See how quickly you change your opinion of me?" Mary cried. "That shows how little you really know about me."

"Mary Beth, you're my little girl. I...." Russ's gentle words conflicted with his angry glaring eyes.

"You don't know me at all, daddy," Mary interrupted. "I'll never be your little girl again. I'm an adult, and what I do is my private business. I didn't come here because D.A. doesn't...." She choked on the words. "He doesn't want me anymore."

"So where were you?" Russ asked. "In a motel with some other man?"

"I don't have to tell you," she replied. "Why don't you call those two busybodies who told you all about me. You believe them more than you do your own daughter. They'll tell you a good story."

"Why you little..." Russ sputtered with rage, his face livid. "One taste of what it's all about and you decide to try it again? Is that what you're saying? You were at that motel again, weren't you? You're no daughter of mine." He raised his hand threateningly.

"No, Russ!" Julie cried.

"I won't tell you where I've been," Mary said, her

voice suddenly very calm in the storm around her. She stood rigidly firm in the center of the large room as her father stomped toward her. "It wasn't with D.A.," she confessed. "I don't care what you all think of me. I've changed, but it's not his fault." She wilted and closed her eyes, resigned to the blow about to fall.

She flinched as she felt something grab her arm. It was hard and cool and metallic. Through her blurry vision, she saw D.A. standing beside her. He carried Annie in his right arm and had taken her own arm in his prosthesis.

"Where did you come from?" she cried, confused by his presence. He tightened his hold on her, and she grew silent.

"Leave her alone!" he said, his voice low and threatening. "Don't you dare touch her or harm her, Russ. She's mine. She belongs with Annie and me. I love her. She's wrong about two things, though. It was my fault for what happened that night, and I do still want her." He looked down at her upturned face. "Very much."

His next words were directed to Russ. "I don't give a damn what tales lecherous old voyeurs like the Sizemore and Johnson women want to spread. You can tell them that Mary is going to become my wife...and soon!" He frowned when he noticed his father covering his mouth with his hand, then he returned his attention to Russ. "Don't you ever try to hurt Mary again," he said, pulling her closer.

Mary stumbled against him as he led her out of the

house. The prosthesis hurt her arm. She had to run to keep up with his long strides or else feel the pain of its pressure as he hurried her to his own house.

"Get inside," he ordered, and she obeyed. "Hold Annie."

Mary watched in bewilderment as D.A. went from Annie's room to his own, shoving a few articles of clothing into his athletic bag. He grabbed their coats and led them out the door.

"Let's go," he said, and he pointed to his car.

"Where?" Mary asked.

"I don't know, but we've got to get out of here!"

CHAPTER TWELVE

MISSOULA WAS A GHOST TOWN. D.A. had forgotten it was the holiday weekend. The hour was late, and the few stores and businesses that had been open all day Friday were now closing again as he drove slowly through the business section of the city.

"Please stop," Mary said, laying her hand on his arm. He'd become progressively somber during the last hour of the long drive. "We need to talk."

He took a deep breath and let it out slowly. Looking ahead, he spotted a fast-food restaurant. "I see a pair of golden arches. We'll get some hamburgers and fries."

Annie clapped her hands joyfully. "Yeah, hamburgers!" she cried, squirming in her safety seat.

"Stay put for a few more minutes, Annie," he cautioned. "I'll get gas, then we'll get something to eat."

A short time later they'd finished their hamburgers, and Annie ran to explore the equipment in the enclosed play area attached to the restaurant. When D.A. came back from cleaning their trays, he dropped down beside Mary in the booth. She turned to him.

"Feeling better?"

"A little." He frowned and looked away. "I said I'd marry you, and I meant it to be this weekend, but we need a license, a blood test, a minister or J.P., and we don't have a single one, damn it." His features softened. "And even if we did, we'd still have to wait seventy-two hours after getting the license. Getting married in Montana is a lot different than a Las Vegas quickie."

Mary stiffened at the mention of his previous wedding.

"Sorry," he murmured.

She leaned closer and touched his hand. "Please look at me, D.A." He turned to her. "Our marriage can't be a quickie. I love you, but running away was wrong." She eased her fingers across the back of his hand, tracing a large vein that ran up to the cuff of his gray cashmere sweater. "I don't want our marriage to start out like this, with everyone who means the most to both of us mad at each other and at us. Are you offering to marry me because you're protecting my reputation? Would you put me in the guest room down the hall like a kid sister?"

She watched him frown and turn his head away, and his hesitation confused her. His face became a blank. She squeezed his hand, forcing him to look at her again.

"You're making another big mistake if you marry me for that reason. You said once that marriage should be forever. You've already gone through one forever marriage that dissolved for reasons I don't fully understand. I don't want to be number two in a string of bad marriages for you. Let Danielle or Jennifer or even that brassy Rose Marie do that. I love you too much for that. I...." Her voice broke, and she hid her face against his knitted sleeve.

He slid his arm around her, nuzzling her hair. "Let me tell you about Sarah."

She shook her head in disagreement, but he silenced her by laying his finger against her lips.

"Yes," he insisted. "When I first met Sarah in the pasture behind the stable on my father's ranch, I literally lusted for her. She became an obsession with me. I saw her a few times before she disappeared. After several months I found her again, quite by accident, and I insisted she marry me. I thought of myself as a knight in shining armor, carrying her away from a life where she had to dance seminude in front of strangers and expose herself to earn enough money to live on. I wanted to give her something wholesome and worthwhile...and traditional. We were married just six hours after I asked her.

"Perhaps I should have listened to Sammy and even you. You were right, Mary. Our union was wrong. The only thing good to come of it is Annie. I don't know why the hell Sarah married me. Her dancing was only the tip of the iceberg for her earnings in Las Vegas. Can you imagine how I felt when I discovered that my wife had been a call girl? That's just a high-class name for a prostitute. Did you know that's what she was...maybe still is?"

She nodded silently.

"You, too, eh? I must have been the last to know. I called one of her former roommates, and she gave me an earful about what my wife was really like. She was earning a thousand dollars a trick before I whisked her away from what I thought was poverty. She and Sid must have had some great laughs over my teacher's salary." He grew thoughtful for a few moments.

"I suppose we both kept secrets from each other. I never told her about my share of the profits from dad's cattle operations. If she'd known how successful the Simmental breeding program has been, she'd have sweet-talked me out of every penny and I would have probably cashed it all in just for her. I was damned gullible. Because I kept quiet, I have a sizable nest egg growing, even though it isn't liquid. When we're husband and wife, you'll share it with me."

"Oh, no, I couldn't," she protested.

He shook his finger at her. "When I become the head of our household, I expect an obedient wife," he said, "and if I want to share my resources with you, you must accept my offer." His smile melted her opposition. "Our marriage will be an open and honest partnership."

"Accepted," she said, "but I come to you with my own dowry, kind sir. Just so you don't think I'm marrying you for your wealth, D.A. McCormack, my father has been putting a share of the profits from his three ranches into a trust fund for each of us kids. We can't touch it until we're twenty-five, but I want you to know you're not marrying a pauper."

They sat quietly in each other's arms for a while. He caught a handful of her dark hair and brought it to his face, touching his cheek with the silky strands.

"We'll have a good life," he promised, winding a thick coil around his index finger and giving it a gentle tug. "You won't believe this, but I was determined to remain a celibate bachelor until that night when you...you told me with your eyes and words and your lovely body that I was acceptable...as a man. Sarah had done something to my male ego when she left me. You were honest with me, Mary. You loved me just the way I am, handicapped physically, but my defects didn't seem to matter to you. That's something Sarah couldn't let me forget. I compared the two of you while you were still asleep that morning after. There's no comparison."

"I know. She's so...."

"You're wrong, love. There's no comparison, because you're the best—prettier, sweeter, more desirable. I love you very much, Mary." He took her chin in his hand and asked softly, "Will you marry me? Be my wife? Help me raise my daughter. How about at Christmastime, in that little Baptist church of yours, with our parents there and a minister?"

"Can we have a double-ring ceremony?" she asked.

"Is that important?"

"Oh, yes," she said. "You know that gold chain that Sammy wears all the time? The one with the blue and green stones in the figure-eight-shaped charm?"

He nodded.

"That symbolizes infinity—their marriage and its permanence. I want our marriage to be like theirs. Sammy told me once that she and your father work at their relationship. I want us to do that." She stopped speaking and studied their clasped hands lying on the seat between them. "I don't know how I'll react when I meet Sarah again. As long as Sammy lives here, Sarah will come back, but...I know it may sound silly, but if we both wear rings to remind us of our vows, perhaps it will protect us from...." Suddenly she smiled. "Did you know that a long, long time ago people thought the wedding ring protected them from evil spirits? That the shape of the ring symbol kept the luck from running out. The Egyptians thought that there was a nerve that ran from the third finger on a person's left hand directly to their heart."

D.A. broke into laughter. "It sounds like you've been doing research on the subject."

Mary reddened. "Lisa and I read a book one time all about weddings. There was a chapter on rings and why they're used at weddings. That's all. It's important to me...and I hope to you, too."

"How would I wear it? It would slide off my left hand."

"I'll think of a solution," she promised. "I think it's important for both of us. And I accept your proposal." She glanced at Annie playing nearby on a merry-go-round. Through the windows she could see the sun slowly dropping behind the western mountains.

"Shouldn't we go back home?" she asked.

"No."

"No?" Her heart fluttered with excitement.

"No, my love," he said. "Our families think we're doing something terribly risqué, so we'll take advantage of the situation. I'll call them later tonight and tell them we're fine. I'd like us to spend the weekend here, away from prying eyes. It'll be the only chance we'll have until after our wedding. We have school and the arrangements, and I'm going to confront those two gossips in town, as well as the dean."

"What does the dean have to do with our wedding?" she asked.

He briefly explained the reason for his preoccupation shortly after the storm, and she was aghast at the seriousness of the women's accusations.

"We'll go see him Monday after classes and explain. He's an understanding and compassionate man," D.A. assured her. "We'll have to start following the proper etiquette for an engaged couple in that damned conservative town though," he teased. He stroked her fine cheekbone with his index finger and whispered hoarsely, "But I want to love you tonight."

CHAPTER THIRTEEN

MUSIC FILLED THE SANCTUARY as the church organist began the prelude to the ceremony. The guests had filled the pews to overflowing, most out of love and affection for the bride and groom, a few out of curiosity. Four-wheel-drive vehicles had plowed through the drifts left from a snowstorm during the night, bringing the McCormacks and the Russells to town.

The women milling around in the vestibule of the small church were chattering excitedly, complimenting the bride-to-be and checking themselves in the mirrors hastily brought in by the understanding minister's wife.

"Let's go," Lisa Russell said, nudging the other bridemaids. "We'll be late." She hurried the two young women out to stand near the double doors leading to the main sanctuary.

Mary Russell's face was alternately flushed with excitement and pale with apprehension.

"Do I really look all right?" she asked her mother. She had tried initially to balance her diminutive body over a pair of four-inch spike heels, then wisely given them up for a pair of satin pumps with a modest two-inch lift. "Why couldn't I be tall and blond like Lisa? I need a miracle," she cried, shaking her hands upward in despair.

"It wasn't a tall, blond woman D.A. asked to marry him," Julie Russell reminded her. "It was you, my darling daughter, just the way you are."

"Do I look stubby? I wish I looked older," Mary said, sighing. "I should have frosted my hair. Or added some eye makeup. Or something!"

"You look beautiful, Mary Elizabeth, just the way a bride should look on her wedding day," Julie said, kissing her daughter's flushed cheek. "Now hold still. Darn it, I don't know how I could have missed this section of the skirt. I was so careful and sewed beads to each flower in the lace overlay, but somehow I missed this entire section."

Julie put the needle between her teeth, picked up a small pair of scissors, and snipped the thread close to the lacy white-rose pattern. "There," she breathed as she carefully replaced the delicate material over the shimmering satin of the gown's full skirt. "Does that look okay, Sammy?"

"Lovely," Sammy McCormack assured her. She made a few final adjustments to the traditional white gown, then turned to her granddaughter.

"Ready, Annie?" she asked. "Do you remember what to do?"

"Yes, grandma. Do I look pretty, too?"

"Of course," and Sammy gave a puff and a pat to the red velvet long skirt of Annie's dress. "Just throw the petals a few at a time," and she hugged Annie and kissed her beaming face.

"We'd better get out there or they might think we've changed the bride's mind." Julie laughed, kissing her daughter affectionately.

"Never." Mary smiled blissfully.

Sammy and Julie hurried toward the entrance to the main sanctuary, took the arms of their respective ushers, Steven Russell and Michael Innes, and were escorted to their seats.

Mary joined her bridesmaids outside the double doors. Lisa, tall and slender, wore a princess-style long gown of red velvet and carried red and white roses. Mary had chosen her two closest friends from high school to be her attendants; Michelle Innes, who was Michael's twin and a cousin on her mother's side of the family, and Joannie Johnson. After a tearful apology from Joannie for her mother's loose tongue, Mary had hugged her and asked her to be a member of the bridal party. Perhaps, Mary had thought, she was partially indebted to Mrs. Johnson's gossipy nature for the impetus it had given to her and D.A.'s relationship.

Ed Russell appeared and came to stand beside Mary. He looked so different in his black tuxedo. Cowboy shirts, denim jeans, Stetson hat and Western riding boots were the clothes she'd always seen him wear.

"You look quite handsome," she said.

The tension in the Russell household had gradually receded when D.A. and Mary had returned to the Rocking R and announced their plans for the future. Mary had been apprehensive and had let D.A. do most of the talking. Aided by Julie Russell's subtle coaxing and nudging, Russ had reluctantly accepted the unexpected marriage of his older daughter.

"You're not losing her, Russ," D.A. had said. "She'll be eight miles up the road. Come see us any time, and we'll do the same."

Her father smiled now and carefully embraced her, trying to avoid crushing her gown.

"You look radiant. This is the way I want to see both of my girls, Mary Beth. In spite of everything, I think you're marrying a good boy. Please forgive me for my big mouth. I was a might...upset...that day." He kissed her cheek, his dark eyes showering her with paternal affection.

He offered her his arm and guided her into the bridal procession as the music changed. Annie was nudged by the minister's wife to begin her walk through the opened doors and down the aisle of the church.

In the distance, Mary saw D.A. and his father standing near the alter. She had known they would both look very handsome in their dark tuxedos with plaid cummerbunds.

David McCormack had laughed good-naturedly when she had asked him to wear formal attire. "I'll wear that monkey suit if I can have a dash of Highland color." The red plaid had blended perfectly with the dark-red velvet of the bridesmaids' dresses.

As Mary saw David McCormack's gray head lean toward D.A.'s curly blond one to exchange some private comment, she felt like pinching herself. Her prayers had been answered. Except for a few wobbly moments, she had never lost faith in her dream. Now she was receiving her wish, finding happiness beyond her wildest hopes. She was approaching a new threshold in her life.

From his station near the minister, D.A. watched the bridal procession glide down the aisle. The congregation stood in unison. He smiled as Annie daintily tossed white rose petals on the crimson carpet. She came to within four rows of the front pew and spotted Sammy. She stopped abruptly, dropped the wicker basket and ran to her.

"Hi, grandma," she said in a cheerfully clear voice as she edged into her grandmother's pew.

"Go back, Annie. Get your basket and stay with Lisa," Sammy whispered, but Annie shook her head and raised her arms to be picked up.

The crowd chuckled, and the minister motioned the remaining participants in the procession to continue.

D.A. focused on the young woman coming toward him. The white of her gown made her hair rich and luxurious under the frothy veil. He tried to maintain his decorum, but a smile tugged at his mouth when she smiled at him.

This was the way a marriage should begin, he thought. He fleetingly recalled the wedding chapel where he had taken his first bride. It was squeezed between two casinos on the strip and had a flashing neon sign. Hurriedly he wiped the image of Sarah from his mind and concentrated on the woman approaching him.

Mary's hand was warm and trembling slightly as he buried it in his own. The vows were exchanged, the promises made, and the rings brought forth.

His father handed him the gold band, and he slipped it onto the small third finger of her left hand. Lisa presented her sister with his larger matching ring, the symbol of their union. Mary reached for his right hand and simply slid it onto his third finger, European style.

The ceremony ended, and he carefully lifted her veil away from her radiant face. He drew her close and kissed her, and she melted against him. For a moment he deepened the kiss. The minister cleared his throat several times.

D.A. eased his bride away slightly. "I love you," he whispered for her ears only, and the congregation issued a mixture of gasps and chuckles when he kissed her again.

His father tapped D.A. on his shoulder. "Enough of a good thing, you two. You can do that later. There are guests waiting," he tactfully reminded them.

In the receiving line during the reception Dr. Loving, the college dean, approached them.

He shook D.A.'s hand and remarked, "All is forgiven, forgotten and understood. Congratulations, my boy. I filed that inquiry where it belonged all along—in the trash! I'll use better judgment the next time those two come to me with their innuendos." Impulsively he kissed the bride's cheek.

D.A. nudged Mary. "Good Lord, where did they come from? Did you invite them?"

Mary glanced up to see Lola Sizemore and Frieda Johnson approaching them. She grimaced. "I had to."

"Why?"

"Mrs. Sizemore is the social chairman here at the church," Mary whispered. "She's in charge of all receptions held here."

He looked at her suspiciously. "And Mrs. Johnson? I suppose she's the co-chairman?"

"No, she's the mother of one of my bridesmaids." Mary smiled sheepishly up at her husband. "Forgive me?"

D.A. chuckled and motioned subtly to Mary as the two women drew nearer. They both wore felt hats with a rainbow of silk flowers around the brim. Their floral print dresses were almost identical in a riot of bright blue, orange and yellow.

"They look like twin parrots," D.A. said under his breath, and Mary giggled.

"Hello, my dears," Mrs. Sizemore greeted them. "Just look, Frieda," she said, pulling her friend closer, "how handsome the groom looks, and the bride. . .just precious in her white gown. Aren't they lovely?"

D.A. put his arm around Mary and hugged her to his side.

"Thank you, ladies, for everything you did to make this all possible," he said.

Both women looked astonished as he quickly shook and squeezed their hands, then moved on to the next guests.

The reception flew by. D.A. and Mary disappeared to change into traveling clothes, reappeared long enough to kiss a sobbing Annie goodbye, and ran out to the station wagon.

After an hour's drive to the Butte airport, they boarded a plane to San Diego. The plane tickets and a suite for four days at the Hotel del Coronado on Coronado Island were a surprise wedding gift from his father and Sammy. They planned to be back in January, when classes resumed.

Throughout the entire flight, Mary felt as though she was literally walking on clouds. D.A. had insisted she take the window seat, and now as they flew over southern California, she could hardly contain her excitement.

"Enjoying yourself, *Mrs.* McCormack?" D.A. whispered near her ear.

"Oh, yes," she sighed. "I think I could adjust to this jet-set life-style very quickly." She laughed. "Only I'd miss the ranch too much."

He brushed her lips with a light kiss. "I suppose the old adage is true that I can take the girl from the ranch but I can't take the ranch out of the girl."

"I suppose," she replied.

"Would you mind living in town for the next semester?" he asked. "We can save a lot on gas. Could you adapt to the city life?"

Her face radiated with love. "Oh, yes," she said, "as long as we're together."

"It would only be for a while," he assured her. "I've retained an architect I know to draw up some sketches of homes. Would you be willing to discuss plans for a new three-or-four-bedroom log home when we get back?''

"Where would it be built?" she asked curiously.

"Somewhere between the old homestead and dad's new house.''

"Oh, D.A., how wonderful!" she cried. "But what about the old log house? Surely you won't tear it down?''

"No, dad's having it renovated," he said. "Sammy is overseeing the move of our things into a rental place in town. I told her to find us a house while we're gone. There's a conspiracy going on behind our backs, and I told Sammy and Dad to do whatever they thought best. We have to trust their judgment since we have no time to take care of matters ourselves.''

She was perplexed. "Why is your father renovating the log house? Who's going to live there?''

"Dad's hired a full-time foreman so he can concentrate on the Simmentals exclusively. He's busier now than he ever was when he worked full-time at Anaconda. I don't think he's been feeling as good as he lets on, either. Sammy's been trying to get him to have a complete examination, but he's too stubborn. He's complained of shortness of breath.'' D.A.'s brows furrowed. "His old lung surgery can't be the cause, and he doesn't smoke. I don't know, but we're both a little worried about him.''

"I hope it's nothing serious," Mary said. "So who's the new foreman?''

He beamed down at her. "Your brother Paul. Dad asked him and he accepted. He'll start the first of the year." He let out a deep breath. "At times I envy the guy. He'll be working with my father the way I used to think I would have if I hadn't gone into teaching."

"Maybe you will someday," she assured him. "I like country living much more than town. I've always felt safer." She gazed at him dreamily. Slowly he brought his mouth down inches from hers, then dipped quickly to kiss her, giving her a promise of passion to come.

She pulled away, blushing against his shoulder, when an airline attendant stopped at their seats to check their seat belts for the plane's descent into San Diego.

"Now you really are a blushing bride," he whispered.

"Be quiet and don't tease me," she replied, but as she leaned against the rigid back of the upright seat she closed her eyes tightly, trying to absorb the joy and excitement that she was feeling.

She wanted her marriage to D.A. to always be a honeymoon. Her thoughts drifted around their future, wondering what events awaited them. She started when his hand reached for hers as the plane bounced onto the runway.

"Sleeping?"

"No, just dreaming... about us."

At the airport they picked up their rental car and drove to Coronado Island. The ornate red-and-white wooden structure of the hotel took Mary's breath away.

"Oh, D.A.," she exclaimed. "It's gigantic. . . and so beautiful. I've never seen anything like it. It must be terribly expensive."

"That it is," he assured her. "But dad and Sammy are footing the bill, so let's just enjoy our stay."

They had been booked into a bridal suite. After registering, they gave the bellman their key and luggage and followed him to their room. As D.A. tipped the young man, Mary turned to survey the room. She almost squealed with delight at the sumptuously furnished suite. It was at least three times as big as her bedroom at home, and on the writing table she caught sight of a chilled bottle of champagne and a huge tray of hors d'oeuvres.

D.A. closed the door, locked it against intruders and turned to Mary. Her hands were pressed against her cheeks, and he smiled at her wide-eyed expression of anticipation.

She looked so sophisticated in her going-away outfit. Narrow ruffles ran down the neckline of her ecru chiffon blouse and disappeared beneath the waistband of her beige skirt. The brown velvet blazer matched her hair and eyes, and the suede boots she wore added three inches to her height. She hardly seemed like the eighteen-year-old girl he'd made love to less than two months ago.

"Well?" he said, stepping closer to her.

"Oh, D.A. I can hardly believe I'm here with you," she said, sighing. "It's as though my fantasy has come true. I know just how the princess felt when she kissed the toad and discovered her own prince charming!''

He raised his eyebrows inquiringly. ''Are you saying that I'm your toad?''

''Oh, no!'' she cried.

''What then?''

She moved backward slightly, concerned that she might have angered him. ''I meant... I just....'' She took a deep breath. ''You *are* my prince charming....'' She discovered she had become tongue-tied and turned away to stare out the window toward the ocean, unable to think of another word to say. A loud popping sound broke into her thoughts, and she whirled around to find its source.

D.A. casually poured champagne into the two glasses, then walked over and handed one to her.

''To us, Mrs. McCormack,'' he toasted, clinking her glass with his.

''To us,'' she whispered, sipping the bubbling champagne. When the glasses were emptied, she set them down near the bottle and slipped out of her blazer. She turned to the window again and watched a sailboat glide past the small harbor, its sail billowing in the wind.

D.A. stepped close behind her, sliding his arms around her slender waist. She leaned against his hard chest, and a wave of peace flowed over them both. She sensed his love, his need... even his uncertainty.

''Just think, D.A., four days without relatives... no school, no laundry, no cooking, no homework or worrying about my computer project and how to make that cursor look like a robin with a red breast, no acid rain, no cows, no gossipy neighbors and, as much as I love her, no Annie.''

He swung her around in his arms. "Be still, my love,'' he said, and his mouth swept down over hers, taking her breath away. His lips gave hers just enough freedom to open, and when their tongues met, all thoughts of home vanished. The heat of his desire ignited a flame in her. He swept her up in his arms and carried her to the king-size bed.

He eased her onto the mattress, and her hands encircled his neck as he slowly unbuttoned her blouse and kissed her throat. Her body became pliant and responsive in his arms as she discovered the meaning of true fulfillment—to love and be loved, to need and be needed, to want and be satisfied.

Later, when they roused themselves from the bed, they nibbled on the snacks. The champagne bottle was emptied and replaced with another. They were free to love and discover each other more intimately than Mary had thought possible, exploring the beauty of each other's body at leisure, without fear of a knock on the door or an intruding phone call.

The days and nights blurred. They made love at midday, with the drapes open and sunlight pouring into the room, no secrets or darkness to hide their passion.

On the third morning Mary awoke with a splitting headache, which threatened to explode her skull when she unwittingly lifted her head from the pillow.

"You've overdosed, my love," D.A. whispered.

"On what?" she asked, holding her head in her hands, afraid to move even a fraction of an inch.

"On love and champagne," he replied. "I'll be back in a minute with Dr. McCormack's marvelously magical hangover remedy."

After he had left the room Mary remained in bed, discouraged. The last thing she wanted was a headache to ruin their blissful stay. Her dazed mind lost track of time, and she drifted into sleep. The sound of D.A. returning jolted her awake.

"I have it," he declared, holding out a glass of thick red liquid and some pills. He went into the bathroom and reappeared with a glass of water.

"Take the aspirin," he instructed, and waited patiently while she complied. "Now the seltzer water." Obediently she drank the fizzing liquid. "Those bubbles will go to your head and absorb some of the champagne bubbles trapped in your brain," he explained with a grin.

She frowned in disbelief until he held out the glass containing the thick red substance.

"What's that stuff?" she asked suspiciously.

"That, my darling, is the magic cure for hangovers. It's tomato juice and Tabasco sauce and a few other miscellaneous miracle ingredients. It'll burn your throat so badly you'll forget you ever had a headache."

Mary choked on the fiery concoction, but D.A. merely wagged his finger at her.

"Drink it all up. It's a proven cure from Mexico to

the Arctic.'' He relieved her of the glass and motioned her to lie back on the pillow. "Rest. I'll read awhile. I bought a magazine while I waited for your remedy,'' he said, moving away and dropping into a comfortable chair near the window overlooking the bay.

An hour later she woke again. Cautiously she sat up and lowered her feet over the side of the bed.

"Do you feel better?'' he asked, concern darkening his handsome features.

She could now nod her head without fearing it might fall off. "I think so. I'm so sorry to spoil everything.''

"You haven't,'' he assured her. "I have plans for us today. Are you feeling up to getting some clothes on that tempting body of yours.''

She blushed and pulled the sheet to cover her bare breasts. "Of course,'' she said, feeling embarrassed and shy.

"I'm going to make you an international traveler. That rental car has been going to waste these past few days while we romped and made love in our room.''

"Too much?'' she asked, her confidence shaken. "Are you tired of making love to me?''

"Of course not,'' he said. "But at my age I need a break once in a while. All things in moderation.'' He grinned. "I thought you might enjoy visiting Tijuana. Want to go south of the border with your husband?''

"Oh, yes,'' she replied. "I think I can get dressed now. I'm going to live, but please, no more champagne. I'm not much of a drinker.''

"That's good. Now you dress while I study the maps and tourist brochures I picked up in the lobby." He dropped down on the bed beside her. "We'll be back here in time for dinner at the hotel. Tomorrow we have to leave."

She made a halfhearted attempt to rise, but he pulled her back and she fell against him. He rolled her over and kissed her throat, nibbling at her earlobe. She was still nude, and his hand began to roam her body.

"Who would have thought that my little shrimpy friend from years back could have grown up to become such a great lover," he whispered near her ear. His hand slid down to rest on her abdomen. "And in a few years the mother of my children."

He pressed her against the pillow and she felt his arousal against her thigh. The thought of his continual desire for her brought a tightness to her heart. She could never have imagined this part of their relationship in her earlier fantasies.

Her breath caught in her throat as he stopped to look down into her enraptured face.

"I thought you wanted a break," she admonished softly.

"You're right, love. I'm making a liar of myself." He eased his body off hers, then grabbed her hand and pulled her out of bed with him. "And besides, I've got to protect you from another overdose."

THE FIREBALL SUN dropped from the sky into the ocean, transforming the horizon into a brilliant palette of crimson, pink and purple.

D.A. and Mary sat on an outcrop of huge boulders at the south end of the public beach on the island. They had eaten dinner in the hotel's main dining room, danced for a while, then wandered through the deserted tennis courts to the sandy beach.

The spray of the ocean waves slapping against the rocks had dampened Mary's shoes and the hem of her dress. D.A. leaned down, slid the shoes from her feet and tucked the dress high across her thighs, exposing her shapely legs to the fine mist. His hand lingered on the silky panty hose covering her legs.

"D.A.," she scolded, slapping playfully at his roaming fingers. "Someone will see us." She quickly scanned the beach, but they were alone.

She leaned against him and felt his arms encircle her shoulders. "Thank you for a lovely day," she said. "The trip to Mexico was great. I had no idea what to expect, but I found it fascinating. I just wish I could speak Spanish."

She settled back into his embrace. "The paper flowers will be so colorful in Annie's room, and I know Sammy will like the onyx stallion bookends, and your father has been saying that he wanted a chess set that was unusual, and I know my parents will like...." She stopped as his lips nibbled her ear, and she turned in his arms. "You should have bought that—"

"My wife talks too much," he grumbled, cutting off her rambling words with a kiss.

Mary wanted desperately to put her arms around him but found herself pinned against his chest. She tilted her head to give him access to the sensitive spot along her neck, and couldn't contain the moan that slipped from her.

He held her in his arms as the sun sank deeper beneath the ocean crest.

"Are you happy, D.A.?" she asked.

"Of course," he said. "But there is something I'd like to know."

"What?" She turned to see his face.

"Where *did* you spend the night when you ran away from your home and your father thought you had come to me?"

"Where do you think I went?" she asked, reaching for his hand.

"Damn it all, I don't know." His features suddenly became unreadable.

She pulled away, alarmed. "D.A., sometimes you frighten me. Your face becomes so devoid of feeling that I don't know what you're thinking at all. What if I didn't tell you? Would you doubt my faithfulness?"

"I just don't want anything to stand in our way of trusting each other." He attempted to sound casual, but his voice was unusually tense.

"I'd trust you," she said. "I wouldn't need to ask."

"I'm sorry."

"Then don't shut me out," she cautioned. "I'm open with you, but I'm still excluded from part of your life. I know that, and I don't like it."

He looked away from her.

Fear gripped her momentarily. "It's Sarah, isn't it? I think she's still in your...thoughts...and you don't want me to know."

"No, it's not that," he replied. "I just wondered where you spent the night."

"I went to the Innes ranch in the Big Hole and spent the night with Michelle. We've been very close friends for years." She sighed as he drew her close again. "Now do you believe me?"

"Of course...damn it, I'm jealous, I guess. More than I thought I could be."

"My psychology professor says that jealousy can be a defense for a person who hasn't been trustworthy himself." She regretted the words the instant they slipped out, but silently she wondered if he could withstand the temptation of his first wife if she was to return. Aloud she said, "There's no reason for you to be jealous, D.A. I'd never be unfaithful to you. I love you too much."

They watched as the sky changed to deep purples and finally to a moonless black. The distant lights of boats in the harbor winked at them.

"Let's go back to the hotel, honey," he said, helping her down from the high flat boulder. "This is our last night alone. We should make the most of it."

He held her close as they walked back along the sandy beach, and she sensed his troubled thoughts. A foreboding hung over her, and momentarily she wished that they could stay there, protected from the unknown dangers that might lay ahead when they returned.

CHAPTER FOURTEEN

MARY MCCORMACK RACED from the clinic, across the lawn to the science building, and down the hall as the warning bell sounded outside the biology classroom.

As she slid into her seat, D.A. frowned at her and erased a mark in his attendance book. She tried desperately to keep the smile from her face and concentrate on her husband as he plunged into the second part of a study in digestion. Occasionally he'd ask a question or call on a class member to comment, but even that possibility didn't stop her mind from wandering.

"Do you agree, Mary?" D.A. asked, startling her from her reverie.

She had no idea what he'd asked, but replied, "Yes," and breathed a sigh of relief as he nodded in agreement. He went on to another student but glanced back at her again, and his frown changed to curiosity. She smiled at him, unaware that her face was reflecting a whole range of emotions.

She turned to the section on reproduction and was soon lost in the chapter. D.A. ignored her the rest of the hour. Biology was their last class of the day.

When the bell rang, she met him outside the door, and they walked to the day-care center to get Annie.

"You look like the cat who swallowed the canary," he said.

"Just a watermelon seed," she replied enigmatically.

"Hmm?" He was paying little attention to her words.

"Nothing," she said. "I just feel wonderful today. Isn't it a beautiful day?"

"Actually the sky is gray, the weather is cold and the wind-chill factor makes it well below freezing. The car is in the garage, Annie's been exposed to chicken pox, and the house plans had three major flaws. Other than that, yes, I suppose it's a beautiful day," he agreed, laughing good-naturedly.

They were within a block of the children's nursery when something clicked in his mind. He stopped abruptly, but she continued to walk on.

"Mary McCormack, you come back here and tell me again what you just said. Why were you late to class? Did you go somewhere?"

She nodded.

"Where?"

"The clinic."

"Why?"

"I wanted to make sure."

"Of what?" He shook her shoulders gently.

She lowered her eyes. "I thought I was safe...you know...that it wouldn't matter."

"What wouldn't matter?"

She took a deep breath and then slowly let it out. "For some stupid reason I forgot to pack my birth-control pills when we...got married...and took our trip. I was so sure that the time of the month was okay that I forgot all about them. I'm afraid...actually I'm not afraid. It's too late for that." She looked up at him. "I haven't had a period since we returned from San Diego. Oh, D.A., until today I was almost sure I was pregnant."

"How does today change things?" he asked. "You said until today."

"Until today I wasn't absolutely positive. But Dr. Morrison says I'll be a mother in September. Oh, D.A.," she said, "I didn't really want this to happen. What will people say? Maybe you don't want to be a father again." She searched his face for his reaction.

"Well, Mrs. McCormack," he said, "I see your dilemma this way. Number one, you are now married, and it's perfectly okay for married women to become mothers. Number two, Annie has always called you momma Mary, and I wouldn't want people to call her a liar, so you've made an honest little girl out of her. Number three, I can't think of anyone else I'd want to have my children. Won't Mrs. Johnson and Mrs. Sizemore be counting on their fingers several months from now." He stepped closer and tipped her chin upward. "I'm old-fashioned myself in many ways...more than I would have admitted a few years ago. My father always wanted a large family, but it didn't work out for him, so we'll take up the McCormack standard and do it for him."

"I won't be able to go to college next fall," she said.

"Disappointed?"

"Not really. I hate to leave Annie each day when I know I could teach her so much myself. We could save money if I stayed home."

"I want you to do what you really want. I want you to be happy, Mary." He kissed her lightly. "Remember when you and I had dinner years ago and you were determined to be a homemaker?"

She nodded.

"Well, you've snared yourself a husband after all," he teased. Before she could reply, he hugged her. "We'll talk to the builder and see if he can't straighten out the construction problems and get us a home before school starts. We'll need those four bedrooms sooner than I'd expected. You can be a country girl again, my love."

After getting Annie from the nursery, they slowly walked the several blocks home.

"Will people talk?" Mary wondered

"What if they do?" D.A. said. "It's none of their business."

"Last week at that party we attended at Dr. Loving's house, some women. . . I think they were wives of three of the professors. . . they were. . . making fun of us. I was in the bathroom, and they didn't know I was there. They made some cutting remarks about me being too young for you, that I'd hinder your career if you wanted to become a department head and things like that. Oh, D.A., I wish I were older. I don't know how to respond when I hear gossip. It always seems to hurt someone. Sometimes I wish I could go to the ranch again and just stay there with you and Annie and all of our unborn children and *never* have to meet those snooty women in town who act like they're better than the rest of us.''

"Mary," he said, putting his arm around her shoulders. "People like those women aren't worth getting excited about. Forget them. They're shallow. How many children we have and when is our private business. You'll be nineteen in a few more months. Those women are just envious of your youth.''

Yet he knew that he, too, would feel relieved when she had her birthday in July. Unconsciously he thought of the other young women he'd known when they had been nineteen. Most of them were quickly fading from mind. Not Sarah. She'd been nineteen when he'd first met her; a sensual, worldly woman, willing to experience things he'd never considered.

Sarah continued to plague his thoughts at the most unexpected times, and he despised himself for it. It made him feel unfaithful to the young woman beside him, who was now his wife, and whose love he never doubted.

"I love you, Mary. You're the only woman in my life," he said, and he vowed silently to make his words the truth.

THE JULY SUN sent a rainbow of color through the droplets from the irrigation sprinkler in the meadow near the house. Tranquility had evaporated like the mist in the field as Sammy returned the receiver to its cradle.

She was still visibly agitated an hour later when she responded to the knock on her front door.

"Come in, Sarah. How are you?" she asked, wondering what could have brought her only daughter from the glittering lights and excitement of Las Vegas to the remote mountain ranch in Montana.

"Hello, mom," Sarah replied, settling herself in a chair. "Sorry for the short notice, but Sid had to fly to New York on business and I thought I'd like to see you again. It's been almost a year since I was here." She lit a cigarette, dropped the jeweled lighter back into her kid-leather purse and crossed her legs. Her hand ran down one long shapely calf before returning to rest in her lap.

"You have a new car?" Sammy asked.

"Yes," Sarah replied, exhaling quickly. "Sid bought it for my twenty-fifth birthday. It's a white Mercedes 280 SL. It's a step in the right direction."

"Meaning?"

"Meaning someday I'm going to have a Rolls," Sarah replied as she tapped the ashes from the end of her cigarette.

"Your dress is lovely," Sammy said.

"It's from the shop," Sarah told her. "Being one of the owners gives me first choice at our designer lines." She touched the white-and-gold pin-striped crepe. "This is by a new designer who's going to make a name for herself soon. I thought I'd give her some business. Everyone needs encouragement at times."

"You enjoy dressing well, don't you?" Sammy asked, recalling her daughter's teen years when she wore nothing but tight jeans.

"I love it. And cars...and traveling. Sid and I have done quite well, and he treats me like a queen," Sarah replied.

"Is Sid still in the construction business?" Sammy asked.

"Sort of," Sarah said thoughtfully. "He sold all his interests in his family's casinos and the...escort service. He devotes his time to acquiring companies to enchance his contracting companies. We recently financed a thirty-story high rise. The lower five floors are shops and professional tenants, and the upper floors are condominiums. We reserved one on the twenty-eighth floor for ourselves. Marvelous view of the desert at sunset." She took another deep drag on her cigarette.

"I'm glad for you, Sarah," Sammy said. "Are you happy?"

"Reasonably. Is anyone really satisfied for long? There are so many experiences I haven't had yet. I want to go to Europe, to the Orient. I want to buy my clothes in Paris, I want to gamble in Monaco, attend the Cannes Film Festival." She laughed. "Sid says I'm impatient and he's right, but I don't want to waste my life doing nothing. Just look at you, mom. You could have stayed with Mastiff Corporation and probably become a vice-president by now. Instead you're stuck here at this godforsaken cow farm. I—"

"Sarah, I'm doing what I want to do," Sammy cautioned. "David and I both could have continued our separate careers up the corporate ladder, but we chose other paths. We're where we want to be. We're free!" She glanced out the window and smiled, her features softening. "David says we have three bosses here. God, nature and ourselves. That's the way we both want it."

"Don't you get lonely?" Sarah asked. "I couldn't stand being away from people."

"There are others living here, and town is just an hour away depending on the weather."

"Speaking of others," Sarah said, a coy twist to her red lips, "doesn't D.A. live here anymore? I saw a stranger leaving his house."

"D.A.'s in town for a while, but he's having a new house built here. You probably saw the construction work near the old log house. It's going to be a lovely four-bedroom log home, rustic on the outside, but spacious and with all the modern conveniences a woman wants," Sammy said, noticing the sudden paleness that came to Sarah's features.

"If the man you saw was tall, dark and rather handsome, he was Paul Russell," she continued. "Paul's our new foreman and doing a fine job. He lives there with his wife and their little boy. David needs relief from the heavier, more time-consuming responsibilities of running the commercial herds. He's...he's not quite as strong as he...he says he's fine, but I think he's not being truthful. Actually, everything is going so well for us. Oh, Sarah, I just can't imagine not being here with him. And when D.A. returns later this fall, the ranch will be like a small town.''

"Ah, yes, D.A. and Annie," Sarah murmured. "I have more money for Annie." She reached into her purse, removed a folded piece of paper, and handed it to her mother. "I appreciate your handling this matter for me. Call it whatever you want, but she's still my daughter. I may have hastily given up any parental rights to her, but I love her in my own way. Use your own judgment as to when and how to use it. D.A. will never understand, but I know teachers don't make enough to live on, and there's no reason for his low income to prevent her from someday going to college. This makes four tens, doesn't it?''

Sammy nodded as she took the ten-thousand-dollar cashier's check and slid it into the patch pocket of her blue poplin skirt.

"Good," Sarah replied. "How is my handsome former husband? He wasn't a very good sport the last time I came to see hi . . . I mean Annie.''

"He's fine," Sammy said.

"I'd hoped to see Annie. I'm sure her doting father is still overprotective of her and hasn't made an effort to remind her of what her mother looks like. She should be old enough to understand that she has two parents. Good Lord, she's three and a half years old, isn't she? Maybe that's still too young. . . .'' She shook her head. "I don't know what kids can do at different ages. We went to visit Sid's sister in New York, but all I remember is how noisy her three children were, screaming and running and never still."

"Sarah, D.A. has remarried."

"What?" Sarah cried. "I don't believe it." She quickly recaptured her composure. "That means Annie has a stepmother. Is she good to her?"

"Oh, yes. She's always been like a mother to her and now that they've married...."

"Wait! Do you mean that D.A. actually married that skinny little girl...what's her name... Marie...Marsha...oh, yes, it's just plain Mary." She began to laugh. "He robbed the cradle, didn't he? How old is she? Fifteen? Sixteen? Isn't that like having two daughters to raise?"

"Sarah!" Sammy said sharply.

Sarah gradually stopped laughing and wiped her eyes. "That's really a surprise. He always preferred sophisticated women, and she's such a timid little farm girl."

"She's very bright," Sammy said. "She's just finished her first year at WMC with honors. She's petite rather than little, and what's wrong with preferring rural life? She's had her nineteenth birthday and yes, she's rather young, but she's a very sweet young woman and a wonderful mother to Annie." She frowned at Sarah. "She loves D.A. very much."

Sarah chuckled again. "I sure remember that about her, but I always thought it was a one-sided crush." She shook her head, feigning bewilderment.

"I never thought he'd actually marry the poor thing."

"Sarah, she's going to have his child in September," Sammy said. "They're on their way here to the ranch. When you called, I assumed you wanted to see Annie, so I told D.A. you would be here and asked him to bring her out. They should be here any time. Sarah, please show a little courtesy to them both. Don't you dare do anything to hurt Mary or embarrass D.A."

"Now, mother," she protested, smiling, "why would I want to do anything to upset the newlyweds. You misjudge me."

"YOU COULD HAVE STAYED HOME," D.A. said as the station wagon rolled to a stop.

"I don't think so," Mary replied, unclasping her seat belt. She couldn't bring herself to look directly at him. Would he have preferred to meet Sarah alone, she wondered?

D.A. got out of the driver's seat, opened the rear door, and lifted Annie to the gravel driveway with a playful swooping motion. Annie's curly dark pigtails bounced back and forth as she skipped along the gravel path toward the house.

"Sarah can be rather cutting at times," he warned Mary as she slid from the passenger seat. She took a few steps before stopping and turning to confront him. She was in her eighth month, yet she'd gained less than ten pounds. Except for the rounded protrusion of her belly she was still slim.

"I wish I wasn't big," Mary lamented, thinking of the shapely Sarah, and unconsciously her hand went to her stomach.

"Don't be nervous," he said, putting his arm around her shoulders.

"I'm just not sure how to be sociable to my husband's former wife. Knowing what she did to Annie and you doesn't help," she said, grimacing.

"Think of her as Sammy's daughter."

"I don't think that's possible." She leaned against him, settling into the curve of his shoulder and arm.

"You're the only woman in my life," he said tenderly, kissing her cheek as they walked up the steps of the porch.

The moment they knocked, the door was opened by Sarah. Mary wondered if she had been watching them from inside.

"Come in, please," Sarah said, the picture of politeness as she stepped back and allowed them to enter.

Annie ran to her grandmother and threw her arms around her.

Sarah strolled over to D.A., who was lingering by the door frowning at her. "Hello," she said, and before he could respond, she slid her hands around his neck, locked her fingers in his curly blond hair and kissed him firmly on his speechless mouth. As she turned to Mary, she purposely brushed against him.

"Hello! You must be little Mary. I believe we've met before, remember? I especially recall the day

D.A. and I came to the ranch to announce our own marriage and you ran out crying. Isn't that right, darling?"

D.A. turned and clasped Mary's hand. "Yes," he said, "Mary and I were married at Christmastime. I'm very fortunate to have found her."

"Probably sprawled at your feet," Sarah remarked without blinking an eye. "Is she more domestic than I was?"

"Very," D.A. replied, quickly dismissing her as he led Mary to the sofa.

Annie left her grandmother's lap and sidled over to Mary. She stood staring up at Sarah.

"She's very pretty, D.A.," Sarah said, studying her daughter. "Does she knew who I am?"

"We tried to explain it to her, but I don't think she's old enough to understand what you did," D.A. told her.

"Annie, come see me," Sarah coaxed. "I'm your mother."

"No!" Annie pressed herself against Mary's leg.

"Come on, Annie. I'm your *real* mother." Sarah leaned closer and reached for the little girl.

"No! Momma's my momma," she cried, and clutched Mary's arm.

"Well—" Sarah shrugged "—I can plainly see you haven't tried hard enough." She gathered up her purse and gold linen jacket. "Mom, I'll be back later this evening or tomorrow. I'm driving to Bozeman to visit a friend who moved there from Vegas. Can I plan to spend the night if I make it back?"

Sammy nodded, relieved at Sarah's unexpected departure.

"D.A., when she's older, maybe you'll try harder to explain to Annie who I am," Sarah suggested. "She really should know that your child bride couldn't possibly be her natural mother unless you slept with her when she was in junior high." Sarah tossed back her wavy dark hair and strolled to the door.

D.A. rose and opened the door to let Sarah out. She turned to him. "I hope you'll be very happy with your little bride, even if you did rob the cradle in order to have a new bed partner. Was legitimacy that important to you? I thought you were more liberated than that. Bye, my darling. You always were a great one in bed." In a parting gesture, she stroked his cheek sensuously with a long manicured red fingernail. He jerked away, but as she swept through the door she made a kissing motion with her lips.

"Bitch," he muttered under his breath, but he couldn't fight the tumultuous reaction in himself that her touch had brought. He turned and saw Mary staring at him. He couldn't read her expression, but he knew she needed his reassurance that she was the important woman in his life. Before going to her, he glanced over his shoulder for one last look at the tall, voluptuous brunet strolling to her expensive white sports car, her hips swinging provocatively as though she knew he was watching.

THE WEEKS AFTER SARAH'S VISIT were tense. Mary found herself unable to express her fears and doubts to D.A. The fact that he went out of his way to convince her that all was well with their marriage didn't reassure her.

She wondered if it was possible for a man to love two women. She was determined to share him with no one, but Sarah was a formidable opponent. D.A.'s tendency to hide his feelings continued to trouble her, but she kept her problems to herself. Her pride prevented her from discussing her worries with her parents or the McCormacks. She grew stubbornly determined to succeed or fail in her relationship with D.A. on her own merits.

She busied herself with refinishing the secondhand baby furniture she'd found in town. Annie's bubbly nature prevented her spirits from sagging, and the thoughts of having her own baby reinforced her confidence in their future.

Only one thing stood in their way. She prayed fervently that Sarah would stay far, far away.

A few weeks later Mary lay on the delivery table, relieved at last of the pressing burning contractions. D.A. held her hand and wiped the perspiration from her damp forehead.

"You did fine, sweetheart, just fine. It's over now." He kissed her parched lips before moistening them with a damp tissue.

"Is it a boy?" she asked, searching his face while they listened to the newborn's cry filling the room.

"See for yourself, Mary," Dr. Morrison suggested

as he laid the newborn on her stomach. Mary stared at the squirming infant draped across her and smiled. "It's a. . . a boy," she said. Gingerly she touched her son, marveling at his existence.

"Yes, my dear, a fine healthy boy," the doctor confirmed.

"I'm glad," she sighed, dropping her head back onto the flat pillow. She clung to D.A.'s hand, and her eyes filled with tears. "It had to be a boy. I didn't want to compete with Sarah." She lay quietly for a few minutes after the baby was taken away by a nurse. Exhaustion threatened to overwhelm her.

"His name has to be David. You know that," she said, and her eyes regained their dark sparkle before she closed them.

A few minutes later she felt a presence near her and reopened her eyes. D.A. stood beside her holding a tiny bundle.

"Would you like to hold our son, Mrs. McCormack?" he asked, beaming with pride. "Let's call him Davy until he's older." Tenderly he placed the newborn infant in her arms.

After the baby was taken to the nursery for postnatal care, Mary settled in her room and soon was napping soundly.

D.A. stayed with her. He sat quietly admiring her pale beauty, and thought of their shared experiences over the years. He'd first met her the summer his father had purchased the ranch southeast of town and they'd moved away from Butte. He'd been a gangling twelve-year-old, just under six feet tall. She'd been a tiny three-year-old, and the bonding between them had begun the moment he'd seen her in the Russell kitchen.

Where had the years gone? Here she lay, the mother of his child, yet hardly more than a child herself.

He remained by her side for more than an hour before slipping from the room in search of a pay phone. He made a quick call to his neighbor's house and informed a jubilant Annie that she now had a baby brother.

Next he dialed the Russell ranch.

"Rocking R. Who's this?" Ed Russell demanded.

D.A. chuckled. "Hi, grandpa."

"D.A., is that you, boy?"

"Yes, Russ. You and Julie became grandparents again about an hour ago."

He had to hold the receiver away from his ear while Russ's booming voice shouted to Julie. "Well, speak up, boy. What was it—boy or girl?"

"It was a healthy baby boy, Russ," D.A. replied. "Don't get mad now, we'll name the next one after you, but this one is for my father. We've named him David Ian McCormack."

"What's that damned middle name?"

"Ian. Ian! It's spelled I-A-N. It's Scottish. David Ian McCormack. He's David, the third, but we'll call him Davy. He's seven pounds and twenty-one inches long. Long and skinny like all the McCormack men, and his head is covered with rusty brown hair. Now, if he has green eyes, he'll be a true McCormack. He's cute as a button, but the little guy won't open his eyes. He has a powerful set of lungs. He entered the world screaming until Dr. Morrison laid him across Mary's stomach. Then he put his thumb in his mouth and started sucking and stopped crying. I think you may have a thumb-sucking grandson, Russ.''

Julie's voice cut into their conversation. "How's Mary?" she asked. "I was concerned with her being so young and thin. She told me she'd gained only twelve pounds, and that's hardly enough. Is she all right?"

"She's fine, Julie, just fine. I was with her all the time. Damn it, that's a marvelous experience. She was fine and did just as she was supposed to do. Those childbirth classes really helped. I've never attended them before and...." His voice wavered as the full emotional impact of the birth registered.

"Can we see her tonight, D.A.?" Julie asked.

"Sure. Meet me at the house. I promised to take Annie to see her new brother. She's just tickled pink about having a brother. Come anytime before seven. I've got to go now. I've got to tell my father and Sammy.''

After a quick call to his father's place, he returned to Mary's room. As he stood watching her, her brown eyes slowly opened.

"You're still here," she murmured, lifting her hand to touch him.

He leaned down and lightly kissed her mouth. "Of course. I wanted to be sure you were okay." Their eyes held for several seconds. "I love you very much, my darling," he said as he kissed her again. "I called both sets of grandparents and Annie, and I've been to the nursery to admire our son. You said once long ago that having children makes a marriage into a family. That's true when the husband and wife are the right match for each other." He gazed at her serene face. "We have the right match."

MARY SAT ON THE BED nursing her seven-week-old son, enjoying the company of D.A. and Annie.

Annie stared at the baby from her position on D.A.'s lap. As her father finished adjusting the snaps on her pajamas, she leaned against his broad chest and sighed. "When's he gonna play with me, daddy?"

D.A. watched in silence as Mary nursed the baby. "He's not old enough, honey. First he'll smile at you, then he'll laugh when you make a funny face. Soon he'll learn to crawl and knock over your toys, and someday when he can walk and run, he'll be outside playing with you just the way you want. Until then you'll have to be patient and wait." He nuzzled the top of her thick curls.

Mary glanced up at D.A., and a spark of desire flashed between them as she moved the baby to her other breast. The baby's small mouth made smacking sounds as he found the nipple, then began to cry as the taut full tip slipped from his reach.

"Hush, baby, don't be so impatient. Here it is," she soothed, and she nudged his cheek gently, guiding him to the source of his nourishment. His tiny fist kneaded her breast, and his eyes closed again.

A small stream of milk ran from his mouth and down his round cheek. D.A. reached for a cloth diaper and wiped the drip from the baby's face. His head was inches from Mary's, and he held her gaze. Without a word between them, she smiled her understanding.

"Ready for bed, Annie?" D.A. returned his attention to his drowsy daughter, whose head had begun to nod against his chest. He eased himself from the bed and reached for her. She threw her chubby arms around his neck and clung to him as he moved from the large bedroom, down the hall, and to her own room.

They had moved into their new home in the compound when Davy was one month old. Sammy had helped them get settled, but there was still much to do. Annie had her own room, and the baby was in the bedroom next to their master bedroom. The remaining room had been set aside for Ed Russell's namesake.

D.A. tucked his daughter into her new bed and kissed her, then hurried down the hallway to Mary. He collided with her as she rushed out of the baby's room, closing the door softly behind her.

"I was in a hurry," she said breathlessly.

"For what, love?" he said, smiling down at her.

She slid her arms around his waist. "For you, my darling husband, for you."

He stooped slightly and picked her up in his arms, standing motionless in the hallway. Her breathing escalated and her heart pounded as she pressed her slender body against his. Slipping her arms around his neck, she drew his head down and kissed him, lingering to see if he would take her hint.

He feigned ignorance, but the glint in his green eyes gave him away. "You have a request, my love?"

"Oh, D.A., I guess every woman has a fantasy, and mine has always been for you to swoop me up in your arms and carry me off to your bed and make passionate love to me until I couldn't stand it anymore, and then have you prove to me that I could."

"Could what?"

"Stand it even more, you thickheaded Scotsman."

"Are you hinting that you're ready to resume our love life?" he teased.

"How much more blatant do I have to make my hints in order for you to understand," she huffed. "I thought you McCormack men were quicker witted than that. Then again, you were rather slow to notice me, weren't you?"

"I'm just a simple country kid, my dear wife. Explain again to me what you want me to do."

"Darling, make mad passionate love to me now. Before I waste away from deprivation...and before the baby wakes up."

He walked slowly down the hallway and into the bedroom, keeping his attention on her face. The darkness of her eyes warmed his ardor as he laid her on the bed and began to carefully unbutton the tricot gown.

He slid it gently from her body. "You're as slender

as you were before the baby," he said, stroking the sensitive area near the dip of her hipbone.

He quickly shed his own clothing and joined her on the bed, pulling her to him and fulfilling both their fantasies.

CHAPTER FIFTEEN

THE BREEZES OF MAY couldn't be accurately described as warm, but after the frigid winter months, the hillsides were showing a hint of green interspersed with golden dandelions, and the tulip beds around the main house were ablaze with color. The last patches of a late-spring snow had melted, and the small creek that ran behind the compound was high with runoff from the mountains.

The Montana sun shone overhead, and Mary sat on a thick picnic blanket admiring her son and soaking up the warming rays on this leisurely Saturday morning. Davy was picking at tiny pieces of grass that had stuck to his moist palms, but quickly lost interest in his hands when a breeze rippled a nearby spindly weed. He crawled away to explore, giggling and cooing to himself.

Mary sat mulling over the coffee-and-sewing get-together at the McCormack ranch the previous Thursday.

Julie Russell had been joining Mary and Sammy for coffee once a week, and recently they had decided to extend an invitation to three nearby ranching women to meet them at the McCormack ranch for coffee and needlecraft activities twice a month. The first get-together had been Thursday. Although the women's hands were busy with assorted crafts, their conversations soon turned to the business of farming and ranching. Both sheep and cattle ranches had been represented, and keeping accurate business records had been a major topic of conversation. The McCormacks' micro-computer system was of special interest, and Sammy had promised to show the other women what she'd accomplished. The women had all agreed the gathering had been successful and expressed their eagerness in meeting again.

Mary found herself envying these women a little. Ranching was the only life-style she truly enjoyed. She hoped that someday her own husband would change his mind and join his father and her brother in running the McCormack operation.

Whenever she had to accompany D.A. to a faculty party or gathering at the college, she felt out of place. The other women talked of golfing and bowling, art shows and alumni events, sororities and their husband's professional organizations, and cocktails at the new restaurant north of town.

One woman would give a glowing dissertation on her husband's recently published article in some professional journal, and the others would nod their coiffured heads in respect but immediately play the game of one-upmanship with tales of their own spouses' accomplishments. Mary doubted if any of the wives had actually read the journals described. She knew all the faculty wives weren't like the ones she'd met, but the others seemed to avoid the cocktail circuit.

Mary had begun to experiment on a micro-computer with a color monitor that D.A. had purchased. At a recent party, when she had tried to explain a game she'd written for Annie and herself to play together on the console, the other women had given her strange looks of confusion mixed with disdain. The experience had left her wondering if they did anything other than socialize and bask in the glories of their spouses. By the time D.A. had sought her out and suggested they leave, she'd decided that she was a misfit in his world of academia, and furthermore, she wanted to remain that way.

She'd tried to adjust, but the social contacts held a pretentiousness she rebelled against. She didn't want to become a showcase for her husband's career. He had the ability to be a success in his own right, and she bristled at the thought that her appearance or actions might be a detriment to his professional advancement.

She glanced up from her reverie and spotted D.A. and Annie playing on the swing set across the compound. She waved to them and smiled as her brother's wife and toddling son joined them. Her brother had married a young woman from Southern California, and her presence gave Mary and Sammy new female companionship. Trips to town for shopping and social events were increasingly infrequent as the ranch geared up for spring roundups and the summer growing season.

She started as a shadow fell over her, and she

looked up into the dark face of Sidney Lansburgh.
She had been badly shaken the previous night when
D.A. had informed her that Sarah and Sid would be
visiting Sammy for a few days. While preparing
breakfast that morning, she'd noticed an unfamiliar
expensive- looking blue sports car parked across the
compound and surmised that they had arrived during
the night.

"May I join you?" Sid asked. He smiled at her obvious surprise. "I realize that I'm probably the last
person with whom you expected to chat. You're
Mary, am I right?"

"Yes on both accounts, but please sit down,"
Mary replied, feeling the flush of embarrassment on
her cheeks. She patted the blanket beside her and
brushed the cracker crumbs away.

"I know who you are," she said with a frown.
"What do I call you? Mr. Lansburgh sounds so formal, but Sidney sounds too...I don't know you at
all, actually. I just know of you." She felt a sudden
determination to smooth the awkwardness she suspected they were both feeling.

"Call me Sid," he said. "Please. And could I have
a cracker? We haven't had lunch yet." He stretched
his arms above his head, then settled into a comfortable position a few feet away from her. "I toured the
ranch this morning with your father-in-law. I grew
up on Long Island and visited city zoos a few times as
a boy, but I'm in an alien world here."

She studied him as he chatted. His iridescent eyes
were pale blue near the pupils but darkened and

gradually changed into hazel, surrounded by a strange brown ring. His complexion was dark, and his black hair had silver wings at each temple. She'd already noticed that he was the same height as Sarah and impressively muscular. From a distance Mary had thought he seemed rather sinister, but as he talked to her, an aura of sincerity and warmth emerged.

"Do you like it here?" she asked.

"It's very different from Las Vegas. No hot asphalt and auto exhaust fumes to breathe, and it's so quiet here. Just the livestock and birds and the wind...and some very nice people. I don't know...." He threw his head back and laughed.

Mary stared at him, puzzled.

"Sarah seduced me into this side trip," he said. "She told me I needed to get away from the pressures and stress of running my businesses and enjoy the beauty of these wild and rugged mountains."

"Sarah did?" Mary exclaimed. "She hates this country! Why would she do that?" Growing alarm at Sarah's motives brought a quickening beat to her already-anxious heart.

"Who knows Sarah's true reasons for doing anything," he said. "I was going to fly to Calgary on business, but when I asked Sarah to accompany me, she suggested we drive instead and stop here. I don't always trust Sarah."

"Neither do I," Mary mumbled.

"What did you say, my dear?"

"Nothing," she said, desperate to change the subject. "Isn't it beautiful outside?"

"Gorgeous," he replied. "I didn't know there were still places like this left in the country. When I went with David this morning we stopped at the barn. A mare was in advanced labor, so we stayed and watched Paul help the mare deliver.

"My God, for the first time in my life I saw a foal born. I got caught up in the excitement and even cheered when the little fellow stood on those spindly legs of his. He was as cute as could be. The manure even smelled good...wholesome...damn it, Mary, I felt renewed. I wish I could get to know David and Sammy better, but with Sarah I know it's impossible. They seem to have found such happiness."

Davy crawled back to the blanket and stared up at Sid. After a few moments he made his way over to Sid and used him for leverage as he tried to stand. The baby lost his balance and fell. Unconsciously Sid reached for his hand and helped the infant steady his wobbly legs. Davy gurgled and sputtered a string of unintelligible sounds.

"I'll take him," Mary said, reaching for Davy. "He'll get your trousers all messed."

"No, no, leave him," Sid insisted. "I don't get to be around babies often. My sister in New York has three children." He smiled at a drooling Davy and remarked, "He's cute. How old is he?"

"Eight months."

"He looks like his grandfather McCormack."

"Yes," Mary agreed, "but his eyes are just like D.A.'s. D.A. and his father look a lot alike except for their hair." She sighed as she reached out and touched the baby's cheek, then offered him another cracker. She gave Sid one, too.

"Thank you," he said. "You love him, don't you?"

"My baby? Of course!"

"No, I mean your husband."

"Oh, yes. Sometimes so much it hurts."

"I know," Sid replied, and patted her hand. "I love my wife the same way."

Mary drew back in surprise, wondering how any man could love Sarah.

"Mary, you're lucky," said Sid. "You and D.A. have this sweet little baby. Sarah refused to consider having a child. Frankly, I wouldn't mind being a father. I'm almost forty and time is passing by. Maybe if Sarah had another child she wouldn't be drawn back here to see her own...." He stopped talking, but Mary could think of nothing to say.

"I never planned to fall in love with any woman," he continued after a moment. "Sarah sabotaged me. I wonder if D.A. knows that I stole his wife."

"What do you mean?" Mary asked. "You mean she didn't go voluntarily? She would have stayed with him?"

He laughed softly. "Perhaps for a while, but sooner or later she would have returned to the excitement of Las Vegas. She wasn't happy with him," he said confidently. "Oh, not that they didn't have their good times, but domesticity isn't Sarah's strong point."

Mary studied the pattern of the blanket on which

they sat. "D.A.'s never talked to me much about her. I don't understand how any mother could just walk away from her child. I know I couldn't."

"Being a female doesn't guarantee the maternal instinct," he observed.

"How did you steal her away?" Mary asked, curiosity getting the best of her.

"Sarah was my uncle's highest-paid call girl and his favorite companion," he told her. "When she disappeared, he asked me to find her. It took me almost a year before I tracked her down in Missoula. When I called her and offered her the old job, I think she was interested right away. By then my uncle had died from a heart attack."

"Oh, I'm sorry," Mary said.

"Thank you, but he was a tight-fisted, power-hungry businessman who's smashed a lot of people along the way," Sid remarked. "Anyway, by the time I found her, he was gone and I'd taken over the businesses. I made her the same offer my uncle had originally discussed with me when he first asked me to find her. I planned to make her my highest-priced girl when I enticed her into returning to Vegas." He glanced across the compound. "The moment she stepped off the plane, something happened. I knew I couldn't let any other man touch her." He chuckled. "My God, she's expensive to keep either way."

He reached for another cracker. "Sarah can be very bitchy at times. I know that," he said. "I warned her not to make trouble for you and D.A. I think she's still attracted to him, more so now that he's remarried and has another child, but she disguises it as motherly concern for her daughter. She knows I don't share my woman with another man, and I can offer her material things that were beyond D.A.'s ability.'' He gave a short laugh. ''I'm usually not so loose-tongued,'' he said, glancing at Mary.

She touched his forearm. ''Mr. Lansburgh...I mean Sid, you shouldn't be telling me these things, but I know how you must feel. It's worse for me. You can buy Sarah all those beautiful clothes and cars and homes, but all I can give D.A. is love. I don't know how much of what you've told me he knows, but every time she comes here, I'm afraid that she and he will.... He says he loves me, but she's so sophisticated and I'm not. She intimidates me. I feel like a little girl beside her.''

''I'm sure he has no regrets now that he has you, Mary,'' Sid said. ''If anything, he'd want to take it out on me for interfering in his marriage. Just remember, if she'd been contented, my offer would have fallen on deaf ears.''

''She keeps returning, and each time I know it upsets him. I don't want him to ever know, but I often wonder if we weren't here and if they were alone, would they....'' Her eyes glistened as she lowered her head. ''That doesn't sound like a very trusting wife, does it? I shouldn't be saying these things to you, either, but maybe you are the only one who understands what I fear most.''

''Here, my dear....'' Sid reached into his pocket and handed her a monogrammed handkerchief. ''I understand Sarah more than she gives me credit. She always wants something that she can't have. When she had D.A. and the beginnings of a nice family, she wanted the excitement and money of Las Vegas. When I gave her those, she wanted the power that goes with the money, and I brought her into my business. She's proven to be very competent at decision making with me. She has an intuitiveness that could be developed if she'd concentrate. But now she's drawn to the very things that she threw away a few years ago.''

He grabbed her forearm and shook her slightly. ''She can't have them, Mary. You've prevented her from continuing to entice D.A. You've become her own child's mother. You produced a son and proved to her that D.A.'s not living a celibate life and waiting for her to return to his bed. She's quite jealous of you. Did you know that? You have what she didn't want, but she's like the dog in the manger. I like to think that she wants what I can give her more than what she could have if she somehow got rid of you and could reclaim D.A. I love her, and I think she loves me in her own peculiar way.''

''Then why does she do *that?*'' Mary asked. He followed her line of vision and watched as Sarah settled herself beside D.A. across the grassy compound, laying her hand on his arm caressingly.

''Damn her,'' Sid groaned as Sarah whispered something to D.A. and D.A.'s head lowered to hear her. Their faces were inches apart, and as she turned to Sid, Mary didn't try to hide the doubt she felt.

"Stay put, my dear." Sid reached out and stopped Mary in her effort to rise. "If she can talk to him, then I can continue to talk to you. At least we can keep an eye on them out here—I'm sorry, I shouldn't have said that.

"Tell me about you and D.A. Oh, not the private stuff, just the things like how long you've known him and what you expect to be doing in a few years... or about his job at the college. Do you have any special interests? I know more about you two than you might think. I've kept my ears open and listened to the good things when my wife carried on about her first husband."

The sincerity in his voice distracted Mary from the activity across the compound, and she began to talk of the future, but she kept one eye peeled for movement across the way.

D.A. HAD LEFT ANNIE to swing by herself and walked a few feet away to sit in the sweet green grass nearby. He had been watching Sid Lansburgh and Mary, wondering what they could possibly have to talk about. The baby, perhaps, he thought, as he watched Sid steady Davy.

The angular lines of his face softened as he thought of his young son. The baby had brought new joy into both McCormack households, as well as the Russells. He was a good-natured baby, and Annie had become a protective big sister, always willing to help Mary care for him.

Annie had lost her toddler chubbiness and showed

signs of becoming a taller-than-average little girl. One more year and she would be going to kindergarten in town. She was bright, and eager to learn. Mary had recently begun to teach her to print the alphabet and to count pinto beans at the kitchen table. Together Mary and Annie had polished Mary's computer game for preschoolers, and a week earlier Mary had mailed off a query letter to a software company to see if the game had market potential.

D.A.'s tranquility was disturbed by thoughts of Sarah. Why had she and Sid decided to visit the ranch, he wondered. At least he had been warned a few days in advance this time. He understood Sammy's reluctance to inform him of Sarah's visits, but the short advance warnings he'd had in the past were intolerable. Finally he'd gone to Sammy and asked that she give him more lead time whenever possible, and she'd agreed.

"Hi." A rich sensuous voice disturbed his reverie.

Sarah's ample bustline almost blocked her face as he looked up to where she stood directly behind him. He steeled himself as she dropped down to the grass beside him. She was careful not to touch him, but one move of his leg or arm and he knew he would be in physical contact with her.

"What brings you two to the Northern Rockies, Sarah?" he asked.

"I had business with my mother, and we were on our way to Calgary. We decided to drive instead of fly. We'll be leaving tomorrow after breakfast. Do you mind?"

"Why should I?" He glanced at Annie, then Mary across the grass.

"Do you still hate me?" Sarah asked, smiling as she touched his arm.

"I neither hate you nor...." He stopped. The feel of her fingertips against his bare skin sent a surge of unexpected desire through him.

"I think you still care for me a little," she said, and moved her fingers around in a light stroking pattern.

"Cut it out, Sarah."

She stopped. "Your little wife looks very pretty. Motherhood seems to agree with her. I guess it goes with being raised on a farm with all the cows and pigs...."

"Take your hand off—" he demanded, as Annie came over to them.

Annie leaned against D.A.'s bent knee and turned her attention to Sarah. "Are you really my mother?"

"Yes, I am," Sarah said, glancing at D.A. "Is that what your father said?"

"Yes." Annie squinted at Sarah and wriggled her nose. She twisted a section of her dark auburn hair around her index finger. "I think you're pretty."

"So are you, Annie." Sarah slipped her hand under and through D.A.'s right arm.

"Why did you go away?" Annie asked. "I don't remember you."

"I went away because...because...maybe I just made an impulsive mistake, Annie," Sarah said, and turned to D.A.

D.A. groaned, torn by the hidden message in her words. He dropped his head to rest on his knees, burying his face in his crossed arms. Sarah's fingers brushed the blond hair near his temple.

"I like my new mother," Annie said. "Her name is Mary, and she's nice to me. She teaches me things. I can count and write my name, and this summer she's going to teach me how to make paper dolls. Did you see my brother? His name is Davy. My grandpa is David and my daddy is David, and my little brother is David, too. Isn't that funny to have so many Davids in one family?" She broke into giggles.

"Yes," Sarah said with a nod. "Now, go play, Annie. Show us how you can swing by yourself."

Annie raced to the swing set, and the silence was deafening.

"Why do you say those things, Sarah?" D.A. asked. He raised his head and turned to her, searching her eyes for a hint of sincerity.

She shrugged her shoulders. "Maybe they're true."

"Isn't it a little late for that kind of talk? I didn't exactly chase you out of our lives."

He tried to deny another wave of desire as she touched his arm again.

Sarah stared across the compound, past Mary and Sid to the pale-blue Ferrari parked behind them. It had been an early birthday present from Sid.

"Then again, maybe this is all for the best," she admitted. She touched his cheek. "There's a difference between wanting *you* and wanting your life-style. I could go to bed with you right this minute and have a great time, but I could never live in this isolated place." She moved her fingers against the blond hairs on his bare arm.

He laid his prosthesis against her caressing fingers. The sight of the stainless-steel terminal hook brought a gasp from her.

"There's also a difference between wanting my stud service in bed and wanting me as a whole man," he replied. "Mary loves me because I'm D.A. McCormack, missing hand and all. She loves me the way I am and is honest about it. You don't really want me. You love the thought of me betraying my wife. You want to hurt her, don't you?

"Well, you can't, Sarah. I don't want you. I'll do whatever is necessary to protect Mary from you. She's a real woman, one who doesn't fake or lie or cheat. I can trust her to be faithful to just me. For years I was too blind to see her, but your leaving me helped me to wake up to her presence. I love her, Sarah, and I wouldn't touch you no matter what you offered. It would crush Mary to think that I'd even want to. You'd better go to your Sid. He seems nice enough, but I really wonder what he sees in a whore like you."

He jumped to his feet and angrily strode across the grass. He was aware of Sarah watching him as he sat down beside Mary and kissed her. He picked up his son and cuddled him on his lap and began talking to Sid. Out of the corner of his eye he saw Sarah disappear into his father's house.

D.A.'S PATIENCE HAD A SHORT FUSE that night as he tried to make love to Mary with a fierceness that frightened her. His thrusts were premature and painful.

"No," she cried. "Please stop. . .it hurts, please."

He collapsed and rolled away from her. "I'm sorry, Mary," he whispered through the darkness. "I'm so sorry, I didn't mean to hurt you."

She knew he'd tried to use her body to exorcise Sarah from his own. "It's her, isn't it?" she whispered hoarsely.

"Who?" he asked, turning onto his back.

She shook her head in disbelief. "Do you think I'm so stupid as to not know? Every time she comes here, you change. You build that tight wall around you as if she doesn't matter anymore, but I know you too well, D.A."

She reached out and laid her hand on his bare chest. "Will you answer me one question?"

"Of course," he replied.

"Do you still love her?"

"No."

She burned with anger. "I think you do."

"You're wrong, Mary," he insisted.

"No, I'm not," she cried, hot tears running down her cheeks.

"You're crazy. I don't love her. . .maybe I never did."

"But you keep acting as though. . . ." He pushed her hands away before she could finish, but she clutched his wrists in despair.

"I hate her," Mary cried, shaking his arms. "She's here, right here in our bed, D.A.! She's turned you from me and built a barrier. She doesn't really want you, she just wants to hurt us." She dropped his wrists and caressed his shoulders. "Please don't shut me out. I love you! Doesn't that mean anything to you? She deserted you. I won't let her come between us now or ever!" She sat up sobbing as he turned his back to her.

He rolled onto his stomach, completely ignoring her. She waited, panic-stricken, but he didn't move.

She dragged herself from the bed and slipped back into her gown, her fingers fumbling with the tiny buttons. After all these months, the suspicions that had lurked in the back of her mind had proven true.

Blindly she stopped near the window, wiped her eyes and looked out at the moon just rising over the trees to the east. The mountain sky was as awesome and spacious as ever, but tonight its beauty was hidden in the darkness. Even the stars seemed to sparkle less. She shivered in the chill of the cool May air. She had forgotten her robe. She knew it lay on the foot of their bed, but pride and pain prevented her from getting it.

If he stayed in the bed, she would know it was a sign. She had asked for truth and now found it ripping their relationship apart. If he refused to come to her, she would have to make a decision, but how could she leave the man who meant more to her than life itself.

If she left him, could she make it alone? Other

than baby-sitting and the summer job in the print shop, she had no working experience. Her whole world had been her beloved D.A. He'd warned her once long ago never to allow herself to become dependent on a man. He'd told her to prepare herself with an alternative career, yet the only career she wanted was to be his wife and the mother of his children.

Her heart ached at the thought of him lying on the bed, already asleep, not caring what plans she was considering, plans that would tear their family apart.

A wave of nausea swept through her, leaving her faint. She groped for the window sill in a futile attempt to maintain her equilibrium. Her heart cracked and spilled some of its lifeblood of hope. Blinded by the tears streaming down her face, she turned from the window. She wanted to go to him once more, but her knees were unsteady.

Suddenly she was caught in a length of fabric. Disoriented, she stumbled and cried out.

"You're cold," D.A. remarked as he draped her robe around her shoulders. "I can tell."

Her sobbing grew in intensity as he tried to calm her. Her shoulders heaved against his chest, and his arms completely surrounded her, forcing her to gradually settle against him. He held her motionless in the moonlight.

"Hush my love, don't cry," he soothed her. "It's only you I want. Not Sarah, just you. I love you, Mary. I want only you as my wife, you to be the mother of my children...just you." He kissed the top of her dark head where the moonbeams glistened. "Oh God, Mary, I didn't mean to hurt you. I love you too much for that."

He eased the damp strands of dark hair from her forehead and cheeks and kissed her wet face. "Just you, Mary. Only you, my darling wife. You are the root of my existence." His mouth covered her trembling lips as he attempted to heal the gaping wound he'd allowed Sarah to inflict.

He led her away from the window, and they stopped near the bed. He turned her to him and removed the robe from her shoulders. "Now just look," he said, tilting her chin and staring down at her upturned face. "How could that woman or any other possibly come between us? You're so close to me, nothing could slip in. Can't you tell how I feel about you?" He pressed her against his long length, forcing her to acknowledge his rising desire.

"I love you," she whispered. "Perhaps too much."

"Never too much," he countered. "You've given your love to me without reservation and I've accepted it, but I've neglected to nourish you in return. I've taken you for granted and that was wrong. You've always been here when I needed you, and I forgot our marriage was vulnerable to outside forces. I've been reluctant to shower you with my love in return. Perhaps I was afraid you'd leave me like...." He tightened his grip on her shoulders.

"I'm sorry," he said, a slight tremor in his hoarse voice. "I know you'd never leave me. The four of us are a family. We couldn't exist without each other.

I. . .I don't know what else to say, my love. Let me show you instead of telling you how I feel.''

His fingers pulled on the silky tie at the neckline of her lavender gown before concentrating on the small tricot-covered buttons that lay in a row down her front.

"Why do designers put so many fasteners on a gown as sexy as this one?" he mumbled. Her hands dropped to her sides to allow him access. As he approached the tiny buttons near her waist, his hand slipped beneath the fabric and caressed her skin.

He brushed the gown from her shoulders and it floated to the floor, settling around her slender ankles. Her dark hair flowed down her back except for a thick coil that covered one breast. He carefully lifted it, allowing his fingers to trail along down her shoulder blade. Her breasts rose and fell as his eyes roamed her slender form.

"You're more beautiful than you were the first time we made love. Motherhood agrees with you. You're fuller here. . . ." His hands brushed across the rosy areola.

"You're rounder here," he said as his hand caressed her flaring hip. "You've left no trace of carrying my child here—" his hand rested momentarily on her naked abdomen "—but I want you here. . . ." His hand slid to the dark triangle below.

"And here," he added, his hand settling at her waist, "but mostly here." He laid his open palm flat against her heart.

"Oh, D.A.," she whispered, reaching out to him.

"I want you because I love you!" he cried out, and he eased her onto their marriage bed.

CHAPTER SIXTEEN

THE FOUNDATION OF THEIR MARRIAGE slowly regained its strength, and they worked at rebuilding their relationship. Sarah was mentioned only when Annie asked about her.

As D.A. attempted to give Annie memories of her life with Sarah, Mary found herself willing to listen to fragments of his own life with his first wife. Annie bombarded her father with questions about the photos he had given her of Sarah, him and Annie as a baby until she grew satisfied. After a week of questions, she took the pictures to her room and arranged them on a large sheet of bright-orange construction paper.

Several days later she awoke from her nap and came to Mary in the kitchen. "May I have a bottle of glue?" she asked.

"Of course," Mary replied, retrieving the bottle from a drawer and handing it to Annie. "May I see what you're doing?"

"Sure," Annie said, and Mary followed her into the bedroom.

Mary watched silently as Annie carefully glued each of the photographs onto the orange paper, leaving a blank area near the bottom of the sheet.

"Can I have a picture of you and daddy and

Davy?'' Annie asked. When Mary found some spare photographs of them all, Annie glued them in a wobbly line on the bottom of the sheet.

"How do you spell me?'' Annie asked.

"A-n-n-i-e,'' Mary replied slowly.

"No,'' Annie said impatiently. *"Me!"*

"Oh.'' Mary laughed. "M-e.'' She wrote out the word on a piece of paper.

Mary watched curiously as Annie took a thick crayon and methodically copied the two-letter word underneath each photo containing herself. She worked diligently, chewing her lip and humming as she labored. Then she went back and drew the number one below each image of Mary and D.A. The number two was drawn under pictures of Sarah.

"There,'' Annie sighed, and leaned back on her heels.

"Tell me about it,'' Mary suggested.

Annie gave Mary a condescending look as she explained the poster. "Me's me,'' she said. "I can't spell Annie or Annette Eliz. . . Eliz. . . .''

"Elizabeth?'' Mary helped.

"Yeah, they're too long for me. Maybe when I'm five,'' she said confidently. "You're my first momma and daddy. My momma Sarah is my second momma. See how lucky I am?'' she cried. "I have two grandpas and grandmas and two mommas.'' She beamed at Mary, then became very solemn. "But I guess I have only one daddy. Sid's okay, but I don't know him. He'll have to wait before he becomes my second daddy. But you and daddy are my very favorite momma and daddy.'' She threw her arms around Mary's neck.

"You're my favorite little girl, too," Mary said, her eyes shimmering with tears. "No matter how many other little girls your daddy and I might have, you'll always be our first special little girl. I love you, Annie." She pulled Annie into her lap and held her, rocking slowly back and forth.

Only when Davy crawled into the room and stood teetering before them did they pull apart.

"Is he your favorite, too?" Annie asked.

"He's my favorite little boy," Mary agreed.

"Are you and daddy going to have more babies?"

"Someday," Mary said. "Someday."

A FEW DAYS LATER a post office clerk called to say he'd received a certified letter for Mary McCormack.

"It's from a company called Educational Fun and Games Corporation," the clerk informed her.

"Oh," Mary cried. "We'll be in later to pick it up."

She told D.A. about the letter during lunch. "I'd forgotten about sending them my computer game for preschoolers and their mothers. Remember...about the robin who uses his beak to pick up the symbols and runs around the screen on his spindly legs and cheeps when you answer the questions correctly?"

"They probably want to buy the game and make you rich on royalties," he teased.

She grimaced. "They're probably just returning my query with a 'Sorry' rejection."

"I doubt they'd waste the money to certify a rejection. Didn't you enclose a self-addressed stamped envelope."

"Yes," she said, and her spirits rose.

When they arrived at the post office, she tore open the thick envelope excitedly and scanned the covering letter. She looked up into D.A.'s smiling face and slowly began to shake her head in disbelief.

"They want to buy the program. My program!" she said. "Me, the little stay-at-home housewife! Me, the woman without a career! Oh, D.A., look at the money they're offering. They'll send an advance when I return the signed contract and...oh, look, they want to see any other programs I've written. They like the instruction brochure I wrote, too. They say it's so easy to understand and...." She scanned the last paragraphs of the letter.

"They want to know if I'd like to try writing instructions for other games...that some programmers can't write clear directions even when the game is brilliant. Oh," she breathed, "just think, my very own money. I had no idea how good it would feel. It's like being set free." Suddenly she realized the implications of her comments. "I didn't mean...." She stopped, fearful of his reaction.

"I couldn't be more pleased for you," he assured her. "I've always said that a woman shouldn't be completely dependent on a man, and I meant it. I'm still the head of this household and that makes me responsible for taking care of us all, but this gives you some financial equality." He kissed her on the tip of her upturned nose. "You can do what you like with the money."

In spite of the other customers at the post office,

he hugged her, lifting her feet off the floor and kissing her soundly.

"My wife has become a professional writer in the computer age," he boasted.

"INTERESTING," D.A. COMMENTED as they lay in bed that night. "Just when you're embarking on a new career, I'm finding myself having doubts about my own."

Mary turned to him in the darkness and propped herself up on her elbow. "What do you mean?"

"I enjoyed growing up in the country and visiting dad when I lived in Missoula. Recently, especially since we've built this house, I've come to realize that I enjoy the summers here working with dad much more than teaching. I still like the research and working with the Big Hole fellows, but the classroom has begun to stifle me. I like the freedom of the open air." He chuckled softly. "At times I even like taking orders from dad. Sometimes I toy with the idea of having a place of my own, but this area is where I feel most at home, and there's no property for sale that I can afford without a big mortage. When I was a kid I used to dream of taking over my father's place, but now...I don't know if my father wants me as a working partner."

"I thought you and your father had discussed that long ago," Mary said.

"We used to, but that was before I left for college and went into teaching. Somehow we've drifted apart over the years. My marrying Sarah caused a rift between us that's never really healed."

His chest raised and dropped quickly as he exhaled. "Sorry to mention her, Mary, but something happened between dad and Sammy that involved Sarah. They've never told me what happened, and I've hesitated to ask. They're loving and warm to me, but I know we're not as close as we once were."

"Why don't you try to talk to him?" Mary suggested. "If you don't like teaching anymore, think about a change. Your father made a career change, and he was older than you are. No one should remain doing something he no longer enjoys if there is an alternative."

"You're right, honey," he replied. "We'll ask dad and Sammy out to dinner in town next week. See if your folks will take the kids. I'll just come out and tell him how I feel and ask him if there might be a place for me here. Between the Simmentals and the Herefords I know there's lots of work to do. When I was younger, my father and I would hug each other and say we loved each other, but the last few years we've let that slide. I think it's time I told my father that I still love him."

DAVID MCCORMACK THOUGHT that everyone was making a big fuss unnecessarily. He'd been selected for the Distinguished Service Award, which was given annually by a local organization, and the evening's program had been arranged to recognize his own award as well as several others. Frankly, he was embarrassed.

He sat on the platform, listening to his friend and

neighbor Ed Russell extol his accomplishments since his arrival in the community seventeen years earlier. David had retired from Anaconda six years before to escape the stress and time-consuming responsibilities of a chemical-engineering career. Recently he had begun to feel that he had merely replaced one burden for another. Breeding Simmental cattle had proved to be a success, but it took a lot of his time and energy. Although Sammy handled the paperwork, he negotiated most of the contracts and oversaw the breeding program.

He wished he'd been able to persuade his son to join the business, but he'd hesitated to discuss it lately. Each time in the past few years when he'd tried to bring the subject up, D.A. had hastily talked about his professional involvement at the college.

As an alternative he'd hired Paul Russell as a full-time foreman, which had freed him from the day-to-day work of the commercial Hereford operation and the feed-production program. Still, he continued to be involved, even though Sammy tried to discourage him.

"Paul's a capable young man, David," she had said several times. "Give him some freedom to do his job."

"I know, I know, but it's hard to let go, Sam."

"Perhaps if you'd practice on Paul, D.A. might change his mind and join you," she had replied. "He's never really said no. He's a lot like you. You can't both be the chief, and he's not willing to be your hired cowboy, David."

He knew she was right, but letting the reins go was difficult. He knew he spent too much time behind a desk and in his truck and not enough on horseback. His weight had shot up to two hundred ten pounds, and his doctor and friend, Bob Morrison, had cautioned him about his sedentary life-style.

"You've got to exercise your body as much as you do your mind, my friend," Dr. Morrison had scolded recently.

Sammy had become concerned and changed her menus to help him lose the unwanted pounds. He had never had a weight problem before, and he found it a humiliating experience. He had had trouble shaking a bout of bronchitis over the winter, and the discomfort in his chest returned whenever he exerted himself. Maybe once he got his weight down to normal he'd feel better.

He looked out at the audience. Sammy was sitting next to Julie Russell in the second row center. He smiled at her and shrugged his shoulders. A few rows behind his wife sat D.A. and Mary. They seemed oblivious to the crowd, their heads close together in a private conversation. Sarah continued to contact Sammy by phone or letter, and each new intrusion brought a strain to his own marriage. He wondered if his son's marriage could withstand some future confrontation. He hoped so. No one deserved a bad penny like Sarah. It was bad enough that Sammy felt a need to maintain the contact. He tried to give her the emotional support to weather the storm whenever Sarah roared into their lives. He wasn't sure if his own son could do the same for his young wife.

He started to take a deep breath, but a steel weight pressed in on his chest harder. He thought of the lung injury he'd had several years ago and knew that couldn't be the cause. It must be the aftereffects of the bronchitis.

The discomfort sharpened, driving a wedge through the middle of his back. He inhaled but found no relief. The seat of his chair suddenly seemed intolerably hard, and his chest really hurt. He had never experienced such an intense pain; even his ulcer had felt better than this. A vague sense of panic hit him as he tried to raise his arm to rub the numbness from his neck and his arm wouldn't respond. Both arms had ached off and on throughout the day, but the primary pain was right in the middle of his chest.

He broke out in a cold sweat, and a wave of nausea overtook him, leaving a bitter taste in his mouth. He was sure Russ had talked for at least thirty minutes. When he glanced at his watch he was surprised to find it had been just three. The pain was becoming more intense. Maybe he should try to leave the stage. He certainly didn't want to do anything foolish in front of all these people.

He tried to rise from his chair but his body wouldn't cooperate. The room darkened. His chest was weighted down with a crushing pressure, and he couldn't get his breath. He thought of his wife and son and all the things he'd meant to say to them. He'd waited too long. He knew he was dying.

Sammy watched as he tried to stand up, gave a soft groan, and sank to the floor. Her scream filled the air, and she bolted from her seat and raced up the side steps to the stage. She shoved her way through the milling crowd and dropped to her knees beside her husband's inert body. Dr. Morrison and Mike Adler, head of the volunteer emergency rescue service, were already administering aid to him.

Sammy clutched her husband's motionless hand. "Oh, David, darling," she sobbed.

Someone laid a hand on her shoulder, and she jerked away. "It's me," D.A. said, and she glanced up into his anxious face.

"It's his heart," Dr. Morrison told her. "We'll get him to the hospital as soon as the ambulance arrives. Mike, where is it?"

"It's on its way, Bob," Mike Adler replied. "Be still, David," he cautioned as David's movements became slightly agitated.

David forced his eyes open and saw the distraught faces of his wife and son staring down into his.

"I...love...." The words he wanted to say were torn away by the excruciating pain.

Dr. Morrison leaned over him, pressing on his chest. He didn't need any more pressure and he tried to tell the good doctor so, but no words came forth. Someone's fingers invaded his mouth and he tried to move away, but again his mind and body were uncoordinated.

Someone placed a small pill under his tongue. He felt a tingling, burning sensation, and the terrible pain began to recede. A needle pricked his arm, and through the darkness he heard Mike Adler giving instructions.

Sammy's voice came to him again, and D.A.'s lower voice comforted her. Why had he taken so long to tell them all how much they meant to him?

Mike Adler and Dr. Morrison were also to receive awards that night, and David hated to interrupt the program. He heard Mike's voice through his receding pain and felt his body being lifted onto a firm surface. The blackness swept him away before he could find Sammy again.

THEY WERE ALL GATHERED in the corridor outside the cardiac care unit. D.A. held Sammy securely against him, and Mary was at her side. Ed and Julie Russell stood quietly a few feet away. Mary touched Sammy's arm as Dr. Morrison approached.

The physician took Sammy's hand and held it as he spoke. "He couldn't have chosen a better spot to have a heart attack—surrounded by experts in emergency cardiac care."

"What if he had been at the ranch?" she asked, though she already knew the answer.

"He probably wouldn't be here with us now, Sammy," Dr. Morrison confirmed. "He's had a moderate myocardial infarction."

"Why?" Sammy asked, her face ashen with disbelief.

"Partly because he's a compulsive doer, because he tends to get excited over everything he does...

partly because he's fifty-two years old and a male. . . because he's been running the ranch from a desk instead of the broadside of a horse and added about thirty unnecessary pounds, and because he has a good case of arteriosclerosis that has become worsened by all the above. He's a classic type-A candidate.'' He patted her hand again. ''In simple, he's a victim of heart disease.''

Sammy shook her head. ''I should have known. I should have recognized the signs.''

''You couldn't have, Sammy,'' Dr. Morrison replied. ''Not if he withheld the problem from you. Now that he's awake and can talk to me, I know he's had several angina attacks before, but he's been able to control them by stopping whatever activity he was doing when they flared. They're caused when the heart can't get enough oxygen due to blockage in his blood vessels, and when he stopped the exertion, his heart and body needed less oxygen. But, Sammy! He ignored the warning signs! Now his heart has rebelled.'' He shook his head angrily. ''He should have come to me, damn it.''

''How is he?'' Sammy asked. ''May we see him?''

''Not yet,'' Dr. Morrison said. ''He knows you and D.A. are both out here. I could see a change in him when I told him. He seems stabilized for now. The staff is monitoring his heart functions. The next several hours will be critical to his survival and recovery.''

''Is he going. . . to die?'' She began to tremble.

''No, he can't,'' D.A. insisted. ''We have things to

work out." His face turned ashen, and tears ran down his cheeks. "He just can't."

"Come with me, both of you," Dr. Morrison said, and he led them away from the others to a cluster of chairs. "Sit down, Sammy. You, too, D.A. No, I don't think he's going to die, but close monitoring will probably make the difference. Sometimes after such attacks the heart really goes wild and a much more serious attack can occur with major heart-muscle damage. Heart muscles don't mend themselves after they die. With our new equipment we'll know immediately if anything happens, and can take preventative or corrective action with medication. He's in very good hands. These nurses and the technicians are the best." He squeezed both their hands reassuringly.

"The physician is the best, too," D.A. said.

"Thanks, son. I think he'll make this one, but he'll be out of commission for several months. He may have to retire again. Perhaps that's a good thing if you want him around."

"I'll cover for him," D.A. volunteered.

"Good," Dr. Morrison replied. "He'll need to know that all is well and in good hands so he won't worry." He stood up. "Try to get the others to go on home. Their love and concern is here in spirit, and they need to handle everything at home. If you two want to stay, fine. I'll let you see him in about a half hour. Wait here. Excuse me now, I must go back into his room. I'll tell him you're still here." He turned and disappeared through the door to the cardiac unit.

The Russells tried to persuade Mary to leave with them, but she insisted on staying with D.A.

"We'll take care of Annie and Davy," Julie said, kissing Mary's cheek and hugging Sammy before leaving.

The nurse led them into the room, and Sammy's heart lurched when she saw him lying asleep in the bed. A monitor tracked his heart activity, two intravenous tubes were inserted into a Y-shaped needle in his arm, and an oxygen tube crossed his cheeks to his nostrils.

Sammy, D.A. and Mary sat huddled together near David's bed. Occasionally one would glance upward to scan the monitor when David's heart activity became irregular. The nurse on duty moved in and out of the room silently, alert to her patient's condition. During the wee hours of the morning, she completed a change in his medication and turned to the weary group.

"He's sleeping soundly now, Mrs. McCormack," she said. "Why don't you get some rest. There's a room down the hall that's empty. Go rest. We'll let you know if anything should happen." She turned to D.A., whom she'd known for years. "Please, D.A., take her there for a while."

He nodded, and slowly led Sammy from the room. As they left the area, he heard the sounds of wheels behind him and turned in time to see a technician push a cardiac-resuscitation cart into the room. "Go with her, Mary," he said. "I'll be with you in a minute."

He caught the technician as he walked out of his father's room. "What's the crash cart for?" he demanded, grabbing the sleeve of the man's white jacket.

"Nothing," the man said.

"Then why take it in there?"

"Just in case, that's all. . . just in case," he said. "Better to have it and not use it than to need it and waste time getting it."

TIME PASSED AT A SNAIL'S PACE as the concerned family waited and prayed for David McCormack's recovery. His progress was frustratingly slow. Continued erratic heart activity troubled Dr. Morrison. A potentially massive attack was brought under control during the second day, but not before some damage was sustained. After more than a week in the cardiac care unit he was transferred to a private room. His physical condition improved slightly, but a new problem developed.

David was experiencing bouts of depression and frustration, with only occasional periods of optimism, and both Sammy and D.A. were concerned. Dr. Morrison had warned them of this reaction, so they tried to be patient.

"Who's running the place?" David demanded one afternoon.

"Paul and D.A.," was Sammy's reply.

"But do they. . . ?" He plunged into a long list of unfinished projects he'd planned to accomplish. "I need to get out of here," he said, and tried to leave the bed, only to drop back exhausted and in pain from the minor exertion.

The next day Sammy found him despondent, the drapes drawn and television soundless. The visit was one-sided on her part. After several days of receiving the brunt of his anger and frustration, she finally lost her temper.

"David, you should be thankful you're alive," she cried. "This has been difficult on us as well as you. Everyone is pitching in and keeping the place going. I come and stay with you as much as I can, and all you give me is this rude silent treatment. Well, I've had it! I'm leaving you alone for a few days to think. You may need a bypass operation, and this negative attitude only makes everything worse. I love you. D.A. loves you. We want what's best for you, but you have to help yourself."

She toyed with the idea of slamming the door, but instead closed it quietly and strode down the hallway, out the exit and to her car. She hoped she was doing the right thing. She loved him more than life itself, and knowing that he'd almost died made it doubly hard to give him such an ultimatum.

She stopped by Dr. Morrison's office and told him of her visit with David.

"Good," he said. "He's had a lot of attention, which he likes, but it's because he's become an invalid, which he hates. I'll talk to the nurses. If there's any problem, we'll call you immediately. Otherwise, take a day or two and rest up yourself. Perhaps he'll realize how fortunate he is to have a family like you and D.A. and Mary and those cute grandkids of his.''

Three days later Sammy returned to the hospital, rested but still concerned over his attitude. She hurried through the door to his room and stopped abruptly.

He smiled and held out his hand. She rushed to his side, and he slipped his arm around her waist. She was alarmed at its weakness but hid her concern.

''What brought this change, darling?'' she asked, kissing his smooth-shaven cheek. ''I was beginning to think I'd married a Mr. Hyde instead of kindly Dr. Jekyll.''

He grimaced. ''I've been acting like an ass,'' he admitted. ''I missed you so much, Sam.''

Sammy chewed on her lower lip in a futile attempt to control her emotions. Her hand slid to the side of his neck, and she rejoiced in his warmth. His breathing was ragged as she kissed his mouth.

''I missed you, too, David,'' she murmured as his fingers ran through her curly hair. Her vision was too blurred to see his own shimmering green eyes.

''I learned something else while you were away, love,'' he said.

She raised her head and was surprised to see him grimace. ''What happened?''

''Yesterday they took me to physical therapy for a stress test on a treadmill.'' He smiled sheepishly. ''I failed the test but met someone I hadn't seen in years. Bea Lambert, the former mistress at the post office was there. She had a stroke several months ago and is just now learning how to use her right arm and leg. She was in a wheelchair and was trying so hard to recover.

"As I watched her, I realized how fortunate I was. I'm willing to have the surgery if necessary because I know I'll make it through it all. I still have lots of things to do. I want to get close to my son again. We've drifted apart. I want to see my grandchildren grow up. And I want to enjoy your company. This is not my time to meet my maker, love.

D.A. SAT AT HIS FATHER'S DESK in the ranch office, trying to make sense out of his father's notes. He'd received two phone calls that morning from out-of-town buyers regarding pickup dates for yearling Simmental bulls.

D.A. wished he'd paid more attention to the details of his father's purebred cattle business. He was confident he could handle any problem with the commercial herd, but the Simmentals were his father's pride and joy, and he was reluctant to make decisions without consulting him first.

He'd stepped quite naturally into his father's shoes, and his only regret had been the devastating cause for the change. Fortunately school was out for the summer, but he was beginning to grow concerned about the fall. His loyalties were divided between family and career, and he'd spent many nights talking quietly with Mary about his problem as they lay in bed.

"I think you should put your family first, but I'm

prejudiced," she would whisper, snuggling in his arms. "You'll have to work it out, and I'll be with you whatever you decide."

A knock sounded on the office door. "Come in," he called.

Sammy entered and dropped into a nearby chair. "Your father and I had a long visit with Dr. Morrison this morning about his lack of improvement. Dr. Morrison has been talking to a specialist in Missoula. David needs surgery."

Her expression grew serious. "Whenever he tries to move, the chest pains return. The nitroglycerin tablets help, but living out here where there's no medical care in an emergency...well, it would be suicidal. Dr. Morrison recommends we go to St. Patrick's Hospital in Missoula. The sooner the better. He can't get enough oxygen to...oh, D.A. he's like a semi-invalid! That makes him angry, and his blood pressure rises and then the chest pains return. It's a vicious cycle. If he doesn't die from another attack, I'm afraid he'll die from the inactivity. Dr. Morrison says the coronary bypass surgery is quite successful in these kinds of cases and his recovery should be just amazing!"

Sammy reached for D.A.'s hand. "There's one big problem, and that's the ranch. David will never be able to work again full-time. He can play at raising the show cattle and working with the Arabian broodmares he bought last year, but the stress of full-time management would be too much. Paul is fine as the working foreman, but we want someone closer to the family as the general manager.

"Oh, D.A., how do I ask you? Would you take over the management of the place? Completely? You've always been his silent partner. You own a third of the capital stock, and each year when the final income statements have been prepared, he's taken your share of the profits and invested it for you. I know how you've tried to avoid direct involvement while he was in charge, but now... now...."

She shook her head sadly. "His will gives half of the ranch to you when he dies, but it wasn't supposed to be so soon."

D.A.'s mind was spinning. "When does he have the operation?" he asked.

"He goes to Missoula by ambulance next Tuesday. He'll check in the hospital for tests, and they'll schedule the procedure if the test results indicate it. Probably within a few days. I'm so frightened. What if he doesn't...I don't want to be without him. I couldn't."

"Sammy, of course I'll do it. How could I say no? I've been thinking about a career change," he told her. "Teaching has lost its excitement for me. I'd rather like the challenge of running the place. It'd give me a chance to show that father of mine that someone else can do things just as well as he can. After all, he trained me, didn't he? Paul and I get along fine, and I think it would make Mary very happy. She's made it quite clear that she likes having me around during the day. This summer has been an absolute delight for us. As for dad's surgery...I'll drive you to Missoula."

Sammy nodded. "I want you near, D.A. I think I'd feel much better having you there with me."

"He's my father," he said, hugging her, "and I love him, stubborn, determined, bullheaded man that he is. He's more than just my father, Sammy. He's my friend. We've wandered away from each other, especially when I lived in Missoula." He squeezed her hand. "And I know that my marriage to Sarah has caused problems for you two. I'm sorry."

Sammy flinched at the mention of Sarah. "She'll keep coming back," she warned. "I hate to see her come, yet I'm relieved to know she's okay. It's crazy, but...."

"I know," he agreed. "It's crazy. But dad's our primary concern now. Mary and I want the best for both of you, but we're also selfish. We're going to make him a grandfather again...no, no, not yet. We've been trying, but we seem to be having a little trouble being successful. Our children need him, too. I think he's very special."

He glanced at the calendar on the wall. "I'll turn in my resignation at WMC. I've signed my contract, but I think under the circumstances they'll understand and let me break it. The timing is perfect with two months still left of the summer to find my replacement. I know a couple of guys in Missoula who would jump at the chance to relocate to this hunter's and fisherman's paradise. Now don't worry. My father has too many plans to desert you now. He's a man of his word."

"WHAT TIME DO WE LEAVE TOMORROW?" David asked.

"Early," Sammy replied. "After breakfast the ambulance will be here. I wanted to go with you, but D.A. and Dr. Morrison think it would be best if I let D.A. drive me. I have a room reserved near the hospital."

He watched her turn and look out the window, and he longed to have her nearer. "I'm scared, Sammy, really scared. I have so much to do. One minute I think everything will be fine, then I get a pain and realize how short life is and how quickly it can be taken away. Does that make me a coward?"

"Of course not," she said, coming quickly to his bed. "You're wise enough to see how precious life is, David." She took his hand in hers and stroked the tanned skin, tracing the veins across its width. "None of us knows when our time runs out. You and I have shared more joys than most people experience in a lifetime. We've weathered the storms because of our love.

"I'm selfish," she admitted. "I want you forever. I've been taught that there is a life hereafter, and I hope it's true. It makes me know that when one of us dies it's only a matter of time until we're together again. God has given us a reprieve, David. He's blessed us again."

His green eyes roamed her face. "I want you forever, too. Selfish of us, isn't it?" A smile softened the lines around his mouth.

"I think in our case, it's okay."

"I'd planned to...."

"It can either wait or D.A. and Paul can do it,"

she reminded him. "David, aren't you the one who always says that no one should make himself indispensable? Why don't you take your own advice, darling? Hasn't the ranch functioned without you for several weeks?"

"I don't know for sure. I haven't been there."

"Well, I have," she said. "It has—and very nicely, too. You'd be proud of those two young men. D.A.'s a natural to run the ranch. He's your son and he's as talented as you, my husband. He'll manage because he has had training from you and education and experience. He's also determined to succeed, just... like...his...father." She patted his hand, emphasizing each word.

"Come closer, Sam," he said.

She sat on the edge of the bed and rested her hand on his waist, marveling at the heat of his flesh through the thin cotton pajamas.

"Do you know that I have no desire to make love to you?" he said with a soft chuckle. "I guess that's proof of the severity of my handicap."

"It's not a handicap," she assured him. "It's just a temporary inconvenience. You'll see. After the bypass is done, you'll be able to do...whatever you want within reason. There's more to our lives than making love. You'll return to the ranch feeling strong again. It's just too dangerous now, with your pain and the possibility of...another attack...." Her voice trailed off.

"Sam," he said, "pray for me. I don't want to die. I have things to do with you, my love." He reached out and touched her cheek. "We haven't had enough time yet."

"You'll make it," she said. "You promised me. I pray for you every day, David. God answered my prayers for you before, and He will again. He knows how much I need you." She bent down and lightly kissed his mouth.

His fingers traced the curve in her arm. "I want to play with my grandson. He's about to have his first birthday, and I won't be there. Strange, but one of the few regrets I have in life is that I didn't have any more children, and now my son is fulfilling that wish by having them for me. Isn't life strange how things work out?"

"The strangest is our finding each other again after all these years. That had to be more than mere coincidence."

"Yes," he agreed.

"Dr. Morrison says you'll be in the hospital in Missoula for three or four weeks, then home to the ranch to recover. You'll have lots of time with Annie and Davy. D.A. wants another child before they stop. I think Mary would have a dozen of his children and be in heaven. As long as Sarah continues to stay away...."

He squeezed her hand reassuringly.

"D.A. told me they've been trying to have another baby, but without success," Sammy said. "I hope nothing's wrong. It would break Mary's heart to be unable to have more children."

They sat quietly for a while.

"When you get well, maybe we can walk to the barn and south pasture like we used to and go riding to the foothills," Sammy suggested. "We haven't done that much lately."

"I know."

"D.A. will be here tomorrow morning to go with us to Missoula. You'd better get some rest, darling," she said. "These next few weeks aren't the end, they're the beginning of a new part of our lives."

"I love you, Sam, very much."

"I love you, too, David. More than life itself."

She rested her hand on his chest, reassured that his heart would once again be strong and healthy. "I'll see you early tomorrow. Bye, darling." She leaned down to kiss him, but he'd already fallen asleep.

HE WAS SOON COMPLAINING that the incision into his chest cavity hurt much more than the angina he'd suffered before. Sammy chided him for his short memory and he grinned.

Three weeks later D.A. arrived to take them home. He hugged his father warmly and helped him into the front seat of the car.

"You look like my father again, dad," he said. "I think you're going to make it for a few more years if you take care of yourself." He winked at Sammy. "Just leave the problems to me. I'm in charge now."

CHAPTER SEVENTEEN

THE MILD WINTER, aided by gentle spring rains, had turned the countryside into a lush green landscape. The creeks and streams cascaded down the hillsides and wild flowers splashed the fields and valleys with color.

Mary talked D.A. into taking the afternoon off, and they took the children on a picnic.

"Aren't the flowers lovely?" she said with a sigh as they gathered up the food containers and packed them away.

"They're just weeds," D.A. said, laughing.

"No, they're not!" Mary insisted. "They're beautiful wild flowers. They're from God's special palette. And the skies! Just look at them. Have you honestly ever seen them so beautiful? Maybe the mountains make them special. Nowhere in the world are the mountain skies so lovely."

"We'd better get you home," D.A. said. "You've become intoxicated on all this fresh mountain air, but I love you anyway." He kissed her soundly before heping her and the children into the cab of one of the ranch vehicles for the rocky ride home over the dirt roads.

Later that evening as she lay in D.A.'s arms listening to the sounds of the night, Mary gave a deep contented sigh.

"What is it?" D.A. asked.

"I think this is the most beautiful spring I've ever seen."

"That's because of the call you received this morning. You said the same thing the last time. I think you view the world through rose-colored glasses when you're going to have a baby." D.A. nuzzled her ear. "You blossom, too. You're as pretty as the flowers outside."

Mary rested her hand on her abdomen. Life was perfect, and in early September she would present her husband with another child.

A FEW MONTHS LATER, D.A. accompanied Mary to Dr. Morrison's office at the physician's request. He waited impatiently in the outside office while the doctor and Mary disappeared down the hallway. He'd given up smoking the previous Christmas, but at times like these he craved a cigarette. Finally they reappeared.

Dr. Morrison was beaming and Mary looked perplexed.

"D.A., thanks for coming with Mary," the doctor said, leading them into his private office. He settled in his chair behind the large wooden desk. "I need to talk to both of you."

D.A. frowned. "What's wrong?"

"No, no, nothing's wrong." Dr. Morrison reassured him. "Mary is now six months along, and it's just that I felt you needed some advance warning." He stalled a moment and lit his pipe, filling the room with a fragrant cherry aroma. "I did an ultrasound on Mary. I've been concerned about her rapid weight gain. She's hit twenty pounds already, and since her mother comes from the Innes family, and Innes women have a reputation for multiple births, I've done a careful examination and a few special tests. I'm almost positive the two of you are going to double the children in your family."

D.A. frowned and looked at his puzzled wife. Then he understood. "Really?" He grinned at the doctor.

Mary was thoroughly overwhelmed. "You mean I'm carrying...twins...two babies...oh my goodness!" She turned to D.A. in amazement.

"Making up for lost time, my love?" he asked.

MARY SURVEYED HERSELF in the full-length mirror. She looked grotesque. Several weeks remained in her pregnancy, and she wondered how she could possibly get any larger.

She had enjoyed her first pregnancy, but this one was so different. Her vision clouded with tears as she quickly covered herself with the loose navy smock. Her ankles were swollen and her face was slightly puffy, and she knew they would be worse by evening. Her hair had become such a problem for her to shampoo and comb that D.A. had finally taken her into town, and she had had it cut to an ear-length bob.

She had always worn it long and was surprised to see a gentle wave appear when the weight had been removed. D.A. had tried to tell her it was attractive, but she thought it made her look like a boy. A pregnant boy at that.

She sat in the chair and tried to reach her foot to adjust her slipper, but her oversized belly blocked her view. She snagged her fingernail on the chair's lower rung and tore it to the quick. She flinched and tears filled her eyes again.

Today was her twenty-first birthday, and D.A. had completely forgotten about it. She certainly wasn't going to remind him. She knew why the date had slipped his mind. Sarah had returned. Why had she come to the ranch and after all this time? When D.A. had told Mary that Sarah would be there for two days, staying at Sammy's, she had felt a great sense of foreboding.

She suspected that right at that moment Sarah was undoubtedly talking to D.A., flaunting her elegantly dressed svelte body at him and making him wish his ugly, pregnant wife would disappear.

Her eyes fell on the desk calendar again. This was such a special day, the day she'd always thought would solve the problem of their age difference.

She heard a soft knock and knew it would be Sammy to help her with the laundry. Since Dr. Morrison had warned her to stay off her feet and take it easy, Sammy had done her best to ease the burden of housework. Lately Mary hated the laundry, the cooking, the cleaning; even Davy who was almost two years old, irritated her. Her promising career writing computer games had fizzled when she learned about the twins, and the only profits she received were royalties from the first game.

If she were one of her father's Angus cows, she would just go hide in the willows by the creek until she delivered. But she was a woman, and forced to endure the often humiliating stares of well-meaning visitors who invariably commented on her size.

As she approached the living room, several people were coming in through the front door, and Mary looked at them in alarm.

Sarah's sultry voice carried to her sensitive ears. She heard the words, "Good breeding stock, D.A.?" and laughter followed. Annie was actually holding Sarah's hand as they walked in behind Sammy. Last to appear was D.A., still laughing over Sarah's comment.

Mary frowned. Who was good breeding stock? Were they comparing her to the livestock? D.A. left the chattering women and walked over to her.

"Hi, sweetheart," he said, kissing her lightly on the lips. "How are you feeling? We've just come from the south pasture. Annie was showing her mother the new foal, and I was telling Sarah about the bloodline of the mare. You look tired, love. Come sit down with me. Sammy, Sarah and Annie have offered to fix lunch for us. Do you mind if they take over your kitchen? I couldn't refuse an offer like that, could I?"

His new responsibilities managing the ranch meant

that he was outdoors most of the time, and he had acquired a deep tan. He looked like a golden Adonis. As he sat down on the sofa beside Mary, his rambling chatter stopped.

"Why so quiet, honey?" He pressed his lips to her forehead. "Mary, don'd let Sarah's visit trouble you. She doesn't bother me at all. Don't let her bother you, either. Hey, aren't you about to have a birthday soon?" He glanced down at the newspaper lying on the sofa.

"Oh damn it, Mary. I'm sorry. It's today, isn't it? I was so caught up with the ranch, the new foal and the meeting with dad and Paul this morning...."

"And *her* visit?" Mary mumbled.

"I completley forgot. Will you forgive me?" He laughed. "No, probably not. How can I make it up to you? Dinner tonight? In town. But would you feel up to it, honey?

Before she could reply he squeezed her shoulder and said, "I'll think of something." With those words he jumped up and disappeared into the kitchen.

Mary wanted to disappear herself and hide in her bedroom, but she was too exhausted to push herself from the comfortable sofa. She leaned her head back and closed her eyes, trying to block out the laughter coming from the kitchen.

THE NIGHT WAS QUIET except for an occasional lowing of cattle in the distance. D.A. finished massaging Mary's back and pulled her gown into place. He helped her turn over, then put an extra pillow beneath her head.

"Lie still." he grinned boyishly at her and left the bed.

She watched him search through a top bureau drawer until he found what he wanted. He dropped it into the pocket of his robe.

"Perhaps this will cheer up my despondent wife," he said, reaching into his pocket and removing a small case. He handed it to Mary.

"We never had time to get you an engangement ring," he said. "I thought perhaps this would make amends." He watched as Mary withdrew the gold ring. In the center of the ring a sparkling diamond caught the lamplight, and this stone was surrounded by six smaller glittering ones.

"Oh, D.A.," Mary gasped, her eyes wide with surprise. "It's lovely. What are the stones?"

"Two sapphires, two rubies, and two emeralds," he said. "It looks a little like a Christmas tree, but Christmas is a special time for us, isn't it?" His eyes met and held hers.

"Do the six stones mean anything special?" She asked.

"Time will tell," he replied, tilting her chin and gently kissing her lips. He took the ring from her and slipped it on her finger.

"You didn't think I'd really forgotten your birthday, did you?" he chided.

She turned her hand from side to side, admiring the flashing stones. "It's just what a stay-at-home wife needs when she does the dishes," she said. "Thank you." Her arms encircled his neck and drew his head closer.

"Damn it," he muttered as they withdrew from a lingering kiss. "This celibate life-style Dr. Morrison has us following is for the birds. A man can only take so much." He kissed her again, leaving her breathless. "A man wasn't meant to be without a woman for long, but I'll try to be patient." He ran his fingers through her short wavy curls. "I really like your hair this way."

"It's not very sexy," she said.

"It is on you."

Thoughts of Sarah intruded. "Why did Sarah come back?" she asked. "Why now? Just when everything is so difficult for me...when I look so awful."

"She wanted to talk to me about Annie. Plans for her future."

"Does she want to take her away? She tried once. You wouldn't let her do that, would you?" Mary's eyes widened with alarm.

"Of course not," he reassured her. "Mary, Sarah really seems changed. She hasn't made one cutting remark since she's been here. That's quite a record for her."

"She still intimidates me," Mary said. "Why do I have to look so terrible? And my short hair *does* make me look like a boy, not a woman who's about to have two more children." She began to cry softly.

He wiped her tears away. "I think you look lovely.

You're too hard on yourself. Your hair will grow long again, and I love you either way. I happen to think you look older and more sophisticated with short hair." He kissed her cheek. "Quit looking for trouble, Mary. Sarah leaves tomorrow night, and the babies will be here before you know it. Just relax." He shed his robe and slid under the covers. Pulling her to him, he rested his hand between her breasts and rounded abdomen.

Mary heard him take a deep breath, and she felt her short hair move as he exhaled. She put her hand on his and closed her eyes. Perhaps she would feel better tomorrow. She was exhausted and had been bothered all day with a faint dull ache that threatened to take control of her entire body. She wouldn't let it. The weeks ahead would be difficult for her, and she needed all her reserve strength to cope.

THE MORNING SUN streamed through the open window as Mary sat in the living room, trying to be content with having nothing to do. She threw down the paperback novel she'd been holding. She'd reread the same sentence several times and still didn't know what it had said.

The compound was quiet. Paul had taken his family to visit the Russells. Sarah, Sammy and David were inside the other house having a final visit before Sarah's departure that evening.

D.A. was working in the ranch office. He had told Mary of a programming bug in a software package he'd purchased for their recently upgraded micro-computer. The program was designed to keep track of the siring records of the Simmental bulls, and a logic problem had caused the statistics of two of their most prolific bulls to become intermingled. Sammy, with her computer-systems experience, had found the problem and made the necessary changes in the program to prevent a repeat, but the damage had been done. Now D.A. was correcting the progeny records in the data-base system.

Annie was down at the barn admiring the new Arabian foal. Her father had said it could be hers. Mary hadn't seen the little filly, but Annie had described it in minute detail at lunch the day before. It had a white blaze running down its face and matching white boots on its forelegs. She had elaborately explained that its dark coat would lighten as it grew older, and had added breathlessly that she would be seven years old when the filly was big enough to begin to ride.

"We can grow up together, momma!" she'd concluded excitedly.

A nagging backache had plagued Mary off and on throughout the night and early morning. She wondered if she might be in false labor. She should probably call Dr. Morrison and describe her symptoms, but she knew it was his day off, and she hesitated to bother his two partners in the medical clinic in town.

Davy was asleep, having an unusual morning nap. Sarah had taken the two children to the barn for a while after breakfast to keep them out of Mary's way. Mary had thanked Sarah, but she was still suspicious of the woman's true motives.

Mary's restlessness grew stronger, and she felt the need for D.A.'s presence. With a groan she pushed herself up from the chair and made her way out of the house. During the long walk across the compound to the ranch office two more contractions racked her body, and she had to stop to catch her breath.

As she left the grassy play area, she saw two heads through the window of the office. D.A.'s head of wavy blond curls momentarily blocked the darker one. Mary thought she saw a hand appear at his waist, and then the two heads seemed to come together. The reflection of the nearby mountains on the window glass obscured her view.

She heard Sarah's voice. D.A. had kissed Sarah. Mary's heart pounded violently as she crept closer to the door, drawn by the overpowering need to confirm her worst suspicions. The door stood slightly ajar and she could hear his voice.

"Meet me here when Mary's asleep this afternoon. I'll show you what I mean." His low laughter sounded suggestive.

"Is that a promise?" came Sarah's sensuous voice.

"Of course. I told you I've needed it. I can't wait any longer. The timing is perfect. I just don't want Mary to find out."

Mary froze just outside the door, then slowly she turned away. A hard contraction swept through her, and she fought to catch her breath.

She had to get back to her own house. She had to get away from the office. Her husband was going to

rendezvous with his former wife, and they would...
when she was asleep...out of the way. She knew
there was a small cot in the inner office. David had
put it there for the long spring nights during calving
season. That cot would become the place for D.A.'s
unfaithfulness while she was supposed to be napping
in their bed.

Fear tore through her.

Another contraction, stronger than before, forced
her to stop again. At last she staggered into the kitch-
en. She clung to the counter as another contraction
worked its way through her. She wanted to lie down,
but if she gave in to her pain, she would only make it
more convenient for him to break his marriage vows.
She had to remain on her feet. Maybe his conscience
would return if he saw her moving about their home.
Maybe....

Another contraction began, and she glanced at the
kitchen clock. Five minutes apart. She couldn't be in
labor. She wasn't due until late August or early September. Dr. Morrison had warned them that twins
usually arrived early, but this was only early July.

She glanced down at the ring D.A. had given her
the previous night. She recalled his words about his
needs and the fact that he was running out of patience. He had warned her. The lovely ring suddenly
seemed a cruel joke. As she leaned against the
cabinets, she held her breath and waited for the next
pain, which she now knew would surely come.

Everything was happening so fast. She needed
D.A. to take her to town, but how could she go to

him now? She tried to remember all the techniques for relaxation and breath control, but they were blotted from her mind by the image of Sarah and her beloved D.A. sharing a moment of passion on the cot.

She gripped her hardened belly and tried to reach a chair. She felt as though her body was trying to push the unwanted babies through her pelvis, and she had to somehow stop the progress. Her ears began to ring with silence. She heard an engine start and wondered who was leaving, but the searing contraction returned and demanded her attention.

Sobs rushed from her throat and tears flowed freely as she slowly sank to the floor, her back supported by the cool wood of the lower cabinet doors. Her body was ignoring her commands and another contraction began. She tried to lie on her side to ease the pain.

D.A.'s voice broke through the roaring in her ears. "Honey, is lunch ready? I'm starved." She hadn't even heard him come in.

"My God! What's the matter?" He was beside her in a flash.

"I...think...the babies...are coming," she gasped. "I'm sorry...to spoil your plans—with Sarah." She couldn't stop sobbing. "Oh, D.A., I hurt. It's not at all like the first time. Everything's going wrong."

"Be still, Mary. I'll be right back," he said, and rushed from the room. He quickly reappeared and knelt beside her.

"Damn it. Dad, Sammy and Sarah went into

town," he explained. "I hoped I could stop them before they got out of the yard, but it's too late."

He carefully lifted her in his arms. "We'd better get you into town. I'll make you comfortable and round up the kids." He took a few steps across the kitchen and stopped. "You're still light as a feather, my love." He smiled down at her. "Remember when I carried you into Sammy's kitchen? You were thirteen. You know, Miss Russell, we've got to stop meeting in kitchens like this or it might lead to something serious."

Mary began to relax in the comforting warmth of his arms. "Oh, D.A., I thought Sarah and you...." She stopped, confused.

He frowned. "What about Sarah and me?"

"I tried to find you earlier, and I saw you with her in the office. I saw you kiss her."

"No, you're wrong, Mary. I thanked her for an offer and she kissed me."

"Yes, but you were going to meet her...later when I was out of the way."

"Out of the way?" he asked, and a hint of anger crept into his voice. "Mary, just what did you think I was about to do?"

"You said you needed to...and you didn't want me to know. You'd meet her there...when I...." The tears began to flow again, and he carried her down the hallway into their bedroom.

"Mary..." he started impatiently, but stopped when she gripped herself. He waited until the contraction eased, then carefully lowered her onto the bed.

"Mary, did you really think I'd...Mary, it's you I love, no matter how you look or feel. Haven't I told you? Oh God, Mary, you don't understand. Sarah offered to help deliver some infant furniture designed especially for twins that I ordered in town. It was a surprise for you. I didn't want you to find out about it until it arrived. I didn't want you to think it was for your birthday, and I almost forgot to give you the ring." He reached for her left hand and touched the sparkling stones. "I was sure you were pretty burned up about my bad memory, so I was determined to keep this a secret until it was here and all set up. Am I right?"

She nodded. "I'm sorry I doubted you. Forgive me. It's just that Sarah has stayed away for so long, and to come back right now.... You said last night that you were tired of...doing without...." She gave up trying to explain her foolish behavior.

"Doing without making love to *you*," he stressed. "Dad took the pickup into town, and they're bringing the furniture home. Sarah offered to help me assemble some of it in the office. That's the only place you usually don't go, my inquisitive wife." He sat down beside her on the bed.

Another contraction started just as Davy called from his bedroom. D.A. waited by her side until the seizure passed. He heard his son call again and suddenly realized he hadn't seen his daughter.

"Where's Annie?"

As he asked, Annie's young voice called from the kitchen.

"Momma, where are you? Daddy? I'm hungry."

"I'll be right back," he said softly. "We'd better get on the road if these babies are going to be born in town." He kissed her quickly, but before he could leave the room she inhaled sharply.

"I don't think there's time," she said breathlessly.

He nodded his understanding and left. He hurried to his son, stripped the wet diaper from his fat bottom and changed him. Grabbing Davy up in his arm he hurried to the kitchen.

"Hi, daddy," Annie greeted him. "I'm hungry. Where's momma?"

"Sit down, Annie," he said as she climbed onto a chair. "I need your help. Are you a big girl?"

Her auburn curls bounced in affirmation.

"Can you watch your brother?"

She nodded again.

"Momma is about to have the babies right here in the house. Now, it's very important," he said taking her shoulders. "I'll make you some sandwiches, and then I want you to stay here with Davy. But most important, I want you to watch for grandpa's truck. They should be back within the hour. They went into town. I *need* grandpa and grandma. Do you understand, Annie?" He shook her lightly.

"Sure, daddy," she said, and a disdainful expression, remimiscent of Sarah, appeared on her pretty features. "I'm almost six, you know."

He laughed aloud. "You're right, Annie." His daughter had begun to consider herself well on the way to being six years old a few days after her fifth

birthday. She was tall, pretty and sharp as a tack.
"You're quite the grown-up helper. Now you can
really be in charge...of Davy. Keep him in here and
watch for grandpa's truck. I'll be with Mary." He
hurried from the room, forgetting all about the
promised sandwiches.

Annie raised a trim eyebrow as he left, then turned
to Davy. "I'll take care of you." She skipped over to
the counter, found the bread loaf and carried it to the
table. Next she went to the refrigerator and removed
a small jar of current jelly and deposited it on the
table beside the bread. She climbed up onto the coun-
tertop and carefully did the necessary gymnastics re-
quired to open the upper cabinet doors.

She smiled when she spotted a jar of peanut butter,
which she eased down to the counter. She found a
knife and quickly began making several sandwiches
for her brother.

Davy sat with his thumb in his mouth, his eyes
round and green, and watched the overhead kitchen
light reflect off the shiny knife as Annie moved it
back and forth across the bread.

"Now eat!" she commanded, placing a mutilated
sandwich in front of his beaming face.

"Drink," he said, pulling his thumb out of his
mouth just long enough to point.

"Okay," she said, and marched to the refrigerator. She returned with a pitcher of fresh milk. She
filled two small glasses and wiped the few drops she'd
spilled. As she sat down and pulled her own sandwich
toward herself, she smiled at her brother.

"See, Davy," Annie said. "I'm big enough to have my own horse and take care of you, so momma and daddy can have babies."

ANNIE HEARD THE CRYING SOUNDS coming from her parents' bedroom and looked round-eyed at her younger brother.

"I think we have a baby, Davy, a baby!" she said excitedly. "Daddy says there may be two. Two babies. One for me and one for you. Isn't that nice?"

"Drink," Davy replied.

She pursed her lips at his indifference toward the births, then cocked her head. From outside came the sounds of her grandfather's truck returning. She raced through the door.

"Grandpa, grandpa!" she shouted. He hurried toward her, and her grandmother followed. Her mother Sarah went toward the ranch office.

"What is it, Annie?" David asked. "Where's your dad?"

"Daddy needs you. Momma is having the babies. I heard one cry!" They raced into the house, down the hallway, and into the bedroom.

"Oh, my God," David exclaimed when he saw the baby pressed against Mary's bosom. A tiny blond head moved slightly, and a whimpering sound filled the room.

Sammy skirted around her motionless husband and hurried to Mary's side.

"When did you call the ambulance?" David asked D.A.

The color drained from D.A.'s face. "I forgot," he said.

"I'll do it," David volunteered, and dialed the number of the ambulance service in town. Mike Adler answered and David gave him the information.

"Bring an incubator, Mike," he added. "It's a premature birth...twins. Hurry!"

"We need something to keep them warm," Sammy said. She surveyed the room. "Where's the other one?"

"It hasn't come yet—it's been almost ten minutes now," D.A. said, glancing at the small clock on the nightstand. "Maybe it knew I couldn't handle two at once."

"I know," Sammy exclaimed. "Heating pads! I have two at the house, and there's one in the office.

"We have one here, too," D.A. said, hurrying to the hall closet and returning with the pad.

"Get me a small clean box," Sammy directed. "Big enough for both babies. I'll make a bed and warm it with the pads. How is it, Mary? Is it a girl or boy?" she asked.

"A boy." Mary smiled. "His name is Russell E., but D.A. won't say if the *E* stands for Edwin for my father or Edward for his father. I think he's all right, but he's so tiny...." She cooed softly to her newborn.

"I'll go get the heating pad from the office," David volunteered, but when he glanced at his son, who had returned to the room with a small cardboard carton, he quickly changed his mind. "No, on second thought, I'll wash up and stay with Mary. D.A., you look like you need some fresh air. Will you go get the pad? And hurry.''

D.A. breathed deeply as he trotted across the yard to the office. He was torn between exhilaration and apprehension.

Would Mary be all right? He recalled the first twin's birth. The tiny head had eased into his hand, and the baby lay motionless until D.A. ran his fingers down his spine and made him start breathing. He was less than half the size of Davy at birth, and D.A. had suggested to Mary that she tuck the baby between her breasts for warmth. What would the next baby be like? Would they both be strong enough to survive? How long would it take the ambulance to arrive? Maybe they'd send the helicopter; it would be faster. Why the hell hadn't he thought to call the ambulance service himself?

He entered the office, still chastising himself. The darkness of the room momentarily blinded him. He closed the door and took a few steps toward the smaller inner office, but stopped abruptly as a movement caught his eye.

Sarah rose from the chair behind the desk. She had changed her clothes since he'd talked with her earlier in the morning. Now she was wearing a pair of white harem pants and a canary-yellow clinging top that stopped just above her navel. Her breasts bounced beneath the translucent material as she hurried to him.

He stepped backward and leaned against the closed

door in a futile attempt to avoid physical contact with her. Her supple breasts pressed against him as she pulled his head down to hers and kissed him with her parted lips. Her warm minty breath left him stunned.

"D.A., I knew you would come," she murmured, her voice throaty. "God, I wanted you this morning, and with little Mary taking her nap, we can be alone." She rubbed her body against him.

"You...." He tried to speak, but she pressed herself closer.

"She'll never know, and I certainly won't tell Sid," she purred. "I've hung around this hick place for days waiting for you to be free." She raised her lips to kiss him again.

He grabbed her shoulders, his fingers and prosthesis digging into her unmercifully.

"Ouch, you're hurting me," she whined.

He pushed her away. "Don't you know, Sarah?" he cried. "Mary has had a baby and she's about to have another—here, in our bed. They're premature and they need medical care. My father is with her now and—"

"He'll take good care of her," she interrupted. "We can still be together."

"Together?" Hatred and revulsion gripped him. "I don't want to be with you. You're scum, Sarah, Las Vegas scum." He shoved her away.

She came toward him again. "No, D.A., there's no way little Mary can satisfy you like I can." She reached for his belt buckle and smiled. "I'm a pro."

He grabbed her hand in his prosthesis and watched her face distort in repulsion. "You never satisfied me, Sarah. You held my manhood hostage and took away my pride. You left me with the only worthwhile act of your life—Annie. Mary gives my life purpose and direction. Get out of our lives, Sarah, for good!"

"You cripple," she sneered. "You never were a real man. I'm glad I left you and that. . .that brat of a baby."

"You're the cripple, Sarah," he snapped, and stormed out the door. He was trembling with rage as he ran across the compound and reentered the house. Upon entering the bedroom, he realized he'd forgotten the purpose of his trip.

"Sammy," he said.

"Yes?" she replied.

"I couldn't find it. Can you get the ones from your house?" She nodded, and D.A. went into the bathroom to wash his hands. He stood in the doorway, drying his hands, and surveyed the room. His father was taking command of the situation.

"Push, honey," David said. "Just a little now." He smiled reassuringly at Mary. "You're doing fine. I think this twin is coming pretty easy. Stay with her, D.A. She needs you."

D.A. glanced at his father's gray head poised over Mary. He sat on the bed beside Mary as she began to groan and strain, and he sensed her pain. He heard his father talking again.

"That's fine. It's almost here, sweetheart. I think it's going to be another blond one. D.A., you've really made your mark on the McCormack clan this time."

D.A. looked at Mary. She still held their new son against her breasts. The intensity of his love for her made his eyes glisten. "Mary, darling, I love you so very much. Don't ever doubt me again. There's no need, sweetheart." He leaned down and placed a gentle kiss on her trembling lips.

"It's a girl!" David exclaimed. "But so tiny." He held the new baby face down in his hands, her lifeless arms and legs dangling limply. He wiped her face, then carefully lowered her to the bed, and began to rub the tiny back and flick the soles of her feet. The baby refused to breathe. Her skin remained a chalky bluish pink.

David shook his head. "It's not good." He picked the baby up again and began to breathe into her rose-bud mouth.

"Oh, no," Mary cried. D.A. reached for her hand and squeezed it reassuringly, all the while holding his own breath.

Time stood still as David continued the gentle, rhythmic motions. One tiny arm jerked slightly.

"Keep it up, dad," D.A. shouted. "She moved!"

They would never know if it was his shout or his father's persistent breathing that made the difference, but the baby brought both legs up and screwed her tiny face into an orange-size prune. A heart-warming cry filled the room. Her color gradually changed to a florid pink, and her chest heaved on its own.

They laughed in relief as the infant reacted angrily to her first encounter with her new world.

D.A. lifted Mary up slightly to watch as David tied off the pale cord, snipped it, and then handed the child to D.A. He held the baby a moment, then gave her to Mary to warm and cuddle against her breasts alongside her sleeping brother.

Sammy returned with the extra heating pads and carefully built a makeshift incubator out of the storage box, the heating pads and some flannel blankets for the new babies. She carefully lifted the little boy into his temporary bed. He was asleep, and his chest continued to rise and fall in a steady pattern. Sammy turned back to Mary.

"It's a girl," Mary told her, staring down at the remaining baby.

"Let's put them together," Sammy said. "They can warm each other, and the pads will help. What are you going to call her, dear?"

"I don't know," Mary replied, reluctantly relinquishing the baby. "I wasn't ready for names."

Sammy placed the little girl up against her brother and tested the pads to make sure they weren't too hot. She tucked a soft receiving blanket around the infants. The box was beginning to feel cozy and warm. As she smiled down at her two new grandchildren, she gave a silent prayer that they would survive.

A helicopter sounded overhead, and the noise aroused the twins momentarily. They whimpered, then settled down again.

Annie had maintained her vigil in the kitchen,

watching her younger brother and listening for the ambulance. She ran to the door and held it open for the rescue team.

The house became a whirl of activity. A gurney was brought in, and Mary was heeled out to the waiting helicopter. A portable incubator was rolled in, and the make shift one abandoned. The babies quickly joined Mary in the helicopter.

Mike Adler listened attentively as David filled him in on the details of the births, and he made notes to give to the medical staff waiting at the hospital.

D.A. knelt before Annie and Davy. "Be good," he said. "I'm going with momma to the hospital. You'll stay with grandpa and grandma until I get back." They nodded their dark heads. He turned to his father. "Thanks, dad, I can't begin to tell you what your help means to us. I . . . ." He stepped close to his father and embraced him.

David hugged his son tightly before releasing him. They were both slightly embarrassed by the emotional outburst and their tear-filled eyes, but their smiles said the words they had difficulty expressing.

"You're my family," David said. "Now go with Mary and the babies. We'll be fine here. Keep us posted."

He watched as D.A. ran to the helicopter. The whirring aircraft lifted off the ground and disappeared over the rolling hills toward town.

Sammy gathered some clothing and toys for Annie and Davy, while David kept them occupied. As they walked out the door, Sarah came storming out of the house across the compound carrying a suitcase. She strutted to her silver-and-black Corniche coupe, opened the trunk, threw in the suitcase and slammed the lid hard.

She spoke briefly to Sammy, who simply shook her head and walked on into the house with Davy. As David passed by with Annie, Sarah arched her finely plucked brows at him.

"I'm sure you two men were very proficient in there," she said, a smile frozen on her features. "But since you've delivered so many cows already, what's one or two more?"

David glanced ahead but Sammy had disappeared. He was thankful she hadn't heard Sarah. He cupped his hands over Annie's ears and tried to shelter her from her mother's harsh words.

He resisted the urge to respond, and Sarah whirled away. She climbed into the luxurious automobile and slammed the door. Dirt flew from the spinning tires as she revved up the engine, and David and Annie watched the car disappear behind a cloud of dust.

"Grandpa, why does she act like that?" Annie asked as they turned to go in.

"I wish I knew," he replied, squeezing her hand.

"I like my mother Mary better. She loves me. I can tell."

He stopped walking, swung her up into his arms and gave her a hug. "I'm sure you're right. And you know what else, Annie?"

"What?" she asked, putting her small arms around his muscular neck and smiling at him.

"Your grandpa loves you, too." He hugged her

once again before letting her slide to the ground. She raced off to find her grandmother and her little brother.

David lingered behind, smiling at his little granddaughter's exuberance. Thoughts of the future with his mushrooming family warmed his heart. The crisis with his own health had been conquered, and he had learned to enjoy life to the fullest. His lovemaking with Sammy had been resumed, and he'd shed his extra pounds by joining her for long rides on horseback to the foothills of their property. He'd turned the management of the ranch over to his son and his daughter-in-law's brother, though he still dabbled in selective breeding of his small but growing stable of Arabians. What he had learned was to listen to his own body, and he'd been made keenly aware of the consequences of neglect.

"Come on, grandpa," Annie called from the porch, breaking his reverie. David chuckled. His granddaughter was almost the same age as Sammy had been when they'd first met. How the years had flown. He wondered if he was getting sentimental in his old age, then chided himself for thinking he was getting old. His uncle Jeff McCormack was still alive and active in his eighties.

Now there were two new descendants to the McCormack line, a fulfilment of the dreams he had had long ago when he'd first seen his own son in a hospital nursery in Butte.

"Coming," he called, waving to Annie. To himself he murmured, "Families do make a difference," and he hurried to his impatient heir.

CHAPTER EIGHTEEN

D.A. AND MARY stood in the hospital nursery, their features hidden behind masks as they studied their children. The twins were the only babies in the small nursery.

"She needs a name," D.A. said, staring down at his daughter.

She had weighed exactly three pounds at birth and was jaundiced. Her tiny head was covered with fine blond curls and was small enough to fit into the palm of his hand. Her arms and legs were no bigger around than his fingers. Because of the jaundice, she spent much of her time under a fluorescent phototherapy lamp, wearing blinders to protect her eyes. He knew the odds were against her survival, and it was important that she have a name.

Mary looked up at him and took his arm. "I love her, even if she is ugly," she whispered. "I'm so afraid for her." She turned away from the enclosed Isolette parked in front of her and buried her face against his chest.

He held her closely against him. "Remember, honey, the doctor said the very fact she's made it for three days is in her favor. In a few days they'll start adding your own milk to the glucose water, and maybe in a few weeks you can even nurse her. At least her lungs seem to be working properly. Dr. Morrison says the natural childbirth without any sedatives definitely gave her a boost in the right direction.''

He tilted her face up to his, slipped the mask down enough to expose her mouth and kissed her.

''She's just got to have a name,'' he persisted. ''She's going to be our little girl. Now what are we going to call her? I named Russell, so you get to name this child.''

''Well,'' she said, taking a deep breath as she turned back to the Isolette, ''I'd like to call her Heather, after your father's Scottish great-aunt, the one who was born here in Montana before the turn of the century. He told me all about her one afternoon when Sammy and I visited him in the hospital in Missoula...that time when you stayed at the ranch.''

She grinned. ''Her middle name will be after me, but not quite. Marissa. Heather Marissa McCormack. Isn't that a beautiful name for our child?''

He was laughing as he spun her around to face him. ''Where in the world did you get a name like Marissa?''

''I always wished my name was something like Marissa instead of just plain Mary.''

D.A. kissed her cheek. ''Sweetheart, there's nothing plain about you or your name. You're warm and loving, you care about others. You're wonderful, and I love you very much. You're wrong about the name Mary. It's been a special name since biblical times.''

He nuzzled her short hair. "Heather Marissa Mc-Cormack, indeed. What if she decides to shorten it to just plain Mari? It would serve you right for putting such a long handle like that on her." He gave her a squeeze. "I pity the poor kid when she's in the first grade and has to learn to spell her name!''

They turned to the second Isolette. Russell looked substantially larger by comparison. He was on a respirator for a breathing difficulty, but his jaundice was less severe than his sister's. His small head was covered with fine platinum hair that Mary was sure showed definite signs of waving.

Russell weighed three pounds ten ounces at birth, but both babies had lost several precious ounces, and the doctor had explained that it might be weeks before they passed their initial birth weights. Their home would be the nursery at the hospital for at least two months, possibly longer.

Medical costs had not been discussed, and D.A. tried not to think of the staggering expenses, which were multiplying daily. The ranch had a group policy on its employees and their families, but he was afraid it wouldn't cover the entire bill. Right now, though, all he was concerned about was his children's survival.

"They're our babies, and I have to talk to them through the glass and see them fed through tubes and IV's," Mary said quietly. "I want to hold them and feed them and kiss them...and go to sleep at night knowing they'll still be with us when we wake up. . . and I can't.''

She gripped his shirt sleeve tightly. "Was it me? Did I do something, especially when I saw Sarah again? I hate that woman! She keeps coming between us. . . and now this has happened. It must be my fault." She groped blindly for an explanation. "I know it's crazy, but sometimes I think I rejected them, because I envied her slender body. Could I have done such a terrible thing?''

"No, Mary," D.A. tried to reassure her. "I'm certain that's not the reason. Didn't Dr. Morrison tell us both that the reason for most premature births remains a medical mystery. Look at me," he commanded, forcing her face upward. "Sarah won't be back.''

"What do you mean, she won't be back?" Mary asked cynically. "She *always* comes back."

"No more," he promised. "When I told you she was meeting me in the office to help assemble the baby furniture, I really meant it, but she thought I had finally changed my mind. Yes, that's right, *finally*. You're the only woman I've made love to since she left me, in spite of what you might have thought. She may have been in my mind a few times, but I've always been faithful to you. I don't doubt your suspicions of me, but it's only you I've wanted or needed. You fulfill me.''

He traced her delicate cheekbone and buried his fingers in her hair.

"When I went to the office for the heating pad, Sarah mistook my appearance as proof of my willingness to climb on that cot with her. She was there waiting for me. I tried to explain what was happening to you, but she ignored my words and said that dad could take care of you and that she and I could still. . . I couldn't believe she could be so callous.

"God, I wanted to slug her. . . but I controlled my instincts and told her to get out of our lives. I'm sure I would have done something regrettable if I'd stayed another moment with her."

Mary reached for his hand. It was his cosmetic hand, but she clutched it as though it was his natural flesh and bone. Her acceptance of him as a whole man swept clean once and for all the tainted scars of Sarah.

"Mary, you've been in my system ever since you were a shy little three-year-old and I stole your chair. It was the first time I ever met your family. Dad and I came to meet our new neighbors, and your mother invited us in for coffee, milk and brownies. You chose me out of that crowd in your mother's kitchen and climbed on my lap and shared my brownie. Remember? You probably don't, but I still do. You were the tiniest little girl I'd ever seen, until now when I look at Heather.

"You stayed loyal to me through all my wanderings—to Missoula, to Las Vegas and Sarah, through those silly young women. Remember Rose Marie?"

She nodded and they laughed.

"Just you, Mary," he said, taking her in his arms. "You were strong enough to stay by me as I searched so blindly for happiness."

D.A. SAT IN THE RANCH OFFICE, trying to concentrate
on the July financial reports that Sammy had prepared for the McCormack Simmental Cattle Company, but all he could think of was his children. They
were five and a half weeks old, and each was doing as
well as could be expected.

Mary had taken a furnished apartment in town to
be near the children. Lisa, her younger sister, stayed
with her during the week. Lisa had a summer job
working on the switchboard for the emergency rescue
service, so the arrangements worked well for both sisters. Mary spent most of her days at the hospital and
Lisa provided company in the evenings. On Friday
nights D.A. would trade places with Lisa, spend the
weekend in town with Mary, and return Monday
morning to the ranch.

He missed Mary. This was the first time they had
been separated other than the two days when Davy
had been born. D.A. wanted her home, and he
wanted his two children home with her.

Russell now weighed four pounds. Mary was helping him learn how to nurse from her breast. His
breathing difficulties had cleared and the tube in his
stomach had been removed. Heather weighed three
pounds eight ounces but was still too weak to withstand the sucking exertion. The doctors were waiting
until she too passed the four-pound mark before at-
tempting a change in her feeding technique.

Dr. Morrison had tried to waive his fee, saying he
had an obligation to his two favorite families and he
considered it a privilege to tend the twins. When

D.A. had insisted on paying, they had struck a bargain. Dr. Morrison had predicted the twins would have Mary's dark eyes. If he was right, no fee; if he was wrong, D.A. could pay him one hundred dollars for each child with light eyes. No argument and no renegotiation.

The financial burden had become a growing concern for D.A. The hospital's administrative head had estimated the babies' care would cost between eighty and ninety thousand dollars each for a stay of eight to ten weeks. The group policy would cover approximately two-thirds of the anticipated bill. That left a mere sixty thousand for him to be concerned about, he thought cynically.

The administrator had assured him that he needn't worry about the time it would take to pay the bill, as long as some effort was made on a regular basis.

"We've never repossessed a child yet," he had assured D.A., slapping him lightly on the shoulder.

Mary's trust fund from her father's three ranches was untouchable until her twenty-fifth birthday, but D.A. didn't feel she should have to pay for the birth of her own children. That was his responsibility. She'd done enough by conceiving them, nurturing them, and now devoting her full time to their care.

A year earlier, he'd told his father to use the funds he'd received over the years to purchase an irrigation system for a new alfalfa field. He'd insisted when he'd heard his father complain about the high rate of interest the local bank had quoted. Then there was the ring. Had its purchase been a foolishly romantic act? It had cost a small fortune, which had seemed inconsequential at the time, but now could have been used more wisely. Yet thinking of the ring on anyone else's finger was unthinkable.

D.A. frowned again at the financial report. On paper the ranch was quite profitable, but most of the proceeds were plowed back into the next planting of feed crops, the next expansion program for either the Simmental herd or the commercial Herefords, replacement equipment such as tractors or heavy harvesting gear, as well as mortgage payments for the two newer houses. His father had recently looked at a large piece of property for sale over the mountains to the south in a broad valley known locally as the Centennial. The McCormack Ranch had joined a grazing association, but summer pasture was always at a premium. The home pastures of alfalfa and natural grasses were harvested for winter grazing, and when winter snows covered the ground, the hay was fed to the cattle from strategically located haystacks. As the temperature dropped, the cattle's feed requirements increased drastically, and advance preparation was a key factor in any rancher's survival.

Utility costs were minimal thanks to his father's solar-energy inventions, and the families grew most of their vegetables in a large communal garden plot and greenhouse. Two Guernsey milk cows and a flock of chickens kept them in dairy products and eggs. The chickens were descendents of those in Mary's 4-H project years earlier. The large walk-in freezer and cold-storage rooms near the ranch office stored meats, and surplus vegetables from the garden were frozen or canned.

D.A. had calculated that he could repay the hospital ten to fifteen thousand each year, but the thought of his children being collateral for the debt didn't sit well at all.

He removed his glasses and rested his head on his arms on top of the papers covering the desk. He was exhausted, both mentally and physically.

A steady tapping on his shoulder awakened him from a fitful nap. He turned around and found Sammy standing behind his chair, a frown on her attractive face.

"Tired?" she asked, touching his arm.

"A little," he admitted.

"May I see you for a few moments?"

"Of course," he replied. "Sit down. Forgive me, Sammy, I'm not in the best of moods today."

She nodded understandingly. "We went to see the babies last night." She laughed. "Russ says they're beginning to look like real babies, almost cute."

D.A. tried to smile, but his financial concerns made the effort a strain.

"We were able to hold each of them for a few moments," she continued. "You should have seen that big softie Russ holding his namesake. It was like a Saint Bernard holding a Chihuahua puppy. He was so happy he actually became teary-eyed."

"Did dad get to hold one?" D.A. asked.

"Yes, he held Heather. They would only let one

person hold each baby, so Julie and I deferred to the grandfathers. Your father is such a compassionate person. He's got to be the most masculine man I've ever met and the most gentle. Seeing him hold that tiny little girl was a very emotional experience. I'm afraid there wasn't a dry eye in the place. The nurses knew he'd not only delivered her, but started her breathing, too."

"I'm glad," he said.

"You're really down, aren't you?" She pulled her chair closer. "Can I help?"

He poured out his concerns to her about his wife, his growing family, his responsibilities at the ranch. He spoke of his loneliness without Mary, and finally his financial woes.

"Time will take care of most of your concerns," she said, taking a deep breath. "But I think I have a suggestion for one of your problems, and a possible solution for the other."

He leaned toward her. "Did I really hear you right?" His green eyes glinted brightly, and he genuinely smiled.

"You look more like your father all the time," she said and kissed his cheek. "You're getting the same wrinkles around your eyes and mouth. You'd better watch it, or you'll also begin replacing that blond hair with silver. It runs in the McCormack family." She leaned back in her chair, smoothing her denim skirt over her thighs, and patted a slight bulge in the patch pocket of her skirt.

"What're your suggestions?" he asked. "I'm open to anything. I'm desperate."

"The first one...why don't you take a week or two off and stay in town with Mary? The babies are doing well enough now that perhaps you and Mary can have sort of a second honeymoon, just the two of you, alone in the apartment. Get to know each other again without interference from outsiders...just the two of you. You both deserve it."

"The ranch...."

"Your father would love to get his fingers in the operations again for a short while. He's feeling great now, and I'd see that he spends only part of his time on it. Paul will be glad to cover the rest of it for you. I've discussed it with both Paul and your father, and they agree wholeheartedly. You really need to get away and be with Mary."

He ran his fingers through his wavy hair and then tried to smooth it again. "Mary has been after me to join her," he admitted. "Has she been working on you, too?"

She smiled. "Perhaps...just a little."

"All right, I will," he agreed. "When I go in on Friday night, I'll stay for two weeks. It'll be good to be with her every night." An embarrassed grin lighted his face, sweeping away some of the fatigue.

"Maybe that's why Mary wanted you to come," Sammy hinted, patting his knee. "See what an intuitively sharp wife you have. Now...about the second problem. How much do you think the hospital bill will be? Do you know how much you'll be responsible for?"

He told her the staggering sum.

"Don't get mad," she cautioned. "I want to loan you some money." She raised her hand to stop his protest. "I knew you wouldn't accept a gift, so I'm merely offering to loan you the money you need. You can repay me however and whenever you want."

He was skeptical. "Where would you get that kind of money? I need sixty thousand! You can't possibly have that much, unless you dipped into the ranch accounts, and I can't let you do that." He shook his head, rejecting the idea.

"Your father and I have been quite successful the past few years, and I sold my home in Phoenix and received quite a nice sum, but you're right. It's not my money I'm offering you." She stared at him thoughtfully. "It's from Sarah."

"Oh, no, Sammy," he said, rising from his chair.

"Sit down, D.A.," she insisted, and he dropped back to his seat.

"How could you even suggest such a thing?" he asked. "That's not fair of you. I can't very well tell you what I really think of that woman and what she's done to Mary and me over the years. She's your daughter, but I'm sorry...no...I couldn't...how the hell does Sarah fit into this? When did you get money from her?"

"It's for Annie."

Her answer startled him, and he could only stare at her.

"She's been sending or delivering money for Annie for several years," Sammy told him. "I didn't tell you before, because I knew how you felt. She gave it me for Annie when she's older. She said she could use it for college or whatever she might be interested in after high school. I know what you're thinking. She swears it's legal money, and not from her call-girl days." Her voice broke and she lowered her eyes.

D.A. was silent, mulling over this surprising twist to his dilemma.

"She insists and Sid Lansburgh confirms that the money is from a dress-design company they financed for a friend of hers shortly after their marriage. She named the line of women's casual wear Originals by Annette. Sid told me privately that she insists most of the profits go to her daughter, and so once or twice each year she mails me a cashier's check. Sometimes she delivers it in person. She always gave me the money first when she visited, almost as though she knew the visit would be short-lived, and she didn't want anything to prevent her from delivering it. I've put it in a savings account, and it's been earning interest for these past few years.

"It's actually Annie's money, but I think if Annie were old enough to understand, she would want you to use it." She touched his hand. "Who loves those babies more than my granddaughter? She's such a little mother. She can hardly wait for them to come home."

"You're right," he agreed quietly.

"It's just a loan," she assured him. "By the time Annie's old enough to need the money, you'll have repaid it. Accept it for me, if not because you need it. I guess I like to think that the money is proof that my

Sarah isn't all. . . perhaps it's a small sign of a conscience. . . ʼʼ she said, her voice wavering.

D.A. put his arm around her shoulders and patted her.

"All right, Sammy," he conceded, "I'll accept it for you, but I don't want Mary to know its source until I tell her myself. I wouldn't even begin to speculate on how she'd react. I'm accepting this for you and those two sweet babies who are proof of our love."

Sammy reached into her skirt pocket and removed a passbook bearing his name and showing an opening deposit of sixty-five thousand dollars.

"I thought I could talk you into accepting the funds," she said, "so several days ago I transferred most of the money into a new account. An interest statement is probably in the mail to you, so I had to tell you about the account before you received the letter and found out about the mysterious money. Please forgive me, D.A." She reached into her pocket again, withdrew a pen and handed it to him.

"Now, if you'll just sign this signature card, I'll take it back, and the account is yours to use whenever you wish."

She waited as he signed the card. "There's just one more thing you should know," she said. "There probably won't be any more money coming." She stared at him for several seconds. "Did you and Sarah have a fight when she was here last?"

"We exchanged a few heated words," he admitted. "Why?"

"Sid called me a few days ago. I told him about the twins coming early. He expressed concern for Mary as well as the children and told me to tell you congratulations. He's really a rather thoughtful fellow, D.A."

D.A. shrugged silently.

"He also said that Sarah returned to Las Vegas irate. She told him that she was going to demand all the money be returned to her. He wouldn't allow it and insisted she grow up and behave like an adult." She gave a wry smile. "He seems to be the only person I know who can handle her. He also said they might be moving back east and that he'd let me know before they left." She slid the card and pen back into her skirt pocket. "I don't want to know what you fought about, but I hope you use the money to make life a little more enjoyable for all of your family."

She rose from her chair. "It's just a loan," she cautioned. "Don't forget, I'll expect regular repayments or I'll be forced to repossess one of those babies. I'd hate to have to choose between them." She kissed his cheek and left the office.

D.A. sat in the quiet office for a long time, staring at the passbook. He wondered how Mary and Sarah would react if they knew what he and Sammy had just done.

CHAPTER NINETEEN

ALL OF MARY'S CAREFULLY LAID PLANS had gone awry. D.A.'s scheduled two-week stay with her had been postponed when a sudden change in the weather forced him to stay home.

The Friday afternoon he was to leave, a freak electrical storm had developed and started a fire in one of the hay barns. The fire ruined almost a third of the stored winter feed, and David had received second-degree burns when a charred rafter fell on his arm. Her brother Paul had dragged David to safety and then driven him to the hospital in town. The rural volunteer fireman had arrived in time to save only a small portion of the hay stored in the barn but had prevented the fire from spreading.

The McCormack men had held an emergency meeting with the Russells the next afternoon to see if, between the two families, there would be enough hay for supplemental feeding in the event of a harsh winter. There had also been talk of a merger of the ranches since the two families were becoming increasingly intertwined through business and marriage. D.A. had told her that a local accountant and two attorneys were preparing a report showing the advantages and disadvantages of such a consolidation.

The legal and tax implications of such business matters didn't interest Mary, and her sister Lisa had recently chided her for being so old-fashioned and domestic.

"Mary, you were born a century too late! Don't you have any desire to have a career, do something exciting, go places?"

"I have a career and I think it's very exciting, and I just want to go home. The computer-game company wrote me again about doing some free-lance work for them, and I've agreed—after the twins are older. I want to be my husband's wife and my children's mother. What's wrong with that? Do I have to leave my home in order to be fulfilled?" she demanded, tears coming to her brown eyes.

The days had dragged into early September. The Labor Day rodeo and county fair had passed. It was the first time in years that D.A. and she had missed the event. The fall roundups were about to begin on the area ranches, and she knew from reading the local weekly newspaper that the first snow of the season had already fallen in the higher regions.

Just when she was sure things couldn't get any worse, another storm with heavy rains had passed through the area, damaging telephone cables and power lines, and now she couldn't even call the ranch. If D.A. didn't show up tonight, she would borrow a car and drive out to the ranch herself tomorrow. The babies could do without her for a day.

She finished nursing Heather and smiled down at her. Her little daughter now weighed four pounds, eight ounces, and was beginning to look like a normal newborn. She was two months old, but it was still impossible to tell what color her eyes were going to be. After careful study and examination, Mary had decided they might be brown. She felt the same about Russell's eyes. She was becoming more confident that these children would both have her brown eyes and D.A.'s blond curls, a striking combination she thought.

Little Russell was gaining daily and would probably pass the five-pound mark the following week. Then they might be able to take him home.

Mary looked out the window at the rain, which had fallen steadily for three days. She wondered if the gravel road to the ranch would be passable.

She sensed movement, and in the rivulets of rain on the windowpane, she caught the reflection of several heads peering through the nursery window. Her back was directly to them, and she felt an uneasiness as she continued to stare at the reflected images. There were two men and a tall woman with dark hair. Was it Sarah?

Mary forced herself to remain calm as she returned the sleeping baby to the plastic bassinet, then slowly turned around.

A sense of rage filled her as she glared at her smiling husband, his despicable former wife and Sidney Lansburgh.

D.A. stepped quickly into the room, blocking her

view of the others. Before she could speak, he grabbed her arm.

"Don't say it, Mary," he cautioned. "If it weren't for them, I wouldn't be here. Now please come out and be civil to them." He led her into the hallway.

"It was my idea this time, Mary," Sid said, reaching for her hands. "I wanted to see your new children. We're moving to New York City for a few years, so I suggested we drive up and say goodbye." He stepped closer and kissed her cheek. "I'm taking Sarah away. Consider it a gift, my dear." He squeezed her hands before stepping away.

"We arrived during the storm," he continued. "Fortunately we made it to your place before the deluge hit. I'm afraid we were marooned there these last three days. When D.A. tried to start his car it wouldn't cooperate, and the other vehicles were all in use. I could see how anxious he was to come to you. We were ready to return to Vegas, so I offered to give him a ride in the Corniche. Nothing like a Rolls Royce for comfort." He glanced toward the sleeping babies. "Your children are beautiful, my dear."

Mary frowned at him, but his sincerity dispelled her anger. When she turned to Sarah her fury flamed anew.

Sarah lifted her chin and looked at Mary through blue-shadowed eyelids. "Sid says you're the best wife for D.A. He's probably right." She turned to D.A. and smiled flirtatiously. "I still think he's a good-looking hunk. Bye for now, darling." She reached up and kissed him on his unexpectant mouth.

Sid groaned and grabbed her by the arm. "Sarah!" he warned, pulling her backward. He quickly said their goodbyes and guided his wife down the hallway. As they turned the corner he gave them a final wave, then a thumbs-up signal for good luck.

Mary remained sullen during D.A.'s brief visit with the infants and the taxi ride to the apartment. Her mouth was firmly set, and only an occasional glare acknowledged his presence.

The rain plastered her hair against her head as they ran from the taxi to the apartment door. She tapped the toe of her shoe impatiently as D.A. fumbled with the key. When the door finally opened, she brushed past him and angrily threw her wet coat down before whirling around to confront him.

"How could you!" she shouted. "You spend three days marooned with *that woman* when you couldn't find time to stay a few days with me." Her chin quivered, and her eyes snapped with anger.

"You don't understand, Mary," he said. "They just came to say goodbye. Besides, we owe Sarah a debt of gratitude."

"What?" she cried. "Never!"

"You're wrong," he replied. "I've been worried sick about paying the hospital bills. You've been playing mother here in town, but I've been stuck out there trying to find a way to foot all these god-awful bills."

"Playing mother?" she echoed. "Is that all you think I do? Play?"

"No, I'm sorry. I didn't mean it the way it sounded," he apologized. "But I've really been in a bind, and now Sammy has given us free use of money that Sarah has been sending to her for Annie's education."

"Well, I won't accept money from that woman!" Mary announced, her voice trembling with rage. "Give it back to her."

"I can't," he said, a grin softening his mouth. "I stopped at the office and paid it all to the hospital. They seldom give refunds. We'll pay Sammy back when we have extra money. Now calm down. You know it's not good for a nursing mother to get upset."

"But I'm only *playing* at this mother business, remember?" she snapped, stepping away.

He reached for her, but she yanked her arm away. His hand brushed her hair, but the short wet strands slid through his damp fingers as she ran down the short hallway, into the bathroom, and locked the door.

"Mary!" He shook the knob and called again, but silence greeted his plea.

Damn it, he thought. What was the matter with her now? It wasn't his fault that the storms had come, that the barn had burned, and that his own father had been injured. He had been as surprised as everyone else by Sarah and Sid's unexpected arrival. Mary was acting as though he'd deliberately chosen to spend his time with Sarah. He couldn't have predicted that the car wouldn't start.

He shook the bathroom door once more. "Mary?"

he called, but she refused to answer. He had half a notion to return to the ranch. To hell with the idea of a second honeymoon.

He frowned as he realized he was marooned in town without a car.

He walked into the bedroom, stripped off his soggy wet clothing, and slid into a warm, forest-green velour robe. He touched the velvety texture. Mary had made the robe and given it to him the previous Christmas.

His glasses were spotted with rain and mud, and he laid them aside, too tired to clean them. He ran his fingers through his wet hair, then went to the hallway linen closet for a towel and rubbed his head dry.

Utter exhaustion swept through him as he dropped onto the bed. Tension from the storms and the damage to the ranch, the unexpected visit from Sarah, concern about the babies and their prolonged hospital stay. . . and most of all, the continued separation from Mary.

He wanted her; her bright smiles during the day, her gentle loving ways with their children, her inquisitive mind when he had problems to discuss, her warm responsive body at night when the house was quiet and still. How he missed her!

He rolled onto his stomach and tried to sleep.

A soft repentant voice disturbed his drowsy mind, and a hand touched his shoulder.

"D.A.?"

Mary literally fell into his arms when he turned

over. He pressed her to him, savoring the feel of her warmth once again.

She raised her head, but he refused to release her. "I've missed you, Mary," he whispered, as his fingers moved slowly back and forth over her full lower lip. "And I need your love." His hand glided up through the silky texture of her hair. "If they hadn't given me a ride I would have walked, even crawled. I had to get here. Can't you understand?"

Her lingering anger evaporated as her lips met his with a burst of desire, and they made love with a burning passion, lost in themselves.

THEY MUST HAVE DOZED. When D.A. awoke, the room was dusky and Mary was gone. He heard sounds from the kitchen, and soon she appeared carrying a tray of sandwiches and twin mugs of soup. Mary clutched her mug in both hands and smiled at him over the ceramic rim.

"I'm sorry I shouted at you," she said. "I don't think I've ever shouted at you before. I must have sounded like a shrew."

"I deserved part of it," he said, grinning at her. "I didn't mean it about your playing at being a mother. You're much too professional about that to ever be accused of playing at it."

She watched him, her eyes darkening.

"I meant it about Sarah's money, though," he added. "The hospital has it, we owed it to them, and Sammy says we can take our time repaying it. Annie won't need it until she's eighteen."

"I know," she agreed reluctantly. "If Sarah's folly can be put to good use for the benefit of our children, so be it." Her shoulders heaved as she reconciled herself to the idea. "I guess I can live with that. I'm just glad you told me now. If I'd found out about it from someone else, I'd be even more upset. It would be as if the two of you were plotting behind my back."

"She doesn't know," he said. "It was Sammy's idea. Sarah had no say in the matter."

"Oh," Mary said thoughtfully. She shrugged. "I guess it's still okay." She removed the empty dishes and joined him again on the bed.

"Did you ever think you'd be the mother of four children when you had just turned twenty-one?" he asked. "Most young women are graduating from college and starting out in the world?"

"Four," she said, tilting her head thoughtfully. "Since they're yours, I love it, but...." Her expression grew troubled. "Sometimes when I look at Annie, I realize how much she looks like her mother, even her mannerisms. I love her dearly, but I wonder if you too see Sarah when you look at her. Sarah has always intimidated me. She's so tall and regal and...so busty. I'm short and skinny and flat. When I saw her today I just lost my temper. The thought of you and her marooned together was more than I could take."

"You're not flat," he murmured. "You're not even small. For your body and height you're just right."

"But...."

"You'd look pretty out of proportion if you were built like her."

"Yes, but...."

"No buts...." He reached for the belt of her maroon robe and loosened it, then eased the front of the robe away from her shoulders until it fell in soft folds around her hips. "You're perfect," he said, brushing his fingertips around the full curve of one breast. "You've spent so much time with the babies. Now it's time for just us, sweetheart."

Her dark eyes smoldered as she returned his gaze, and her short wavy hair formed a halo around her oval face. He scanned her form.

"Your body is fuller than before," he said.

"You mean fatter?"

"No...rounder, more womanly. I think you've left your girlish figure behind, and now your curves are firm yet soft...just right." He stroked her waist, easing his touch as it dropped to her flaring hips.

"D.A.?"

He looked at her. "What's troubling you, love?"

"Sometimes I want to...make love to you," she said. "But I'm not sure how...and then I'm afraid you'll be reminded of *her*...her profession I mean.... I love you and I want to please you.... Sometimes I want to touch you in places where I don't know if it's all right...and I'm hesitant to try." She stopped, a plea for understanding in her eyes.

"Mary, if we both like it and it feels good to both of us, how could it be wrong?"

She looked down. "I bought a book last week. . . on sex."

"Oh? Does this mean we must make love step-by-step from a sex manual?" he teased.

A blush colored her cheeks. "Please don't make fun of me. You're the only man I've known, and if I can't learn from you, who can I learn from?"

"You're serious, aren't you?"

"I don't want our lives to get boring," she said. "I'm afraid you'll get bored with just me."

"Maybe you're right."

Her eyes grew wide with concern. "You mean it's getting boring?"

"No, no. What I meant to say is if we don't talk and learn together, it *might* get boring. Mary, maybe I have treated you like a child, or worse yet, I've put you on a pedestal and been afraid of doing certain things with you. Maybe, because of your innocence when I first made love to you, I assumed it would shock you."

"Shock me? Like what?" A shiver of anticipation passed through her.

He grinned. "Are you looking forward to practicing some of the techniques in that damned book? For your information, my love, there's probably not one technique that I don't already know about. I've just been too inhibited with you. Here, let me see that book."

She grabbed the small book from the nightstand and hid it behind her back. "Don't treat me like a saint on a pedestal, D.A. I want to be your woman.

Not your child bride anymore, but your woman!''
She held his gaze, and he gradually became aware of
her wandering hand.

"Tell me, D.A. Tell me what you like," she pleaded, and he began to tell her what pleased him. The
power in her slender fingers as they explored his body
was awesome. When he knew he could stand her
touch no longer without losing complete control, he
grasped her hand and rolled her onto her back to in-
troduce her to new pleasures.

As the heat of his mouth seared her body, her nails
dug into his muscular shoulders. She was unable to
prevent the moan from deep in her throat or the
tremors of her convulsing body as she writhed in explosive ecstasy.

He returned his lips once again to her panting
mouth, and his body became fused with hers as they
explored new heights together.

At last they lay spent in each other's arms. D.A.
stirred and left the bed. Mary stretched lazily and sat
up.

"I usually go to the hospital about this time," she
said. "Is it still raining?"

He peeked out the window and shook his head.
"It's stopped. The storm outside has blown itself
out, too," he said, coming to her, his nude body
shadowy in the twilight.

She reached out and touched his bare thigh.
"Should we call the taxi again?"

"Let's walk," he replied. "I can see the moon and
lots of stars." He dropped to the bed and touched

her cheek. "Just like the stars in your eyes," he said, and brushed her lips with a kiss. "It looks like a gorgeous night. You can nurse those cute kids of ours, and then we can come back to this place and study that book you purchased. We have two weeks to practice. Everyone at the Russell and McCormack ranches has received instructions to stay away. That includes phone calls, unless it's a real emergency."

He held out his hand and assisted her from the bed. "Are you willing?"

"Very," she replied.

They dressed quickly. Mary was wearing flat-heeled shoes, and D.A.'s height made it difficult to reach his mouth when she tried to give him a final kiss.

She clung to his neck and he lifted her off the floor, gradually covering her mouth with the hot, intoxicating pressure of his parted lips.

She was breathless and light-headed when he finally withdrew.

"Oh, Mary," he said, his eyes glistening, "you're D.A. McCormack's woman and I love you, today, tomorrow and always."

Yours FREE, with a home subscription to HARLEQUIN SUPERROMANCE.

Begin a long love affair with
HARLEQUIN
SUPERROMANCE.™

Accept LOVE BEYOND DESIRE **FREE**.
Complete and mail the coupon below today!

- -

Harlequin reaches into the hearts and minds of women across America to bring you

Harlequin American Romance ™.

Enter a uniquely exciting new world with

Harlequin American Romance ™

Harlequin American Romances are the first romances to explore today's love relationships. These compelling novels reach into the hearts and minds of women across America... probing the most intimate moments of romance, love and desire.

You'll follow romantic heroines and irresistible men as they boldly face confusing choices. Career first, love later? Love without marriage? Long-distance relationships? All the experiences that make love real are captured in the tender, loving pages of **Harlequin American Romances.**

What makes American women so different when it comes to love? Find out with **Harlequin American Romance!**

Send for your introductory FREE book now!

Get this book FREE!

Mail to:

Harlequin Reader Service

In the U.S.	In Canada
2504 West Southern Ave.	P.O. Box 2800, Postal Station A
Tempe, AZ 85282	5170 Yonge St., Willowdale, Ont. M2N 5T5

YES! I want to be one of the first to discover **Harlequin American Romance.** Send me FREE and without obligation *Twice in a Lifetime.* If you do not hear from me after I have examined my FREE book, please send me the 4 new **Harlequin American Romances** each month as soon as they come off the presses. I understand that I will be billed only $2.25 for each book (total $9.00). There are no shipping or handling charges. There is no minimum number of books that I have to purchase. In fact, I may cancel this arrangement at any time. *Twice in a Lifetime* is mine to keep as a FREE gift, even if I do not buy any additional books.

Name _____ (please print)

Address _____ . Apt. no.

City _____ State/Prov. _____ Zip/Postal Code

Signature (If under 18, parent or guardian must sign.)

This offer is limited to one order per household and not valid to current Harlequin American Romance subscribers. We reserve the right to exercise discretion in granting membership. If price changes are necessary, you will be notified. Offer Offer expires January 31, 1985   154-BPA-NAWA